Lifelong romance addic
New Zealand. Writing
with happy endings and
create. You can follow
www.facebook.com/jch
jcharroway and www.tv

Alexx Andria is a *USA TODAY* bestselling romance
author who writes about bad boys with a tough
exterior but a soft, warm heart deep down. She loves
sweet but dirty romance with lots of witty banter—
and, of course, sizzling scenes in the bedroom…
or kitchen…or wherever they happen to end up—
and a guaranteed HEA. Learn more about her at
authoralexxandria.com.

If you liked *Her Dirty Little Secret* and
The Marriage Clause, why not try

Unmasked by Stefanie London
Inked by Anne Marsh

Discover more at millsandboon.co.uk

HER DIRTY LITTLE SECRET

JC HARROWAY

THE MARRIAGE CLAUSE

ALEXX ANDRIA

MILLS & BOON

First Published in Great Britain 2018
by Mills & Boon, an imprint of HarperCollins*Publishers*
1 London Bridge Street, London, SE1 9GF

Her Dirty Little Secret © 2018 JC Harroway

The Marriage Clause © 2018 Kimberly Sheetz

ISBN: 978-0-263-26641-2

MIX
Paper from
responsible sources
FSC™ C007454

This book is produced from independently certified FSC™ paper
to ensure responsible forest management.
For more information visit www.harpercollins.co.uk/green.

Printed and bound in Spain
by CPI, Barcelona

HER DIRTY LITTLE SECRET

JC HARROWAY

MILLS & BOON

For G.

For pushing me, supporting me and cheering me on. x

CHAPTER ONE

THE FOUR-INCH HEEL of her hand-dyed shoe caught on a cable, one of a hundred that snaked over the bare concrete floor. She stumbled with a curse and a roll of her ankle that made her eyes water. Harley Jacob sucked in a breath, waiting for the pain to subside, and then frowned at the scuff in the leather—petrol-blue to perfectly match her cashmere dress, the signature piece from her fashion line's autumn collection.

She sighed, funnelling her frustration into determination, her mission here today more important than a hundred pairs of hand-dyed shoes. Careful to avoid further injury, she picked her way across the cavernous space, her hesitant steps avoiding the hazardous maze of plastic dustsheets, vicious-looking power tools and stacks of dusty building materials.

Stupid jackass property developer.

Whoever was at the helm of Demont Designs Architecture and Property Development not only had a packed schedule, but he'd suddenly stalled on their deal for her purchase of the Morris Building. A deal that was days away from completion. And he'd stalled without explanation.

Harley headed towards a huddle of men at the far

end of the room, swallowing down the humiliation of
the hard hat and fluorescent vest combo—for someone
with her eye for fashion, it represented the ultimate insult. She straightened her shoulders, mentally smoothing any wrinkle that dared to sully her immaculate,
poised exterior and stepped around a nest of ducting
pipes dangling from the ceiling like the building's in-
testines spilling out.

Her determination to close this deal increased with
every step. Not because of the reputation of her family
name, one of New York's elite and synonymous with
real-estate royalty, but because she'd literally sweat
blood and tears to ensure her fashion label and her
social enterprise business, Give, succeeded.

And this deal was personal. She couldn't fail again.

As she approached the group of men, who were
similarly attired to her in safety vests and protective
gear, the whine of machinery and the constant staccato of hammering lessened slightly. Harley breathed
a sigh. At least she'd be able to hear Mr Demont's excuses. And hopefully his reassurances and apologies.
He owed her a pair of hand-dyed shoes, but she'd take
his signature on their contract in recompense.

The group, perhaps hearing the clack of her heels,
turned at once.

Conversation stopped.

A perfectly timed lull in the background hum of
construction noise gave a moment of skin-crawling
silence. Ten pairs of eyes landed on her, some curious,
some surprised, some wide, no doubt taking in her inappropriate footwear and now cloying woollen dress.

Harley lifted her chin. She hadn't come here to plas-
ter a wall or plumb in a bathroom. She wouldn't be

dismissed this time and she was well versed in holding her own in male-dominated environments.

Like her siblings, she'd grown up working school holidays at the family firm. But where her brother and sister had filed documents and answered telephones, Harley's dyslexia meant she'd been relegated to fetching coffee for her father's executives and emptying the office trashcans.

'I'm looking for Mr Demont.'

The group parted. The workmen closest to her stepped back, amused stares swivelling to the man at the centre of the group, who straightened from his stoop over an open laptop, his stare pinning her with twice the intensity of the bystanders', their eyes now round with curiosity.

'I'm Jack Demont.'

The air whooshed out of her lungs and heat slammed through her body—instant spine-tingling awareness. *No.*

It couldn't be.

Harley locked her knees, her fingers clutching the file in her hand.

Jack?

Jacques?

Jacques Lane?

Her disbelieving eyes scanned the man she'd come here to see, taking in the sexy, powerful, urbane demeanour he wore like an expensive suit. A man grown from a younger version she'd known, lusted after and once imagined herself in love with.

'Can I help you?' He showed no signs of recognition, but it was definitely him. The barest hint of a French accent—one that curled the toes inside her designer footwear. The same shade of azure-blue eyes, piercing her now as if she'd shrugged off the cashmere and stood before him naked. The scorching surge of hormones pounding through her bloodstream, clouding her reasons for seeking him out.

His stare didn't waver, but darkened. Annoyed by her stunned dithering or, like her, reeling from the frisson of sexual awareness snaking between them like the myriad cables on the floor?

Harley pressed her thighs together, astonished by how quickly her own annoyance and frustration had morphed into burning arousal. Arousal for a man she no longer knew. A man from her past. A man who'd stalled their deal for no reason.

Why was she here? She searched her scattered thoughts, mind clunking into gear. Yes…the Morris Building.

His stare still burned into hers. Caught on the back foot, she jutted her chin forward, employing her haughtiest tone.

'Could I trouble you for a moment of your time?' Damn, even her vocal cords spasmed at the sight of grown-up Jack, her strangled voice emerging all breathy. She cleared her throat. Time to claw back the upper hand.

If he wanted to pretend he didn't recognise her and had no idea why she'd hunted him down, she could play along. So what if her erogenous zones lit up like sparks from a welder's torch under his continued scrutiny? She refused to back down or slink away. And the fact they'd known each other—intimately nine years ago—was irrelevant.

She'd forgotten they were there, but, as if sensing

the tension thickening the air, the other men dropped their gazes to their steel-capped toes. Harley stepped forward, dropping her file and her purse on top of the blueprints on the table.

If Jack Demont thought she'd be intimidated by this testosterone-charged environment, or the fact their families had parted on bad terms nine years ago, he'd clearly forgotten the reputation of her hard-ass, cut-throat father, a man who'd raised her with his own personal brand of subtle put-downs, constant reminders of her failings and barely concealed disappointed looks.

With a twitch of his lips, Jack looked away, closing his laptop.

'Gentlemen, excuse us. Any queries, speak to the foreman.' The bite of his tone and the astute stare he levelled on her slammed her mission back to the forefront of Harley's lust-addled mind.

Mission. Contract. Signature.

The group disbanded, dispersing one by one until all that separated her from the man who now went by another name was a heap of ancient history and the crackle of sexual tension that rent the air like the buzz of power tools.

Her paper-thin confidence wavered, blurring the lines between past and present. Yes, for a few heady months she'd believed herself in love with teenaged Jack, back when the idea of love and naïve romantic ideals had ruled her head.

But perhaps she was alone in this renewed violent surge of attraction. Perhaps he *didn't* recognise her. Perhaps her ending their relationship had been insignificant to him then, easily forgotten the minute he'd returned to France with his family. And the subsequent heartache and guilt she'd felt on calling it off without explanation had been completely unnecessary.

She used the stalemate stare down they had going to reacquaint herself with the object of all her teen-aged fantasies on the perfect man. Of course, now she understood there was no such thing.

Time had changed him, but for the better. His dark blond hair was shorter, the unruly flop of youth now cropped at the sides and back, still a little wild on top—a place to slide her fingers. His face, still hand-some, had lost its boyish charm, his square, clean-shaven jaw was more pronounced and the cleft in his chin, which, from memory, perfectly fitted the tip of her index finger, was still prominent. How she'd love to test the scrape of his stubble against her skin. To kiss the curl of derision from his sexy mouth.

But one thing was glaringly obvious—the boy of her childish recollections had left the building. This man before her, dressed in a button down with the sleeves rolled up to reveal tanned muscular forearms, and tailored pants, oozed testosterone from every pore. The scorch of his stare alone told her he was in charge. Power dripped from him, the proud breadth of his chest, the dominating height of his stature and the de-termined jut of his arrogant chin.

Harley sucked in a breath.

'I—'

'What can I do for you?'

Their words clashed.

Their eyes clashed.

Harley swallowed, her resolve solidifying despite the flare of lust drawing her back in time. Now she'd met the man on the other end of their broken deal, she wouldn't leave without being heard out. She stood taller. She'd leave with his signature on the contract and they need never cross paths again.

The animosity between the Lanes and the Jacobs gave her an edge—know your enemy. And this was *her* turf. *Her* dream at stake. And despite not quite fitting the mould, she was a Jacob.

That Jacques Lane, or Jack Demont, now held that dream in the palm of his sexy, grown-up hands— hands she'd like to reintroduce to her traitorous body— provided an additional hurdle.

But she'd learned harsh lessons from her father's years of disapproval. Hardening herself to others' expectations and battling, daily, the personal limitations of dyslexia had become her norm. It would take more than his brooding sexuality to trip her up.

He continued to stare, his eyes sultry, as if they'd already peeled the layer of wool from her body. But still, he showed no hint of recognition.

Harley faltered, her composure fleeing, replaced by the ingrained insecurities that hovered close to her polished surface. But his cluelessness could be to her advantage. Time to throw *him* off balance. Why should she be the only one floundering and ignorant?

'You don't remember me?'

'Oh, I remember you, Harley.' He grinned, a superficial mask that didn't reach his eyes, which glittered with sparks as they traced her from head to toe. As if he'd plugged her into one of the sockets scattered about and attached her to the mains, his lazy perusal lit her up from the inside. And then his words registered and an all-over-body chill replaced the heat of moments ago.

He'd known the identity of his purchaser and deliberately stalled the sale. What other explanation could there be? Was this delay tactic some sort of petty revenge for the bad blood between their families? Or just revenge against her?

Harley jutted out one hip and fisted her hand there. If he'd stalled over some historical family feud…that was easily ironed out.

'You do?' She shifted her weight, her limbs liquefying under his molten stare.

She expected his dismissal or anger. After all, she'd unceremoniously dumped him years ago. But she hadn't expected the instant buzz of attraction or the urge to rip him out of his fine tailoring and see what havoc age and maturity had wreaked on his sublime-looking, rangy body.

But the clenched muscles in his jaw told her he not only remembered her, he also recalled the bitter feud between their families.

'Of course.'

Heat of a different kind crept under Harley's skin. She'd learned more than how to break someone's heart that summer. She'd learned about the lies adults told, the deceit hidden in plain sight and the true value of her so-called love.

Rearing back from memories of that time and her foolish infatuation with the boy Jack had been, she started when he stepped closer, encroaching on her personal space so she was forced to look up at him if she wanted to maintain eye contact. His heat burned into her, shunting her body temperature so high, she regretted the cashmere even more.

'I remember you, just fine.' His stare dipped to her mouth and she licked dry lips, an unconscious gesture.

Why, despite the harshness of his expression, did his words slide over her like a caress from the finest silk? He'd barely spoken, but the husky drawl of his voice reverberated viciously between her legs.

Just as it had at seventeen, her body reacted to him. But this time, she too was all grown up and her libido seemed to have multiplied exponentially in his potent presence.

But she wavered, caught between the successful entrepreneur of today here to seal the promised deal and the smitten schoolgirl of yesterday—insecure, lonely even within her family and infatuated by Jack's abundant confidence, his exotic accent and his cocky smile.

No.

She bit her lip, trying to dampen the licks of arousal coiling in her belly.

Not her.

Not him.

The events of that ill-fated family holiday with Jack's family had completely overwhelmed seventeen-year-old Harley, ripping apart everything she'd known to be true. In her confusion, fear and disillusionment, she'd abruptly broken things off with Jack, despite her rampant crush.

So her libido now had designs on this man. But time hadn't altered her opinions on relationships. And Jack would be the last man she'd ever consider had she any interest in changing that stance.

As if in slow motion, he gripped the front of his safety vest, his stare lingering on hers, and he tugged, ripping apart the Velcro and exposing a crisp blue shirt, which lay open at the neck to reveal a glimpse of golden chest hair.

Mmm...keep going...

Where had that come from? She was here for their deal, her building. Her eyes darted back to his in time to see a flash of what looked suspiciously like triumph simmering there. Caught with her hand in the cookie jar and drool on her chin.

'Did you just come to ogle me?' He lifted a brow, stepping closer. 'Or perhaps you like getting dirty.' He glanced down.

She followed his line of vision to the toes of her pumps, now covered with a layer of grey building dust.

Conceited asshole.

But the way he'd said *dirty*, his sensual accent wrapping around the word—she wanted to roll around in the sound, cover herself from head to toe and emerge completely filthy.

She snapped back to reality when he tossed the vest onto the table and began rolling down his shirtsleeves, his amused eyes dancing over her hot face.

'I came to get these contracts signed.' Not indulge in fantasies of the sexual prowess he'd developed over the years. Prowess she'd been denied.

'I have offices.' He slipped his hands in the front pockets of his pants, tugging the fabric taut across his manhood. 'Perhaps you should make an appointment to see me there. I think you'll find the ambience more...forgiving to your wardrobe.'

Arrogant, conceited asshole. And staring at his crotch...really?

'I've tried on multiple occasions to see you at your

offices, as I'm sure you know.' Heat boiled through her veins.

A shrug. A French tilt of his head.

Her fingers twitched. She longed to angle that head for her kiss. Rile him up and dismantle the control he now wore like a second skin. Redress the power play on display.

Harley lowered the pitch of her voice. It wouldn't do to show him he'd affected her professional composure or her personal interest.

'I'm here to discover why our deal stalled. And only days from completion?' Not that she'd known the run-down commercial property she was in the process of acquiring had anything to do with Joe Lane's son. Would she have walked away if she'd known? And had he really known Hal Jacob's daughter was on the other end of the Morris deal? He'd yet to confirm her theory.

'I hope you're not going to tell me you've applied the brakes because of some ancient family feud?' One look at the chips of ice in his eyes told her the answer.

'My lawyers advised me to dot the i's and cross the t's. You can never be too careful in business.' A wry twist of his sexy mouth accompanied the minute narrowing of the stare he settled on her. 'And they uncovered a mistake with the paperwork.'

'A mistake?'

No.

Harley's cashmere clung, her skin growing clammy. She'd checked and double, no, triple checked the forms before passing them to her lawyers. And she paid them fat bonuses to compensate for her...limitations. Limitations that had dogged her whole life.

'So it has nothing to do with the fact I'm the purchaser? *I*, after all, haven't changed my name.' She stepped nearer, the subtle, manly scent of him warming the air between them and sending her head into a tailspin.

The hard smile returned.

'I admit, when I contacted the Give Foundation to discuss the misfiled documents, your name was... familiar. But I assure you, Ms Jacob, I have no ulterior motives. I'm a straight-up businessman—no agenda.' A shrug. 'What you see is what you get—delivered with a handshake, of course.'

Harley leaned in, her feet welded to the spot. If he expected her to be intimidated, or even conciliatory, he'd chosen the wrong sparring partner. She was used to being one step behind, used to criticism. She usually came out snarling to compensate. Another Hal Jacob lesson...

'I assure *you*, Mr Demont, as the purchaser, any... mistake is an oversight and easily rectified.'

Please let it be easily rectified. If this deal collapsed, Hal would find out. Bad enough he was already fiercely opposed to this purchase. In fact he was opposed to all of his youngest daughter's choices.

'There's no reason to delay. I'm watertight.' She lifted her chin. *Fake it 'til you make it.*

But inside the familiar icy sweats erupted. Her whole life, dyslexia had thwarted her every ambition, but this mistake carried ten times the impact. She wanted the Morris Building—perfect for her needs and in a prime location.

But she'd messed up. Again. She could almost hear her father's flat-voiced disappointment. The unspoken 'I told you so' she'd been hearing since the sec-

ond grade. The last thing she needed was to prove Hal
right, or, worse, let herself down once more.

She forced her breaths to slow, talking herself back
from the ledge as she'd done many times over the years
when the familiar panic set in. New York had plenty
of real estate. She knew that better than anyone. Even
though he hadn't approved of her latest venture, Hal
had offered her a bargain deal on an alternative building, keeping it in the family.

If she weren't so determined to go it alone, she
could capitulate. But then she'd have to confess to her
father she'd sabotaged her project, one Hal Jacob considered a waste of time, through a simple clerical error,
which a five-year-old could probably spot.

Nope. Not going there.

'Watertight? Are you?' A dubious sneer. 'Jacob
Holdings have been known, in the past, to act with a
ruthlessness that I find…off-putting.'

Was he actually looking down his straight nose at
her? Her shoulders dropped a notch. She'd grown used
to condescension, was used to being dismissed. She'd
spent her whole life feeling stupid, embarrassed, un-
worthy. Not that he knew that. But his words stung as
if he'd struck at the most vulnerable part of her with
pinpoint accuracy.

'I prefer to deal with more…agreeable clients.' He
gathered his belongings from the table, tucking his
phone into his pants pocket. 'And until the documentation is corrected…' Another shrug.

Harley's pulse ricocheted around her body. So her
instincts had been right. He carried the Lane/Jacob
grudge, the same grudge that had soured not only their

respective fathers' business dealings, but also their families' friendship.

'I'm not Jacob Holdings.' She forced her fingers to relax. 'This deal has nothing to do with my family.' If only she hadn't messed up, her words would pack more punch.

His eyes flicked over her as if she hadn't spoken, or her arguments carried little weight with him. He'd made his opinion. Nothing, it seemed, would shake it.

'We'll see.' Completely unfazed, he offered her a tight smile and strode across the cavernous space towards the bank of elevators.

Taking a split second to admire his muscular ass under the fine wool of his pants, Harley hurried after his ground-eating strides, which made light work of the obstacles littering the floor, her own footfalls hindered by the clingy, tight-fitting dress.

Damn her dyslexia. Would its insidious grip on everything she tried to achieve never lessen? She'd personally handed him the ammunition to shoot down her dreams for the Morris Building. Another of her dreams destined for the 'Harley tries hard, but…' pile.

Part of her wasn't surprised—the little girl inside who'd always craved the same pride afforded her siblings' achievements. Of course those achievements could be measured academically—the right degree from the right school.

But how dared Jack insinuate the company she'd painstakingly built single-handed in spite of her father and her dyslexia, and Jacob Holdings, the family-run business with Hal at the helm, were bedfellows. She'd fought long and hard to forge her own path unencumbered by her surname.

Her turbulent hit-and-miss education, her enforced deviation from the Harvard to Jacob Holdings fast track her siblings had pursued and her determination to make it alone meant she'd forsaken her family name, despite its power to open any door in Manhattan.

She'd deliberately named her company Give for anonymity. Of course, it was impossible to completely disassociate herself from her New York heiress reputation. Fighting not only her family, who would see her firmly back in the fold, but also the few men of her past, who failed to understand why she eschewed a life of vacuous privilege to make it alone.

Dammit, why was he so tall, his legs so long?

'Wait.'

The elevator doors slid open. Jack disappeared inside and Harley trotted the final few paces to catch up. If he thought she'd simply slink away with her tail between her legs and their deal in tatters, he'd underestimated her.

So she'd made a mistake—she could own it and make it right. This was *her* deal, *her* dream—to build a dyslexia school with state-of-the-art practices and affordable to all. Nothing would stand between her and fulfilling that dream. Not Hal, not her fierce reawakened attraction to the man dangling the deal overhead like some sort of petty revenge and especially not the arrogant asshole Jacques Lane had become. In fact, as today had proved, the only thing that could derail her plans was Harley herself.

She'd almost made it to the elevator doors when her spike heel caught on a plastic dustsheet and her body lurched forward, destined for the concrete floor. She flailed her arms, clutching at nothing but dusty air.

Her file of documents and her purse hit the floor and then she slammed against a wall of solid chest. The air left her in a thump as Jack caught her, hauling her entire body up until every inch of her from shoulder to thigh was pressed against a firm mass of lithe muscle and hard man.

In less than a second she'd gone from seething after him to the sublime thrill of full-on body contact.

Her muscles froze.

Her brain forgot even the most basic of functions.

Her calm and compelling argument died on her tongue.

Jack's scent washed over her, vaguely familiar and enticingly foreign—clean, spicy, male—triggering a cascade of emotional memories and a flood of scalding need. His body warmth scorched her through the luminous yellow safety vest and the stifling layer of cashmere. Every slab of taut muscle pressed against her, spoke to her weak-willed body.

She looked up.

He looked down.

Their faces only inches apart.

Their mouths only inches apart.

The past nine years evaporated. She was seventeen again. So infatuated with the handsome, eighteen-year-old French boy, she'd begged him to take more than a kiss that last Aspen holiday their families shared. Not that he'd obliged—young Jack had had scruples, integrity and enough willpower for two.

But he'd kissed her as if she were dying and given her her first orgasm, all the while disentangling himself from her keen, persistent attempts to get him naked and take things at a pace quicker than he would allow.

But this Jack?

He was thick against her belly. His nostrils flared as if he too tried to relearn the nuances of her unique scent. His eyes turned stormy, as if he remembered the stolen minutes of ecstasy they'd snatched on those twice-a-year shared family holidays.

While their fathers had discussed business and their mothers had tanned, she'd imagined herself falling for him.

Right up to the moment she'd been rudely awoken with a lesson on relationships that had shifted her world view for ever. Another Hal Jacob lesson—this one harsher and more devastating than any before.

His mouth curled and his breath gusted over her parted lips. But instead of reminding them both of the passion and heat of those kisses she'd craved, he set her on her feet.

'Careful there, Princess. You might break a nail.'

Bastard.

Harley battled the lust raging through her and smoothed down her dress, which had ridden up to mid-thigh during her tumble. She shrugged out of the hideous fluorescent vest and, seeing Jack had removed his, tore the hard hat from her head.

So he thought her pampered, living off her trust fund, dabbling in real estate. He knew her no better than she knew him.

And so what if her body was stuck in the past— the torrid rage of hormones he'd once inspired more potent than ever? That meant nothing. She had a mission, one she intended to fulfil.

'Mr Demont. I refuse to be sidelined. I'd like your assurances my purchase of the Morris Building won't be unnecessarily delayed. I have developers on standby and a deadline for opening.' She scooped her belongings from the floor, ignoring the sizeable bulge in his pants and the hard look he shot her as the doors closed. A look laced with delicious heat she tried to ignore.

Jack pressed a button on the control panel, but, rather than commencing its descent, the elevator remained static. Just like their deal.

He stared for long uncomfortable seconds, feet spread, unruffled, his hands casually hooked into his front pockets as if highlighting his considerable manhood for her greedy stare.

Look what you missed out on.

Harley dragged her eyes away, throat hot, like the rest of her. Close up, his manly body displayed obvious and sizeable advantages over the younger one she remembered. She'd never actually seen him naked back then, but, damn, if she didn't want to strip him of more than his arrogant smirk.

But she wasn't an eager virgin any more, naïve to the games people played and the lies they told. So she still found him attractive. Big deal. It wouldn't stop her getting what she wanted. And if she'd learned anything since she'd last seen Jack, it was that sex was overrated and relying on others, for pleasure, business, or anything else, only led to more crushing disappointment.

He slouched against the wall of the elevator, dismissive stare raking her, leaving her hot in all the wrong, or right depending how she looked at it, places.

'Used to getting what you want, are you?'

'No.' The opposite in fact. She lifted her chin. 'This

development, the Morris Building—it's important to me. How can we get this deal back on track?' She leaned against the facing wall, the scant distance between them increasing a fraction. Not that she gained any relief from the inferno between her legs or the rampant thumping of her heart.

He narrowed his stare, holding hers captive.

'Are you trying to influence due diligence?' He stepped closer, stalking, stealing some of the air from the elevator while he looked her up and down in that delicious way that left her short of breath.

She leaned back against the handrail, gaining another couple of millimetres from his potent domination of the small car. She rolled her eyes, fighting to get her hormones under control and focus on business.

'Of course not.'

'You think because you're a Jacob you can rush a flawed business deal? Grease the wheels?' He invaded her personal space again, which had grown twice the size in his presence as if she was acutely attuned to every move he made.

'I told you before.' Her breaths grew choppy as she fought the lure of his closeness. 'This has nothing to do with my family. The Give Foundation is mine and mine alone.' The air, tinged with his scent, his warmth, thickened, as if she were trying to suck syrup into her lungs.

His gaze swept lower, tracing her mouth and then back up again. His tongue darted over his lush lower lip seconds before his breath gusted over her, and his voice dropped to a husky whisper.

'You think our past, what we shared, will influence me?'

Her legs quivered and she clung to the rail. How many more physical intimacies would she love to share with this version of Jack? She bit down on her lip to stop herself answering. Or worse, succumbing to the urge to shut him up with a kiss.

'You think you can show up here dressed for a runway, dazzle me and get whatever you want?'

Fire sizzled through her blood vessels, hot colour pooling in her face. She couldn't work out which was stronger—the buzz of arousal between her legs at his proximity, his heated stare and his sensual reminder of her first sexual awakening or the boiling rage clouding her vision at his lazy taunts.

She swallowed down the arousal, forcing out an affirmation she was far from believing.

'I'm a savvy and professional businesswoman, Mr Demont.' *When I'm not making simple errors that sabotage my own deals.* 'We had a contract, a promise, a sale and purchase agreement. Nothing more. Nothing less.'

Harley leaned forward, prepared to burn up to make her point.

'Is this some sort of payback?' She narrowed her eyes, fighting the surge of lust he instilled. She should be outraged, appalled, furious. But all she could muster was simmering annoyance eclipsed by the raging desire to tug his mouth down to hers.

His hard eyes glittered, holding her in limbo for long, torturous seconds where her breath stalled and her pulse throbbed in her throat.

Harley's toes flexed of their own accord, lifting her a few millimetres closer to those lips.

Her breath mingled with his.

The air between them crackled, hot and potent.

His eyes swam before her, a flash of the familiar sparkling in the depths of his irises. He sucked in a breath, as if on the verge of a decision. The verge of an action.

'Make an appointment, Ms Jacob.' He stepped back, seemingly unaffected by the past few seconds of intense sexual awareness, and pressed the descend button.

Harley, by contrast, hovered on the edge of spontaneous combustion. She must have misread the rampant lust burning in his eyes. Perhaps because her own underwear was on fire, she'd imagined he felt the same.

She gripped the handrail, too uncertain of the integrity of her wobbly legs to keep her upright, and bit the inside of her cheek until she tasted blood. His dismissal left her desperate to hide. To crawl away to lick her self-inflicted wounds.

'I've tried on numerous occasions to make an appointment. In fact, your assistant, Trent, and I are on first-name terms. Perhaps you should employ more staff, run a more professional outfit if you find yourself so over-committed.'

He pulled his phone from his pocket and dialled a number, a small smirk on his handsome face.

'Perhaps you should try my London or Paris offices. I'm often there. Perhaps you'll have more luck. Excuse me, I need to make this call by eleven.' Lifting the device to his ear, he spoke in French as the car stopped and the doors slid open to the ground floor foyer.

Without a backward glance, he strode to the reception desk, deep in conversation. An obliging building attendant handed him a tailored jacket that matched his pants and he dropped the hard hat on the counter and slung the garment over one broad shoulder.

Harley stood floundering in the tiled entranceway while he exited the building and climbed into the back of a sleek Mercedes-Benz waiting at the kerb.

She'd been brushed off before, belittled, ridiculed, sidelined. She'd never grown used to it. And she expected it from Jack Demont; after all, she'd once carelessly dismissed *him*.

And this time, she only had herself to blame.

Perhaps Hal was right. Perhaps she was wasting her time with…hobbies. Harley followed Jack outside, texting her own driver.

Their fathers might have instigated the Lane-Jacob war, and Harley might have jeopardised her tactical advantage, but she wouldn't lose this battle to Jack without a considerable fight.

CHAPTER TWO

JACK DISCONNECTED THE call and tossed his phone onto the seat beside him. 'Home, please, Will.' He pressed his lips together, offering a silent curse. He didn't normally bark at his regular driver, but the older man had the good sense to nod and pull out into Manhattan traffic without comment.

Jack gnashed his teeth together, sucking in air through flared nostrils, willing his body into submission. Despite himself, he'd been hard since he'd laid eyes on Harley, her white-blond hair askew under the ridiculous orange hard hat, her womanly curves barely concealed by the baggy safety vest and the demure woollen dress that covered her from knee to neck, and her flawless face pinched with confusion, her astonished stare quickly unleashing sparks of fire in the wake of his barbed taunts.

And then he'd touched her, not intentionally— initially he'd forced his hands to stay by his sides, battling the urge to reach out and test if her skin was as soft and fragrant as he remembered. But then she'd literally fallen into his arms, slotting against his body and fitting him like a glove.

Her delicate scent the most potent aphrodisiac and

her green stare clinging to his as if begging him to taste her again. Just as she'd begged him at seventeen. He shifted, adjusting the steely ache in his groin.

Fuck his integrity, his sense of honour. He'd held back then, never got to explore her the way he'd wanted, to see if the passion burning in her eyes could be fanned to an inferno. Because she'd dumped him. Out of the blue. No *Dear John*, no explanation, no regret.

And then his life had turned to shit. Jack rubbed a hand over his face, swallowing back a surge of bitterness.

What an idiot he'd been—on multiple levels. His naïve belief he'd have time to explore his budding relationship with Harley. His foolish conviction she'd cared for him and his complete lack of understanding when it came to the complexities of relationships.

He closed his eyes—even the word carried a bitter aftertaste. Sucking discipline through his flared nostrils, he willed his body back under control. But without the visual distraction of his surroundings, the memories amplified.

The feel of her against him in the elevator. Her soft curves pressed to him, flooding his body with renewed life as if he'd been dead all these years and she'd jump-started him with forty thousand volts. Her nipples peaking through the fine wool of her dress. The tantalising swipe of her pink tongue brushing across her plump lower lip. The flawless creamy skin flushed with…arousal or just anger?

Stop.

He raked his hand through his hair. At this rate, he'd

have to wait out his hard-on before he could enter his building and take a cold shower.

Of course, he'd known she'd show up some time. The minute he'd discovered the CEO of Give, the company purchasing a run-down piece of commercial real estate in the Bronx, was the girl who'd broken his young heart.

But like an idiot, he'd underestimated the impact of seeing her again in the flesh. Even with the hard hat, the impractical footwear and the blaze of belligerence, she was as achingly beautiful surrounded by building dust as she'd been at seventeen.

And even more so, because she'd matured into a sophisticated and, from the glimpses he'd seen today, savvy and determined woman. All woman—every curve waking primal urges within him, every plane of her exquisite face a bittersweet reminder of his youthful naiveté.

But he was no longer a besotted teen. And Harley had taught him his first relationship lesson—that 'love' vanished as quickly as it appeared and meant nothing.

His parents' divorce, which had followed in close succession to the sour business deal between his father and Harley's, had taught him the second lesson, and life as he'd known it had spiralled out of control, changed for ever.

He cursed. He tried not to think of those times, but Harley had stirred up more than his libido.

His father had never truly recovered from the implosion of his joint business venture with Hal Jacob or the demise of his marriage. And Jack had vowed never to be as vulnerable to that level of devastation, fighting damn hard through his late teens and early twenties to survive the crumbling of his once-happy family and to forge his own career path independent of his father's failing business.

Every step of that hard-won journey had been achieved by taking control of his life, making the decisions and shelving pointless sentimentality.

He rubbed his still-buzzing lips. He'd come so close to kissing her. Some caveman part of him demanding he give her both a taste and a demonstration of what she'd been missing.

Fuck, he'd come close to hoisting up that reveal-nothing wool dress and plunging inside her right there in the elevator of the building he was renovating.

He cracked his knuckles, stopping just short of punching the wood-panelled door. He'd once been a stupid kid, a dreamer. But he'd be damned if his residual and frankly irrelevant sexual attraction to her would rule him this time, even if it was clearly reciprocated.

Harley could no more hide the shallow breaths and fluttering pulse at her throat than he could hide his steely length in his pants.

The chemistry still raging between them affected her too. Perhaps she wanted more from him than the Morris Building. Perhaps she craved a taste of what she'd once callously thrown away.

He snorted, the idea growing in his mind. It had merits.

A game.

A mutually satisfying interlude that served a dual purpose—show Harley what she'd missed out on and scratch this insistent itch they'd sparked in each other.

Only this time he'd be firmly in control, as he always was. His rules, his playbook.

Being confined in a slowly moving vehicle with Harley in his head tested every ounce of his usually abundant patience. But that too could be channelled to serve his purpose. He reached for his phone to dial his assistant.

He dismissed polite preamble. He'd apologise when his mood improved and his head cleared of Harley's image.

'Find out if Give has any connection with Jacob Holdings.' He'd vowed long ago never to do business with Hal Jacob, the man who'd shafted his father professionally, stripping him of his self-confidence to make good decisions. A vow he intended to keep, despite the way his body responded to Harley.

'Yes, sir. We've already completed those checks,' Trent reminded him.

'Double check.' He wouldn't make the same mistakes his father had made. If Harley's business, her foundation, was tied up with Hal Jacob, he'd ensure the Morris deal stayed dead.

He hadn't lied to her. There *were* irregularities with the contract that required ironing out. But he'd been handed a gift, one he'd take full advantage of if he discovered she could be as deceptive as her father.

'Employ an industrial investigator. I want it ironclad.' One luxury of being head of your own multinational was the enviable position of being able to cherry-pick your business associates and clientele. A luxury that satisfied his need for control. He'd worked too hard to be led by his dick.

Fuck, perhaps he needed to get laid. He'd neglected

himself in recent months, building up his New York contacts, renting offices, finding the right apartment to renovate as a showpiece for his architecture clients.

And he hadn't spent the past nine years living like a monk. His life was full—personally and professionally satisfying. He'd made good on his promises to himself, his business going from strength to strength and the women in his life taking a gratifying but always temporary back seat.

'Mr Demont,' Trent interrupted, 'Mr Lancaster is in town. He's sent over a ticket to a function tonight. He'd like you to join him and Ms Noble.'

Perfect. That was what he needed. A night out with his cousin and his fiancée, somewhere glamorous with the distraction of plenty of gorgeous women. Women beautiful enough to chase away the memory of Harley's pert breasts pressed against his chest, her heartbeat thundering against his.

'Send the ticket over, Trent. And let Mr Lancaster and his fiancée know I'll be attending.' It didn't matter the nature of the function. He needed a diversion. Fast. It had been months since he'd had a woman in his bed. Too long.

The thought of sex flooded his mind with imaginings of Harley. Her blond hair fanned out over his pillow, her naked body wrapped in his sheets, her delectable scent clinging to the bed linens long after she left...

At this rate he'd have to bang one out before he left his apartment for the evening. He scrubbed his hand through his hair. Why hadn't he prepared himself for the sight of her? He should have guessed she'd take umbrage at him stalling the sale while his team investigated the error they'd unearthed at the eleventh hour. An error, it turned out, that originated with her.

Typical Harley. She'd breezed over that fact. And her family already owned half of Manhattan—of course she'd charge in and simply demand what she felt she deserved.

But he'd be damned if he'd give it to the pampered princess, no questions asked. He wouldn't trust Hal Jacob to the end of the street and he wouldn't make the same mistakes his father had made by becoming embroiled in a Jacob Holdings deal.

He'd witnessed the devastating fallout of that decision—his father's confidence, all his future enterprises and even his marriage fell victim to his miscalculation.

Jack credited his own business success to his determination to step out of his father's shadow, even shucking his father's name, literally reverting to his mother's maiden name to keep their businesses distinct, untainted by association with Hal Jacob.

No way would he allow his dick to lead him back into that viper's nest. No. This time, he'd keep Harley Jacob where he wanted her—under contract or under him, if she wanted a sample of what she'd missed.

The car pulled up to the kerb outside his Midtown apartment building and he strode inside, impatient for a shower to wash away the memory of Harley and her lingering scent on his clothing.

When he exited his private elevator on the top floor, his feet skidded to a halt and his heart bucked against his ribs.

Harley.

How had she beaten him here? She sat on the loveseat beside the doors to his penthouse, her eyes trained on the elevator and trained on him.

In seconds he was back to rock hard.

'How did you know where I live?'

She stood, her long eyelashes fluttering on a series of blinks.

'Some people would call this stalking.' Damn if her persistence didn't ramp up his interest. Was she keen for more than her precious building?

'I looked you up and tipped the doorman.' She shrugged. Clearly she'd grown up her father's daughter, not above bending morals to suit her personal needs.

But, man, had she grown up. And damn if he didn't want to drag her inside and give her the guided tour, starting with his bedroom. Fuck the bedroom. He'd unwrap her from that sheath of expensive wool, splay her over the minimalist slate-topped console table he'd imported from France in his foyer and go down on her until she sobbed out his name and forgot her own. That would be difficult for her to dismiss.

'I'm on my way out. Make it brief.' Swiping his key card through the reader, he ushered her inside, ahead of him, his innate good manners accepting nothing less, regardless of their past.

She paused in his entranceway, her gaze flitting around his space as if she'd been invited here and had every right to touch his home with her beautiful, perceptive eyes.

He used the time wisely, his stare tracing her curves, lingering on her luscious ass, which, despite the demure dress concealing it, was high and toned.

He groaned inwardly, his cock twitching with renewed enthusiasm.

With a flick, she tossed the swathe of silver, silky hair over her shoulder and lifted one brow in question. He dragged his mind away from her naked on all fours in front of him and led the way into the living space, throwing his suit jacket over the back of the sofa.

Knowing she stood behind him, no doubt assessing his choice of décor or the views from his windows, his shoulders tensed. He was proud of his home. The five-thousand-square-foot apartment dated to pre-war, but he'd renovated it with a flair for modern, while keeping some of the original features, a look that worked if his growing clientele were any judge.

'Drink?' Why was she here? Did she think he'd change his mind so easily? Sign a flawed contract just because she came from real-estate royalty? Or perhaps she thought he was still the love-struck sap he'd once been, willing to give her anything she desired.

'No, thank you.'

He selected a frigid bottle of still water from the fridge, unscrewing the cap and finishing it in three swallows, wishing for a split second it were Scotch. But the last thing he needed around Harley was any lowering of his physical inhibitions. He was close enough now to showing her what she'd been missing all these years.

And the way she looked at him, as if she wanted the lesson, made it increasingly difficult to ignore the hormones raging through his blood. But hadn't she been engaged? He vaguely recalled something in the society pages. Surely she'd found some Jacob-approved yes-man to show her a good time.

The water sloshed inside him, bitterness lingering in his throat. He checked her ring finger, finding it bare before his eyes flicked away. Not his problem. If she was here for sex, who was he to deny her the ride of her life?

'You changed your name.' She hadn't moved from her spot just inside the doorway, her back only centimetres from the wall as she eyed him warily. They were, after all, strangers.

Nine years ago, she'd made no attempt to let him down gently, stay friends, or keep in touch. And he'd channelled his dislike of her ruthless father and his impotence at his crumbling family into determination, driving his own success. Forgetting all about the Jacobs and that tumultuous time of his life. Forgetting about Harley.

He shrugged, his eyes raking her immaculate appearance. How would the heiress look undone by pleasure, rumpled and replete?

'I went to university in England. Jacques became anglicised over the years.'

'And Demont?' She licked her lips.

His eyes followed the swipe of her tongue, fresh blood pulsing in his groin. He needed to get her out of here before he offered that tongue another occupation than questioning his attempts to be a better man than his father.

'My mother's maiden name. A business decision.' He lifted his chin, daring her to question.

She nodded, the move small and thoughtful. Then she rolled her shoulders back, game face on.

'Look, I want you to know. I plan to turn the Morris Building into a school. A special school.' Colour seeped into her cheeks, heightening her attractiveness. Would she flush like that as she climaxed? Was she ashamed she'd come here begging? Or just struggling to beg him, a man she deemed of little consequence?

Regardless, damn if he didn't want to poke at her, to see the flashes in her eyes as she lambasted him turn to that sultry warmth as he kissed her the way her eyes had begged him in the elevator earlier. *Sick bastard.*

'Yelling at me didn't work, so you thought you'd try guilt?' He stepped closer, the flare in her eyes a jolt of electricity to his chest. 'Tell me, if I resist your demands long enough, can I expect a full-blown sexual charm offensive?' Not that he'd mind—he'd be up for a little…inducement if that were how she planned to get her own way.

In fact, if he decided to toy with her, her tactics played right into his hands. A little revenge sex might be just what he needed. Of course, he'd ensure she enjoyed it too. Perhaps she'd even fall for him? Then he could walk away without hesitation as she'd done to him.

How she must hate coming to him of all people, cap in hand and clearly so turned on she couldn't stop her gaze flicking to his crotch every few minutes.

Her hand clenched, and he expected her to slap him.

'You really have matured into a world-class asshole.' Her stare narrowed, hip jutted to one side.

He shrugged, impervious to her insults. She'd done her worst nine years ago. Cast him adrift without explanation, allowing him to fill in the blanks while he rode the storm of his imploding life.

In fact, she'd done him a favour, her rejection shaping him, clarifying his priorities, laying the foundations for all future liaisons with the opposite sex, which had been, without exception, on his terms.

'Not that it's any of your business, but I plan to build a dyslexia school.' She hesitated over the word *dyslexia* as if it was bulky in her throat, but then she tilted her chin, eyes hardening to emerald chips. Vulnerable or manipulative?

And why a dyslexia school? Did he care enough to ask?

'There are lots of dyslexia schools.' Instinct told him the Morris Building was more than important to her. It was personal.

This kept getting better and better.

'Not in the Bronx.' Her eyes darted away.

His fingers itched to tilt up her chin, to keep her open to him, in case he'd imagined the flashes of defensiveness. His skin tightened, as if he'd stayed still for too long. He closed the distance between them, unable to resist the pull.

Her watchful eyes grew rounder. Her lips parted, breaths short and choppy, lifting her pert breasts with each inhale.

'Why are you here, Harley?' If she'd come to demand he jump through her hoops, he'd kick her out. Fuck, he should kick her out anyway because the longer she stayed, the harder it became to ignore her mentally undressing him with those big eyes.

Power surged through him, flooding his muscles, demanding he act.

'I…' The pulse at her throat fluttered and her eyelids drooped to a sultry half-mast.

His body tensed, on high alert, an effect of her closeness and a side effect of his raging need to touch her again. He focussed on her mouth—plump lips parted to emit those breathy little pants that called to his dick.

'Did you come for a sample of what might have been?'

He took another step.

Her huge eyes glowed, deep pools that a lesser man could drown in. But he'd never again lose his head. This close, her pupils dilated as she looked up at him. Did he imagine the regret hovering in the depths of her eyes? Less obvious than the excitement she couldn't hide.

Had she come to explain why she'd called things off between them? The last thing he needed was to hear her belated let-down.

He braced himself to turn away. This trip down memory lane was over. Best to leave the past undisturbed. After all, he'd made damn sure he moved on. And this buttoned-up heiress, polished, sophisticated and accomplished, was a complete stranger to him.

'Time to leave. Whatever it is you came for, you won't be getting.' Unless all she wanted was a fuck for old times' sake.

She touched his arm, closing the distance between them, fingertips digging in. Her purse hit the floor with a thud that matched the pound of his pulse as she stepped up close and lifted her face to his.

His strung-taut body acted on instinct. A cathartic release of pent-up frustration as he reached for her.

'Yes,' she hissed seconds before his mouth covered hers, swallowing the tiny moan she released. He pressed against her, fanning the flammable connection that had sparked to life in the elevator earlier.

As her fingers tangled in his hair and her lips parted, giving his tongue access, the past grew foggy.

He didn't need to trust her to enjoy the feel of her body in his hands. And she was right there with him, succumbing to the searing chemistry, as physically attuned as cream and coffee.

Her soft moans punched him in the gut, his balls heavy. She twisted her fingers in his hair and pressed herself against him as she'd been in the elevator, but this time her body writhed, as if she too was trying to quench an insatiable fire inside.

Perhaps it had been as long for her as it had been for him.

He cupped her ass, drawing her heated centre to his rock-hard dick, pressing her closer, to their mutual delight if the gasp she gave was any indication. He could practically feel her wetness through their layers of clothing.

She wanted him as much as he wanted her. Why wait? Why deny this? Why not slake this mutual physical need? No strings attached.

Reaching for the hem of her dress, he worked his hand up one bare thigh, the silky softness of her skin a roadmap leading him home. She shifted, opening up and giving him the access he sought. Still with him. On the same page.

As his fingertips stroked her soft lips through the lace of her panties she gasped, pulling back from their kiss to stare at him while he worked his fingers back and forth with increasing pressure.

She was clearly as turned on as him. He'd barely touched her, but her panties were soaked, and her eyes were soft and heavy with desire. He pressed himself to her hip, making his intentions clear.

'Do you remember your first orgasm?' He cupped her, his index finger working inside the wisp of lingerie to find her wet, swollen. So ready.

She nodded, her tongue darting out to trace the cupid's bow of her top lip.

'Tell me.' A test. Did she really remember? Had it meant something to her as it had to him or was she just desperate to get off?

Her eyes rolled back, her mouth open on a broken gasp as he located her clit and brushed the nub of nerves with the pad of his finger. Her moisture slid down his fingers, and he widened his legs, pushing her thighs open with his to get closer to her centre. When he pressed home, two fingers plunging inside her tight warmth and his thumb zeroing in on her clit, her eyes flew open, her stare beseeching.

'Tell me you remember, Harley.' She'd get what she wanted when he did. Confirmation that, if only briefly, he'd once mattered enough.

But fuck, she was responsive. Her thighs juddered, bumping his working fingers as if she were seconds away from coming on his hand. Just like the first time he'd made her come, her cries muffled into his shoulder.

She could barely speak, her breathy voice punctuated with staccato moans that matched the rhythm of his plunging fingers.

'We were at the…lodge, in Aspen. You said…that you'd make the next one better. Oh.'

Triumph surged through him, and he ramped up the circling of his thumb. Her breath caught, her head fell forward. She clung to him, her nails gouging his arms as she held on tight, her bold, uninhibited sexuality a wet dream come true.

His own desire ramped so high he searched his mind for the location of the closest condom, reluctant to move too far from this spot before plunging inside her.

Every muscle in his body tightened to snapping point. He pressed closer, grinding his erection between the crush of their writhing, jerking bodies.

'I was a kid then.' He twisted his wrist, his fingers probing deeper, curling forward to rub her walls. 'I'm not any longer.'

As firsts went, he'd been damn proud that he'd taken her there. But he'd honed his skills since then, never had any complaints. If she wanted it, he'd show her everything she'd thrown away.

No emotions.

No entanglements.

And just like her, no regrets when he walked.

'Look at me, Harley. Look at me and I'll make this one better.'

Her head lifted, her eyes heavy, swimming with lust. He cupped her breast with his free hand, his thumb brushing her nipple erect through the layer of frustrating wool.

He ground his teeth. It wasn't what he wanted. He wanted her naked. He wanted her laid bare so he could touch every inch of her sexy body. He wanted his mouth on her, every part. Laving and lapping until she went off like a rocket and screamed his name. He wanted to be inside her so bad he had to bite his cheek to remind himself he didn't know this woman aside from his ability to get her off.

He tweaked the bud, twisting and rolling her nipple between his fingers.

'Yes.' Her mouth dropped open.

Euphoria pounded through his blood. She was close. She would come for him, just like the first time. He held her eyes captive. A roar in his head deafened him to everything but the frantic little whimpers she made as he worked her higher and higher.

His hand started to cramp, but he'd die before stopping, something primitive in him demanding her orgasm, showing her the man he'd become.

'Kiss me.' His voice wasn't his own. Gruff. Challenging. But getting him what he wanted.

She cried out, cupping his neck and yanking him down roughly to meet her needy mouth. Her tongue welcomed his, every surge and retreat, every slide as perfect as the first time they'd kissed, the excitement of firsts eclipsing the awkwardness back then.

But there was no awkwardness now. He wasn't a fumbling teenager any more, and she was all woman, writhing on the verge of climax.

She pulled back, wild eyes clinging to his.

'Jacques… I—'

With her use of his French name, he groaned, the bittersweet wash of memories unleashing his raw need to stamp his mark on her as Jack Demont, not the dismissible Jacques Lane.

Her kisses turned frantic and then she tore her mouth from his, her orgasm slamming her against the wall as she cried out, her hooded stare wildly flicking between his eyes. Spasms rocked her and she rode his hand with sublime abandon.

Fuck. Perfect.

He kept up the pressure, his hand slowing but not retreating from between her legs and his thumb circling her peaked nipple. Still she twitched around his fingers, her body lax in his arms as her breaths slowed.

Finally she pushed his hands away, and he released her. A flush caressed her cheeks, her eyes slumberous, and a small, satiated smile tugged her red and swollen mouth.

She rested her forehead on his chest, the gesture so familiar, something in him recoiled from the intimacy. He pressed his body along the length of hers.

Just sex.

'I'm a man of my word, Harley.' She couldn't deny she'd had a good time, and once he got inside her, he'd take her there again.

A small sated sigh. 'We'll see,' she mumbled against his shirt.

He froze. Ice water replaced his blood. Had he heard her right?

He stepped back, steadying her by the forearms until she stood tall, taking her own weight.

'What did you say?'

The post-orgasmic flush in her cheeks darkened, but she lifted her chin.

'I said we'll see. You've certainly broken your word on the Morris Building sale.'

His balls shrank as quickly as if she'd kneed him in the groin. A red film lowered over his vision— he'd always assumed that was an exaggeration, but, no, he was definitely seeing red. Hearing red. Fucking feeling red.

So she doubted his integrity, his professionalism, still blamed *him* for the delay despite *her* mistake?

He shook his head. *What a fool.* He stepped back, adjusting his diminishing hard-on.

'I'm my own boss. I call the shots and I choose who I do business with. The cock up with the Morris contracts came from *your* office.' His enamel creaked where he ground his teeth together.

She pushed down her dress, eyes blazing.

'I told you, Give has nothing to do with Jacob Holdings. I'm my own boss, too.' Her eyes flared but colour highlighted her cheekbones, and she looked away. 'So I messed up the paperwork. But we're not so different, you and I.' She retrieved her purse from the floor, glaring at him again. 'You're so desperate to disassociate yourself from your father and the mess *he* made with his business, you've changed your name.' She mashed her lips together, breathing hard through flared nostrils.

Perhaps he imagined the moment's regret on her face. Either way, he was done. This—whatever this had been—was over. He turned away, gathering the last shreds of his resolve. His fingers formed a fist, frustration with his stupidity tensing every muscle in his body. How had he been so blinkered? Harley was a Jacob. She knew as much about him as he did her, but she'd already tarred him with his father's brush. Used him to get off and then insulted him. Clearly thought no more of him today than she had nine years ago.

At least the timely reminder of the distrust between them had finally cured his hard-on. He turned back,

keeping the emotions from his face. The best advice
his father had ever given him—show no weakness.
Not that he was weak, professionally. Only, it seemed,
where his dick and Harley Jacob were concerned.

'Well, I guess we both have something to prove.'

He needed this deal like he needed a hole in the
head. He'd been half tempted to renovate the Morris
Building himself. And, until the issues resolved and
he was certain Hal Jacob had no hand in it, the deal
stayed stalled.

'I'll have my lawyers contact yours when the issues
are rectified to my satisfaction.' He loosened his tie.
'If the timing was that important to you, perhaps you
should have taken better care to avoid errors.'

Her fuming glare followed the path of his fingers
as he popped his shirt buttons but the satisfaction was
short-lived.

'I'm going to take a shower. You know the way out.'

Even with the water switched to arctic, he couldn't
wash away the scent of her, which clung to him as if
he'd doused himself, head to toe. Nor could he banish
the flash of hurt in her eyes as he'd walked away, leaving the society princess to put herself back together
and show herself out.

CHAPTER THREE

LOFT 333 IN CHELSEA, a chic industrial space in the heart of the Garment District, provided the perfect venue for an intimate fashion show showcasing some of New York's most exciting new designers. Harley emerged from the makeshift backstage area into the cavernous space, which vibrated with the thud of techno music, the kaleidoscopic lighting bouncing off the stark white walls.

A buzz at her temples threatened to become the perfect and fitting end to the shittiest of days.

And it was all Jack's fault.

Starting with the stubborn pig-headedness that had caused him to cancel their meeting, ruining her favourite shoes at his Swiss cheese building site and ending with him unceremoniously kicking her out of his apartment.

She couldn't blame him for the part where she'd surrendered to her fierce sexual attraction to him—that was all her. Stalking him to his building, practically eye-fucking him and then unashamedly riding his hand to orgasm…

Yep, all her.

Forcing her mind from the memory of his voracious, demanding kisses and his exceptional manual skills, she scanned the venue, her critical eye for detail and high expectations cataloguing the packed rows of seating, the smartly dressed wait staff and the professional, if not headache-inducing, audio-visual display.

Shame her thoroughness with the Morris deal had let her down. She sighed, slinking further into the shadows.

Part of her, the old Harley, baulked at her own success. Yes, she'd had every privilege in life. But without her team behind her—her dedicated assistant, her competent store manager, her siblings—her dyslexia meant she struggled with the very basics.

To outsiders, she had it all. And yet the planning alone for tonight's show—the lists, the running order, the spreadsheets of which model would wear what for which designer—was enough to make her head explode.

Jack was right. She alone had responsibility for sabotaging the Morris deal. She'd failed. Again. Shot herself in the foot.

She leaned back against the wall, maintaining a low profile. She rarely lauded her own shows. Her fashion label, the only aspect of her life that offered her contentment, meant everything, but she'd decided from the beginning she wouldn't use the Jacob name to garner publicity, make connections or grease the ladder rungs. If she made it in what was a competitive, often fickle and rapidly shifting industry, she'd make it on merit alone.

And it was the creative process—from sketching a new design, to sewing a sample garment and then styling an entire outfit—that allowed her a brief glimpse of chest-tingling pride. At least she was good at one thing.

But she wasn't here to see her own designs paraded.

Harley snagged a glass of champagne from a table laden with exquisite crystal and located a quiet, dark corner to watch the show. She'd missed most of the first half, staying backstage to help the other designers dress their models.

The collective of young, emerging fashionistas she mentored had worked tirelessly for months putting this show together and she was here to support them, knowing first hand the importance of a leg up onto the bottom rung. The fashion industry, as cut-throat as any deal Hal Jacob peddled.

She released a small snort—she'd learned from the master. Not that Hal had ever dedicated any time to her education, preferring to hurl money at the situation, his 'problem daughter'.

She'd known from an early age she was different. But her difficulties had gone undiagnosed through elementary school, until the age of twelve, when she'd been no longer able to hide her challenges and one particularly insightful teacher had suggested to her parents she might benefit from formal testing. Hal had struggled with her diagnosis, denying the label and preferring instead to employ a series of tutors to put his *unmotivated* daughter through the wringer.

Dyslexia affected sufferers differently. Harley struggled with the full gamut of challenges. The fact she'd learned strategies to mask her shortcomings had delayed confirmation of her diagnosis until well into sixth grade. By which time she'd become a bullied, socially isolated black sheep of her over-achieving family and a constant disappointment to Hal.

Harley gulped a mouthful of champagne, forcing down the shame and humiliation. She scuffed the toe of her shoe on the parquet flooring, cursing her stupidity with the Morris paperwork.

She'd checked and double checked until her eyes watered and her temples screamed. Then she'd run everything past her assistant. Not that she blamed Alice. The mistake was all Harley's. And she was used to making the most simple of errors. But why did it have to be on that deal? With him?

Perhaps that explained her uncharacteristic rudeness. Heat crept up her neck as she recalled the shutters covering Jack's heated stare earlier when she'd questioned his integrity. She'd obviously inherited her vicious tongue from Hal, too.

She smoothed her damp palm down the length of her form-fitting dress—a simple bias-cut sheath in black silk. Elegant, timeless, modest. Or as her twin sister, Hannah, would say, boring. But Harley preferred fading into the background over standing out.

She scanned the two-hundred-strong audience, sipping her champagne to chase away the demons that lurked beneath her polished exterior. Although her eyes focussed on the show, her mind wandered.

Back to Jack.

Her initial shock at seeing him again had faded quickly. Her annoyance at him holding the sale of Morris Building to ransom simmered. But the few stolen moments in his apartment this afternoon…? They played in a continuous looped film reel behind her eyes, every intensely erotic, libidinous moment relived over and over.

Surely she'd exhausted her supply of female hormones? She shifted, pressing her thighs together and leaning back against the wall in case she slid to the hardwood floor in a puddle of lust.

Just like the first time he'd touched her so intimately, he'd commanded her body, turned her inside out, thrust her so hard into an intense orgasm she'd literally seen stars.

She'd never known anything like it, not even with her ex-fiancé, not since the first one, also at Jack's hands. And what talented hands they were.

She swallowed, face flushed with heat. Of course, there'd been one or two others since Jack. Not many, her troubled teens merging with her underwhelming early twenties—a time when most girls spread their sexual wings. But Harley had been too preoccupied with overcoming her dyslexia enough to prove her father wrong and get her college degree, albeit in a subject Hal considered more of a hobby—fashion design.

She'd even come close to marrying, again in an attempt to improve her standing in her father's eyes. If she couldn't be a Jacob Holdings' executive, she could marry one… But she'd quickly realised her error—she and Phil, although he was Hal-approved, were ultimately too different. And she had no intention of becoming a Hal Jacob puppet by proxy. Hal and Phil, cut from similar cloth, shared too many opinions about Harley's career, or, as they saw it and frequently commented, her lack of one.

The hairs on the back of her neck lifted seconds before the warm breath whispered across her skin. She

froze, either instinct or her body's imprinting onto
the only man with whom she'd discovered such overwhelming pleasure warning her it was Jack.

'Still stalking me, I see.' His low voice vibrated
against the sensitive skin of her neck, tingles spreading to her toes via her in-sync-with-Jack clit. It seemed
she possessed an inexhaustible supply of hormones
where this man was concerned.

She spun so quickly, she sloshed champagne from
her glass over the back of her hand, a few spots landing on the front of her dress. Jack gripped her elbows,
steadying her, his eyes amused in the red and green
lighting bouncing off the loft's every, whitewashed
surface.

Jack's stare pinned her and his lips twitched; he was
clearly enjoying her rattled composure. He reached
inside his breast pocket and withdrew a crisp white
handkerchief. He pressed the square into her free hand,
and she wiped the spill from her dress.

'What are you doing here?' She scanned the crowds
behind him. Had he come here with a date? There
were plenty of stunning women in the audience and
Jack was by far the most handsome, put-together man
present—not a bad accolade considering the number
of male models present.

Harley's pulse thrummed in her throat and between
her legs as she flustered around with the handkerchief,
avoiding his stare.

She'd come propped against the wall in his well-
appointed living room this afternoon, writhed and
bucked against his hand, getting herself off like a sex-
starved nympho. Trouble was, she *was* sex-starved,
at least starved of the high-calibre variety of sex she

was sure came as this man's standard. Not that her and Jack had ever hit a home run. Not nine years ago, and certainly not now.

'I have a ticket.' He tapped his breast pocket and her fashion-tuned eye took a few indulgent seconds to admire the cut of his suit—this one steel blue. His tailor really was excellent, but then Jack was every designer's dream model. Tall, athletic, muscular but not buff—every inch of him expertly and expensively attired. His black shirt, open at the neck, brought out his fair good looks and highlighted the gleam in his eyes. A gleam levelled directly on her.

'I see your label is up after the interval?' He accepted the return of the handkerchief, slipping it back inside his breast pocket.

She nodded, marvelling at the way he could speak on such a mundane topic, all the while his eyes seemed to be stripping her bare. Was he recalling her libidinous display earlier?

Or perhaps it was just wishful thinking on her part, the wisp of silk she wore transforming into a bulky, itchy straightjacket, begging to be tossed so she could get down and dirty with him again.

'Yes.' So he'd done his homework. The Give Foundation she'd established after college comprised an ethical fashion house, a cruelty-free cosmetic line and a charity arm. The dyslexia school, if the purchase of the Morris Building proceeded, would be her latest acquisition and, she hoped, her most rewarding endeavour to date. If only she could pull it off.

If only the paperwork had been properly filed.

She kept her mind on business, perhaps then she'd

stop eye-fucking him or drooling over her vivid imaginings of the real deal.

'So have you reconsidered? Will the sale go ahead?' She might as well work on rectifying her mistake while she had him here. It took her mind off dragging him backstage and stripping him out of that suit and demanding a replay of this afternoon.

His sinful mouth quirked up.

'So you don't trust me, but you still want my business?'

She swallowed. A hundred answers forming on her tongue. Trust him? She barely knew him. She just wanted their deal back on track so she could forget she'd ever…reacquainted with him.

Kissed him as if the world were ending. Used his incredible skills to get off and then slapped him back.

'I've spent six months searching for the perfect building. I have an architect on standby for the renovations and I didn't say I didn't trust you.'

Trust…? She knew little of the man he'd become. But she craved the searing chemistry between them with a fierceness she didn't recognise as her own.

He grinned. 'You didn't have to say it aloud.' His eyes lingered on her mouth, his own lip curling. 'Don't worry, I don't trust you, either.' His lazy stare dragged slowly down the length of her body, and he stepped close, his voice dropping to a sultry murmur that skated over her ear and slid down her neck.

'And yet you trust me with your body? With your pleasure?' His lips grazed her earlobe as he straightened, the only point of contact between them. And just like that she returned to a state of full-body meltdown.

She leaned forward as he pulled away, as if her

entire being were magnetised and drawn to his, opposing poles. Memory of that pleasure snaked south, a flood of heat dampening her panties. Damn him. How could he do that to her, with a few husky words? He seemed to have a direct line, a retinal scanner and magic wand to her libido.

A round of applause heralded the end to the current show. Harley ignored the heat fizzing through her veins and the more potent heat rising from the man next to her. She placed her champagne on a nearby table to clap as the designer took the stage with his models for one last walk.

'Your turn next,' he said as the lights went up, heralding the start of a fifteen-minute interval. Why did his every word scrape at her nipples? His sexy accent, the deep timbre, the accompanying smoulder that seemed to be tailored specifically for her.

'Oh, I don't walk at my shows.' She picked up her champagne flute, giving her restless hands something to do other than touch Jack as she busied her stare with the audience, who rose from their seats, many heading to the bar.

'Why not?' He sipped his own drink, his tongue taking a slow swipe across his bottom lip. A lip she'd tasted, scraped with her teeth, sucked at while kissing him as if her life depended on it. Would it feel as amazing gliding over the rest of her body?

She lifted one shoulder, heat of a different kind infecting her buzz. Should she justify her rather unorthodox choices to him?

In the past, explaining her beliefs and opinions to the men in her life had only led to criticism. And she'd heard enough of that to last a lifetime. Could she tolerate it from Jack, of all people?

'I find my label does better without the often adverse publicity of the Jacob name.'

His brow dipped, as if puzzled by her revelation. She was about to elaborate when they were joined by another couple, the man tall and immaculately tailored like Jack, and the woman elegantly understated in that trendy, New York way.

Jack stepped aside, welcoming the couple into their space. 'Harley, I'd like you to meet my cousin, Alex Lancaster, and his fiancée, Libby Noble. Libby is a New Yorker, too.'

They shook hands, exchanging warm, polite greetings, and then the gorgeous couple took flutes of champagne from a passing waiter.

'So, how do you two know each other?' asked Alex, eyeing his cousin.

Harley jumped in. 'We…' What could she say? Their liaisons, both then and now, too complicated for polite conversation.

'Harley and I are in business negotiations.' Jack flicked her a look that replicated the effect of his fingers teasing her nipple earlier. She clamped her mouth shut in case she actually whimpered out loud. How did he do that? He hadn't even touched her.

With his eyes still on her, he spoke to his cousin.

'Her company is purchasing the Morris Building.' He could have used different words, other explanations.

We holidayed together as kids. Our families were once friends. We shared hot and heavy make-out sessions during stolen teenaged moments.

Highly attuned to the erotic tension coiling between her and Jack, she avoided his eyes. But she couldn't avoid the memories—those innocent moments of sexual awakening hijacked by an awakening of another kind, one that had killed that innocence, changed her view on relationships for ever and tore their two families apart. Hal's explanation had been a business deal turned sour. But sadly, Harley knew better.

She swallowed the bitter aftertaste those memories always evoked, along with the harder to overcome shame.

Alex looked at Jack, who still stared at Harley.

'Oh…' Alex glanced between Harley and his cousin '…are you the person responsible for the cock up?' He grinned, his expression teasing mischief. But the barb went deep, with the accuracy of a medical laser.

Harley winced, looking away.

'Libby, are you enjoying the show?' Jack deftly saved her from answering and changed the subject in one move.

But the damage had been done. What did Alex know? Had Jack talked about her? Blamed her stupidity for the stalled deal? Credited the error to some girl he'd known nine years ago, playing at business but woefully underqualified?

Did he congratulate himself on his disentanglement from her, from her dysfunctional family and now from their business deal? A close escape from dumb Harley and her ruthless old man. Oh, she could almost hear the conversation. No doubt Joe Lane had badmouthed her family as much as Hal had maligned his.

Her shoulders fell. Jack owed her no loyalty. And it was all true, mirroring how she saw herself.

As Libby and Jack discussed the first half of the show, Harley offered Alex a tight, polite smile, her face flaming. 'Excuse me.'

Alex frowned. 'I'm sorry. I—'

She almost comforted him; he seemed so contrite.

'No problem.' She forced her facial muscles to relax. Her blood pounded hot. Spreading fire. Whatever Jack had said about her to his cousin, she didn't need to hear. 'I need to check things backstage.' She made to sidestep away from the group, away from the awkward exchange that had brought all her insecurities to the surface.

Despite the front she presented to the world, deep inside her self-esteem was shaky at best. Her undiagnosed dyslexia, a lifetime of never quite fitting in, even at home, and years of listening to her tactless and selfish father had shredded every scrap she possessed.

That was why her 'projects', as Hall called her business enterprises, carried such importance. They represented a chance to feel pride in her hard work. A chance to make a difference.

She'd barely moved when Jack's hand found the small of her back, his fingers pressing with possession. She shot him a look, his own expression unreadable as he stared at her over the rim of his glass.

Harley smiled for Libby and made her excuses. He might have set her body alight, showed her the good time he'd promised, but he didn't own her, didn't even know her. And she owed him nothing.

She wasn't that naïve schoolgirl any longer. She understood how the world worked, how people used each other, wrecked lives for a few minutes of selfish pleasure. She could compartmentalise sex. And she and Jack hadn't even shared that.

As she wove her way backstage she made a vow. Tomorrow, she'd set her dreams back a few months and start looking for another piece of real estate for her beloved school.

Fuck, he'd blown it.

Harley had disappeared. He'd waited for her to emerge after her show but there'd been no sign of her. Why hadn't he kept his mouth shut? Why hadn't he had a better explanation ready for his inquisitive cousin? He should have known Alex would put it all together—sharp, astute bastard. He bit back another curse.

Alex and he had attended the same university. Their bond more akin to brothers than cousins. Alex had witnessed first hand the fallout from the abrupt, un-explained end of his relationship with teenaged Harley, his first relationship. And he knew all about the bad business, the rift that tore his and Harley's families apart.

Without Alex's friendship, he'd never have weathered his parents' divorce, nor the financially turbulent years that had followed as everything his father had worked for had crumbled. If it hadn't been for his mother's family money, they'd have even lost their home.

A lead weight settled in his gut. It had seemed as if he'd thrown Harley under the bus. But any composure he might have displayed as his past and his present collided had been shot to pieces by the sight of her at the fashion show.

From the moment he'd arrived at the glamorous

event she'd been on his mind. Instead of scoping out the guests for a beautiful and sophisticated distraction as he'd planned, he'd replayed the vision of her pleasure, rapt and clinging to him, her glorious mouth swollen from his kisses and her cries of ecstasy echoing around inside his skull, until the catwalk show had blurred before his eyes.

Then an inexplicable burn at the back of his neck had forced him to turn around. And there she was. As immaculate as ever but cloaked with an air of vulnerability. He'd watched her, shadowed in a dark corner, his whole body shocked into nerve-tingling life. A quick scan of the previously untouched programme in his lap and he'd slotted all the pieces together.

And then Alex had correctly guessed that the woman on the end of the Morris deal was the one that got away. *No, ran away.* He knew his cousin just as well as Alex knew him and Alex's searching stare spoke a thousand words.

Her face at his cousin's playful jibe haunted Jack—he'd supplied the ammunition to embarrass her over the botched contract. He'd never seen her anything but composed.

He clenched his fists. She'd looked as if she'd taken a blow to the chest. She'd shuttered the flash of hurt behind her huge luminous eyes, shot him a *fuck you* look and swanned away with a sway of her sexy ass.

He understood that the Morris Building, her plans for it, formed a personal crusade, but surely someone in her team should have spotted the clerical error his lawyers and hers were currently untangling. Didn't she have a scapegoat to blame?

He slammed out onto the landing. Why did he even

care that she'd been humiliated? Why was he so knotted up over this? He never allowed personal to interfere with business. Perhaps it originated in his persistent sexual frustration—he'd failed to get laid, despite a steady stream of interested looks from the abundant women here tonight.

But once he'd seen Harley again, he hadn't been able to muster one tenth of the enthusiasm she inspired. Perhaps the revenge fuck idea carried more merit than he'd acknowledged.

He snorted out his frustration. He'd go home, have a second cold shower and try to wipe Harley from his mind.

But at the top of the stairs, he halted.

She stood on the next landing down, her focus on the phone clutched in her hand as she paced, worrying at her lip. He slowed his stride, taking the stairs at an easy pace while he willed his heart rate and breathing into submission.

He paused three stairs above her. At least he'd have a chance to apologise for Alex's clumsy comments. He should never have mentioned the Morris deal to his cousin—business indiscretions were beneath them both.

'Libby loved your collection.'

Harley looked up, her hand flying to her chest.

He should have coughed, warned her he was there. He offered an apologetic tilt of his head. 'She said you understood real women's bodies.'

She recovered quickly, cold eyes darting away to street level.

'Thank you.' She glanced back down at the screen of her phone as if he weren't there. He deserved that—

he should have been more circumspect. But he'd voiced his frustration to Alex before he'd discovered it was Harley behind the Morris deal.

And he owned his mistakes, big and small.

'I'm sorry about earlier… Alex.' A shrug. 'I'd mentioned my latest deal was held up because of an oversight. I didn't know of your identity at the time.'

'Don't worry about it.' She shook her head, a humourless grin on her face as if she expected nothing less. 'I'm used to making mistakes and paying the price. And who you choose to gossip with is none of my business.' She glanced down the stairwell, her bottom lip taking another punishing.

What the fuck did that mean?

'I don't gossip. I discussed a stalled deal with a business colleague.'

And he's an insightful pain in the ass with a really good memory.

'You're upset.' His hand inside his pants pocket curled into a fist. 'He was just teasing. He's English.'

He thought she might smile at his outrageous explanation, but she shot him a frosty look and then returned her attention to her phone, which buzzed with an incoming text.

He took another step closer.

'Why *are* you upset?' Why did he care? He should walk away now. He'd proved his point both in relation to their aborted contract and their newfound sexual chemistry.

Her glare wavered, as if she grew fatigued by the weight of it. 'I'm not upset. I'm…disappointed with myself.' She deflated.

'Mistakes happen.' He willed himself to stay on

the stair. 'The lawyers should have picked this one up sooner.'

She shook her head. 'I'm responsible.' She looked up at him then, her eyes deep pools of vulnerability. 'I have dyslexia.' Just as quickly she looked away, her shoulders rolling back so she was once again composed and untouchable. 'I usually triple check everything then ask my assistant to triple check too. I guess I was just so keen to start the renovations...'

This time she used her finger to push her bottom lip between her teeth, her gaze distant as if she was lost to her self-flagellation.

Pieces of the puzzle slotted into place. This wasn't his problem. So she'd messed up. So she'd confided something intensely personal. So she carried a lifelong learning challenge.

It changed nothing.

His feet moved as if of their own accord. He took the last two stairs until they shared the small landing.

'Why didn't you tell me?'

She lifted her chin, her stare hard.

'Why would I have told you? I'd just met you. And I already felt foolish enough.' Her shoulders lifted a notch and he quashed the crazy urge to touch her. To wipe away the small frown crinkling her forehead.

'But you haven't just met me.' He shoved the other hand into his pants pocket, away from temptation.

'I didn't know that about you.'

She shook her head, eyes darting away.

All those holidays, the time they'd spent together— she'd never once mentioned dyslexia and neither had her family. Perhaps she was only mildly affected? No, that wouldn't explain her obvious disappointment in herself.

'I... I struggled to talk about it back then.' She lifted her gaze to his—clear, unguarded. 'It's not easy being the dunce in a high-achieving family.'

Something visceral shifted in his chest, and his throat tightened. What the actual fuck...? He knew Hal Jacob was a world-class asshole, but surely he valued his daughter and her extensive achievements?

Not your problem. Keep walking.

Her phone beeped again. She read the text with a curse.

'Problem?' So he was a glutton for punishment.

She sighed, her shoulders sagging. 'There are press outside. My driver is stuck.' Her eyes slid to his—fatigue-tinged and wary.

'Camera shy?' Surely she was used to that. He'd seen her photographed many times over the years at some high-profile event or charity gala. She was New York elite after all, her status rendering her practically a celebrity.

She pinned him with a hard stare.

'I wanted to keep a low profile tonight. The other designers...' She sighed. 'I know how hard it is, starting out. If they see me—' she pointed down the stairwell, indicating the press '—they'll concoct some story about how I'm using the Jacob name to promote my label, my own interests. It's...' she mashed her lips together, her perfectly arched eyebrows knitted '...distracting.'

He stepped closer, his movements slow and easy as if he feared he'd spook her. Or perhaps he was simply stopping himself from touching her again.

'I have a car. Want a lift?' He held his breath, her answer way too important for someone who shouldn't care if she walked across Manhattan alone in four-inch designer heels.

No. It was the least he could do after Alex.

She looked up, a small shake of her head.

'Your car is probably snared up in the same jam as mine. It's chaos out there.' She fingered her temple, her brow furrowed.

His hands twitched, the inexplicable urge to pull her close, to feel her feminine curves pressed against him again, relentless pounding waves. It must be the chemistry or sexual frustration on his part. Or the way she looked at him, as if she too liked the idea.

He retrieved his phone from his pocket and fired a quick text to Will. There was likely a back entrance to this building. Aside from everything, Harley looked beat. And despite what she thought of him, he wasn't an asshole...revenge fucks aside.

'I'll sort something out.' He pocketed his phone, his hands staying safely tucked in his pockets. Hands that remembered every contour of her and how readily she'd embraced their physical connection, her greedy abandon at his apartment the biggest turn-on.

She still wore the frown, eyes wary.

'Why are you helping me?'

He shrugged, hiding the rush of skin crawling her question and the look on her face caused.

'I'm a nice guy.' She'd have once known that if she'd stuck around.

Not that their tender, naïve relationship would have lasted. After his parents' acrimonious split, he'd re-

evaluated all areas of his life, not deeming entanglements worth what it cost him in the control stakes.

He swallowed the surge of bitterness, forcing dangerous thoughts from his mind.

Her tongue darted out to moisten her top lip as she
dissected him with her stare. A shot of lust zapped his
balls. She favoured cherry-red lip-gloss; he'd noticed
that this afternoon and again this evening. What would
those pouty, luscious lips look like wrapped around
his cock, leaving behind a red print? Damn, he really
did need to get laid.

Her stare flicked south.

Was she thinking the same thing? Did she, like him,
want another taste?

Perhaps this would tick all the boxes. He'd settle
the score and she'd get a sample of what she'd missed
out on. After all, he'd never had any complaints and
she'd been keen enough this afternoon. She couldn't
hide her physical interest, no matter how much she
disliked or distrusted him.

'Do you want to hang about here in a draughty stairwell or shall we talk about the orgasms?'

Her eyes widened, a pretty pink flush staining her
neck and cheeks. She shifted, crossing one foot over
the other.

He held back a smile. So his words struck home.
He could control this. Them—his physical craving for
her and her reaction to the chemistry neither of them
seemed able to resist. On his terms. They'd both get
what they needed.

She tilted her chin, eyes blazing with challenge,
and, he hoped, lust. 'Orgasms?'

He nodded, slowly encroaching until her body heat registered and her delicious scent tickled his nose.

'We established earlier, there's little trust between us. But we don't need to trust each other outside of the bedroom to have a good time.'

Her pulse fluttered in her throat and he let his stare linger there, letting her know he saw that she wanted him.

'You trust me with your body.'

She laughed, a nervous snort she used to conceal the rush of excitement lighting her eyes. 'Cocky much?'

He nodded. Slow, sure, sincere. He'd show her a good time. For old times' sake. A taste of what she'd never got to experience and what she clearly craved.

His blood pounded harder, her excitement ramping up his own.

'Here's how it's going to go.' He rolled his shoulders, enjoying the kick of satisfaction when she looked him up and down, her tongue darting out onto that glossy red lip.

'I'll call the shots, and you'll reap the orgasms.'

She lifted one brow. 'Plural?'

Another nod. Another inch closer. 'Think of this afternoon as a prelude—not my best work.' He allowed his eyes to linger on her parted lips, her soft rapid pants encouraging him. 'The next one will be better. And better...'

She stared as if he'd proposed a naked run through Central Park. 'Call the shots?'

He held his ground, but she stepped half a step closer. Perhaps she wasn't even conscious of it. Now only a sliver of air separated them, practically sparking with erotic possibility.

He nodded, his hand sweeping the swathe of her hair behind one delicate shoulder, while his stare searched hers.

'Are you done?' He lifted a brow, tempting. 'Or do you want more?' He leaned in, his eyes practically closing as her warm scent bathed him. 'You know I can give them to you. The question is, how much do you want them?'

She placed her hand on the centre of his chest, fingers flexing with enough pressure that he wasn't sure if she'd push him away or curl those fingers into a fist around his shirt and pull him in.

Fuck, perhaps he'd played too hard? Miscalculated?

No. The unfinished business between them went beyond the stalled deal for the Morris Building. He knew it. She knew it.

Would she submit to his proposal, pick up where they left off earlier, leaving everything but sex at the bedroom door? She called it cocky, but he was a man of his word, he'd prove that to her, even if he had to drag that understanding from her one orgasm at a time while he worked this itch from beneath his skin.

She came to him, her petite frame pressing into his body from breast to thigh, and her breath gusting over his lips. The eyes she lifted to his glowed, the passion and defiance he'd guessed at earlier clearly on display.

'I'm not sure that one earlier can be topped.' Her fingers curled into his shirt.

His blood surged, thick and powerful.

'Oh, I'll top it.' Lust slammed through him. A primal roar. Game on.

With a swoop from him and a tug from her their mouths collided. He manoeuvred her against the wall and kissed her, pouring every scrap of frustration into the slide and skim of lips and tongues. The surge of lust that had simmered beneath the surface since this morning at the building site flooding through him, breaking free, seeking fulfilment.

She whimpered, as if he'd held back for too long and she was as starved as him for the ferocious kisses. She palmed his cock, drawing a hiss from him, and he tugged the hem of her clingy dress, exposing bare, toned thighs. Pale and smooth—a place a man could lose himself.

She spread them, her fingers hooking into his belt loops to pull him between her legs, her hands as grabby as his, her need matching his with every stroke. He ground his erection into her, the clothing barriers hindering his goal—to get inside her and take them both over the edge. Over and over until she begged for more.

He pulled back from her hungry mouth, his gaze flicking up and down the stairs in case they were being observed. Harley kissed and nibbled a path to his neck, tonguing his earlobe until his eyes rolled back.

Was he seriously considering fucking her in a stairwell where they could be interrupted at any time by someone leaving the fashion show or someone entering from the street? Harley seemed up for anything. Her hands found his belt buckle, tugging and grappling as she returned her mouth to his.

Reality dawned.

He stilled her hands just as his phoned buzzed in his pocket. He soothed the rejection by palming her fantastic ass, pressing her centre to his hard length while he twisted away from her kiss to read the text.

'Car's here,' he mumbled against her swollen lips.

Pocketing his phone, he pulled back, sliding her dress back down her shapely legs, and bit back a curse. He'd lost himself in the moment, almost fucked her in a public place.

He cupped her flushed cheeks, pushing her dishevelled hair back from her face. Her lip-gloss had vanished, her hair was tousled and her breasts, pressed against his chest, lifted and fell with her rapid pants.

She nodded once, stepping aside and tweaking her hair and her dress so she was once more the immaculate goddess.

With a flick of her blonde tresses, she followed him to the fire exit and his waiting car, where they made their escape into the night.

CHAPTER FOUR

HARLEY HOISTED HER dress to mid-thigh and clambered astride his lap to continue the frantic, almost desperate kisses that had begun the moment the car's doors closed. She couldn't get enough of the chemistry that arced between them. It was as if she'd been living under water, everything dull and muted. This…lust… flared hotter than anything she'd ever known.

Combustive. Addictive. Uncontrollable.

And in this moment, she'd never wanted anything more than to pick up where they'd left off this afternoon in Jack's apartment.

She reached between them, rubbing him through his pants until he groaned into her mouth and bared his teeth on a hiss. It wasn't enough. She craved him naked, every inch of his magnificent body hers to explore. She yearned for him sweaty and determined above her, pushing her over the edge as she instinctively knew he could.

She didn't give a damn about his driver, or the passing traffic. She'd had a brief taste this afternoon and she wanted more. More of what he offered. Just sex. The amazing, sheet-clawing kind.

When he'd suggested a ride home, she'd reasoned

that accepting provided an opportunity to try one last time to convince him to push through the sale of the Morris Building. But honesty won. She wanted him. Plain and simple. And she wanted the orgasms he promised. Why shouldn't she take what she could get? A fling she could walk away from, hopefully clutching the Morris contract in her hand.

They weren't kids any more, clearly both capable of separating sex from the rest of their lives. And right now business, their pasts, their families, were the last things on her mind. A mind full to capacity with this sexy, grown-up Jack, his mouth, the rumble of his deep voice, the hard body under her exploring fingertips.

Kissing him was like kissing two different people—the teenager she'd once swooned over and the man he'd become. Familiar and foreign. Larger than life. Sexier than her wildest imaginings—more demanding, more intuitive, more everything. When combined with the hint of forbidden…she hovered close to orgasm just from kissing him alone.

The journey to her Fifth Avenue apartment was blessedly short. Just like when they were teens, Jack applied the brakes more than once during the ride, literally removing her hand from his underwear and slowing things down, where she would have ridden him in the back seat, onlookers be damned.

The touching, kissing and groping continued into her building and twice she dropped the electronic key card to her private elevator in her haste to get him upstairs and get him naked. To continue this clandestine connection behind closed doors.

Once inside the deserted car, he pressed up behind her, his erection slotted between her buttocks shooting tingles up her spine. His hand swept her hair aside, and his lips found the back of her neck, nibbling.

'Do you live alone?' His voice, thick with arousal, scraped over her nerve endings, speaking directly to her clit. She could barely stand upright.

When he held her hips still in his large hands, pressing himself home, she twisted her head over her shoulder to capture his mouth.

'Yes.'

Her older brother, Ash, lived in the apartment above, but she didn't want to stop kissing him long enough to explain that unnecessary detail.

As the elevator ascended Jack once more shimmied her dress up her thighs to her waist, his hands trailing fire along the bare skin he exposed. He reached for her hands, lifting them and curling her fingers over the brass handrail at waist height. 'Hold on.'

She had no time to luxuriate in the thrill pounding through her at his command or what it meant. Jack dropped to his knees behind her, nudging her legs apart and kissing first one cheek of her ass in an open-mouthed caress and then the other. The scrape of his teeth skittered down the backs of her thighs and weakened her knees.

What was he doing to her? Why was she such a willing accomplice? Her breath stalled in her lungs, and she clung to the rail with enough force to ruin her manicure. But it was worth it.

With a shuffle and a sexy grunt, he manoeuvred her hips backwards so she bent over at the waist, her ass in the air. Jack slid the thong of her underwear aside and plunged his tongue inside her quivering sex.

Her cry joined his throaty groan. His fingers curled

around her hips and his stubble grazed the sensitive skin between her legs. She clung to the handrail as the sensations assailed her. Jack's raw hunger and the carnal urgency with which he took what he wanted sent thrill after thrill trickling along her spine.

Jack slipped one hand between her thighs, rubbing at her clit while he continued to plunge his tongue inside, sending jolts of fire to her toes.

She sank deeper into the sensual haze, uncaring of where she was, every nerve in her body focussed on the havoc Jack wreaked between her legs.

With a judder she couldn't be sure originated outside her body, the elevator stopped. Harley opened her heavy eyes. The polished brass of the car's wall reflected her image. Wanton, dishevelled, lust-drunk. There was no hiding the effect he had on her or the abandon he'd effortlessly instilled. Abandon that left her willing to partake in public sexual acts. Twice in one day.

His mouth left her and her knees wobbled. He slid her dress down and took her hand. Within seconds, they were inside her darkened apartment. A single lamp shone on the table just inside the entrance.

'I'm sorry,' said Jack, leaving her side long enough to carefully place the designer lamp on the floor.

Hormones pounded Harley, fogging her mind. 'Why?' Had he changed his mind? And why was he shifting the light fitting?

His mouth covered hers once more, tongue delving as his hands tugged the dress back up. He broke free, a fierce look on his face. Harsh need. A thrilling wildness.

'Because the first time's going to be right here.'

He indicated the table and a fresh wave of moisture slicked her panties. He shucked his jacket, tossing it to the floor, working his belt free with one hand while he scooped the other around her waist and kissed the breath from her.

Harley's lust-addled mind caught up with dizzying euphoria, and she couldn't help him quickly enough, dropping her purse and lifting the dress all the way up and overhead. An ominous tearing sound accompanied her efforts, but she tossed the garment without ceremony, desperate now to have Jack inside her. No more skirting around. The hard length of him through his clothing…she wanted him. Now.

'Fuck.' He paused to cup one breast through the lace of her bra, his thumb tracing the nipple as his eyes devoured every inch of skin. Then she was airborne, Jack's hands splayed around her waist lifting her onto her antique hall table.

They were wild for each other. Her hands fumbling alongside his to free his erection, her lips clinging to his, tongues duelling and her thighs holding him captive. She'd get what she wanted this time. No more unfinished business.

With a grunt, he tore his mouth from hers, pulling his wallet from his pocket, locating a condom and tossing the rest over his shoulder. He tore into the foil with his teeth, sheathing himself while his hot stare toured her splayed-out body clothed only in scanty black lace and four inch heels.

Harley worked on his shirt buttons, ignoring the mild discomfort of being perched on the table, desperate to see more of him. To touch every inch of him.

To feel the spring of his chest hair on her face and the taut ridges of muscle under her fingers.

She'd barely pushed the fabric over the rounded contours of his ripped shoulders exposing his well-defined pecs and a glimpse of rigid abs when he circled his arm around her hips and tugged her ass to the edge of the table. Clearly Jack was as close to his limit as she was.

'This needs to go.' He tugged at the filmy black thong, scraping it down her thighs with impatience and a look of fierce concentration on his handsome face. Halfway down her legs he stopped dead, his mouth grim but eyes hot.

Harley stopped breathing. Her pulse thundered in her ears. Please don't let him change his mind; leave her hanging here on the edge of ecstasy.

But he simply stared between her legs, his jaw clenched and his nostrils wide, breathing hard.

'Fuck, you're beautiful.' He traced the narrow strip of blond hair until his fingertip rested on top of her clit, his greedy stare drinking her in while she fought the urge to squirm and close her legs.

She'd never been so thoroughly inspected. So devoured. Warmth spread from her belly, burning beneath his motionless fingertip and snaking a tingling path along her thighs.

'Later, I'm going to eat at you for hours.' He lifted his eyes to hers, so intense, so full of carnal promise. Just like his words. 'But now, I need to get inside you.'

She nodded. Speech impossible. Totally down with that plan. Grown up Jack was hot as hell and she longed to go up in flames.

The finger on her clit began a slow rhythmic stroke.

Harley whimpered, her head falling back against the wall and her eyes fluttering closed. She snapped them back open again when he stepped closer, widening his feet and spreading her thighs with his.

'Stay with me, Harley. Look at me.' He continued to stroke her clit as he notched the head of his cock into her entrance.

She'd never been so open before, her previous sexual encounters rather robotic and perfunctory. But Jack completely commanded her body and wheedled his way into her mind, saying exactly the right thing to banish any awkwardness and make her hotter, more desperate, closer to the edge.

She gripped his waist. They were really doing this. Her breathing turned choppy. Short bursts of air that did little to quench the burn in her lungs or the buzz in her head.

Jack's jaw bulged, his hot eyes locked with hers as he pushed inside, one slow, delicious inch at a time. She battled the desire to close her eyes, fighting the immense pleasure he kindled, attacked from all angles. Her thighs gripped his in a feeble attempt to control so much stimulation—stretched from the inside, her sensitive nerves petted outside by his clever fingers, the pulse of endorphins from his eye contact flooding her bloodstream. She was embarrassingly close. And he'd yet to move. She bit down on her lip, staying the waves of delirium, savouring the seconds, the sight of Jack half naked, face taut with the pleasure of being inside her.

'Yes,' he hissed, flaring his nostrils and fluttering the pad of his finger over her clit in light swipes. He licked his lips, eyes raking over her body. 'Pull down the cups of the bra.' He gripped her hips in his large hands, a move that both pinned her to the edge of the table and pulled her towards his steady, shallow thrusts.

She obeyed, her hands clumsy in her haste to do anything he asked. Because she knew she'd reap the rewards. Already this was better than anything she'd ever experienced. She didn't consider herself a prude, but she was far from an adventurous lover. But the way Jack made her feel, effortlessly drawing out the hidden exhibitionist she hadn't known was inside her... she'd become a veritable nympho for the orgasms he promised.

With her breasts pushed up over the cups of lace, she lost his eyes. He groaned. Then his stare slammed open, his lids heavy as he gazed at the tight peaks of her breasts. He leaned forward over her, lowering his mouth, which couldn't quite reach due to the awkward angle of her unconventional sprawl on the furniture.

'Help me.' Frantic eyes darted between her face and her nipple. 'I want to taste you.'

'Yes... Oh, yes.' She cupped her breast, lifting it to his hot mouth. Her cry stuck in her throat as he lashed the aching peak with strong swipes of his tongue.

Then he began muttering in French, words garbled around the flesh filling his mouth, his hips still rattling the table against the wall and his finger still stroking a sublime pulse over her clit.

She'd never mastered his native language, had no idea what he said, but it didn't matter. The look on his face told her all she needed to know. He was there, with her, climbing this euphoric peak. And he could have been reciting a grocery list—the foreign language naturally sensual. Or perhaps it was just Jack and the way his sinful mouth caressed the sultry words.

When he released her breast, new determination shone in his eyes. He jerked his chin, voice gruff. 'Touch them. Don't stop. I've got you.' He gripped her hip tighter, fingertips flexing.

Perhaps he meant he wouldn't let her fall from her perch on the table. Perhaps he meant he'd take care of her orgasm, they'd take care of it together. But she had no time to ponder. She followed his instructions, embracing the libidinous woman he unleashed, all self-consciousness forgotten.

She let go of the edge of the table and used both hands to stroke her tingling nipples to attention. The more his eyes darkened to pools of molten metal, the faster she strummed, releasing her cries and moans unhindered.

Jack grunted a sound of approval, his hips picking up speed and his finger pressing down on her clit with greater pressure.

Harley whimpered, losing the battle to keep her eyes on his. The table banged the wall as he pummelled her again and again. She locked her ankles behind his thighs, holding him captive, drawing him closer.

When she opened her eyes again, his stare burned her breasts. 'Tweak them, Harley, as firm as you like it.'

Her teeth clamped down on a wail as she listened, pinching and rolling her tortured nipples until her blood sang, a direct path to her clit.

'Yes.' Another hiss. 'You're swelling up.'

How could he tell? And yet it seemed he was correct, because he thickened or she tightened, the friction between them building in intensity. 'You're going to come soon. Look at me.'

Every command, every bitten-out order should have irked her, but had the opposite effect. Because his words were more like prophesies. And he was spot on. Her nipples ached. Her sex grew slicker, tighter around his shuttling cock. Tendrils of fire shot out over her belly and thighs from beneath his working finger and as she opened her eyes to the unbridled lust burning in Jack's stare the lightning struck.

'Jack.' Her throat closed on his name as her orgasm hit, firing every nerve in her body. She clung to him—her eyes, her legs, her sanity latching onto the source of such overwhelming pleasure like a lifeline.

He gripped her tighter, his fingertips punishing. She didn't care. She still pulsed around him. Wave after wave of euphoria. He'd lifted his finger from her over-sensitive clit, but continued to softly stroke her belly, her thighs and her buttocks, intensifying the after-shocks that rattled her from head to toe.

But there was no time to recover. His pace picked up once more. Harley clung. Sweat beaded his brow as his jaw muscles bunched and his hips lost some of their smooth rhythm.

He looked down at her, his fervid stare darting over her breasts then swooping down to where they were joined until he gorged his fill.

His face twisted as he met her stare. 'I want to make you come again…' He shook his head, his chest heaving.

Harley gasped, all the reaction her boneless body could muster. 'I can't.'

He nodded. A flash of regret. 'You will. Next time.'

Was he seriously lamenting his stamina after the single most erotic sexual experience of her life? She had no time to comment. He hammered into her, his hips jerking erratically and one hand trailing a hot, possessive path over her breasts and down her belly.

His shout, when he came, echoed off the walls. He collapsed forwards, every muscle taut as he pumped into her and kissed her through the last of the pulses racking his body.

Reality returned. The edge of the table dug into her butt and although he wasn't placing all his weight on her, his arms braced beside her hips, and she struggled to breathe.

She brushed her lips over his ear, enjoying the tickle of his hair on the end of her nose.

'Next time?' She stifled a delighted, if a little girlish, giggle. Wow. She doubted she'd be able to walk after that performance. But already she looked forward to the promised next time.

He groaned into the side of her neck, his scruff scratchy, no doubt leaving its mark on her skin. 'Give me ten minutes.' He disengaged from her and helped her down from the table.

The narrow space between them widened. Harley pulled up the cups of her bra, wishing she'd chosen a less sheer design, and yanked up her panties, which were tangled around one ankle.

He stood in her entranceway, his urbane clothing rumpled and dishevelled, his softening cock still wrapped in latex and his clear blue eyes still touching on her near naked body with impressive hunger, considering the wall-banging session that had just taken place.

Harley reached for her purse and handed him a tissue.

What now? Invite him in? Offer him a drink? Suggest he stay the night?

The chill of the dark apartment infected her, and she sought her likely ruined dress while Jack tucked himself back inside his pants.

'There's a washroom there.' She indicated a door to the right, grateful for the few seconds of reprieve while he disposed of the condom.

He opened the door and flicked on the light. While Jack binned the evidence of their coupling and washed his hands, Harley dived for her dress, holding it in front of her nakedness in a ludicrous display of modesty that left her cheeks hot.

She'd just come like a supernova around him, touched herself in front of him, allowed him to fuck her on an antique table she'd inherited from her grandfather. Now she back-pedalled?

Jack returned, scooping his wallet from the floor and pocketing it before reaching for her hand. He made no comment on the dress shield, slanting her a crooked grin as he tugged her closer and swiped his mouth over hers with surprising ardour.

She opened her mouth, her tongue sliding over his. Her arm came around his neck, the dress barrier forgotten as she indulged in another of those drugging kisses.

'Harls? You home?' A disembodied voice blasted from the intercom next to the entrance door.

Harley jumped away from Jack, her eyes wide and

her heart hammering in her throat. She darted to the intercom, pressing the button to speak to her brother.

'Yes.' Harley winced, clutching her dress with one hand, her temples with the other. She turned her back on Jack, head bowed. Why hadn't she just ignored Ash? Her back burned and she clenched her butt, hoping the heels she still wore presented her ass to its best advantage.

'You alone?' said Ash. They often got together late at night, sharing a nightcap and tales of their day.

Damn. What could she say? *No, I've just fucked the enemy on Pop's antique table...* If she told the truth, tomorrow she'd have her brother here for breakfast on a fact-finding mission. And then she'd have to confess she'd messed up the Morris deal, too. Another dose of humiliation.

'Yes, of course.' Shoulders high, she scrunched her eyes closed, the lie raising the stab of a thousand pinpricks over her exposed skin. She could practically feel the chagrin pound her back in waves. Or perhaps it came from within.

'Pour me one. I'll be down in two.' The ominous silence from the intercom started a deafening countdown. Harley turned to face Jack, an apology bubbling up in her throat.

He'd already donned his jacket and buttoned his shirt, his face blank.

She clutched her dress tighter, holding it to her sides with rigid arms.

'I...' What could she say?

I didn't want my brother to know I just had the best sex of my life with Joe Lane's son.

Manhattan was small enough. With a little digging,

Ash would easily discover Jack was the head of De-mont Designs. That he'd re-entered her life. Crashed back in, bells, whistles and horns blazing more like.

Jack stepped closer, one finger brushing the hair from her cheek.

'*Bonsoir*, Harley.' His hand dropped to his side, and he slipped the other hand into his pants pocket, a casual move that reassured her and irked her at the same time.

She swayed towards him, her eyes begging him with words she couldn't articulate.

He stepped aside, turning at the door. 'You'd bet-ter look in the mirror—you look well fucked…a look I personally like, but one I doubt your brother will appreciate.'

With those parting words and a blank expression, he left.

CHAPTER FIVE

JACK SLID THE scissors under the wide red ribbon, his smile finding the handful of camera lenses aimed his way. The hospital administrator gave him the nod and he cut the ribbon to a round of applause from the small crowd gathered outside the new wing of the Bronx Hospital for Children.

While the sense of pride he felt for donating his professional time for free to certain worthy projects warmed him, his face ached with the pressure of maintaining a benign smile. He despised ass kissing, both dishing it out and receiving it, preferring to judge and be judged by action.

His usual tolerance for making polite small talk deserted him. He blamed last night. Harley's abandon to their explosive chemistry had shifted something in him, a piece he hadn't known was out of sync until she'd entrusted him with her body and her orgasm.

The memory of her splayed under him, hair wild as she teased her pert breasts, her languid stare trained on him as he'd pounded them both to completion made his cock twitch. She'd unfurled before his eyes, stunning, uninhibited, claiming her pleasure like a goddess.

He'd been right. The sex between them had surpassed his imaginings. He'd planned to spend the entire night making her come. Reacquainting himself with her body and discovering every facet of the fully fledged woman she'd become.

And then she'd dismissed him. Again. Her denial to her brother as good as kicking him out of her apartment before the sweat had dried or their heart rates had settled to normal.

Hadn't that been a knee in his still-throbbing balls? But it shouldn't have bothered him. After all, he'd got his revenge fuck, hadn't he? And while spending the night between her shapely thighs might have been a pleasant added bonus, he'd always planned to walk away—she'd simply expedited matters.

He choked down the bitterness, the contrast of her perfect abandon and her awkward brush-off still grinding his teeth. But it was a timely reminder that, although physically they were thoroughly attuned, she'd abandoned him once before.

With a fixed smile on his face, he accepted several handshakes from hospital officials, the mayor and patient representatives, his encounter with Harley souring the morning. He cast a discreet eye around the parking lot for Trent, keen to get out of here now he'd done his ribbon-cutting duty.

His eyes slammed to a halt.

Harley stood to the side of the lot, her big stare on him and her fine wool coat flapping open in the light breeze. Seeking him out for the third time in two days? Damn, she just couldn't get enough.

At his small nod of acknowledgement, she crossed the lot, her hips swaying and a glint of determination in her green stare. Only Harley would come here this morning, after unceremoniously kicking him out last night, with an agenda. Hadn't he already declared this…fuckfest would happen *his* way? On *his* terms?

Nevertheless, his body reacted to the sight of her. He forced his muscles into submission and adopted a casual pose while his heart thundered and his blood surged, hot and thick.

She stalked him. Sassy, confident, probably determined to get whatever she wanted, whether it was her beloved Morris Building or the orgasms he'd promised.

Her presence here, her stalking him down, offered a new and intriguing dimension to their game. How far was she willing to go? How far could he take her? Push her?

Fuck, what a turn-on. The urge to taste her in the back of his car flooded his mouth with saliva. He'd had a brief sample last night in her private elevator, but it wasn't enough and he'd planned to gorge himself, smashing his dry spell apart. Until she'd invited her brother to join the party.

He excused himself from the thanks and congratulations around him, his lips twitching, and met her halfway across the lot. He placed a perfunctory swipe of his mouth on both her cold cheeks.

'Careful—' he glanced left and right '—we might be seen together.'

Her cheeks flushed pink, the colour reminding him of her nipples as she'd circled them with her fingers. Her chin lifted, wisps of blond catching in the light breeze.

'I…' She glanced down at her toes, seemingly lost for words.

Rather than a surge of satisfaction at calling her

out, he missed the light in her eyes, now dull with embarrassment.

Damn, what was wrong with him? But he was still uncertain of her motives, especially after the way she'd ruthlessly ejected him from her apartment last night. And he wouldn't be duped; better she understood that from the start.

'If you think last night changed anything, if you've come to plead for a fast track on the Morris Building, save your pretty mouth. I haven't changed my mind.' Although the things he wanted from that pretty mouth had certainly clarified.

Her head shot up and she stared at him for long, silent seconds.

'I came to apologise.' No demands, no coercion, no bargaining.

His tie flapped in the breeze. He tucked it inside his jacket and fastened the button.

'For?' He stared her down, guard firmly in place. Yes, he knew the way her breathy moans caught in her throat seconds before she climaxed and he'd learned the perceived thrill of being caught excited her, but she was largely a stranger.

She rolled her eyes and then sighed, shoulders dropping. 'I behaved rudely last night. I…' A bigger sigh, her sincere eyes lifting to his. 'I wasn't thinking straight.' She laughed and flushed at the same time, reminding him of her pretty, post-orgasmic glow. 'Damn, I could barely think at all.'

So she'd had a good time. Perfect. Fresh lust slugged him in the gut along with another emotion, harder to quantify. Not that he was given to flights of intro-spection.

'I…' Her neck turned red.

He bit his tongue, fighting the urge to be the gentleman and put her out of her self-inflicted misery. She sighed, meeting his stare head-on.

'Could we get some coffee?'

He hid a smile, tossing her a lifeline. A small one.

'Sure.' He tilted his chin. 'There's a deli across the street.'

She swivelled her gaze in the direction he indicated. Her pert nose wrinkled.

'What? Too good for the Bronx?' Why had she followed him here? If he could nudge her out of her comfort zone, perhaps she'd be as honest about her motivations as she was when it came to claiming her pleasure.

She smoothed her features. 'Sure.' With a flick of her long silvery ponytail, she stepped around him and headed towards the crossing.

In two strides he'd caught up with her, her light perfume wrapping around him. He'd worn her scent all the way back to his apartment last night—when mixed with her arousal its heady aroma amplified a hundred times over and he'd been torn between showering or spending another night hard and alone in his bed.

'Did you design the new wing?' She tilted her head in the direction they'd come from, her eyes sliding over him as if searching for something. A missing piece, perhaps. One she hadn't bothered to hang around long enough to see nine years ago.

He nodded. His mouth tingled to kiss her perfectly glossy lips again. If only to remind himself he wasn't alone in his need to taste her. She wore a nude colour today, light make-up, professional clothing. How he longed to mess her up, rumple her a little, unleash the sex goddess he now knew lurked under the sophisticated elegance she designed and wore like a suit of armour.

'And they asked you to open it?' She tilted her head, ponytail swinging.

He shrugged. 'I'm a benefactor. I worked for free so they insisted.' Whatever her opinions of him, whatever prejudices she believed about the Lane name, she didn't know him. He had nothing to hide and nothing to prove.

She stared, not quite open-mouthed, but he'd take it. The lights changed. With his hand tingling in the small of her back, he guided her across the street and into Martinelli's.

They ordered espresso, the delicious aromas almost enough to make him hungry for something other than Harley, but not quite. At a table for two in the window, he pulled out her chair and took the seat opposite.

'So, you wanted something else from me?'

His ambiguous statement hung in the air. Spot on target. She flushed, fidgeting with her coat and her purse in her lap, her eyes dancing anywhere but on him.

Intriguing.

When she looked at him, she swallowed, her delicate throat lifting.

'I have a proposal.'

'I'm listening.' And his cock was pretty interested, too.

She tilted her head so her hair swung over one shoulder in a way that made him want to reach out and touch.

'I'm…' she pressed her lips together while she chose her words '…between relationships right now…' her stare hardened '…and I assume you're single.'

He stayed silent, offering a small nod, desperate to see what angle she'd play. He'd already experienced her negotiation skills for her beloved building. He couldn't wait to see how she'd broker whatever deal brewed in her smart, determined mind.

'We could…meet up, you know, occasionally.' She stuttered to a halt. She shrugged, as if the words meant little to her, but the tension around her full mouth told a different story, and her chest worked on rapid, shallow breaths.

Jack leaned back in his seat, legs spread, giving nothing away. A surge of triumph warmed his chest. So she craved more. Had played right into his plan to get even and get them both off.

Part of him could tolerate being her sex toy, if it meant he'd get to gorge himself on her sublime body. But a bigger part, the hard-wired version, had some demands of its own.

'So you want to fit me in for a fuck between gym sessions and mani-pedi appointments?' He clenched his jaw. He wasn't as outraged as he made her think. In fact, his hard-on was raring to go. Shame for both of them he wasn't that easily led.

Her eyes widened and she pinned him with a glare. 'No, I…'

What a fucking turn-on. She'd come here to explore the sex between them, sex good enough to keep him awake last night even after she'd lied to her brother and kicked him out.

Clearly he'd been on her mind too. Good to know

he wasn't alone in this rekindled-to-the-point-of-combustion attraction.

Their coffees arrived.

Jack caressed the handle of the espresso cup, a kick of satisfaction warming his gut when her stare followed the path of his fingertips. Yes, she was definitely in this, the physical connection between them hard to ignore.

'So last night was good for you?' His ego didn't need stroking and her internal muscles had clenched him like a vice, but he enjoyed the pink flush of her skin, and if he could persuade her beautiful, cultured mouth to talk dirty, all the better.

She sipped her coffee, her eyes glaring above the rim even as her cheeks obliged with another rush of colour.

'Mmm.' A shrug, as if sex that good were commonplace. But then she wouldn't be here if that were true.

His lips twisted. 'Your orgasm better than the previous one?' He'd take the confirmation he was a man of his word.

She rolled her eyes, shoulders sagging with a sigh. For a moment he thought she'd refuse to answer. After all, it likely wasn't every day she sat in a Bronx deli discussing the quality of her orgasms.

The moment she decided to be candid, she met his stare, head-on.

'So good, I stopped breathing. But you know this.' She flicked a fallen strand of hair behind one ear and adjusted the neck of her blouse.

He did know. He'd witnessed her unrestrained rapture, revelled in it, the surge of triumph almost making up for his unceremonious dismissal. Almost.

He instinctively knew her body as if he'd had the past nine years to learn every plane, every contour, every pleasure point. And she wanted more?

He tilted his head, staring into her eyes until she squirmed. After a pause, he reached for his coffee cup and took a sip, all business. Energy flooded his limbs, the way it did when he negotiated any deal, but more, the best deals hard won. And here she was, the ultimate prize, not above begging for what he offered.

'If we do this, you're going to need to allocate some dedicated time.' He placed the cup back on the saucer, taking his time to find her wide eyes again.

At her crinkled brow, he continued.

'I'm not a stud to be slotted into your busy schedule whenever you've got an itch.'

Tightly pursed lips. Shoulders back. 'I didn't assume—'

He lifted his hand.

'I'll call you any time. Any place.' He shrugged. 'If you want more…' He had boundaries, too. She wanted to explore their explosive chemistry until it fizzled out? He could oblige. But on his terms. His agenda. His timescale.

He took another sip of coffee, waiting, the bitterness on his tongue lingering like her taste. If the deli weren't crowded with office workers seeking a caffeine fix, he'd pay the owner to close the place and go down on her at this very table, until the only word spilling from her parted lips was *yes*.

A thousand emotions flitted across her sea-green eyes as she warred with herself.

Time to reorder your priorities, ma belle. You want

me, yes. But how far are you willing to go for my prom-
ised orgasms?

'Okay.' A hoarse whisper, barely audible over the
general noise of the busy café, but he'd take it.

Blood flooded his groin, his belly tight with anticipation. He smiled.

'So, *chérie*. I'll be your dirty little secret.'

She shook her head, the excitement in her eyes dulling.

'It's not like that. I—'

He held up a hand, keeping his expression light
and easy.

'I get it. Family is everything, right?' The bitter
coffee taste grew more pronounced.

Yes, their families were enemies. But, they'd set the
rules in play. The game, it seemed, was on.

'Has the green silk come in?' Harley asked Belinda,
the manager of the Give concept store on Fifth Avenue. The other woman nodded, indicating a display
rack near the fitting rooms, and answered the phone
with an apologetic shrug.

Harley went to the rack, her expert eye assessing
the new garments. Her hand trailed over the luxurious
fabric, its sensual glide over her fingertips reminding
her of Jack and the way he'd touched her. With rever-
ence, with possession, as if he knew her body inside
and out. As if he wanted her so badly, he couldn't
stop himself touching. Her own fingertips tingled. She
knew the feeling.

She hadn't seen him since their shared coffee two
days ago. But her every waking thought and some of
her sleeping thoughts too were of his command of her

pleasure as he'd lured her to the edge with hoarse encouragement, addictive praise and cocksure prophecy.

You're going to come soon. Look at me.

And he'd been spot on. She shivered. Delicious reminders fluttering low in her belly.

She flicked impatiently through her beloved autumn collection, the hours of hard work, luxurious fabrics and form-flattering designs completely lost on her. Her skin itched. Every second she didn't hear from him increased her longing to have him inside her again, no doubt exactly the reaction he intended.

Bastard.

She'd tried to banish the constant ache, diminish his power over her. She'd masturbated only this morning, her tepid C-grade orgasm mocking her efforts. And it hadn't helped. Clearly her body refused to return to mediocre self-pleasure. Having experienced the fully grown, man-with-serious-bedroom-skills Jack, it craved the A-grade variety with a side of sheet-clawing, hoarse-throated OMG. And that was currently to be found only with Jack.

Belinda finished her call and called out an apology as she scribbled a note. Harley surfaced from her trance and glanced over her shoulder at her competent manager with a smile. She didn't really need to be here, her business a well-oiled machine staffed by competent and trustworthy people who understood Harley's priorities and her limitations.

In fact it operated better without her…interference. She'd learned early on to leave the ordering, invoicing and bookkeeping to someone else. The one time, when the store first opened, she'd sent Belinda out on a lunch break, she'd had to hide in the back room to conceal her panic attack from a customer who'd insisted Harley use the computer there and then to order in a particular garment in her size.

She relied on her staff, perhaps more than she should. But she compensated them well. And as her beloved workroom was above, she regularly visited the boutique-style store to ensure everything was as it should be for her loyal and growing clientele, who favoured the luxury-with-a-social-conscience brand she offered.

'Let's feature this in the window, shall we?' Harley pulled a size two green silk dress from the rack and began to remove the protective tissue wrapping. 'Let's team it with the tan suede pumps.' The spreadsheets, marketing and correspondence might be above her, but she understood how to put an outfit together, her eye for accessorising and layering contrasting textures spot on.

Belinda nodded, her attention snagged by someone entering the store behind Harley. She waved Belinda away. Her store manager moved to the front of the shop to intercept the customer.

Harley hung the dress on a hook outside the fitting room and stooped to snag the pumps she'd wear with this particular dress. *Yes. That worked.* She'd designed a faux-fur bolero that would finish this look to perfection...perfect for the opera, or theatre or...

Her phone buzzed and she snatched it from her purse, her shoulders drooping when she saw the message was from her assistant, confirming her lunch date with an A-list celebrity who loved her brand and wanted to discuss an endorsement. Then they dropped again when she realised she'd never actually given Jack her number.

'Waiting for an important call?'

His breath warmed the back of her neck, raising the hairs. Harley jumped, but then the shock dissipated, leaving behind the throb from her pebbled nipples, an inconvenient thrill brought on solely by Jack's husky voice. She closed her eyes, breathing hard, and fought the urge to lean back into his solid chest.

She schooled her features to neutrality and spun, slowly, to face him. The impact of him all suited up and sexy as fuck sent electricity zinging between her legs. She swallowed.

'Shopping?' She fisted a hand on her hip. 'Can we help you find something?' It wouldn't do that he knew the effect he had on her body—but that didn't mean she couldn't enjoy his.

She ogled him shamelessly. He was dressed in a dark charcoal business suit and a blue shirt and tie—could she close the store, send Belinda on an early lunch break and persuade him out of his immaculate tailoring?

Harley held her breath as, in return, he eyed her up. Please let him be here for sex. Her panties turned slick and desire coiled in her belly as the uncontrollable lust poured through her system.

One eyebrow arched, his sinful mouth twisted. 'Perhaps.' He tilted his head and opened his jacket to push his hand into his pants pocket. 'Do you have time for a tour?'

The vest he exposed matched the suit. She wanted to unwrap him layer by layer—yet to see him completely naked—and take her own tour of his sexy, cut, mature male body.

He waited, giving no indication he'd read her thoughts, or shared them. She flustered. He seriously wanted to look at couture, not peel her out of her clothes in the back room?

'Sure.' Harley placed her purse on the counter where a discreet Belinda busied herself at the computer. Her heart thumped with more than sexual anticipation.

Her business, her passion—it was more than a job for her. Would he understand what she tried to achieve? How hard she'd worked? What she'd overcome to have her own Fifth Avenue store turning over enough profit to fund initiatives she considered important?

He wouldn't know how whole she'd felt the first time she'd created something with her hands, the summer she'd stayed with her grandmother, who'd spent long patient hours teaching her to sew. For the first time in Harley's life something had come easily, when all else—reading, maths, writing—seemed like traversing the Grand Canyon on a broken pogo stick.

Would he get her, or dismiss her, like her father and Phil? She cleared her hot throat, meeting his stare, one of genuine interest.

'Give is a concept store.'

He nodded, his thumb and forefinger stroking his cleft chin as his eyes scraped over her. She looked away, unable to witness any judgment from him, if it came. She moved to a wall of exquisite shoes, each designed by her and made in the US.

'For every pair of shoes we sell, every purse, every

item of clothing, the profits are turned into food and clothing in Third World countries.'

He frowned. 'All the profits?'

She nodded, jutting out her chin. She'd heard it all before. *Crazy. Naïve. Ridiculous.*

'I take a modest salary. The rest…it's surplus. I'd rather see it doing real good than sitting in the bank.' Her face grew hot. Why should his approval matter? 'And I have no shareholders to pacify. The store is leased. A lot of the business is clicks, not bricks, so overheads are minimised.'

She moved to the make-up area, acutely aware of his proximity behind her. 'All Give's cosmetics are cruelty-free and packaged by disabled adults here in NYC.' The surprise and admiration she saw in his face flooded her body with warmth, bolstering her sense of pride in what she'd painstakingly created and she herself often failed to enjoy. She'd spent too long compensating for her challenges. Too long doubting herself and her abilities to break the habit and take full ownership of her achievements, at least on the inside.

She warmed to her topic, basking in his interest.

'Even our lingerie line contributes.' She ran a hand through a rack of skimpy silk and lace, holding his stare. 'Sales funding global women's issues initiatives.'

Jack glanced at the froth, his fingers tracing the lacy edge of a rose-pink thong.

'And you design everything here?' He stepped closer, eyes hot, searing, probing deep inside her until she wanted to hide.

She nodded, pressing her thighs together as his fingertip lingered on the silky fabric. The air thickened, heat from his closeness making her dizzy with longing. He wasn't even touching her but she was ready to combust.

He took the garment, if such a filmy scrap could be called that, from the rack and lifted it between them, eyes wicked.

'You're very…talented.' Low, seductive, innuendo dripping from his tongue. His eyes flashed. He was picturing her in the thong he held in his hand.

Harley tilted her head, a challenge, half tempted to dash to the fitting rooms and oblige. To wipe that cocky smirk from his face, replace it with the burning lust he'd shown her that night in her apartment.

'Would you like to see my workroom?' Air caught in her chest. Why had she said that? Her inner sanctum? The creative space the only place that settled her mind and gave her a modicum of confidence in her abilities.

He nodded and followed her to the back of the store and up a narrow flight of stairs, the lingerie still in his hand.

Light spilled into the room from the floor-to-ceiling windows, and she cast an eye around the space, guessing at what he would see. Two long, wide cutting tables dominated the room, racks of paper patterns lined one wall and rolls of fabric occupied every corner, nook and cranny.

'I'm working on my spring collection.' She indicated the sketches and swatches cluttering the nearest table. Her shoulders lifted as he silently surveyed her work.

'Do you sew the designs yourself?' He pointed to a dressmaker's mannequin draped in a half-finished kaftan-style dress.

She nodded. 'Just the samples. To see if the design works as I see it in my head.'

The warmth in his stare made her shiver. He sobered, placing the lingerie next to her sketches. 'I'm impressed, Harley.'

Her blood ran hotter, her chest expanding with his praise. 'Thank you.'

He smiled—her first glimpse of the boyish smile the younger him had frequently worn, and she sucked in a gasp, the expression so reminiscent of the carefree boy he'd been, an ache took up residence in her stomach.

She had the insane urge to blurt out the reason she'd called things off between them. She bit her lip.

'I remember you were always drawing.' It was the first time either of them had directly mentioned their past relationship, if it could be classified that way. A heavy silence settled. 'You're very talented, and you've created something worthwhile.'

She practically sagged to the floor. So he remembered her favourite pastime as a teen, but that he understood how important Give was to her left her speechless. Was she so desperate for praise, for affirmation from someone else that her vision was a worthy use of her time and talents?

He reached inside his jacket and withdrew an envelope.

'Some documents for you to sign.'

She stared, her jaw slack. 'The Morris Building?'

He nodded, the heat from his eyes eclipsing the effect of his smile. He leaned in, not bothering to hide the long, indrawn breath as he breathed her in and whispered, 'Wait until I leave to open it.'

His stare dipped to her mouth, which she was certain was open while she panted and drooled.

'I hope you're free tonight?'

She nodded, the gesture automatic, as if he'd tugged a thread directly linked to her throbbing clit. And then she sobered, pressing her lips together.

'Damn. I can't. I have a charity gala.' If she'd plunged into a bathtub of ice, she couldn't have doused her excitement more effectively. *Really, Harley? So desperate for sex?*

She expected his disapproval; after all, she'd fallen at the first test of this new…arrangement. But he said, 'Where?'

'The Hammerstein Ballroom.' Could she sound any more deflated? What had begun as a much-anticipated event on her social calendar now turned into a torturous exercise in self-denial. Because a promise lurked beneath Jack's stare, a promise of more of the explosive chemistry between them. Getting blown to smithereens at Jack's hands…there were worse ways to go.

'What will you be wearing?' His eyes caressed her from head to toe, the gleam of approval obvious. 'Something a little more provocative, perhaps?'

Her temperature soared again, only this time the heat prickled, instead of burned. It wasn't his fault. He didn't know her sensitivity to being judged by her looks.

She'd been thirteen the first time Hal had described her to a colleague as 'the pretty one'. And every time he quoted his self-satisfied moniker, she recalled that first time he'd said it, the sting still jabbing like a thousand pins.

She pressed closer, playing Jack at his own seductive game. Her lips brushed his ear and he sucked in a breath. She grinned, enjoying the tendrils of power that snaked south to join the constant fizz of her blood in his presence.

'You don't like the way I dress?' A whisper with a sting in the tail.

He leaned back, his hands settling on her hips. 'On the contrary.'

She smiled, sickly sweet.

'Good, because I dress for myself. I'm not a clothes horse.' She rarely wore the more provocative things she designed. She favoured professional clothing over sexy. It was her way of owning her worth as more than her appearance.

He latched onto her stare, his own smouldering as he studied her.

'I've touched a nerve?'

She dipped her gaze as heat rushed up her neck.

'Hal struggles with having a daughter without a Harvard degree. He likes to justify my…limitations by labelling me the face of Jacob Holdings.'

Poor Harley, her grades are appalling, but at least she can fall back on her prettiness.

His throat bobbed on a swallow, jaw bunching.

'You're a beautiful woman. There's no hiding it, no matter what you wear.'

She shrugged. Her father had often tried over the years to tempt her into working for Jacob Holdings by suggesting she front their advertising campaigns.

'No. But I'm more than my looks, as you are more than yours.' When she'd told Hal she had her own dreams of a degree in fashion design, starting her own label, his dismissal had been predictable, but no less devastating.

Jack tilted his head, in acknowledgement, something that looked like respect lingering in his eyes. His expression turned from playful to serious.

'From what I see—' he glanced around the workroom '—your career, your vision is very worthwhile.'

She shrugged, stepping back from the precipice of vulnerability. She'd been determined to go it alone away from Hal and his constant comparisons with her Harvard-educated siblings. But doubting her worth, a lifelong habit, was hard to break.

He stepped closer, not touching her, but dipping his head until his breath tickled her neck and his spicy scent engulfed her.

'But know that whatever you wear tonight, I'm going to be stripping you bare down to that perfect pussy of yours and eye-fucking you all night.' He straightened, eyes hot. 'I hope that ruins your expensive lingerie.'

Harley gaped. Her underwear took a punishment, as he'd predicted, damn him.

Jack placed a perfectly chaste, almost dismissive peck on her cheek and, with a wink, disappeared down the stairs, all swagger.

Round one to Jack.

As she recovered her mind concocted a revenge plan. With a small smile, she made her way back to the store and selected her size of the rose-pink thong he'd fingered earlier and a matching strapless bra from the rack.

'Belinda, add these to my account. Can you finish the window without me?'

Her store manager nodded and wrapped the lingerie in tissue embossed with the Give logo.

If Jack wanted to play, she could play.

CHAPTER SIX

HARLEY STIFLED A yawn and forced her attention back to the man holding her captive. The older gentleman, a business associate of her father's who claimed he remembered her in pigtails and braces, had monopolised her company for thirty minutes with a monologue on the merits of doing business with Jacob Holdings.

People mingled around them, but the old guy showed no sign of releasing her, his ass-kissing completely wasted on Harley, although Ash was here somewhere carrying the Jacob banner.

Harley's eyes darted regularly around the glittering Hammerstein Ballroom, from the ornate, hand-painted ceilings to the tables decorated with thousands of fairy lights. The only thing keeping her at the Women for Women Gala, now that the important fundraising and awareness-raising part of the evening was over, was the promised appearance of Jack.

Would he come? Was he already here? Every few minutes, shivers danced over her bare shoulders, as if he watched her, unseen. She stifled a shudder, one that covered her in goose bumps. *Wishful thinking.*

His note, written in the confident penmanship she remembered from the love letters he'd mailed to her from France during the long months between their joint family holidays, played over and over in her mind.

I'll think of you naked every second until I see you again. Know that I'll bring my A-game to-night. Better and better.
J

Her legs wobbled, the thought of anything better than when he'd fucked her so thoroughly on her hall table leaving her weak-kneed. Her eyes scanned the ballroom once more for his tall frame decked out in the expensive and immaculate tailoring she'd grown used to.

She slid her eyes back to her tedious conversation partner, cursing that her natural good manners prevented her from simply walking away to scour the upper balconies for Jack.

And then he was there. Only ten feet away.

Her breath caught in her lungs, and her eyes watered at the sight of him. Something visceral shifted inside her as she took in the air of manly sophistication he carried.

He too was engaged in what she assumed was small talk with the Chairperson of Women for Women. When his stare found hers across the room, holding, sparking electricity across the space that separated them, her pulse surged to a frantic rhythm. The heat blooming in her belly threatening to incinerate her on the spot.

He'd gone all out, his black tuxedo ridiculously flattering and the gleam in his bright blue eyes, as he sent her a sly sexy smile, outshining the glittering ambient lighting.

Harley looked away, praying her face didn't show off the excitement bubbling inside her. She'd never get rid of pops here if he misinterpreted her enthusiasm.

She escaped moments later, the fizz of anticipation thrumming through her blood. Jack had disappeared from the spot she'd last seen him. She deflated, the room losing a little of its sparkle as her gaze searched nearby. She craned her neck over the sea of heads in the crowded ballroom.

'Harls, great fundraiser.' Ash cupped her waist and stooped to kiss her cheek. She smiled, distracted, forcing her eyes to her brother rather than scouring the mass of glamorous socialites in search of her quarry.

'You look beautiful tonight. Is this one of yours?' Her brother, her biggest fan, dipped his chin at her outfit, a strapless bias-cut gown with a thigh-high split.

She nodded, her admiring stare taking in her handsome sibling. 'You look good too. Here alone?' Ash never went far without some statuesque beauty on his arm. Not that they lasted long enough for Harley to learn their political leanings or career aspirations. Ash had been badly burned once.

He grinned. 'I am. Why? Spot someone promising?' He glanced around, scanning the crowds.

She nudged him with her elbow. He winked, the cocksure expression that had rescued him from endless childhood misdemeanours, and turned away to snag them a couple of glasses of champagne from a circulating waiter.

Then she winced, herself turning in the opposite direction as Old Man Jibber-Jabber returned and collared her brother, calling him Jacob Junior, a name Ash hated. Ash stilled her escape with his hand on her arm and drew her back into the conversational circle with a tight smile and a glass of champagne.

With flight temporarily thwarted and her brother occupied by the bore, Harley sipped her drink and glanced around surreptitiously for another glimpse of Jack.

This time, when their eyes met, he made his excuses and, not once taking his eyes off her, stalked her way.

Harley's throat dried. Her feet shuffled half a step in his direction as he approached. The silk of her dress scraped across her sensitive skin, her nerve endings tingling to life as she held his bold, seductive stare with what she hoped was one of her own.

How did he fray every scrap of her composure, easily unravelling her with an arch of his thick brows or a heated look that seemed to speak directly to her rampant libido? Rampant for him.

She swallowed and glanced at Ash, who was still trapped in conversation, but cognisant enough of her bid for freedom to shoot her a warning glare.

She stood her ground, waiting, anticipation twice as potent as the champagne. She fingered the skirt of her dress, enjoying the appreciative gleam in Jack's eyes.

She'd dressed with him in mind, selecting her favourite gown and donning the rose-pink lingerie, which contrasted well with her creamy skin tones and showcased her ass to its best advantage. If, as he professed, he had X-ray vision, he certainly had an eyeful right about now.

At last he reached her side, all handsome masculinity, impeccably dressed and eye-fucking her, as he'd promised.

'You look beautiful.' His words whispered over her neck as he bowed to kiss first one cheek and then the other in that French way of his.

She sucked in his scent for an indulgent, unguarded second. 'Thank you. This is one of my favourites.' She indicated the dress.

'Mine too. Beautiful and talented.' His voice was low, murmured, so that even surrounded by people, with Ash only a few steps away, he effortlessly created a bubble of intimate privacy.

She laughed. 'I could say the same about you.' She eyed his tux, once more enjoying the breadth of his shoulders and the way the pants stretched taut across his slim hips. 'Italian?' She lifted the jacket, inspecting the whimsical flash of colourful lining and the cut of the tailoring.

He quirked his mouth, tutting.

'French. An emerging designer.' He touched her waist, drawing her closer. 'I'll introduce you if you like, next time you're in Paris.' He dipped low again, his lips brushing her ear so only she could hear.

'Are you wet for me? Been dreaming, all afternoon, of the orgasm I'm going to give you?'

She swayed towards him, righting her posture at the last minute to deny herself the feel of his firm chest and strong arm around her. She looked up, all innocence, face blank.

'Perhaps I couldn't wait for you. Perhaps I saw to my own needs.'

Instead of scolding or expressing shock, he laughed,

his head shaking and his eyes alight. 'Good. Practice makes perfect when it comes to orgasms.'

How did he know that? Was he some sort of sex guru in his spare time? Did she care as long as she reaped the obvious and abundant benefits?

Another body entered her personal space, putting an end to the frisson of lust sparking between her and Jack. Ash grinned, clearly oblivious.

'Is my sister working you over for a donation? She's tenacious when it comes to her causes. Be warned.'

Harley dipped her chin to try and conceal the heat blooming in her chest. She had yet to work Jack over the way she wanted to. If she looked at him now, Ash might see that written all over her face.

Her brother eyed Jack, his hand outstretched in greeting and his polite smile drooping slightly as he tried to place the other man.

Damn. She'd forgotten about this eventuality.

'I'm always happy to contribute to a worthy cause,' said Jack. 'Especially one important to Harley.' He shook Ash's hand, squaring up to her brother with a puffed-out chest in that way men faced off.

Silence stretched as she gaped at Ash to see if he'd recognised Jack. Her jaw worked as she looked between the two men but no sound escaped. Lost for words. Struggling to label this thing with Jack and reluctant to expose herself to Ash's likely criticism.

Jack cast a lifeline. 'Jack Demont. You're Ash Jacob.'

Harley awoke from her trance, her hand instinctively reaching for Jack's arm as she clarified the introductions. 'Jack is a property developer and architect. Remember, I'm purchasing the Morris Building?'

Ash nodded, the cogs of his mind visibly clunking into gear as he flicked eyes dawning with recognition between them. Harley let her arm fall to her side, but Jack stepped close, his hand proprietary on her hip. Had he just laid claim?

'You remember me, I'm sure. I'm Joe Lane's son.' He lifted his chin, staring her brother down. A face-off pissing contest ensued as the men gleaned the measure of each other the way men did. Silently assessing, fixed grins in place. Giving little away.

Harley, too, stood her ground, although she longed to waft away the testosterone permeating the air. After years of trying to fit into the Jacob mould, she wished she were past caring what her family thought of her choices.

Hating her dyslexia every time she saw a flash of disappointment in Hal's eyes or he openly compared her to her two high-flying siblings, she'd tried to forge her own path—doing something she loved, something she was good at, and measuring herself against her own goals, the only way she could claw back a shred of her tattered self-esteem.

But her self-doubts were deeply ingrained. Her shoulders twitched with the effort of staying straight-backed. To his credit, Ash concealed whatever he thought behind a thin but polite smile.

'Of course. It's been a long time. So, have you re-located to New York?'

Harley's heart sank. She knew that look. She had a reckoning to face. And then her blood froze as another thought occurred to her. Had Ash found out about the real reason for the Lane-Jacob bust up? After all, he worked every day with Hal. Would he let it slip now?

Throw it into the conversation as some sort of macho put-down?

Jack tilted his chin. 'Temporarily. I've recently opened offices here, although most of my business runs out of Paris and London.'

'And you two are…' Ash pointed his finger between them, hedging.

'We—' Harley jumped in, stuttering to a halt. What could she tell her brother?

We're having the best sex of my life? I propositioned Jack over coffee? Before the night is over I hope to be screaming out his name loud enough to wake you? And, no, I haven't told him about Dad's affair with his mother so keep your mouth shut?

Her stomach flipped.

'I was thrilled to discover Harley's interest in a property I'm selling, especially when I discovered what she has planned for the Morris Building.'

Her gaze flew to him. Her heart skittering in her chest as the fear subsided. Jack flicked her a look, adding a wink, and his fingers flexed on her hip. Warmth flooded her body and centred between her legs. As he turned to glance at the band, which had returned to the stage, Ash briefly widened his eyes in Harley's direction.

She shook her head and then looked away. She knew what she was doing. Exploring intense sexual attraction. It was no one's business but hers who she fucked. Certainly not her brother's and most definitely not her father's. And she and Jack weren't serious—no need to drag up ancient history.

'So, are you…?' Ash left the question hanging. Harley shot him a *shut up now* look, but the unspoken sounded loud and clear.

What are you doing? Dad will flip when he finds out.

'About to ask your sister for a dance? Yes.' Jack tilted his head to the dance floor, providing a perfect socially acceptable distraction for two old friends recently reacquainted. 'Shall we?'

Harley nodded, her feet immediately lighter. She reinforced her kiss of dismissal on Ash's cheek with a warning squeeze of his arm, and for once her brother stayed silent and kept his opinions to himself.

Sometimes it sucked being the baby of the family; no matter how old or successful you were, you could never outgrow the role. Although she only qualified as the youngest by seven minutes. And of course she'd never be successful enough by her family's standards.

The fact she was sole recipient of the knowledge of Hal's philandering turned her stomach. But she pushed that from her mind, determined to enjoy Jack's company without interference from her family.

Harley sank into his arms, grateful for his confident steps and firm grip on her hand and waist leading her around under the lights. She checked his demeanour. No annoyance. No harbouring ill will. And certainly not concealing his interest in her, picking up where they left off before Ash interrupted. Clearly he didn't give a damn what her brother thought of him.

If only she could achieve that...

'So tell me about this orgasm.'

His change of topic was so abrupt, Harley's neck protested as she leaned away to confirm the wicked gleam in his eyes. She glanced around. Bodies moved around them but no one seemed to have heard.

He laughed, a low rumble reverberating through his chest and zinging her nipples to life.

'You brought it up, *ma belle*.' He licked his bottom lip, pressing his thick length into her belly as he swayed them indecently close. His lips grazed her ear. 'Did you think of me when you touched yourself?'

It was pointless to deny it. If he had any observational skills, he'd feel her accelerated heartbeat thud against his chest and see the flush of arousal her strapless dress failed to conceal.

She lifted her chin, meeting his bold stare. 'Yes.'

Triumph sparked in his eyes—the cocky kind that expected nothing less. 'How was it?'

Predictable. Tepid. Hollow.

'Perfectly adequate, thank you.' His ego needed no massaging from her.

He smiled, confidence unwavering. He stopped dancing, gripping her tighter, pressing every inch of her body to his while he stared intently.

'May I put my number in your phone?'

Her insides turned gooey. The way he asked, like an old-fashioned knight accepting her favour with polite courtesy.

'Why?' She fought a smile. But she fished her phone from her clutch and handed it over while her pulse fluttered, double time.

His eyes gleamed as he typed his details in with one hand and held her with the other. When he passed it back, he resumed their slow dance.

'Next time you have the…urge, you can call me. A little phone sex might liven up the mundane. I'll join you.' His lips twitched, fire in his eyes. 'We can talk each other over.'

Nothing about sex with Jack, the phone variety, she guessed, or any other, could be described as mundane. And she'd been wrong about his politeness. A black knight, perhaps.

Certainly, the memory of that session on her hall table still had the power to make her internal muscles clench. The thought of him stroking himself while she did the same, their vocalisations and filthy words of encouragement the only contact between them, left her light-headed. Would he revert to his native French at the height of passion?

He sighed, his warm breath sliding down her neck.

'Although the image of you pleasuring yourself… I'd travel a long way for such a sight.' The look he settled on her left her trembling with anticipation and torrid arousal.

How could he do that with only a few, albeit explicit words and an intense look?

Then his eyes turned devilish. 'So, are you coming home with me? Or are you sufficiently satisfied for today?'

Her belly quivered. Would she ever get enough of his sexual prowess? And he'd ramped up the anticipation so successfully, if he didn't touch her more intimately soon, she'd probably spontaneously orgasm, just by walking across the room.

She pressed her lips together, her face straight.

'That depends. Will it be worth my while? Better and better, you said.'

He nodded. Self-assured. He dipped low, his lips

caressing her ear once more, setting off a cascade of tingles.

'I have something up my sleeve.'

She smiled, fingering the expensive cufflink at his wrist. 'Well, let's undo this, and see what you have planned, because I'm on a promise.'

The minute she entered his apartment, his needs solidified into a hot ball of determination. He'd strived for what he wanted every day of his adult life, and right now the only thing on his agenda was getting Harley completely bare to him so he could demonstrate that determination over and over again, until she was one hundred per cent convinced.

He'd deliberately kept his hands to himself in the car, building the anticipation until his own skin itched and every muscle raged at him to touch her. But the wait would be worth the denial for both of them.

Since he'd visited her store, witnessed her passion and dedication to her career first hand, he'd thought about her constantly. Not what she would wear tonight or how she would look naked on his bed, his floor or anywhere else they might end up.

But how she'd opened up to him, showing him her workroom, her sketches, even her vulnerability over her asshole father's cruel taunts. But he shoved that from his mind before he broke something. Not that it was his business.

Tonight was about pleasure.

'Is there anything you want, besides me between your perfect thighs?' He stepped up close as she cast her eyes around his dimly lit living space and whispered the words on a husky drawl—part intentional because he enjoyed the fine tremors of her reaction, and part because his own needs choked him to the point of oxygen deprivation.

This was physical. A game. His reminders to himself grew more frequent and more resolute.

She shook her head, her scent wafting on a cloud of warmth tinged with a hint of the arousal she was powerless to conceal. His hands glided to her hips, his fingers finding the dip beneath the jut of her hipbones.

He'd arrived at the gala at least thirty minutes before she'd finally spotted him, circling her like a cat, waiting for the perfect moment to strike. But he'd forced himself to observe her from afar, building the anticipation self inflicted torture. He'd ached to touch her, her creamy skin aglow under the dancing lights. And now he had her here. Had all night to indulge. But first he had to make good on his promised orgasm. Tonight, at least this first time, was all about her.

'Come.' He nudged her forward in the direction of the bedroom, his hand clasping hers to ensure she stayed with him. When he'd lit the bedside lamps, casting the masculine space into warmth, he dropped her hand and loosened his tie and the top buttons of his shirt.

'Show me how you plan to torment me for my clumsy comments earlier—I know you're hiding something under there.' His gaze flicked down the swathe of rose-coloured silk to the toes of the sexy, peep-toe heels he'd glimpsed when she'd stepped from his car.

He hadn't intended to question her dress sense earlier, merely fuel his own fantasies with visions of her draped in some figure-hugging garment or other.

What kind of a man would make her doubt, for one second, a single iota of her true worth as a human being, a woman?

And what kind of man seduced someone for some sort of twisted revenge?

Breathing hard, he focussed on Harley. The night he had planned. For her pleasure and his. Questioning himself only led to doubt—and he didn't do doubt.

She lifted her chin, passion and sass warring for control of her expressive eyes.

'Why would I bother to dress for you? You either want me or you don't.' Her pupils narrowed, the hint of vulnerability dimming the flecks of gold in her irises.

'Well, that's not in question.' He clasped her hand, pressing it to the front of his pants, over the steely erection he'd sported most of the evening. 'You're a sexual woman. A woman who knows what she wants and isn't afraid to get it. Whatever is under that dress—your creamy skin, a hint of rose in all the right places, or the most provocative lingerie—will torture me until I can get my hands and mouth on you.' He dropped said hands to his sides and curled them into loose fists, waiting. Biding his time.

With a small sigh and a look that made his balls tingle, she lowered the side zip on her dress and shimmied it down until it pooled at her feet.

He'd been right.

Pure torture.

Her toned body, curves generous enough to scream one hundred per cent woman, was scantily clad in the same rose pink, almost translucent underwear he'd fingered at her store this afternoon. Her rosy nipples, visible through the lace of her strapless bra, seemed to strain towards him. His mouth watered, reminding him of other tasty parts of her.

The narrow strip of blond hair was just visible through the sheer panties, and when she turned to place her dress on a nearby chair, her glorious ass came into view, the high-cut thong framing the creamy cheeks and disappearing into the crack between them.

'Wait.'

He shucked his jacket and took the dress from her, placing both on the ottoman at the foot of his bed. 'Why don't you sit there?' He indicated the chair, which was decadently upholstered, wide and incredibly comfortable. Perfect for what he had in mind.

She smiled, tilted her head and reached up to remove the pins from her up-do until her hair fell around her shoulders and kissed her pert breasts, which lifted with her arms like an offering to the gods.

He was so fucked.

Jack bit back a groan. His cock strained at the front of his dress pants and he removed the belt and loosened the button at his waist. He made light work of his shirt and took the hairgrips from Harley, placing them on the dresser with his cufflinks.

When he turned around, she'd settled into the chair, her luminous eyes watchful and her cheeks flushed the same colour as her nipples and her sex.

Jack heeled off his shoes and removed his socks, impatience clawing at him. But she was worth the wait. He should know. He'd had another taste, the nine years since they'd fooled around as kids, the ultimate in delayed gratification. Sprawled under him on her own console table, coming around him while she'd tweaked her own nipples, she'd been any man's fantasy.

But, as usual, he was firmly in control of his needs and about to test the limits of Harley's. How badly did she want him? How far would she go for her orgasm? Only time would tell.

He dropped to his knees. With his hands, he spread her thighs, a punch of lust winding him when he met no resistance. He lifted first one foot, removing first one shoe, before kissing her delicate anklebone, and then the other. She watched his every move. Her eyes lit from within. Her chest rose and fell with her shallow pants, her nipples twice the size as when she'd removed the dress. Dark and ripe.

Saliva pooled in his mouth. 'Lift your hips, *chérie*. Let's see if my memory of your taste is as good as the reality.'

Fuck, he loved the flush of her skin when he talked bluntly. And her compliance—that she was momentarily outraged or flustered but went along with it anyway—exquisite.

Harley gripped the arms of the chair, her pink polished nails digging into the fabric as she lay back and granted his wishes.

He peeled the wispy garment down her thighs, the slight flicker rippling down her muscles telling him the ferocious, all-consuming need pounding through him was likely matched in her.

When he'd freed the lace from her pretty feet, he held it aloft, dangling the wisp from one finger. The scent of her arousal hit him square in the chest. He clenched his jaw, fighting the urge to rush this, finish it too quickly for his intended plan. Her pleasure.

'You ruined these.' He tutted and she shrugged, her eyes flicking to the scrap of pale lace.

More colour rushed up her neck.

'It's your fault.'

He nodded, a slug of triumph straightening his spine.

'Apologies. I'll replace them.' He tossed the panties, his gaze raking over the slick pink flesh between her legs. He licked his lips, his stare settling on hers as he lifted first one leg and then the other over the wide, cushioned arms of the chair, splaying her open for his flagrant perusal.

In twenty minutes, she'd either hate his guts, or be begging him for a replay. His blood pounded with renewed force. Resolve strengthening.

'That is a beautiful sight.' He let his stare linger, slowly, almost reluctantly meeting her sultry stare. 'Your pussy is exquisite.'

She gasped, whether from the coarse term or the lightest swipe of his finger over her clit, he couldn't tell, but some Neanderthal part of him enjoyed shocking her. 'Perhaps you prefer the French, *la chatte*.' Another swipe.

Her eyes grew heavy. 'You're completely filthy.'

He shrugged. '*Oui*. And I'm going to enjoy every second of this.' He leaned down to kiss first one pale thigh and then the other, holding her stare throughout. 'I hope you will too.'

Waiting was over, anticipation played out. He gripped her thighs with both hands. If he didn't taste the delights before him soon, he'd lose his mind.

And then he did lose it, because before he could get to her Harley slipped one hand down her belly, her perfectly manicured fingers forming an inverted V over her sex. She spread them open, parting herself to his stare, her mouth slack on a ragged sigh.

An offer and an invitation.

Fuck. He almost came in his pants at the sexiest sight he'd ever seen. This woman was made for sex. Sheer, uninhibited perfection.

With a groan that gave away his desperation, he dived for her, batting her hand away as he sank between her thighs and covered her glistening sex with his mouth. Her taste hit him, filling his senses with her essence. His cock lurched, and his hands gripped her thighs, holding her open as she acclimatised to his tongue on her most sensitive flesh.

This angle, her sprawled in the armchair, afforded him a view of her reactions—every broken cry, every glorious gasp, every streak of ecstasy across her beautiful face.

Her nails clawed at his scalp as she tried to control the angle of his working mouth and depth of his plunging tongue. He ceded, ramping up her pleasure until her thighs trembled against his face and her breathing grew choppy, punctuated with mewls of delight.

And then he stopped.

She cried out, neck arching.

The anguished sound lodged a lump in his stomach. But he leaned back, blowing cool breath over her quivering sex. Wordlessly, ignoring the drunk but slightly bewildered expression on her face, he encouraged her into a sitting position so he could undo the bra and toss it to the floor. He wanted to see all of her, every inch of her creamy skin, every freckle and scar, every shard of ice in the confused glare she levelled on him.

Her questions flittered across the stormy green of

her eyes as her breaths slowed. He looked away, soothing the sting of his desertion with a long, languid pull of his mouth on each nipple that left her panting once more. When her hand slipped between them towards her clit, he grasped her wrist, gently restraining. He lifted the hand to his mouth, kissing each fingertip in turn. 'Patience, *chérie*. I've got you.'

She'd start cursing soon. His balls tightened at the flecks of defiance flickering in the hot stare she levelled on him. Good for her.

'Now…' he licked his lips, his eyes burning over her again '…where was I?'

Before she could speak or even whimper, he dived back in. This time, her clit swelled almost immediately, the primed nub pouting towards his eager lips and tongue. He laved and sucked, smiling at Harley's shocked curse and bitten-out cry of triumph as she renewed her clasp on his head.

Not content to take her medicine, this time, she lifted her thighs over his shoulders, her heels pressing his back, urging him closer. Not that he'd be anywhere else.

For now.

She mewled out her pleasure as he sucked down hard, gifting her his finger inside her tense warmth.

'Yes,' she cried. 'Oh, right there, yes.'

He pumped the finger, finding that sensitive spot inside her that had her twisting his hair and rocking her hips into his mouth.

This time, he steeled himself. At the first flutter of her internal muscles around his finger, he pulled out. His mouth left her, muscles straining to overcome the clamping of her thighs around his neck.

'No,' she yelled, her head thrashing. She glared at him along the length of her naked body, her beautiful breasts jiggling with her seesawing breaths.

His voice was thick, transformed by his own lust battering down on him. 'Soon.' He kissed her thighs, which trembled under his lips. 'I promise it will be worth it.'

At his words, realisation flicked across her face. She rolled her eyes, her face twisted with agony as she flopped back on the cushion. Her thighs clenched, tiny spasms twitching her abdominal muscles.

The wait killed him. He stroked her trembling thighs, the cheeks of her ass, her flat stomach, quiet, reverent words of encouragement and reassurance spilling from him in French. Not that she understood his praise or his declarations of her beauty and what she did to him, but she must have gleaned the tone, because she looked down at him, trust shining in her passion-glazed eyes.

This time, he gave her everything. Two fingers burrowed into her tight channel, his mouth feasted like a starving man and he growled out his own frustrations against her swollen lips and clit.

He'd primed her so effectively, it took seconds to send her over. Her whole body lifted from the chair when she came, the power of the climax arching her back to an almost impossible angle, her cries bordering on screams and her fingers clamped around the short strands of his hair as if she'd tear it from his scalp.

He was relentless. His mouth working at her until his jaw ached, he sucked every drop of her arousal, swallowing her taste over and over again. All the while testosterone roared through his blood, triumph hot

on its tail. In those protracted seconds she gave herself completely. Her sublime reactions, total surren-
der, beyond his wildest imaginings. Her buy in to his
one-upmanship challenge with himself a hundred and
ten per cent.

Perfect.

Spent, she pushed him away. Her stare shone from
beneath heavy lids and she whispered, 'Wow.'

'Was it better?'

She nodded. 'So good. You're clearly some sort
of sex guru. Architect by day, orgasm whisperer by
night.'

He laughed and eased to a standing position, his
cock rigid, tenting his pants. She sobered. Her sexy
stare traced a path up his thighs, along his abs, finally
settling on his eyes.

She licked her lips. Slow. Seductive. Salacious.

He hardened further, although he wouldn't have
thought it possible. He needed to get out of these pants
before his balls turned blue. Her mouth, the flushed,
plump lips, the peak of her tongue, the twitch of a
smile, held him captive. Fuck. Payback would slay
him. If he ever saw that mouth around his dick...
Game over.

'Does it work for you too?'

Clearly her mind was more attuned to his than he
realised. She slithered from the chair, settling on her
knees at his feet, eyes wide, hair gloriously tousled,
a satisfied glow to her creamy skin. She tugged at
his zipper, her bottom lip trapped beneath her teeth
on one side. His mind turned to mush. What had she
asked him?

'What?' Fuck, was that his voice? He needed to get

a grip. Now. If she put her mouth anywhere near him in his current state…

'Orgasm denial. Does it work for you too?' She yanked the trousers over his hips, the tight cotton boxers following until he was trussed at the ankles by his own clothing. Hell, no. No way could he last if she thought to torture him as he'd done her.

He cupped her cheek, his thumb brushing her lower lip, wiping away the indentations left by her teeth. He should claw back control. Find a condom and finish this inside her, but clearly the memo stuck in his brain, his legs rigid and his feet glued to the spot before the goddess at his feet.

Clearly she'd waited long enough for his answer. She gripped the base of his cock and closed her eyes, running the tip of her nose along his length as she dragged in a deep breath. She moaned, her eyes opening as she reached the tip, her mouth placing a chaste kiss there.

Every muscle strained towards her, his cock bobbed before her and she smiled, a feline grin that both chilled him and boiled his blood.

Could she be any hotter?

And then she stopped.

How he managed to keep the roar inside he'd never know. She sauntered to the end of the bed and retrieved her clutch. With a small smile that didn't bode well for him, she reached inside and retrieved a tube of lip-gloss. With two quick swipes, she'd painted her mouth that shade of blood red that almost brought him to his knees.

With her eyes fixed on his, and her lips parted, she returned.

'Now, where was I?'

He cursed at his words repeated back at him. Harley dropped to her knees again, her hands at his hips as she stared up at him, all wicked eyes and pouting lips. While he clenched and uncurled his fists, struck dumb, she dipped her head. Her tongue peeked out tracing a path from the base of his shaft. At the most sensitive area, just below the crown, she paused, her tongue swirling there, before placing a firm kiss on him. She leaned back, eyes sparkling, admiring her handiwork.

'And what do we call this in French?' A small smile and a tilt of her head.

Fuck, he loved her sass, her playfulness.

'Harley.' The bite of warning gave his voice a harshness he'd regret if he weren't so close to plunging inside her and taking what he wanted. What his strung-taut body craved.

She smiled, the merest brush of her lips over his crown. 'It will be worth it, I promise.' Her eyes sparkled. And then she engulfed him. Her hot, tight mouth practically swallowing him whole, while she held his stare to ransom.

The pleasure was so intense, his eyes started to close. He slammed them open, the visual of her on her knees, that pretty red mouth of hers wrapped around him, too good to miss. His hips jerked of their own accord, shunting him deeper inside her warm, wet cavern. She nodded and groaned, taking him further to the back of her throat. So close to losing it.

No. Show some stamina.

He pulled back and she gripped her hand around the base of his cock with just enough pressure to send his hips in the opposite direction once more. Her other arm circled the steel of his clenched thigh, anchoring them together so he couldn't escape, even if he wanted to.

His world shrank to the single entity of Harley on her knees with her mouth on him. Her sultry eyes, burning with erotic promise, mesmerised him, the tiny streaks of green a siren's call. An endless ocean where a man could drown.

He cupped her face, his fingers anchoring into her hair as she bobbed her head and slid her tongue over his shaft with a frantic rhythm that left stars flashing behind his eyes.

His clothing, still around his ankles, held him prisoner. Without pulling from the warm clasp of her mouth, he lifted one foot free and widened his stance. When she gripped his flexed buttock, nails digging, he lost the battle to keep still, to let her guide the pace, and began plunging into her mouth with shallow thrusts.

She hummed, her head nodding her assent and he touched the back of her throat with a grunt.

She reached for his balls, her small hand cupping and rolling, all the while tiny groans vibrated from the back of her throat to the tip of his cock.

It was over.

'Harley,' he barked in warning. He tried to back away, but she clung, her hand squeezing his shaft like a vice, and gave a small shake of her head.

Heat slammed through him, from the base of his spine to the tip of his cock. Fire raced, spasms rocked him and he emptied himself down her throat. He forced his eyes to stay open, willing himself to suck every second of rapture from the wonder of the woman giving him the best head he'd ever experienced.

Her fingernails grazed his sack as the last spams tore through him and he registered the yell—harsh, broken, and from his own throat.

She released him with a final suck that made him wince. He panted down at her. She gazed up at him, her own chest working hard and brushing her nipples across his thighs. He hauled her to her feet, crushing her body to his.

Emotions expanded inside his chest. He pushed them aside, crediting the high, the euphoria to the physical release. It was just sex. Tremendous sex.

Out of nowhere, a question slammed into the forefront of his mind. One he'd shelved long ago.

Why? Why had she dumped him all those years ago? Swallowing hard, he sucked the scent of her fragrant hair into his lungs to stop the words escaping. The past was done. He'd started this to show her what she'd missed out on. And he'd made his point. Exacted his revenge. There was nothing more.

He'd end it soon, when the novelty had worn off. When they'd exhausted the burning chemistry. With those words running on repeat in his head, he dragged her to his bed, and collapsed alongside her, his grip on her suspiciously tight.

CHAPTER SEVEN

JACK'S MADISON AVENUE pre-war apartment was renovated to an exquisite standard. Clean minimalist lines
made the most of the light spilling in from the east-
facing wall of windows. The masculine space could
have been sterile, but it worked—a perfect balance of
soft furnishings and art softened the look and made
Harley want to curl up in the contemporary white
leather armchair and enjoy the sunrise over the Manhattan skyline.

At the thought of armchairs, she grew hot and achy.
Memories flashed—last night and what he'd done,
wringing her orgasm from her with complete profi-
ciency the way a skilled seamstress manipulated oddly
shaped pieces of fabric into the most exquisite of garments. Her bare toes curled on the polished hardwood.

Forcing her thoughts away from toe-curling orgasms and back to the job in hand, she lowered the heat
under the griddle and flipped the pancake with a small
smile. Teenaged Jack had loved pancakes. They'd often
met early, before the others awoke, to share breakfast
at the Aspen lodge their families rented every year for
skiing holidays. He'd always chosen blueberry pancakes laden with maple syrup.

When she'd roused early, before the dawn, and padded out into Jack's comfortable living space in search of coffee, the idea to make him breakfast had struck. She'd eventually found the hidden latches on the kitchen cabinets, which had at first seemed like an intimidating wall of brushed steel worthy of an operating theatre. And she'd almost squealed with delight when she'd found blueberries in the freezer.

She plated the golden pancake dotted with blueberries and poured a generous helping of mixture into the pan for a second.

The trip down memory lane stirred up unwanted emotions, which dampened her sexed-up high, the associated memories of the bust up between Hal and Joe bringing an abrupt end to their trip that year and the demise of the friendship between the two families.

Of course, she'd already withdrawn from Jack, her fear and confusion over discovering her father's and Jack's mother's affair leaving her reeling and running scared.

She flushed with heat, her throat tight. She could have handled their break up differently, with more maturity, and she'd never explained any of that to Jack.

But she couldn't go there now. Too much time had passed for excuses. And the truth…

Harley sprinkled blueberries onto the second pancake and flipped the disc as her stomach lurched.

Did he already know about Hal and his mother? It would explain his reluctance to have any business dealings with her father. Not that she blamed him. She herself had made vows never to do business with and, more importantly, never to behave like Hal Jacob.

Although aren't you doing just that—Jack, your dirty little secret...?

She shook her head, dragging her mind from past regrets. The bedroom was in darkness when she carried the tray loaded with pancakes and coffee back to Jack's bed. She placed it on the dresser while she opened the curtains, allowing golden morning light to spill over the polished hardwood floors that appeared authentically original.

Jack slept on his stomach, his back muscles clearly delineated even in sleep, and the thick white sheets pooled around his slim hips. Golden hair dotted his arms, the same golden hair that covered his chest, and led, by way of a happy trail beneath his navel, to the thatch at the base of his spectacular cock.

Harley pressed her thighs together, marvelling at the vision of him naked. She crawled onto the bed, pancakes forgotten as she traced the dip of his spine between the well-developed ridges of muscle with her mouth. He groaned, stirring. She slipped one hand under his hip, burrowing for the magnificent appendage that was, blessedly, fully hard.

She gave him a couple of experimental strokes, and then released him as he started to rouse fully awake to shuck the T-shirt of his she'd donned to cook breakfast.

He rolled over, his hands reaching to cup her breasts even before his sleepy eyes had fully opened. He scraped the pads of his thumbs over her tender nipples, sending shock waves south.

'Fucking fantastic morning...' His voice was thick with sleep, but his cock, jutting above his belly, was thicker and Harley couldn't help rising above him and sliding her slippery sex down his length as she kissed him, agreeing wholeheartedly with his assessment.

She nibbled a path across his scruff-covered jaw to his ear while he teased her nipples and palmed her ass, guiding her hips where he wanted her.

'I made pancakes.'

His eyes opened wide. 'Blueberry?'

She smiled with a nod, his obvious delight turning her insides to goo.

His expression sobered as he studied her, as if she'd snooped through his office files rather than cooked him breakfast. Perhaps she'd overstepped the mark. Outstayed her welcome. Perhaps morning-after chat should be limited to *I'll call you.*

But he'd fallen asleep spooning her. He hadn't suggested she leave and his body was certainly up for round two. Perhaps breakfast had been a step too far. Too couply.

She shrugged. 'I should have asked.' She reached for the T-shirt, her high dissipating.

He gripped her arm, stilling her retreat.

'No. It's fine. Thank you. I just…'

Whatever he'd been about to say, he stopped, kissing her instead. Her mind grew hazy under the constant stroking of his thumbs over her nipples.

Forcing her thoughts from his confusing reaction to pancakes, which was only destined to destroy her burgeoning orgasm, she gripped his cock, using her own moisture to lubricate the glide of her hand along his length. He groaned, rolling them so she no longer straddled him but lay sprawled beneath him, thighs open. Wet and ready.

His hips stilled. He stared down, his eyes so close,

the brilliant blue hazed out of focus. His mouth met hers with the barest of whispers. He swept the hair from her face with a tender touch, both hands lingering in her hair. She stilled beneath him, pancakes and even orgasms forgotten as she got lost in his eyes. Lost in this precipice of a moment.

Emotion trapped in her chest, pushing aside vital organs to make room for the unnamed feelings springing up. Did he feel it too?

A ringtone killed the anticipation. Harley railed between heart-thudding relief and skin-crawling frustration.

Jack scanned the nightstand, his body tense. He flicked apologetic eyes back to her, one hand raking his hair until it stood up on end in all directions.

'It's my personal cell. Only a few people have the number.' He softened against her belly but still covered her, pressing her into the mattress.

'Of course. You should get it.' She made to slide from under him but he held her firm, his mouth covering hers again while his hand patted the nightstand until he located and silenced his phone. He pulled his mouth from hers with a sigh, lifting the device to his ear.

'Yes?'

His face changed from mild frustration to relaxed and happy and then he spoke in rapid-fire French she had no hope of following, even if her command of the language stretched beyond the few sex words Jack had taught her. Not that she'd really been listening, too caught up in his sexy mouth and its power to send her shooting to the stars.

Harley let her hands explore his sublime body, tracing his shoulders and back and then fingering the silvery scar on his elbow where he'd broken his arm ski boarding aged sixteen and had required surgery.

He smiled, his eyes following the path of her fingers, and then kissed her, his conversation continuing between chaste presses of his mouth to hers, her neck, even her fingertips.

And then he stilled. His relaxed and happy expression morphed into a small frown but then his French became more animated, punctuated with laughter.

A twinge settled under her ribs, a slow burn that burrowed deep. Who had put that look on his face? What made him so animated? She knew so little about his life now. Aside from his work, his sexual skills and penchant for bilingual dirty talk.

Harley tried to escape again, to offer him a modicum of privacy to finish his call. His arm tightened around her waist, and he pressed his lips to hers once more, stilling her retreat.

Harley made out a female voice on the other end of the conversation. She breathed deep, trying to still the thrum of her pulse in her head and rein in her wildly spinning imagination. He must have sensed the tension she held in her body because he pulled away, his brows dipped as he peppered her lips with kisses, presumably waiting for a break in the conversation.

With his stare fixed on Harley, he said, '*Chérie*, I'm not alone. Can I call you back?'

The response came in French and he ended the call, tossing the phone back onto the nightstand and returning his undivided attention to Harley. 'I'm sorry.' A soft kiss. 'That was rude of me.'

Harley wriggled again, desperate now to dress in

last night's ball gown and call her driver. To get out
of here and take her confusion and her confessions
with her.

'No problem. I need to leave anyway.'

He let her wriggle free, a small frown crinkling
his brow.

She'd just made it to the edge of the bed in a sitting
position when his arm scooped her waist, first hauling her back against his hard chest and then tumbling
her back under him.

He was fully hard again against her thigh. His
mouth swallowed her gasp and any objections. When
the slow, thorough kiss ended he reared back to pin
her with an open and sincere look.

'Isabel. You remember my little sister. She got married this summer.'

She nodded, recalling the girl who looked like a
female version of Jack.

His mouth tensed, the playfulness draining away
as he absently stroked her collarbone.

'You don't approve?'

He frowned. 'It's not that.' He rolled onto his back,
resting his clasped hands under his head.

Harley slipped the T-shirt back on and retrieved the
tray from the dresser. If Jack was anything like Ash,
he'd be more communicative well-fed. She placed the
tray on the bed, and he smiled, sitting up to take one
fork and offer her the other. Half a pancake in, he
found his voice.

'She wanted to let me know I'm going to be an
uncle.' He studied the plate, his fork hovering.

'And that makes you frown?'

A small snort and a shake of his head. When he

looked at her, his eyes blazed. 'I just worry... She seems so happy, but...'

Harley fought the urge to squirm. What was going through his mind? Perhaps if she kept still he'd offer more of an insight.

The prongs of his fork prodded at a blueberry. 'It's all bullshit, don't you think?'

She held her breath, her gaze dipping to the half-eaten pancakes. 'What do you mean?'

He sighed, his fork clattering on the plate. 'Relationships. It's bad enough risking it for yourself, but to bring a child into the mix...' He ruffled his hair and jumped from the bed, all pent-up energy. Stalking to the dresser, he located a pair of cotton boxers, tugging them up his thighs with brisk, almost angry movements.

Harley mashed her lips together, her mind racing and her appetite forgotten. She agreed with him. Discovering her father's affair, the devastation of everything she'd known, and the subsequent mockery he'd made of his marriage afterwards had solidified her stance on love.

And in her brutally honest moments, she could admit her initial feelings for Phil, a man she'd been engaged to, had been more about fitting into a Hal-determined mould than any real feelings.

But Jack had been hurt. By her ending their childish, teenage infatuation, or something else? Unease lifted her shoulders.

'But she's happy?' Her eyes slid to a family photo she'd spied on the dresser, all four of the Lanes smile-laughing at the camera, captured in an unguarded moment, young Isabel's smile the biggest.

Jack snorted, his tense back to her while he rifled through his drawers.

'She's delirious. But marriage is like that—dreamy one minute, disintegrating the next. I mean, look at my parents. I would have thought Isabel would have learned something from them.'

'Your parents divorced?' The few mouthfuls of pancake settled in her stomach like concrete. She'd always liked the Lanes. Jack's parents had always been nice to her, and Isabel, two years younger, had emulated a seventeen-year-old Harley, not that she'd ever understood why. What had happened to them following the demise of the friendship between the Jacobs and Lanes? Had Joe discovered the affair? Had Amalie confessed? Was Hal to blame for their family breakdown?

Jack slammed the drawer closed. '*Oui*, spectacularly.'

He didn't know.

If he knew about his mother and Hal, he wouldn't be able to look at her right now, let alone tolerate her in his bed. Her throat turned scratchy. She couldn't look at herself.

'That doesn't mean Isabel's marriage will fail.' Yes, it took two to tango, but the far-reaching poison Hal had spread… Harley covered her mouth in case the she blurted out words that would kill this dead.

He pulled on the white T-shirt and shrugged. 'I just don't understand why she's so keen to play happy families.'

She should tell him. Her stomach cramped with the familiar burden that knowledge brought. For years she'd struggled with the secret, desperate to share it, lighten the load, but too scared of the repercussions.

And in some sick way, knowing about Hal's affair gave her a connection with him no one else had. They'd never discussed it, but she'd loyally protected him all these years. So desperate for his approval. So fearful of his disappointment.

The pancakes threatened to make a reappearance. But why should she have to clean up Hal's mess? If she told Jack, she'd have to tell her mother, too, in case Dulcie heard of it from another source.

It had been bad enough discovering them that last shared holiday in Aspen, bringing an abrupt end to her childhood and naïve notions about love and happy ever afters. Compounded by the shameful years of keeping the secret, she'd allowed her discovery to shape her own relationships. Keeping her guard up. Never falling too far.

And now? Why should she enlighten Jack on the choices their parents had made? Harley knew first hand the devastation the knowledge carried—Jack's relationship with his mother would be tarnished for ever.

If she told him her father was responsible for his parents' split and she'd known all along, he'd hate her perhaps more than he hated Hal—was she ready for things to be over?

Harley swallowed. It shouldn't matter if he was done with her. After all, what they shared was just sex. Why then did she want to run and hide so he couldn't see the truth written on her face?

'Perhaps she is happy.' Whatever her own motives, Isabel deserved to share her joyous news with her brother, unencumbered by Hal's actions. 'And you're happy for her.'

Jack wasn't his father or hers. He deserved to find happiness for himself. And he deserved to embrace his soon-to-be uncle role.

He paused in the hunt for more clothing, his jaw bunched but his shoulders sagging as if in defeat.

'Wanna go shopping for baby clothes?' Harley said.

His mouth twitched into a reluctant grin as his eyes searched hers. She swallowed, her throat hot and achy.

'Congratulations, Uncle Jack.'

He laughed, striding back to the bed and pulling her up for a thorough kissing. Something like relief poured through her, pushing aside the guilt keeping Hal's secret had always created. But as she succumbed once more to her physical connection with Jack she acknowledged neither emotion had any place in a short-term relationship composed solely of great sex.

Harley kicked off her shoes in the foyer of her apartment, allowing a surge of blood back into her tired feet. She padded up the connecting stairs to Ash's apartment above. He'd texted her thirty minutes ago saying he wanted to talk, so she knew he was home. After a day spent with Jack—baby clothes shopping, lunch and then a walk in Central Park—the last thing she wanted to do was face her brother's inquisition.

But Ash had a stubborn streak a mile wide. Better to hear him out and put him straight. The sooner she got it over with, the sooner she could wallow in the tub, something she'd been dreaming about for hours, the ache of underused muscles the only downside to fantastic sex.

She keyed her code into the entry pad, letting herself into her brother's apartment, which, size-wise, was a carbon copy of hers. They'd both inherited the Fifth Avenue apartments from their grandfather, an Irish immigrant turned real-estate magnate and founder of Jacob Holdings.

'Ash?' She found him in his office. Eight-thirty on a Saturday night and Ash was still working. As Jacob Holdings' leading corporate lawyer, he pulled horrendous hours, but he seemed to thrive off it. Another reason she could never have worked in the family business—their father's ridiculously high expectations stretched beyond her below-average grades, poor test performance and her choice of degree.

Ash looked up from the screen of his laptop and smiled.

'Hey, Harls.' He stood, flicking off the lights as he led her back into the living space and poured their usual Scotch and soda nightcap.

Harley settled into one corner of plush sectional sofa that faced a state-of-the-art minimalist fireplace and sipped her drink. The hairs on the back of her neck prickled, but she breathed through her apprehension, giving her beloved brother the benefit of the doubt. Sadly, he let her down.

'I'm just gonna come out and say it.' He crossed one ankle over the opposite knee and glared. 'What the hell are you thinking?' Ash gripped his glass so tight, the tips of his fingers turned white.

Harley sighed.

Really?

She was twenty-six years old and he still wanted to play 'big brother knows best'?

'To what are you referring?' No way would she make this easy for him. If he wanted to overstep the mark into her personal life, he'd have to do it unaided.

'You know what I mean. Jacques Lane, or whatever he calls himself these days. The old man will flip.' Ash rubbed his forehead and took a glug of Scotch.

'And it's no more his business than it is yours.' She rolled her bunched shoulders, refusing to ruin her happy, sated, shopped-out mood. 'Besides, we're just fucking.' That should shut him up. She tucked her feet under her and snuggled deeper into the cushions, her eyes drawn to the flickering orange flames over her brother's jaw-dropping glare.

Ash scrubbed his hand through his hair, his own curse hissed under his breath.

'Didn't you dump him? Didn't some major shit go down that winter, between his parents and ours? Dad never spoke of the Lanes again unless it was to bad-mouth Joe's shitty business dealings. I am remembering this right, yeah?'

Heat spread from the swallow of Scotch, flooding her with fire.

'So, what does that have to do with us? Besides, it was more than you know, more than Hal let on. The bad business between him and Joe was only part of the story.'

'I know what happened, the collapsed docklands deal. Joe Lane lacked the backbone for it, messed up and the deal folded, Hal lost thousands, blah, blah, blah.'

Harley snorted, shaking her head. 'Right, that's the version we heard from Hal. Don't you ever question him? Our father is a ruthless businessman. Don't you think that ruthlessness might spill over into his personal life?' She swallowed, her throat hot. During her speech, she'd uncurled from her relaxed position and leaned towards her brother, who looked at her with an infuriating unreadable expression.

But he'd touched a nerve. One that lay exposed and raw, permanently close to the surface and vulnerable to attack. Her blind faith in Hal was as thin and filmy as gossamer. And just because Joe Lane hadn't matched Hal Jacob for cold-blooded business deals, didn't mean Jack followed suit, not that it was a bad trait in Harley's book. Fortunately, from what she'd witnessed, Jack shared neither of their fathers' qualities.

'Perhaps because you're the golden boy, you've never experienced Dad's…acerbic tongue and brutal honesty.'

Ash huffed. 'I work with the guy every day. I've experienced plenty. I'm surprised *you* have.'

Harley smiled, sickly sweet. 'I'm the pretty one—remember when he called me that for the first time? Well, I was smart enough to see he'd written me off academically. Too stupid to go to Harvard—'

'You never even applied.'

'Because I was scared of failing again, disappointing him again.'

Ash stared, open-mouthed.

'He still tells his friends I'm the face of Jacob Holdings because he's too embarrassed by what I do, what I've built, to show any pride.' Harley slammed her tumbler onto the coffee table, and glared at her brother, daring him to defend their overbearing, often tactless father.

Shortly after that fateful last skiing holiday they'd

shared with the Lanes, Hannah had made it into Harvard Business School and Ash had passed the bar, to much family rejoicing. Harley, by comparison, had applied to the New York School of Design to study fashion. Hal's reaction, his obvious disappointment, had sealed the deal on their relationship. But his harsh comments had stung, nonetheless, shoving her firmly into the role of the family dropout.

Ash shook his head, his glass in his lap, seemingly fascinating.

'I'm sorry he made you feel like that. He's an asshole. We've always known this,' he said, his voice quiet and his expression remorseful. 'So what do you know that I don't?'

Harley shrank a little inside, the memory of Jack's face this morning crushing her when he relived the pain of his family's implosion. She couldn't bring herself to tell Jack. But could she tell Ash? The words hovered on her pressed-together lips, forcing their way out as if they'd taken on a life of their own.

'Hal had an affair with Amalie Lane.' The cathartic rush was almost head spinning but the words sickened her.

Ash gaped. 'Bullshit.' He slugged a mouthful of Scotch.

She nodded, the flames of the fire turning hazy as her heart thudded too fast. Now she'd spoken the confession aloud, should she repeat them to the person who had a right to know? A man who was still hurting from the consequences of Hal's actions.

'I saw them. That last holiday in Aspen.' She'd never been able to look at Hal the same way again, their already shaky father-daughter relationship irreparably tarnished by stumbling across the illicit liaison and thrust into the middle of a very grown-up issue.

At the time, she'd taken her anger and pain and fear and internalised it, withdrawing from Jack the only way she'd known how to deal with such momentous knowledge. Doubting everything she'd believed, seeing her father clearly for the first time, and terrified the secret would come out.

'Fuck. Does Jack know?' Ash gripped the back of his neck while his mind spewed out questions. 'Does Hal know you know? Does Mom know?'

Harley shrugged, the swirl of nausea intensifying. On the surface their parents' marriage seemed solid. But Jack was right. Who knew what went on behind closed doors? No relationship was invulnerable. And love…? Well, that was a sham.

'You've known all this time and didn't say anything?'

'I was scared at first…and then.' She shrugged. 'It's an impossible position—if I tell, I'm ruining someone's life. If I stay quiet, I'm condoning it. Colluding.'

'I'm so sorry. I had no idea.'

Harley nodded. That was the trouble with secrets. They ate away at you inside, and if you let them escape, you simply spread their power, allowed them to infect others with their poison.

At her sigh, Ash held up a placating hand. 'I'm sorry for sticking my nose into your personal life. I was looking out for you. But I see you don't need my protection. I just didn't want you to get hurt again. I mean that idiot, Phil—'

'I wasn't hurt by Phil. I ended it, remember.' Harley stared at the tumbler of amber liquid on the table.

Aside from making her feel small, Phil and Jack didn't belong in the same conversation. Besides, she'd never allowed herself to get close enough to Phil to get hurt, despite being engaged to him.

She could at least thank Hal for that. On discovering his deception, she'd seen a man she'd looked up to her whole life, one whose approval was constantly worth chasing, and she'd vowed to be nothing like him. To be guarded when it came to relationships, because from what she'd seen they led to lies, heartache and betrayal.

But Ash was right. She and Jack hadn't talked about the past and her part in it. Perhaps she'd hurt him with her rejection more than she realised. And now she'd hurt him all over again if she told him what she knew about Hal and his mother.

Perhaps he'd be able to forgive her for being young and clumsy with his feelings. If she'd been able to discuss what happened with her father, she might have worked through her confusing emotions and let Jack down with more of an explanation. More consideration.

But now? How could she explain that she'd kept such a monumental secret from him? From everyone. A secret that must have played a major part in the breakdown of his parents' marriage and the implosion of his family.

He detested Hal—once he discovered she'd covered for her father, he'd hate her too.

She sucked in a shuddering breath, reminding herself she and Jack were just fooling around—a casual fling, great sex. Enlightening him on the real reason for the family feud and his parents' subsequent divorce when they were just having a good time—what was the point? All these years later?

Jack had moved on from that then and he'd soon move on from her now. Harley rubbed her temples to banish the vice gripping her head.

'I did a little fishing.' Ash pressed his lips together the way he did when delivering bad news in the boardroom.

She pinned him with a hard glare.

He held up a hand. 'I know, but I'm your brother. It's my job to look out for you. And this is business.' He sighed, eyes softening.

Of course Ash would dig. It was his job, one he excelled at. And reading people—he'd always told her that was the key to being a good attorney.

'I can take care of my own business.'

He continued as if she hadn't spoken, a trait he'd inherited from their father that made her teeth grind. 'The Morris Building... It was scheduled for demolition a year ago. Did you know that?'

Damn.

She glanced away, shoulders heavy. Why didn't she know that? Something else she'd overlooked? Another mistake? The throb intensified at her temples.

Ash leaned forward, his elbows braced on his knees. 'Perhaps he's hiding something from you too.'

Inside, Harley shrank into the sofa. Fatigue dragged her down. She was so tired of doubting herself. So tired of expecting to fail, no matter how hard she tried.

Ash took her hand. 'If he's such a stand-up guy, why is he trying to sell you a building that was only good enough to be knocked down? Do you think he's out for some sort of revenge?'

Good question. Her sore head spun, nothing to do with the Scotch. It was bad enough that she doubted herself, without her brother checking up on her every move. When would people see past her dyslexia? See what she'd built?

She wasn't some green sap, playing around with her hobby business and falling back on her trust fund. Shock turned to anger.

'Thank you for pointing that out to me.'

'Harls—'

'There must be an explanation.' She had no patience for Ash's interference, no matter how well intentioned. 'But don't you think I did my due diligence? Don't you think I vetted his company prior to commencing negotiations, even before I knew that Demont Designs was Jacques Lane?' Anyone with a lick of business savvy would do the same. And she might not have the MBA, but she'd gleaned enough business skills from her family her whole life by watching and listening. It wasn't enough to satisfy Hal. She'd never be enough. But she'd expected more from Ash.

Her shoulders, now somewhere around her ears, twitched, her body draining of fight and energy. He was right. She'd made another mistake. Missed critical information. How long had Jack owned the Morris Building? Was he even aware himself about the aborted demolition? Was he keeping his own secret?

She stood, her fatigue multiplied tenfold since she'd trudged up the stairs twenty minutes ago. 'I'm going to bed.' She'd heard enough. There was only so much self-flagellation she could tolerate in one day. And where Jack was concerned, her head chased the same problem around and around.

Ash stilled her, his hand reaching for hers. 'I'm sorry. I only have your best interests at heart.' She nodded, her throat too tight and her brain too fuzzy to speak. She was lucky—Ash always had her back.

'Do you want me to look over the contract? You haven't signed it yet, have you?'

She had. It was in her purse, ready to be couriered first thing Monday morning. She swallowed a swirl of nausea souring the Scotch in her stomach, and shook her head. Whatever mess, or not, she'd got herself into, it was her job to extricate Give from the clutches of a bad decision. And extricating herself from Jack...? Would that be as easily achieved?

She squeezed Ash's fingers, letting him know she understood his sibling interference and his motivations. He kissed the back of her hand, regret shining in his eyes.

She was almost to the stairs when he spoke again. 'Love you, Harls.'

She nodded, too choked to speak, and hurried down the stairs heading straight for the bath she'd promised herself. Perhaps, by some miracle, the hot water would scald all her niggling doubts and insecurities away. One thing was glaringly obvious. She didn't know Jack beyond his astounding bedroom skills. Why, then, did the tumult spinning around her head and crashing behind her ribs feel suspiciously like emotions she had no place feeling? Stupid, naïve emotions she'd left behind long ago?

She sighed, submerging herself fully under the hot water.

Emotions or not. Business was business.

CHAPTER EIGHT

THE FOLLOWING EVENING Harley adjusted the halter-neck top and fluffed out her hair. Taking an hour to primp and preen, try on multiple outfit choices and perfect her make-up stopped her from checking her phone every five minutes. So determined to ignore the hateful device, she'd not only switched it off, but she'd also put it inside the fridge for good measure.

Jack had sent three texts throughout the day. A series of flirty, suggestive missives that yesterday would have made her toes curl and her panties wet. But Ash had planted his seed of doubt deep in the fertile soil of her mind. And her dilemma to tell him about the affair drained all her residual energy. She just wanted to forget the mess her life had become in a relatively short time. Personal and professional.

Probably the reason she'd accepted an invitation to go clubbing with Hannah, who was celebrating a promotion amongst the Jacob Holdings ranks. One thing about Hal Jacob—he believed in his children working their way to the top. Nepotism at its finest.

Harley jumped when the buzzer sounded, announcing the arrival of her sister and her friends, and reached for her clutch.

Hannah had chosen one of New York's chicest nightspots, a place frequented by the elite. As they spilled from the car and tottered towards the entrance, bypassing the queue, a series of photographs flashed behind the cordoned-off area. On the rare occasions she partied with her friends, Harley preferred the quieter clubs, ones less likely to be filled with celebrities, and therefore less likely to attract paparazzi. But this was Hannah's night.

Harley turned her head away and tugged her sister towards the entrance. The sooner she made it to the dance floor, the sooner she could banish the restless energy pounding through her.

The club heaved with bodies, glamour and good times on the agenda. Hannah had reserved them a VIP booth, which eased Harley into the groove, one she struggled to feel despite hoping it would provide a distraction from her doubts over Jack and her disappointment with herself. She downed a couple of shots, trying to get into the swing for her sister's sake. But she wore her reservations and fears like an extra layer of clothing—thick and itchy and hard to shake.

After a suitable length of time drinking with Hannah's friends they headed for the dance floor. Harley closed her eyes, and succumbed to the heavy beat of the dance track thrumming through the floor and into her bones. The vodka-dancing combo worked its magic. Her mind settled, all thoughts of Jack and her botched business deal relegated to the corners while she lost herself to the thumping beat and the flashing lights.

Hands settled on her hips and her eyes fluttered

open. Expecting to see Hannah's smiling face, she faltered when the recipient of the hands came into focus.

Phil.

Her stomach flopped. Of course he'd be here. Perpetually single, her ex collected beautiful dates like trophies. His lucrative salary at Jacob Holdings and his social-climbing sense of entitlement meant that clubs like this one provided the perfect hunting ground for him.

He shot her a grin that carried nothing friendly. He'd never quite forgiven her for breaking off their engagement. But for her, Phil would be heir to a large chunk of the Jacob fortune, his way to the top practically guaranteed.

Harley's feet shuffled to a standstill. Her first instinct was to pull away without speaking to him. She was halfway there when he dropped his hands from her hips and moved just outside her personal space, dancing.

Damn. Now she'd have to make nice with small talk.

The dance floor was packed with bodies. The music so loud that a cursory *how's it going* and some rudimentary sign language was sufficient communication to tick the social-etiquette-for-an-ex-lover box.

She glanced around, her feet moving to the music with less enthusiasm, but her chest lighter when she spotted her sister and the group of girls nearby.

Subtly sidling closer to the girls, Harley practically swayed into her sister. Phil followed, joining their group with a nod to Hannah and immediately engaged one of her friends with his oily smile and whispered banter. If he'd hoped to prick her jealousy, he clearly didn't pay enough attention. Aside from polite dance-floor camaraderie born of an innate civility, her interest in her ex ended there.

What had she ever seen in Phil? She'd been young. Too young. Barely nineteen when they'd first met. She'd been dazzled for all of five minutes—Phil's ambition and drive an attraction until she'd realised it was all he cared about and couldn't tolerate anything less in others, especially her. As their relationship had continued, he'd seen her independence from the family business as a hobby, a lack of direction. When he'd told her, during a recurring argument, she was stupid to renounce her place in the family business, a cash-cow future mapped out before her and that Hal agreed with him, she'd finally broken free of her inertia and called things off.

She glanced at him again, recalling their lacklustre intimacies. Nope. Nothing. Not even a flicker of her pulse.

As the track ended she tilted her chin at Hannah, indicating her departure from the dance floor. She'd chug a bottle of water, use the restroom and then find Hannah, let her know she was heading home. Phil's presence had put an end to the promise of the evening, not because she had feelings for him, but because the glaring contrast between him and Jack had plunged her once more into the pit of doubt she'd come here to forget.

She shook off the emotion—it was the sex. It had to be the sex.

Perhaps that was why she hadn't confronted Jack already. Stalling the inevitable? Was she really too scared to risk what she'd found in Jack's bed?

She rounded the corner on the way back to their booth.

Jack blocked her path.

The air whooshed out of her lungs as she almost collided with him.

'Oh, hi.'

His lip curled, eyes dancing. 'A tepid greeting for an intimate acquaintance.' His lips grazed her cheek, the cool formality grating on her nerves already stretched taut with indecision, confusion and the constant burn of need.

His lips hovered over her ear. 'Have you already forgotten how it feels to come around my cock?' His breath blasted the tiny hairs on her neck and then he leaned away, eyes sparking, and took a swig of beer. She glanced back to the dance floor. Phil, a head taller than most people, looked their way, his eyes narrowed even as he pressed up behind the woman he'd singled out for his attention.

Harley looked back to Jack, who gave no indication he'd seen her dancing with another man or that he cared one iota. Good. She wasn't Phil's. And she wasn't Jack's. She could dance with whomever she pleased. If only her libido understood.

'Are you here with friends?'

He nodded once, his stare dipping to her chest and continuing down to her bare legs. 'Alex and Libby. But perhaps I also stalked you here, like you stalked me to get what you wanted that first day.'

Did he? Did she care? Goose bumps snaked down her arms and she fought the urge to hug herself. Her nipples peaked, chafing on the gossamer fabric of her halter-top.

'What do you want?' Her voice carried a tremulous quality. Fear of his answer? Fear he'd ask her the same question?

He stared. The barest of shrugs. Then he clasped her fingers, his own cool and damp from the beer bottle.

'I… I'm here with my sister. She's celebrating.' Why did she feel the need to explain herself? Why so unsure of this man she'd entrusted with her pleasure, her body? A man she allowed, no, begged, to push her boundaries, her a willing accomplice to their sexy game. A man she wasn't certain she could trust, but wanted anyway. How messed up was that?

Another nod. His hand found her hip and he tugged her close, her body going willingly to slide along the length of his. Hannah and Phil danced only metres away, the Morris Building could be one big dud, her mind buzzed with secrets, doubts and humiliation that she'd let herself down one time too many, but she didn't give a damn.

All that mattered was the warmth from his body, the curl of instant lust that sizzled up from her belly the moment she saw him and the frisson of uncontrollable need he inspired as easily as a quirk from his sinful mouth.

His lips glided over the skin below her ear, curling her toes.

'I'm not the jealous type, *ma belle*. You either want me, want what I can give you, what we have together, or you don't. Simple.'

So he had seen her dancing with Phil.

She shuddered, his warmth and spicy scent a combination more potent than the vodka she'd drunk. Was it simple? It should be. Just sex. Spectacular orgasms. No strings.

Why did her second-guessing his motives and doubting his integrity complicate everything? Why, after years of her shoving it to the back of her mind, did Hal's indiscretion hover on the tip of her tongue every time she looked at Jack? Because she'd developed feelings beyond physical gratification?

'There's a reason you didn't marry him.'

There were hundreds of reasons. Harley pulled away. 'You knew I was engaged to Phil?'

He shrugged. 'You're an heiress. I saw the announcement.' His fingers flexed at her waist. 'What happened?'

Not one shred of envy marred his expression. If anything, he looked at her with hunger, as if he was seconds from kissing her, a look she'd grown accustomed to and a need reflected in her for anyone to see.

She sighed, Phil the last thing she wanted to talk about. But she had nothing to hide.

'He…didn't approve of me, said I wasted my birthright in pursuit of what he deemed a hobby.'

Jack's eyes flicked to the dance floor, slivers of steel solidifying there. Then he was back with her, his lips brushing her temple.

'I'm glad you saw through him, for your sake. A man who needs to put you down, one who couldn't even get you off…not worth your time.'

'How do you know he couldn't get me off?'

He shrugged. 'An educated guess. If he met your needs, you'd be happily married by now.'

She shuddered. 'I was naïve. I never loved Phil. But part of me wanted to conform. And Hal approved.' She shook her head at her own stupidity. She largely shared Jack's cynicism about the marital state, at least for her. That didn't mean she wasn't sincere in her comments about his sister's happiness. She'd learnt her lesson, both from Hal and Phil.

Ash's words rang in her ears. Was she a good judge of character? Yes, she'd seen through Phil. She'd realised her relationship with him had been more about her relationship with her father and trying to please him.

But had she grown sloppy, or been mesmerised by her physical attraction to Jack and missed a crucial character flaw? Was he the kind of businessman who had more in common with Hal than she realised?

Her empire, her dyslexia school in particular, meant everything to her. But she'd walk away from their deal in a heartbeat if he'd deliberately deceived her. Especially if, as Ash suggested, he'd used her for some sort of revenge. She cringed. If he'd managed to dupe her because the documents and contracts pertaining to the Morris Building swam before her eyes and made her head hurt...

Or perhaps *she'd* put everything she'd built up in jeopardy with her constant challenges. Perhaps Hal was right. Was it time to stop messing around and return to the safety of the family fold?

Jack stepped closer, his erection grazing her thigh. Her limbs quivered as if she'd drunk more than she had, her nipples peaked through her top and chafed on his shirt and her sex clenched in anticipation. She swallowed, her eyes closing and her forehead leaning against his firm chest.

What was wrong with her? Doubting his integrity

and professionalism one minute, about to claw at his clothes and ride him the next. Was the sex with Jack really that good? Good enough she couldn't walk away if her business interests dictated their connection over? No regrets? If he'd lied to her, duped her...

She closed her eyes tight, the sexy beat of the music and the rhythmic swipes of Jack's thumb on the bare skin of her waist lulling her into sensual waters. Unlike the forgettable Phil, everything this man did, said and was lured her there.

And she did want what they created together. Something she'd failed to find with anyone else. This searing connection, flammable chemistry, a forbidden addiction... Until she'd had chance to fully investigate Ash's claim, could she really abandon it, abandon him again, so easily?

And while she hadn't known Jack for the intervening nine years, the man she'd spent the day with yesterday—the same one who'd picked out tiny giraffe-printed romper suits and a cuddly snowy-white swan for his pregnant sister—she just couldn't reconcile that man with one who orchestrated dodgy deals, professionally. Perhaps *that* made her stupid, an emotion she'd grown up with.

Jack's lips grazed her temple and she opened her eyes.

'You didn't answer my texts.' Not a question. He buried his nose in her hair and inhaled. She leaned into him, following the slight sway of his body, which moved them in time with the sensual beat of the music in a dance of their own.

'No.' Why did swaying on the edge of the dance floor with this man feel a hundred times more intimate

than anything she'd experienced with her ex-fiancé, a
man she'd almost married? Harley looped her fingers
into the belt loops on his jeans so their hips moved
in unison. If she closed her eyes, kept this moment,
her dancing with Jack, alive, she could avoid thinking about the doubts, both of him and herself, eating
her away inside like acid.

Jack stilled.

Harley opened her eyes, reluctant but a realist.

He looked down, expression unreadable. Not angry.
Not even insulted that she'd ignored him without explanation, it seemed.

He placed his beer on a nearby table and took her
hand. No explanation. But she didn't need one. She followed him, her pulse thrumming between her legs as
their bodies weaved through the crowds. Heat curled
inside her. She couldn't be sure if it was shame that
she'd sidelined her concerns and succumbed to her
constant physical need for Jack, or the heat that rarely
dissipated from her body when he was around. Either
way, she offered no resistance, which was how, moments later, she found herself in a darkened corridor
off the club, the chill of the air and the dulling of the
music shutting out everything but Jack, his body warm
and insistent against hers.

He crowded her and she tugged him with her as
she leaned back against the wall. He scooped the hair
from one shoulder, his fingers brushing her skin as
his eyes held her captive.

'Tell me…' a small frown dulled the searing intensity of his stare '…did I imagine your cries, your satisfaction yesterday?' He slotted one leg between hers,

the scrape of denim against her inner thighs firing her nerve endings to screaming life.

She rubbed herself shamelessly on him, her hips undulating as he found the sensitive skin beneath her ear and caressed it with his mouth, waiting for her answer.

Her head hit the wall behind her, eyes rolling back.

'No,' she whispered, uncaring of the needy catch in her voice or the way her nails clung to his rippling shoulders as he pinned her to the wall.

His hand eased between her legs, which parted without resistance, his fingers slipping beyond the scant barrier of her panties, fingertips strumming her clit.

She pulled him closer, her mouth finding his. The hollow ache between her legs intensified. She wanted him. Here. Now. Her sister or her ex could come searching for her any moment, but all she could think about was Jack inside her, fucking her against the wall. The ecstasy she knew he'd deliver, the sex, between them so easy.

The only easy thing in her life right now.

She scrunched her eyes closed, willing the rapture she knew was out there. But it hovered just out of reach, her mind warring with the needs of her body and, for once, coming out on top. Her timing sucked, the need to prioritise answers over her body's demands.

'What's wrong, *chérie*?' His eyes cleared. His fingers stilled. He removed his hand from her panties and smoothed her skirt over her hips, hands lingering there.

She looked away. Still confused. Still balanced on

a tightrope, afraid to look down for fear of what she might see. She shook her head.

Outside their business deal, she had no right to probe. But their conversation about Isabel and her doubts about the Morris deal dragged up questions.

Did he hate her family enough to deliberately conceal facts about the Morris Building? Her mouth opened and closed. She folded her arms across her waist. She had no right to answers when she herself kept a secret from him. And did she really want those answers when they could mark an end to the best sex of her life?

'I—' Her throat scratched. How could she question his motives without telling him the full story of the reasons for their families' rift? Demand complete honesty from him, while concealing something so enormous herself?

He sighed, adjusting himself before putting his hands in his pockets. When he looked at her again, she shivered.

'Are you letting me down gently, this time?' His mouth tightened a fraction, or she might have imagined that because his tone stayed light. 'Are you done with our little game?' His neutral expression gave nothing away, as if he didn't care either way. As if he could walk away, right now. Tonight. No regrets.

But could she?

His hand scrubbed his stubbled cheek as if he was about to say more, but held back. What would he say? *We were just fooling around...? Au revoir?*

Harley shrivelled inside.

His jaw bunched and then he smiled an unconvinc-

ing smile and shrugged. 'It's your choice.' He swiped
a kiss over her parted lips. And without a backwards
glance, he left her reeling, as confused as ever.

CHAPTER NINE

TRENT BUZZED HARLEY in seconds before she swanned into Jack's office with little more than a cursory knock. Eight-fifteen in the morning and her eyes sparked with fire, burnishing the green to gold, the resolute tilt to her chin announcing she had an axe to grind.

He rose from his chair and rounded the desk to meet her, his cock twitching at the sight of her all elegant, sexy as fuck and clearly pissed with him.

Could he blame her? He'd thrown down the gauntlet last night then tossed and turned, his mind racing at the possibility this was over. He'd come to know her well enough to see she hid something from him, and whatever she concealed should be none of his damned business. But the hypocrite in him wanted to pry, while keeping his own feelings securely locked behind the fantastic sex.

'Trent said you were alone,' she said by way of explanation, not that he assumed for one second she was here for a Monday-morning quickie to start the working week off with a bang. He rested on the front edge of his desk, feet spread and cast his eye over her from head to toe. Her tight skirt outlined the flare of her hips and her nipples peaked through her blouse. Pissed but aroused.

He slipped one hand into his pants pocket, discreetly adjusting his semi. 'What can I do for you?' Apart from unzip that skirt and bend that delectable ass over his desk so they could both feel better and delay the inevitable showdown. That he'd awoken alone, a hollowness gnawing at him, had already soured his day.

She held out the sheaf of documents he'd hand-delivered to her store last week.

'I came to personally deliver these. All signed.' She dropped her arm, her glare intensifying. 'Tell me. Did you know the Morris Building was earmarked for demolition a year ago?' Her chin lifted, eyes sparking as she popped out one hip and stared him down.

So she'd done a little digging. Doubted his motives? Assumed he'd allow their past to influence his business ethic? He bit back the first retort to form on his tongue and stared, poker-faced, until the flush from her chest spread to her neck.

His stomach rolled—he'd known going in they lacked trust between them, but the sting flayed him just the same. He clenched his fist in his pocket—why should it bother him now? Hadn't he started this as a game of revenge? To show her what she'd been missing? Yes, that had fulfilled his need to control this searing chemistry between them. But could he really say his hands were spotless?

'You know—' he rubbed his jaw, fingers itching to get hold of her despite the wall that surrounded her, ten feet tall '—I can't decide whether to kick you out—' he rested his hands on the edge of his desk beside his hips '—or fuck you over my desk until we both have a do-over on this Monday morning.' A partial lie—his mind already on board with option B.

She gave a small snort, her head shaking.

'Answer my question.'

Jack pushed away from the desk and strode to her, reaching for the signed Morris contract and flicking his gaze over the first page, which bore his signature and hers. His insides boiled with a sickening mix of frustration and arousal. And perhaps other emotions he refused to dissect.

Slowly, deliberately, he lifted the pages to eye level between them, holding the challenge in her stare with one of his own. He tore the entire document in half, the kick of sick satisfaction stirring in his belly as her eyes widened.

'Wh-what the…?' she stuttered.

He returned to his chair via the waste-paper basket, dropping the contract in the trash. He settled back against the leather, willing himself calm. He never lost his unflappable business exterior, his tight grip on control, but dealing with Harley pushed him to his limits. Professionally and personally.

He shrugged, his fingers steepled in front of his face. 'Without trust…' a shrug '…we have nothing worth having.'

'So you're back to refusing to sell?'

She would think that. Another blow to the gut. Perhaps physical communication worked best for them. They certainly had no concerns in that department.

He leaned back in his chair, fighting the urge to kiss her. 'No. Not at all. I'll draw up another contract, only this time I'll put my money where my mouth is.'

She fisted both hands on her curvaceous hips, her lush mouth tight.

'Or you could just answer my question.'

'My actions speak for me, *chérie*. Consider that contract null and void.' He rubbed his jaw with a sigh. 'To reassure you, Ms Jacob, the Morris Building is sound. The previous owners saw more value in the land than the old building.' The moment's hesitation flitting across her face gave him no satisfaction.

'I had planned to renovate that building myself, until other projects demanded more of my time.'

She dropped her defensive stance but kept him on the hook.

'You perhaps should have mentioned that to a prospective buyer.'

He tilted his head, conceding. Fuck, she was magnificent—smart, determined, taking no bullshit.

'I didn't set out to dupe anyone.' Only to use their mutual attraction to level the score—not his finest moment. But he couldn't tell her that. Because admitting she'd hurt him nine years ago took this…fling way out of the realms of casual sex. A place he never set foot.

'That information is public record. You perhaps should have had your team unearth information that's clearly there for anyone to see.'

She flushed and he winced. Fuck, he'd wondered about the quality of her lawyers, but she'd take that as a personal attack. He softened his tone.

'I'll make you another deal.'

What was the real issue here? Her checks and the documentation he'd provided with the sale agreement would have highlighted any major structural issues with the building. This, her doubts, her easily under-mined trust, went way deeper.

Prying again? What did it matter if she didn't trust him? And why did he want to crawl out of his skin right about now?

'I'll sell the very sound Morris Building to Give, if you bring me on board to renovate, pro bono.'

She rolled her eyes. 'That's completely unneces-sary.'

Not to him. 'The price of my integrity is worth ten times that to me.' *And the price of your trust.*

Fuck—there it was again. He'd always known she'd held back. And he didn't need her trust outside the bedroom. He focussed on her wary stare, refusing to dissect his motivations.

'Would I sell you a dud building and then attach my name to the development?' The irony that if she agreed they'd be in partnership together on this deal, just as their fathers had been all those years ago, made him wince. Only the stakes seemed to soar much higher. And for Harley...? He had no clue where her head was. Only her body.

She regarded him for so long, he expected her to walk out. And then her shoulders dropped by the mer-est fraction. 'I don't think you'd sell a dud.'

'And yet you doubted me anyway?' He shouldn't care. But a vice constricted his chest. Yes, their fami-lies were enemies. Yes, he'd initially sought payback for the way she'd callously abandoned what they'd had nine years ago. So he'd toyed with her a little, used their chemistry to show her that he was twice the man she'd discarded... But now...?

He swallowed, throat tight, too terrified to go there.

'I—' She mashed her lips together as if she feared what would emerge. Hiding something herself?

'Nothing to say?'

Emotions flitted over her exquisite features, a battle raging within. Her shoulders dropped and her guard followed until all that remained was the stark honesty and candour he'd seen every time they'd connected physically. But he longed to see it outside the bedroom, too.

With a sigh, her words rushed out. Heartfelt, stripped bare, and setting off a tidal wave of relief through his body. 'I want you.' A small shake of her head. 'I'm not ready for this to end.'

So she didn't trust him fully, but she wanted him anyway. Euphoria pounded inside him, flooding his muscles until his body screamed at him to act. To remind her how good they were together. How much better things could be…

No. This was all there was.

While he stood mute, pushing aside his own dangerous thoughts, Harley kicked off her shoes, tossed her purse on a chair and began unbuttoning her blouse.

His cock surged against the front of his pants. Barely nine in the morning and he seriously contemplated fucking her in his office? His mind filtered through his calendar for the morning—nothing that couldn't wait.

Without waiting for his reaction, Harley locked the door she'd stormed through only minutes earlier and sauntered his way, hips swinging as she crossed his office on stockinged feet. She perched her delectable ass on the edge of his desk between his spread thighs. With a little shimmy, she'd lifted the figure-hugging skirt to mid-thigh and he got a glimpse of lace-topped stockings.

Fuck. He was so done for. Although this form of communication, all they had, worked for him, part of him, the small niggle at the back of his mind, for the first time, entertained the possibility of more.

He came to his feet and Harley yanked on his tie, pulling his mouth down to hers. She took, pressing her tongue into his mouth with a whimper that pounded need through him. But that part of him held out for more.

He'd had his revenge; he'd proved to her again and again his worth as a lover. But he was nowhere near done, his need for her evolving, morphing, transforming.

He kissed her back, ignoring the 'why' in his head. He'd draw out her faith piece by piece if he had to.

His hands grasped her hips and he slid her ass forward to the edge of the desk and onto his rock-hard erection.

'Do we have a new deal?' He wouldn't let her hide. He ground his hips into her, one hand cupping her breast, his thumb honing in on her puckered nipple. He wasn't her toy, available to scratch any itch she might have. If she still wanted to play, he wanted her assurances, her belief in their professional partnership at a very minimum. A starting point.

Her head fell back. She spread her thighs wider, pressed her heat closer. 'Yes. I'm sorry.' Her sincere stare burned into his while she waited, poised, like him, on the edge of a new precipice. But he was as powerless to this physical need as she seemed. He slanted his mouth across hers, pouring his passion, his honour, his commitment into the kiss that stole a throaty gasp from her throat.

She loosened his tie, undoing shirt buttons with impatient hands. His hand slipped between them, his fingers probing beneath her drenched panties. He found her clit, primed and plump, and rubbed the pad of his thumb there as he tore his mouth from hers and said, 'Do you trust me…to help you build your school?' Fuck, what was wrong with him? Why push this? She was ready, begging him.

Her hips jerked and she reached for his belt.

'Yes.' Her mouth traced his jaw, his neck and between his pecs. She groaned, her face buried in the hair on his chest. 'Yes, Jack, I do.'

Appeased for now, he ripped at his fly, the scent of her arousal as potent as the hit of his morning coffee, his stamina at its limit.

'Quick… Hurry.' Her frantic hands freed him from his boxers, shoving his clothing over his hips as she returned her mouth to his with nibbling kisses that drove him perilously close to the edge.

He left her briefly to stride to his personal bathroom and locate a condom. When he returned, tearing into the foil with his teeth as he crossed the room, she'd shimmied out of her panties and lifted her skirt to waist height.

Her sophisticated look would be ruined, but she didn't seem to care, any more than he cared that her ass was crushing some blueprints and his laptop was at risk of hitting the floor.

Within seconds, he filled her and they groaned together, chests heaving as if they'd held their breath for too long. The rightness of it, of her, made his head

swim—euphoria or trepidation? He couldn't tell and
didn't want to look too closely.

As he pounded them both to a torrid climax that
left Harley wailing loud enough for the whole building
to hear, he made himself a vow to discover what she
held back. He didn't stop to question his own motives.

Two days later Harley wished Belinda goodnight just
before closing time, her mind, as always, on Jack. He'd
flown to Paris the day she'd confronted him about the
Morris Building, a prior business meeting requiring
his attention. He'd made sure to send the revised contract over before he'd left, along with a personal note
that left her reassured and cranky at the same time.

> *Looking forward to our new working relation-
> ship. I have to be back in Paris in a week but
> hope to begin on the Morris plans before I leave
> again.*

The more she thought about him, the more restless
she grew. Had this, somewhere along the way, shifted
from just sex? Every time he popped into her head,
her chest pinched. Every text alert sent her heart rate
soaring and then plummeting, and she counted down
the hours to his return tomorrow.

She braced herself against the bite of the evening
chill as she stepped out onto the street. Then she came
to a halt.

Jack stood at the kerb, leaning up against his car
with his phone in one hand and a bouquet of flowers in the other. Seeing her, he quickly pocketed the
phone and strode in her direction, his grin lighting

her up inside as much as the sexy smoulder coming from his eyes.

With a certainty that stalled everything but her thudding heart, she had her answer.

'Bon anniversaire, ma belle.' He handed her the flowers and swiped a cold kiss over her mouth, one that finished all too soon.

She swallowed, throat tight.

'You remembered my birthday?' A flush warmed her from inside while her head whirled. She was never more certain of anything—she'd fallen for him. How had that happened, and what did she do with the information?

He tilted his head in that French way. 'Of course.'

He'd never given her any indication he wanted more than sex. His cynicism about his sister's happiness, the impact his parents' divorce must have had on him and the demise of his father's business, confirmed he shared some of Harley's own reservations about relationships. But the look he shot her seemed to peel back her layers until she stood before him, exposed.

Memories of her seventeenth birthday surfaced. They'd been at her parents' house in the Hamptons. Jack had waited until everyone else was occupied in various parts of the house before suggesting a walk on the beach, where he'd not only presented her with a book on the life story of Coco Chanel, one of her favourite fashion heroines, but also kissed her for the first time. She still had that book on her shelves at home.

She pressed her tingling lips together.

'How long have you been waiting?'

He stepped close, his hand on her waist as he looked

at her as if he wanted to devour her, right here on the street within gawping distance of half of Manhattan.

'That doesn't matter.' His eyes searched hers and she blinked, uncertain what he saw and unsettled by the probing depth. 'Do you have plans?'

She shook her head. She'd celebrated with Hannah and Ash last night. All she'd planned for tonight was food, a bath and sleep. But now Jack was back a day early…a birthday girl could find some energy for whatever he had in mind.

His lips grazed her temple as he scooped his arm around her and huddled her into his side, away from the wind.

'Send your driver home. I want to feed you and fuck you in that order. I missed you.'

The return sentiment bubbled up from her throat, but she swallowed it back, too terrified to let the words free. Because, for her, the words now came with feelings. And feelings changed everything. They carried added responsibility.

The weight of the secret that wasn't hers to tell pressed her into the sidewalk. She should tell him, before she fell deeper? Before too much time passed and he'd never be able to forgive her for concealing something so momentous.

She wouldn't carry the burden any longer, refused to be like Hal, refused to be his accomplice through her silence. Jack deserved the whole story.

But finding the right moment…

Jack looked at her expectantly. As birthday presents went, what he offered was up there with the best. She forced a smile, shelving her confession like a coward, and quickly spoke to her driver before joining Jack in the back of his car.

He'd chosen her favourite restaurant, a chic, intimate establishment in Soho. They sat side by side in a booth with mellow lighting that lulled her into embracing the moment.

He touched her often, a hand on her knee, a clasp of her fingers, frequently brushing hair back from her face while he told her about his trip home and asked about her ideas for renovating the Morris Building.

Over dessert—her favourite, a classic chocolate mousse—he pulled a gift from his breast pocket. Harley licked a smear of the rich chocolate from her lip, finding it hard to swallow.

He handed her the exquisitely wrapped gift, a small, rectangular box. 'This designer, a Parisian, reminded me of you. You share a vision, I think.' He smiled, his hand on her knee under the table.

Harley tore into the paper, anything more than a hoarse 'thank you' beyond her.

Eyes alight, he watched as she opened the box. 'She uses reclaimed precious metals and ethically sourced stones in her designs.'

Harley fingered the delicate gold bracelet, her burning stare lifting to his. That he'd put so much thought and effort into her gift choked her. She urged him to help her fasten the fine strand of gold around her wrist, laughing as they both fumbled with the tiny clasp.

He could have bought her diamonds. He could have spent enough to feed a family for a year. But he understood her. Saw her. Eschewed flashy ostentation for the simplicity of a gift that, like her range of fashion and accessories, carried a message and a social conscience.

She kissed him, a surge of emotions welling up to paralyse her vocal cords. She snuggled into his side and focussed on the simple bracelet that sparkled on her arm while she breathed through her feelings.

That was how they left the restaurant, arm in arm, her close to his side. The flashes startled her from her dreamy state. Two or three paparazzi crowded the sidewalk outside the restaurant, their cameras popping as they fired questions and called Harley's name.

Jack gripped her waist, guiding her to the car, which idled at the kerb. His other arm shielded them from the most insistent pap as they hurried inside the vehicle.

'Drive,' he barked at Will, looking over his shoulder at the photographers they'd left behind. He gripped her hand.

'Are you okay? Does that happen often?' He looked ready to break something, nostrils flared, jaw clenched.

Harley shrugged, the adrenaline dissipating and leaving her limbs heavy and her head fuzzy. Way to kill her birthday buzz.

'Only if there's no one more gossip-worthy to pester.'

Jack pulled her into his lap, his nose nuzzling below her ear as his own breathing slowed to normal.

'You look tired.' A soft, undemanding kiss. 'The birthday fucking can wait.'

She pouted, wriggling on his lap until he groaned and dropped his head back on the leather. She rose up onto her knees astride him, leaning above him to swipe her mouth over his, coaxing.

'But I want my birthday fucking and you promised. Better and better, remember?' She'd missed him, whether or not she could say it aloud. Four days without their searing physical connection seemed like a year. She rubbed herself over his lap, her mouth parted as the tingles between her legs snaked along her belly.

Jack held her face between his palms, his gaze flicking over her face. 'Fuck, woman, what are you doing to me?'

She laughed, swooping to kiss a trail along his jaw until she arrived at his earlobe and sucked. He gripped her waist, fingers flexing. And then he pushed her away to pass his hot, mischievous stare over her.

'Take your panties off.' A gruff order, one that she hurried to obey.

She slid to the seat beside him and shimmied her underwear down her thighs. She dangled them from one finger, her breath catching at the look of unbridled lust on his starkly handsome face.

He took them from her, holding them to his nose and inhaling deeply before tucking them inside his pants pocket.

'Touch yourself.' He leaned back in the seat, relaxed, unhurried, confident of her compliance.

Harley glanced at Will through the privacy glass, her body temperature rocketing into dangerous territory. The driver couldn't see or hear, but with the thrill of the illicit—her pleasuring herself as they travelled the darkened streets of Manhattan—she couldn't act quickly enough.

Jack stroked his chin as if waiting for a conference call, face blank, seemingly bored. As Harley trailed her fingers up her thigh, he grasped her wrist, his voice low and rough.

'Slow. Don't come.' And then he settled back to

watch, a stare so hot, so intense burning on his face as he traced the progress of her hand along her thigh, she feared she'd have to disappoint him.

How did he do this to her? Turn her into an exhibitionist? But as she located her clit, her eyes fixed on his, all thoughts other than Jack fled.

It was the longest and the shortest journey home. By the time they made it inside her apartment, Jack barking, 'bedroom', in between stripping her, stripping himself and kissing her senseless, she was already so worked up, she doubted he'd have time to get inside her before she went off.

When he had her naked but for the hold-up stockings, he slowed things down, stepping behind her to cup her breasts from behind as he pressed himself between her buttocks.

'Do you trust me?' His breath lifted the hairs on the back of her neck.

She sagged against him, desire turning her blood to thick syrup.

'Yes.' No hesitation.

His expert fingers worked her nipples into peaks— firm, insistent, enough pressure to send licks of flame down to her clit. She clung, desperate to stay aware of every touch, every caress, even as she slipped into the fog of arousal.

He palmed one cheek of her ass, his large hand kneading and stroking, warming her flesh.

'I want to see this gorgeous ass while I fuck you.'

Her knees buckled, and he wrapped one strong arm around her waist. With a nudge, he urged her towards the bed where she climbed onto all fours. She sucked air in through her nose, anticipation setting her belly aflutter. The crinkle of foil pushed her heart rate higher, and then the bed dipped as he leaned over her, his chest to her back.

His hands found her nipples again, and she arched back into him like a cat.

He groaned.

'Soon…soon.' His voice hypnotic.

He pulled her up to a kneeling position, her back to his front as he continued torturing her breasts and scraped his teeth over the skin where her neck met her shoulder.

She swayed into him, her head spinning and limbs languid. How would she survive what he did to her without blurting her feelings or her confession? She bit her lip, holding the words inside.

One of his hands covered hers and he guided their linked fingers down her belly, through her strip of hair into the wet folds of her sex.

'Touch yourself.' His fingers moved beside hers as, together, they set up a rhythm that had her crying out his name while she clung to him with her free arm. Her anchor.

'Keep going.' He positioned her on all fours again, and she balanced her weight on one arm to carry out his husky instructions, once more locating her clit and stroking herself as he'd commanded.

'Jack, hurry.' She was already so close and she wanted him inside her, too empty without him.

Gripping her hips with both hands, he pushed inside, slowly, one inch at a time. Harley's back arched as he filled her up, her fingers strumming faster to counter the stretch with a thrill of fiery heat burning beneath her clit.

'Slow, Harley. Not yet,' he warned as his hips moved, steady, sure and so deep she gasped.

'Fuck, I love your ass.' He gripped her hip again with one hand, caressing the opposite cheek with the other as he rocked into her over and over. 'So fucking perfect. Just watching you walk, these gorgeous hips swaying, is enough to make me hard.' All the while he spoke, he slammed into her, filling her up with his cock and his words of admiration.

He loosened his grip on her hip to stroke the length of her spine, from between her shoulder blades to the small of her back, the flat of his hand splayed over her in an act close to possession. She closed her eyes, slipping deeper. In that moment, his.

The lightest pressure from one fingertip hovered at the top of her crease. Harley's eyes slammed open.

'Ever played here?' His finger delved between her buttocks with feather-light touch over her rosette.

She whimpered, the foreign sensations so good she struggled to utter a single word. She shook her head, too turned on to speak. Too full of him, her mind, her body, her senses crammed full with Jack and the way he strummed her body alive.

He growled what she assumed could only be a French expletive, his finger lingering over her sensitive flesh.

'Want to try it? I won't hurt you.' The pressure of his fingertip increased slightly, and she pushed back, her own fingers circling wildly between her legs.

'Yes. Oh, please…yes.' Harley closed her eyes again, strung out on sensory overload. Every nerve in her body sang. Jack pummelling her from behind, her slick clit throbbing between her fingers and his husky voice, tempting her to push boundaries, safe in his hands.

'Tell me when you're close,' he gritted out, his hips rocking the entire bed and his fingertip skating over her rear entrance with every pound, thrilling.

When words began to spill from him, French, broken English, garbled sounds of how good she felt and how good he wanted to make her feel, she lost it.

'Jack!' As the climax hit, bombarding her from all sides, his fingertip pushed inside, and she cried out until her throat burned. Wave after wave struck, the orgasm so intense, she broke the sublime contact with her clit to brace both arms on the bed, the covers clenched in her grasping fists.

'Perfect. You're perfect,' Jack muttered just before he yelled out himself and went rigid behind her, his steely thighs pressed against hers and his hands pulling her hips back with almost bruising force.

They collapsed together, side by side. Limbs tangled and breaths harsh in the quiet.

'Better?' He pressed a chaste kiss to her forehead.

Speech impossible, words lost apart from the ones trying to escape her wildly thundering, but terrified heart, she nodded.

CHAPTER TEN

THE WEAK LIGHT of dawn bounced off her, turning her flying hair to silver as she rocked above him. He took a second to enjoy the sight of her riding him, the intense bite of pleasure from her tight warmth gripping him.

Then he rolled her without slipping from the warm clasp of her body, linking his fingers with hers as he pressed her hands into the mattress beside her head. She glowed. Her green eyes hypnotic, boring into his until he was forced to bite his tongue from fear of spilling his guts, confessing feelings—too much, too soon.

Fuck if he even knew where they came from, but they arrived, undeniably insistent. This was no longer a game for him, his motives way beyond revenge sex. But labelling this scared the shit out of him. And if he was to confess anything, shouldn't it be that he'd used her attraction to him, at least in the beginning?

Damn, he wasn't ready to go there. He focussed on her body under his, covering her bobbing nipple with his mouth, drawing the flesh inside until she clenched around him. So tight he growled. So close. Two more thrusts and she flew, milking him, calling his name and breaking the intense eye contact she gave him as the pleasure overwhelmed her.

He followed, pumping all he had into her while he clamped his lips against her shoulder to stop the feelings he was too terrified to name aloud spilling free.

After a quick trip to her en-suite bathroom, he returned to the bed, drawing her onto him until her body covered his, the sprawl of her hair over his face, the strands clinging to his morning scruff. Her scent cloaked his skin. He never wanted to move.

She snuggled closer. 'I need to get up.'

He nodded. He had an eight a.m. meeting, himself. Fortunately, he'd gone straight from JFK to her store last night after returning from Paris, so his luggage had been in the trunk. Right now, he couldn't think of leaving this bed, her nakedness pressed to him, ever again.

Harley's heartbeat slowed against his. She lifted sleepy eyes to his, hair wild around her face. Breathtaking. He cupped her cheeks. Pushing the curtains of silk behind her ears.

Her eyes flicked between his and then dipped.

'Can I ask you a favour?'

Fuck, he'd give her anything. Couldn't she see that? He nodded. Too unsure of what would come out of his mouth to speak.

She smiled, the almost giddy, girlish smile he remembered, climbed from the bed and padded out of the room naked, her glorious ass swaying. Jack groaned inwardly, his cock twitching anew.

He stretched out his hands behind his head, sated but his skin tight with new realisations. She returned moments later with a folder tucked under one arm and two steaming mugs of coffee.

Jack shelved his restlessness for now, content with

her hesitant smile and her request for help. And naked coffee deliveries? A man could get used to that kind of wake-up.

Used to it…? There was a permanency to that that squeezed his lungs.

'I wondered if you'd show these to Isabel.' She handed him the folder and perched on the edge of the bed, sipping her coffee. 'Since our shopping spree the other day, I've been thinking about a maternity and infant range. There are so many gorgeous fabrics out there.' She fingered some swatches next to the designs.

He studied the drawings, respect for her swelling inside, choking him. She looked away, her teeth gnawing at her lip. He wanted to kiss her and never stop until she saw the talented and beautiful woman he saw.

She still struggled with her dyslexia—her self-esteem seemed thin at best despite the accomplished and poised exterior she presented. She'd hinted at her social isolation growing up, how difficult things had been at home with her parental expectations and comparing herself to her siblings. What he wouldn't give to see her fully embrace her authenticity. Believe in herself.

But the trust issue, still a barrier between them, made him likely the last person she'd believe. And did he have any right to suggest improvements when he himself battled substantial transformations he wasn't ready to admit?

He kept his eyes down, his voice soft. 'Do you want *my* opinion?'

She shrugged, her eyes heartbreakingly wary. Then offered a small nod.

'These are really good.'

She rolled her eyes. 'They're just drawings.' She snorted. 'I remember the first time I told Hal I wanted to be a designer. I was fifteen. He called my sketches scribbles. I think that was the last time I actively sought his advice.'

He gripped her free hand, his blood boiling. 'Hal's an asshole.' He smiled, coaxing a reluctant giggle from her. 'These are more than drawings. They're your passion, your talent, your heart on a page.' His voice almost cracked. 'I...love...that you would show me these.'

Jack forced his muscles to relax. If he ever got his hands on Hal Jacob, he'd punch him. He swallowed bile, forcing a smile for her sake. She placed her coffee next to his on the nightstand and curled her arms around his neck, kissing him so vigorously he had to scramble the drawings aside so she didn't crush them.

She pulled back, eyes glowing.

'I thought we could use organic cotton for the baby wear, merino wool from New Zealand, and we can link the profits to a charity that provides infant vaccines in Africa.'

He couldn't resist her, a no doubt goofy, indulgent grin splitting his face.

Her phone pinged and she leaned over him to retrieve it. Her breasts hung before his face. Just one taste; rude not to.

He'd just formed his lips around one tasty bud when her body turned rigid above him. 'Bastards.'

He sobered, releasing her and sitting up. 'What is it?'

She held out the phone, showing him the headline.

Real Estate Heiress finds New Beau.

Harley stood abruptly and slipped on a white silk robe, a garment designed for modesty that did nothing to douse his hard need for her as it draped over every contour and his photographic memory of her body filled in the blanks. She paced the room, fingers tapping her thigh.

He didn't enjoy seeing his own face on the gossip column, but her reaction seemed out of sync with what was essentially a photo of them leaving the restaurant last night and a few lines speculating on their relationship status.

'Don't worry about it. Who cares?' He tossed the phone, capturing her hand on her next pass.

She gnawed at her lip. 'Everything I do. It's never enough. If I support a charity I'm a spoiled brat.' She made air quotes. 'If I go out with friends I'm squandering my trust fund. If I—'

He squeezed her hand, bringing her back to him.

'Harley. What's the real issue here?' He tugged her down to sit beside him on the bed. 'Are you worried about your family's reaction?' His insides shrivelled.

She evaded his eyes, toying with a loose thread. 'Aren't you? I'm a Jacob, remember. Don't tell me you need the hassle this will bring.' She pointed at the phone.

He shrugged, slotting his fingers between hers. 'It's not anyone else's business but ours.' He lifted her hand to his mouth, kissing each knuckle in turn.

Her eyes darted away and his gut churned. Was she still worried what her family thought? Still keen to keep him a sordid secret?

'I… I need to tell you something.' She wouldn't look at him, her eyes flitting anywhere else. Her lip took another punishment from her teeth and Jack released her hand to cup her face. He sucked in a breath, wishing for a do-over on the morning.

When she did look up, he stopped breathing.

'Remember that last holiday in Aspen?' Barely a whisper.

His mind scrambled to keep up but he offered a curt nod. Why was she going there? He needed to relive that year of his life like he needed root canal. And now, with his brain already trying to make sense of what had changed in him...

'I...'

'Harley...' She was ending this. Again. Just when his feelings had emerged from hiding.

She shook her head, determined. 'I hurt you, but I want to explain why.'

He squeezed her fingers.

'That's ancient history.' He'd been a naïve kid—all hormones, wearing his heart on his sleeve. He clenched his jaw. He didn't need the reminder.

She nodded, expression sombre. 'But the press has a way of...unearthing things. And I... I don't want to keep secrets from you any more.'

Hairs on the back of his neck stood to attention. He released her hand and climbed from the bed, his limbs impatient for activity.

Secrets? He jerked on his pants and shirt. Whatever she had to tell him, he needed some armour. The weight of her confused stare, guilty and hurt, dragged at his shoulders.

'Tell me, then.' He faced her, his skin crawling as if he were trying to climb out of his own body.

Her eyes filled with a sheen of moisture. 'Your

mother and my father had an affair. I saw them together. In Aspen.'

What. The. Fuck.

He speared his hair with his fingers, gripping tight while he paced the room, too restless to stand still. Too shocked to stop his thoughts spinning.

'Are you fucking kidding me?' Memories bounced around inside his skull with dizzying speed, churning his stomach.

She shook her head, her gaze dipping to the comforter.

An affair? All these years he'd assumed it was the financial impact of the bad business decisions, which began with the aborted deal with Jacob Holdings, that had put a strain on his parents' marriage. But on top of everything else, he'd been lied to, deceived.

His fists curled until the bones of his hands ached. Anger, white hot, pounded him. At Harley. At Hal. At his parents. And the lion's share for himself. Fuck… so stupid. She'd kept this from him. Then and now.

He'd been a stupid kid nine years ago; a trusting besotted fool. And now? He'd convinced himself he was safe from the kind of pain he'd witnessed diminishing the man his father had been to the broken version who'd almost lost everything. But, like an idiot, he'd slipped up, lowered his guard, developed…feelings for Harley.

'You knew? All this time? And you said nothing.' Too much energy pounded through him. His voice scraped his throat raw, emerging eerily calm. She'd played him. He'd confided in her his concerns for Isabel, told her the origin—his parents' marital implosion.

And all the time she'd known a major contributing factor in that divorce.

She pulled the front of the robe tighter across her chest, her hands clutching the opening.

'I was a kid. Shocked, horrified by what I'd seen, confused. I was too ashamed, too scared to tell anyone, to make trouble.' She snorted. 'I'd been in enough trouble with Hal back then.'

Fuck Hal…couldn't she see she'd never get his approval until she stopped seeking it and believed in herself?

'So you said nothing? You kept Hal's secret. And you're still keeping it?' He sat on the foot of the bed, shoving his feet into socks and shoes, unable to look at her.

'Jack…'

He turned on her, frustration spilling free, his control reaching breaking point. 'All these weeks, all the time we've spent together—you couldn't have told me?'

'What good would it have done?' Her stare searched his beseechingly. 'I didn't want to hurt you. Didn't want to damage your relationship with your mother.'

'So why today?'

She pinned him with her stare and for a second his chest, which had been encased in concrete, expanded.

'I… I'm done with hiding Hal's actions. Why should I, we, carry the legacy of our parents' choices?'

Her words filtered through the fog in his mind, making sense. But the rock in the pit of his stomach left a bad taste behind. Too little too late? He scrubbed his face. He needed time to think.

He retrieved his jacket from the chair and reached for her phone, tossing it onto the bed before her.

'You hate Hal's choices so much? Careful you don't become just like him, *chérie*.'

Her stunned expression and shocked silence escorted him from the room but the emotion snapping at his heels… That smacked of fear.

CHAPTER ELEVEN

THREE DAYS LATER Harley stepped into the bright, welcoming kitchen of her childhood home and embraced her twin sister, Hannah, clinging for a few seconds too long, absorbing unspoken and unconditional comfort. They'd always been close, despite a lifetime spent hearing Hal point out their differences. It could have driven a wedge between them, but this was one relationship Harley refused to allow Hal to influence.

She'd had no contact from Jack since she'd made her confession. She'd tried to avoid it, but she'd hurt him anyway, as she'd predicted. But, she hadn't wanted to keep the secret from him for one second longer. She'd fallen in love with him and the deeper she fell, the heavier the burden of her silence.

Respecting his wishes, giving him time, destroyed her. Each second she didn't hear from him ticked like a bomb in her head. How much time would he need? And would she break before then, rush to him, spill other confessions she suspected he wasn't ready to hear? Especially now she'd been the bearer of such devastating news.

Dulcie kissed both her daughter's cheeks and handed Harley a mimosa before joining Ash and Hannah at the island where they shared *The New York Times*. Weekend brunch had become a Jacob tradition. If they missed a week, Dulcie complained about their lack of commitment to family time. And despite the newspaper spread over the marble counters, business discussions at the table were strictly prohibited.

She had no good news on that front. The Morris deal, like the rest of her relationship with Jack, hung in the balance. The only communication she'd received from his office a set of plans for the renovations, emailed by Trent.

Ash glanced up from the article he read.

'Dad wants to see you.' Worry dulled his eyes, forcing Harley's stomach to twist. She gulped the delicious mimosa. In her experience, nothing good ever came after sentences that began that way.

'What about?' Had Hal seen the photo of her and Jack leaving the restaurant together on the day of her birthday?

Three blank faces greeted her, eyes sympathetic. Whatever he wanted, she was on her own. And she could guess.

'He's in the office,' said Ash.

'Here, take him one of these,' said Dulcie, squeezing Harley's shoulders and then handing her a second mimosa, 'and tell him brunch will be ready in five minutes.' Harley reluctantly left the family room in search of Hal, steeling herself against the inevitable criticism to come.

The minute she stepped across the threshold her hackles rose. The day of reckoning had arrived. She placed his drink on the desk.

'Mum said brunch in five.'

'Sit down, Harley.'

She sighed, old demons surfacing. She rolled her shoulders back.

'I'll stand. You wanted to talk about something?' If she stayed on her feet, she could leave quicker. Her scalp prickled, just as it had as a kid when she'd got a particularly bad grade or had been called to the principal's office for 'wasting time' or 'daydreaming'.

Hal pursed his lips in that way that conveyed his displeasure. It had terrified her as a girl, when she'd first realised she was different from her siblings, and crushed her as a tender teen, when his excuses for her poor academic performance had cut deeper than his outright criticism.

But now it simply irked her. She was no longer that kid, desperate for his approval, desperate to be valued like her older, successful, conforming siblings.

Hal jumped straight in. No preamble.

'I hear you're in business with Jack Lane, or Demont as he goes by these days.'

She pressed her lips together. She had no intention of justifying herself. She shrugged. Evasion in a tight spot—he'd taught her that.

But he wasn't giving up.

'Dammit, Harley. That family has no drive, no instincts when it comes to business. Why would you get involved with him of all people? It's bad enough that you're wasting your money on that derelict piece of real estate.'

Harley bit and then released her tongue. She shouldn't have to defend herself. Or Jack. Who was Hal to judge others?

'I refuse to live my life based on some ancient deal

that turned sour for *you*. Jack Demont has built a very successful global brand. And who I choose to do business with is really none of your concern.'

'Of all the men in Manhattan…' The rant continued as if she hadn't spoken. 'And messing around with…a school? Really? The number of opportunities you've squandered.'

'Opportunities?' She bit back a sardonic laugh. 'I want to build a school so kids, like the kid I was, have a safe environment to learn. One where they're understood and encouraged, their skills nurtured, their challenges overcome not belittled.'

His mouth formed a thin line.

'I did my best for you, Harley.'

She snorted. If that was his best…

'By denying my learning difficulty? By postponing the diagnostic testing? By ignoring the fact your youngest daughter was an isolated, lonely kid struggling both at school and home—a place where she should have found encouragement and acceptance?'

'You're not a child any more. I'm talking about you messing around with your projects. I thought when you and Phil got engaged that you'd be married by now, have a couple of kids…'

She didn't even bother defending her aborted engagement, a relationship based on trying to be a daughter he could be proud of.

'You're right. I'm twenty-six years old. I no longer seek, nor need your approval. And I've created my own opportunities, ones that suit me.'

He stared, long and hard. Harley prepared to leave, done with this pointless conversation. And she should thank him—this reckoning was long overdue. She practically hovered off the floor with the lightness finally confronting him brought.

'Are you…personally involved with him, too?' His lips puckered, tight and disapproving. 'It certainly looked that way from the photos. The Lanes have a reputation—be a little more discreet.'

Reputation? Well, if that wasn't the pot calling the kettle… She'd stayed silent all these years, protected *his* reputation out of some misguided need to gain her father's approval.

Harley swallowed bile, her body flooding with scalding heat. Jack was right. She'd inadvertently kept him her dirty little secret out of loyalty to a man with only half his scruples. Half *her* scruples. And Hal's respect wasn't worth having.

She lowered her voice to a hiss the others wouldn't hear. 'Are you seriously giving me relationship advice?'

Hal's nostrils flared. A sure sign of his rising temper. This wasn't going his way.

'What does that mean?'

'I know about you and Amalie Lane.'

Hal curled his lip as if he'd tasted something foul. 'You can't trust anything the Lanes say. That's why I advise against getting involved with one of them.'

'I saw you together, Father.'

Realisation dawned. Hal had the good grace to turn puce and look away. So the mighty Hal was fallible after all.

He leaned back in his chair, the inscrutable mask he wore most of the time firmly back in place. He stared for so long she almost squirmed before him. But those days were over.

'Have you told anyone?' She'd never seen him so cold, so calculating. The last veil slipped from her eyes.

'I told Jack.'

He snorted, shaking his head as he did when he was frustrated with her.

'Well, that explains why he wants to see me—'

'Wait, what?' She braced her palms flat on the desk. Jack had approached her father? Why? Did he plan to confront him over the affair?

'You didn't know? So he has his secrets, too?' A flash of mischief sparked in Hal's eyes, and Harley realised her mistake.

Show no weakness.

Harley's mind spun, but one fact emerged, time and time again. She trusted Jack. Whatever his reasons, they'd be sound, measured, fair. A polar opposite of her father—perhaps the reason she'd fallen in love with him.

'Why did you tell him? Making trouble?' Hal's eyes darted to the door behind her.

She sighed, checking the clock and calculating how long it would take her to get to Jack's apartment through Sunday morning traffic.

'I told him because I'm in love with him. He's a good man, an honourable man. If *he* wants me, I must be good enough.'

Did he still want her? It was too much to hope he reciprocated her feelings, but she was ready to give him her trust. Give him everything she'd held back.

Hal scoffed.

Harley saw red.

'I know I don't stack up against Ash and Hannah. I

never have. But guess what? I no longer need your approval. I'm successful as measured by my own yardstick. My foundation donated over ten million dollars to charities last year. In three months, my dyslexia school will be open to all, not just to those who can afford the tuition fees, and Jack Demont is helping me to build it. We may not have the cut-throat business acumen you value, but what we do makes a difference to someone other than ourselves. Can you say that?'

At his stunned silence, she turned on her heel and glided out of the room, lighter than air.

So what if words and numbers jumped on the page before her eyes and she struggled to memorise lists? She would never do well in formal testing or enjoy reading for pleasure. But she'd built something from nothing. Something worthwhile, with her own hands.

It was time to believe in herself.

With her heart hammering against her ribs, she stepped back into the family room, crying off brunch with an invented headache that threatened to become a reality as her euphoria dwindled and Jack's hurt expression reappeared before her eyes.

So she'd had a realisation—that didn't mean Jack was ready to forgive her or that he shared her feelings.

Dulcie walked her out, shrewd eyes apologetic. 'I'm looking forward to your show tonight.'

Harley winced. She'd barely given any thought to the catwalk show, part of New York Fashion Week. She nodded feebly, her head still full of Jack and tracking him down. Offering him another explanation…even begging, if required.

Dulcie paused at the door and stroked Harley's shoulder. 'I love this sweater. One of yours?'

Harley nodded, too distracted to answer.

A sigh. 'I know what he's like.'

Her mother gripped Harley's fingers. 'Don't take any notice of the old fool—I haven't for years.' Dulcie's intelligent eyes pierced Harley.

Harley's stomach flopped. 'You know, don't you?'

Dulcie's eyes flicked away.

All these years Harley had been keeping the worst-kept secret. Her throat burned, making her eyes water. She'd even allowed the knowledge of Hal's infidelity to shape her own relationships, tainting her authenticity through fear, shame and cynicism. And, most importantly, she'd jeopardised what she'd found with Jack—the most real thing she'd ever had. But was it too late to redeem?

'I had no idea you knew, darling. I wanted to protect all of you.' Dulcie fingered her immaculate hair.

'Well, you didn't. I may not have the correct diploma on my wall, but I'm an intelligent woman. He's your husband. It's your business that you stood by him. But until you're ready to take me, my career, seriously, perhaps it's best if you stay away from my show.'

Ignoring the flare of anger and then hurt in her mother's eyes, Harley left, her stomach rolling but her spirit free.

With renewed energy and sense of purpose, she hurried down to the street and gave directions to her driver, her head full of one thing only—Jack.

Could she persuade him that what they had surpassed ordinary? That the foundations were solid enough to build upon, if that was what he wanted? That she was a Jacob and he a Lane, but that didn't mean they couldn't break free of the choices their respective parents had made? Be themselves? Free to trust in something as delicate as gossamer on the surface but shot with threads of steel?

At his building, she raced to his floor, forgoing the elevator and arriving out of breath for more than one reason. Her knuckles stung as she rapped on his door, the frantic rhythm matching her thundering heart.

Seconds stretched to hours. Harley sagged at the knees when the door swung open, everything she wanted to say backed up on her lips, ready to spill free.

Her face fell.

Her heart dropped like a stone. Her mouth clamped shut.

Too late.

A beautiful, petite brunette stood in Jack's doorway looking perfectly at home.

Harley's pulse stuttered back to life as recognition slammed through her. 'Isabel?'

'*Oui*, Harley. *Enchantée.* It's been so long.' Isabel pulled Harley into a one-armed embrace, drawing her over the threshold and closing the door. She welcomed her as if she'd been expecting her, as if they'd only seen each other yesterday.

Isabel waved the sheaf of papers she held in her hand.

'I'm only here to email Jacques some documents he left behind. Trent is travelling with him, so I end up as substitute assistant. On a Sunday.' She rolled her eyes. 'So, tell me, how are you? You look great.' The younger woman spoke in accented, rapid-fire sentences as she led Harley into the great room—hard to follow, but Harley caught the gist, and her insides shrivelled.

'Jack's not here.'

Isabel paused, a frown dipping over her huge, hazel eyes. 'No. He's in Paris. You didn't know?'

Harley shook her head, sinking into the plush, leather sofa as all her adrenaline drained away. Of course. He'd mentioned another trip overseas. She'd been so caught up in rectifying the mess she'd made, dissecting her feelings and preparing for her show tonight, she'd lost track of the days.

'Do you know when he'll be back?' She'd sent him some tickets for her show, but all she'd received in return was a single line, receipt and thanks reply from Trent. Nothing personal.

Way beyond too late.

Isabel joined her on the sofa.

'The day after tomorrow, I believe.' The younger woman frowned. 'Would you like coffee?'

Harley shook her head, eyes scrunched closed, her fingers pinching the bridge of her nose. Why hadn't she woken up sooner? Recognised the incredible man in her life and what an amazing and rare thing they'd discovered?

She sniffed, shifting to the edge of the sofa, new resolve straightening her spine.

'I know this sounds a bit stalker-like—' hysterical laughter rang in her ears as she remembered the first time she'd stalked him here that fateful day he'd re-entered her life '—but would you mind giving me Jack's address in Paris?'

She'd get through her show tonight and then she'd fly to Paris. Stalk him to his apartment again. Tell him how she felt. Apologise for hurting him. He might not be ready to hear it, but she was done with suppressing her feelings to please others.

Isabel laughed. 'Of course.' She touched Harley's arm, eyes dancing. 'You know my brother can be an idiot, right?' She tilted her head—the way Jack did when he made a point. 'I mean, I get it. Our parents' divorce hit him hard and he's always been a bit hung up on integrity and doing the right thing. I think he'd kind of given up on love bullshit.' She snorted. 'How many times have I heard that cynical tirade? I mean, he didn't have a proper girlfriend until his last year of university and she didn't last long…'

Harley's stomach rolled. She'd played a part in that. She'd hurt him more than she'd known, more than he'd let on.

'But I'm so glad you're back in his life. He's much happier now.'

Was he? His face the last time she'd seen him… surely all she'd done was bring him more pain? Drag up devastating emotions from his past and pour salt on the wound.

'So you have a show tonight? I hope you don't mind but Jack gave me the tickets you sent him. I loved the sketches he showed me, by the way. He's right—you're very talented.'

Right, her show.

All she cared about was getting it over with and going to him.

'Of course. You must come. I'll be backstage most of the night, but I'll look out for you.' The hours until she could catch a flight to Paris would drag but she owed it to herself, her years of hard work, to give one hundred per cent to her label.

She stood, her limbs jittery, restless. 'Congratulations by the way.' She forced herself to smile. Forced her mind back into work mode. She'd toiled too hard—her team had too—for her to lose momentum now. But after tonight? All bets were off.

'I'll text you his address.' Isabel pulled out her phone and Harley reeled off her number, her brain already racing with plans of what she would say to him and calculations of the time difference between New York and Europe.

The next thirteen hours couldn't pass quickly enough.

CHAPTER TWELVE

JACK WINCED, THE volume and throbbing tempo of the music scraping his eardrums raw and echoing around inside his skull. He scanned the audience, the familiar sight of her petite but curvaceous silhouette nowhere to be seen. Fuck. Had she left already? Had he missed his chance? He should never have left without telling her how he felt.

He curled his hands into fists to stop himself hurling the nearest vacant chair at the wall. Not that there were any. The New York Fashion Week show was packed. Standing room only, which suited him just fine. He wasn't here for the couture.

Just for Harley.

His body tight with frustration, he slammed out of the auditorium and scanned the foyer for a door that would take him backstage.

With a quick introductory call to Harley's sister, Hannah, he'd grovelled sufficiently to score himself a VIP backstage pass. He gripped the plastic card hanging around his neck like a life preserver and flashed it at the bouncers manning the doors that led to the warren of behind-the-scenes corridors.

He followed the noise, his impatient strides ground

eating, until he arrived at the scene of utter chaos, so far removed from the glamour parading the runway.

She had to be here somewhere.

He wove between the crush of bodies—models in various stages of dress, designers and dressers tweaking outfits and barking orders, and runners with clipboards and bottles of water—stepping over clothes and shoes haphazardly strewn on the floor and skirting garment-laden clothes racks.

No sign of her.

He scrubbed his face with both hands, cursing his stupidity. For a fully grown, intelligent man, his short-sightedness astounded him. How could he have been so blinkered, so pig-headed?

Somewhere between guarding himself from further pain and losing himself in their game, he'd fallen for Harley. Hard. As far as a man could fall. But he'd messed up, banging on about her lack of trust in him, when he'd been too scared to trust his own feelings.

Like an idiot he'd tried to control what they had, telling himself it was simply amazing sex, but it had long ago surpassed casual. He'd just been too terrified to admit it.

His chest pinched as he cast around the frenetic room, searching her out.

He spotted her.

The air slammed from his lungs with a whoosh.

Every nerve ending buzzed to life as he took in her flushed, excited face as she laughed with the model she dressed. They battled with an enormous headpiece that complemented the scanty lingerie the model wore.

But his eyes were solely for Harley. He muscled his way through the crowds. Time to tell her how he felt.

Yes, his timing sucked, but he couldn't wait a second longer. Perhaps, even now, he was too late.

She didn't see him. Tweaking the outfit of the model in front of her, she looked slightly frazzled but achingly beautiful. And then she looked up, straight at him.

The visceral blow knocked him back on his heels. Her face fell slightly, eyes wary.

Another blow.

'I need to talk to you.' His throat was so tight his voice emerged way too gruff.

She stared, the models around her disappearing to join the line waiting to walk on stage. Her eyes flicked over his shoulder, brows pinched together, and he stepped in front of her.

'Please.'

She swallowed. 'What are you doing here? How did you find me?'

His lips twitched, memories of the first day she'd literally stumbled back into his life crushing his chest.

'I looked you up, and I tipped the doorman.' He waved the VIP pass at her, his grin widening when she pressed her lips together as if she held in a smile. He had one or two stalker skills, too.

But his apology so far sucked, because she wasn't in his arms where he wanted her. Sucking in a deep breath, he scraped the bottom of the patience barrel. She was working. He'd wait for her—as long as it took.

'I'll wait for you. After the show.' His muscles twitched with the urge to reach for her. But this was her moment, and he'd always support all of her passions.

She nodded once and moved past him.

His whole body sagged as he spun to watch her walk away. And then she was back, leaping into his arms and pressing her mouth to his, her kiss filling him to bursting point, but all too fleeting.

'Wish me luck.' She pushed at his arms and he reluctantly loosened his grip around her waist, letting her slide down his body to the floor.

'Good luck.' He snatched another kiss, uncaring that he now likely wore more of her lip-gloss than she did. 'But why do you need it?'

She smiled, eyes alight, stealing his air.

'I'm walking. It's my label, right?' She stepped back, smoothing her hands down her immaculate outfit, a goddess. 'I'm proud of it. No more apologising for who I am.' And with a wink that boiled his blood, she hurried after her models, the sway of her sensational ass smacking him between the eyes.

He stripped her, his touch reverent, relearning every exquisite inch he exposed, pausing often to reconnect through searing kisses, as vital as air. Words he'd almost waited too long to say spilled from him, French words she wouldn't understand, but he hoped she'd glean their meaning from his face and his actions.

Her hands weren't idle, exposing him piece by piece until they stood before each other naked, with nowhere to hide. He cupped her face, peering into her soul as his fingers worked into her hair, his grip firm and possessive.

'*Je t'aime.* I'm sorry it took me so long to see it.' How had he ever believed he could walk away? How had he fooled himself for so long that this was just about their astounding physical connection? That it was enough?

'I love you too. I'm sorry I hurt you.'

He shook his head, the past slotted where it belonged. He wasn't his father any more than she was hers. All that mattered was them. Together.

He'd show her, every minute of every day, what she meant to him. They'd work the rest out between them. Their own way.

She tugged his neck and his mouth covered hers as his hands cupped her breasts, tearing away from their kiss with a grunt to take one tight, perfect nipple into his mouth. She arched towards him, clinging to his shoulders as his lips tugged and her knees weakened.

Fuck, he loved her. Perfect, as if handmade for him.

Through frantic kisses and roving hands, they made it to the bed, where Jack covered her body with his, their legs slotted together, her breasts crushed to his chest until her scent, the tickle of her wild hair and her breathy moans completely surrounded him.

Bringing him home.

He poured himself into kissing her, his hands tangled in her hair, until her lips swelled, rosy red. When his control stretched paper-thin, he slipped his hand between her thighs, finding her soaked and ready for him.

He groaned, breaking away to quickly fish a condom from the nightstand. She took the foil packet from him, stroked the length of him and rolled the latex over his erection.

He took her hands, slotting his fingers between hers as he pushed inside her, her warmth clasping him inch by scorching inch, and his stare locked on hers.

His chest seized. She was everything he hadn't known he needed, the intensity of the rightness vaporising the air in his lungs. Who needed oxygen?

Jack moved above her, gauging her every reaction, as in sync as their matched heartbeats. His thrusts first slow and long grew faster as he pounded her into the mattress. She clung to him with her thighs and her feet and her eyes, riding with him on tumultuous waves of pleasure.

They crested together, she crying out his name as the climax struck and he with a guttural yell and his mouth slamming back over hers, stealing her air for himself. He wrung the last spasms from her, the jerks of his hips subsiding as he groaned and she panted.

Time passed. He grew soft and slipped from her body, shifting to remove the condom and toss it onto the floor before collapsing back on top of her.

They lay in the dark for what seemed like hours. Silently tracing every inch of each other with lazy, indulgent touch. Jack pressed his lips to her stomach and she tangled her fingers in his hair, stroking the strands back from his face.

'Thanks for coming to my show.'

He grunted, too comfortable, too satiated to move.

'You were amazing. I'm honoured to know the woman you've become.' She wriggled from under him, holding his face between her palms.

'And you're an incredible man, one I can look up to, without fear of ever being diminished.'

'Harley...' He rasped out her name, and then he kissed her again.

When he let her up for air, his length already hard

against her thigh, her eyes sparkled, flooding his body with renewed lust.

Fuck, would he ever get enough of her?

'So what about our game?' She slid one foot up the back of his leg and he sank deeper into the cradle of her hips. His lust-fogged mind struggled with her meaning as her soft lips caressed his earlobe while she whispered, 'Our better and better game?'

He grinned, grinding his hips into hers. 'I'm happy to continue playing, if that's what you want.' His lips captured her nipple, and she squirmed, wriggling free, but not out of reach.

She pressed her lips together as if stifling a smile.

'But surely it's over. Nothing could be better than that last one.' Her fingers traced a torturous path across his chest and down his abs until her hand circled him, slowly pumping.

With a speed that made her gasp, he slid her back under him, pinned her wrists to the bed and parted her thighs with his own. 'Oh, man, I love a challenge.'

She laughed, the sound trailing off to soft moans as his open mouth travelled her neck and chest. He paused to lap at each nipple in turn and then he released her hands and sank beneath the sheets.

Employing his best effort, he channelled all his energy into rendering her speechless for a while, unless it was to cry his name and confirm he'd succeeded.

Better and better.

EPILOGUE

One month later

'OH, JACK, IT's going to be amazing.' Harley bounced on her heels, her wide stare scanning the reconfigured space, which was still shrouded with dustsheets, the ceiling dotted with disembowelled cables.

Light spilled in, filtering through the dust, which covered everything, even the toes of her dove-grey suede boots. But she didn't care. From the building site before her, her school appeared in her mind's eye, her vision come to life.

When Jack had suggested lunch, she'd jumped at the idea. She'd hardly seen him over the past week, another trip to London taking him away. But then they'd crossed the river and she'd guessed he was taking her to see the progress on the Morris Street School.

'So this will be your reception area.' Jack, dressed just how she liked him in one of his immaculate suits, stretched out his arms, spinning to highlight the spaces she'd only seen depicted on plans.

'Disabled bathrooms there, sick bay further back and these doors open out to the courtyard.' He took her hand and together they picked their way over cables and around abandoned tools as they made their way to a wide set of French doors, which were still covered in a film of protective plastic and, like everything else, draped in dustsheets.

'I love it.' She tugged him to a stop. 'I love you. Thank you for helping me make this happen.'

He shrugged, his lip curling. So French. And so fucking sexy.

'You'd have done it without me. But I'm honoured I'm here.'

Her belly flopped and heat bloomed in her chest. She leaned close, eyes closed, her mouth finding his. She wound her fingers into his hair, tilting his head to get a better grip on him and a deeper angle for her kiss. With a growl, he grew against her stomach.

She slipped her hands inside his jacket, casting her mind around for a suitably clean, dust-free surface so she could take this to the next level. But then pulled back, frustrated.

The whole place was one, big, hazardous death trap. Hardly romantic. But her hormones couldn't care less.

'Do we really need to eat? We could do something else with our lunch break?' She cupped his firm ass, which flexed under her palm as he tilted his hips and rubbed himself between them.

His lips traced her neck, whisper soft. 'So you want something better than what I have planned, *chérie*?'

Harley tilted her head to one side. 'I always want *you*.'

He kissed her forehead, taking the heat down a level in his gentle way.

'Let me show you the courtyard first. The land-scapers finished yesterday.' He softened the blow by fondling her ass. 'Then I promise to fuck you and feed you in that order, agreed?'

She nodded, all smiles. Was there any better way to spend an afternoon?

Jack grappled with the door, shoving the billowing plastic sheet aside. She followed him outside. As she crossed the threshold, her heel caught on the dustsheet and she stumbled with a cry.

The fall never came. Jack's arms caught her, gripping her to his firm chest and hauling her up so she was once more pressed to him from shoulders to thighs.

They laughed at the replay and then he sobered. His lips slid over hers, taking advantage of the position, not that Harley had a single complaint, too mesmerised by the man she loved to much care about the finished landscaping.

He pulled back.

'I wanted to tell you something.' His face turned serious and her shoulders tensed. She nodded, bracing her hands on his biceps. But he clung tighter, refusing to release her.

'Now this project is almost complete, I'm planning a new venture.' The crinkle between his brows was starting to freak her out. Where was her charming, relaxed Frenchman and his lunch-break promises? She swallowed, her throat dry.

His gaze settled on her, unreadable.

'I'll need a business partner. And as we work so well together, I wondered if you'd be interested?'

She touched his cheek, the air leaving her in a whoosh.

'You had me scared for a moment.' She laughed.

'I thought you were going to say you're permanently relocating to France.' She shivered, looping her arms around his neck and standing on tiptoes to press her lips to his. 'I'd love to work with you again. But how tight is the timeframe? My second store is opening soon, and I have another fashion week to plan.' She brushed a speck from the shoulder of his impeccable suit.

He pressed his lips together, clear disappointment tightening his mouth.

'The timeframe is tight. I need an answer today.'

Harley sighed, stepping back so he lost his grip around her waist. 'I wish you'd given me a bit more notice. I don't think I can commit to anything more right now, otherwise, when will we see each other?' As a couple they were busy enough—no way would she compromise her Jack time. And he felt the same. Why was he being so mulish?

He pinned her with a hot look.

'Don't you think you should ask me what the project involves, before you turn it down? I've even spoken to Hal about the opportunity.'

'What? You discussed business, with my father?' Why would Jack take Hal's advice and what was so important?

Jack nodded. 'He's fully on board with this project.'

She snorted, fisting her hands on her hips, feathers well and truly ruffled. 'Hal can kiss my—'

Jack pressed his fingers against her lips, blocking the tirade.

'I really think you should reconsider.' He took her hand, pressing her knuckles to his mouth while he slanted his bedroom stare her way.

'Since when are you and Hal partners?' This was news to her. Yes, she and her father had come to an understanding for the sake of family harmony—he butted out of her life and she was polite and respectful for her mother's sake. But Jack, Hal and her working together…? Had he lost his mind?

'Just look over the proposal.' He reached inside his breast pocket. 'If it's not for you…' Another Gallic shrug. But this time his eyes danced with a mix of passion and playfulness.

She looked down.

Jack held out his hand, slowly uncurling his fingers.

Her brain shut down completely. Her heart thundered into her throat.

In the centre of his palm sat an exquisite gold solitaire. Harley's burning eyes shot to his, which shone with love and promise and so much more.

'Harley, you were my first love. Will you be my last? Will you marry me?'

The tears blinded her. But then she was in his arms, where she belonged. She peppered his laughing face with frantic kisses.

'Yes, yes, I will.'

Jack took her hand and slid the ring home. 'This belonged to my grandmother Demont. She was an heiress, a humanitarian, and a fighter just like you. Never change.' He pressed his mouth to hers, and she sank into him, never needing to be anywhere else.

He held her close, her head tucked under his chin. The stone gleamed on her finger, a perfect fit.

'So you're not going into business with Hal?'

He chuckled, the sound rumbling through his chest under her cheek.

'No, apart from becoming his son-in-law.'

Harley pulled back.

'But you went to speak with him? That couldn't have been easy.'

He shrugged. 'You're worth it.' He grew serious. 'And I didn't want to be at war with the family of the woman I love. I'm not made that way. I don't play dirty.'

'Good. I don't want you dirty.' She pressed her mouth to his. 'Well, not outside of the bedroom, anyway.'

He laughed, his heated stare wicked.

Jack tugged her closer, his voice dropping to a sexy growl.

'Now there I can be as filthy as you like, *ma belle*.'

'The best,' she whispered.

They sealed the deal with a kiss.

* * * * *

THE MARRIAGE CLAUSE

ALEXX ANDRIA

MILLS & BOON

Dedicated to the dreamers who have the tenacity to become doers.

Every success story started at the beginning of a long road.

Don't be afraid to take that first step...and keep walking.

CHAPTER ONE

Luca

MY NAME IS Luca Donato. You may have seen my mug on the cover and in the pages of *Forbes*, *Fortune* and the *Robb Report*, because my family is ridiculously, obscenely rich.

I'm talking Saudi prince–level money.

I could wipe my ass with hundreds for several lifetimes and still not make a dent in the family trust.

My family descends from Italian aristocracy—some royal connections if you go back far enough—and we've done well enough with our investments in Donato Inc. to never have to work again if that were our choice.

But unlike some in similar positions, the Donatos haven't grown soft with privilege. If anything, our wealth has made us harder, hungrier—all about the victory.

We decimate our opponents, and the word *no* really isn't part of our vernacular.

In fact, I can't remember the last time someone refused to cave to my demands.

Until a certain redhead came along.

The one I'd chased to the airport.

Ah, there you are, you gorgeous pain in my ass.

Katherine Cerinda Oliver…my runaway fiancée.

If Katherine had thought to blend in, that spectacular head of burnished auburn hair was her downfall. Stubborn tendrils escaped her messy bun to curl around her delicate jaw, teasing wispy ends that tickled and caused her to rub her nose without thought.

My hands itched to twist in those sweet, silky curls and bury my nose against her skull. Immediate hunger threatened to override my decision to play it cool. The thing was, she was so damn beautiful sometimes all I could do was stare. I'd been a fool to play fast and loose with her heart years ago.

Now I was paying the price.

Our marriage, arranged by our powerful fathers when Katherine was only a girl, was about to be *un*-arranged if my runaway fiancée had her way.

If Katherine had any inkling how difficult the last two years—giving her the space to do her own thing while I focused on the Donato empire—had been for me, maybe she'd be less inclined to hiss at me like a wet cat.

But that didn't seem likely, given that over the last six months, anytime we were in the same room together Katherine did everything she could to avoid me.

We were supposed to be working toward building a partnership, courting each other, even. But Katherine wouldn't even sit through a single dinner unless it was insisted upon by my parents.

And now she was running away from me—*literally*.

I watched unnoticed from the jet bridge, allowing others to go ahead of me to find their seats on the massive commercial plane. I couldn't remember the last time I flew commercial—preferring the Donato private jet—and I saw little to compel me to do so again.

So she thought she'd gotten away, had she? Believed she'd outsmarted the Donatos by draining her accounts and leaving without notice, paying with cash for every purchase, including her direct flight to the wilds of California.

But as our wedding date loomed—it was set for this spring—and preparations had hit a fever pitch, I'd sensed something was up. My gut feeling only deepened when our last dinner engagement had gone spectacularly sideways and Katherine had practically tripped on her own feet in her haste to get away.

And when your bride-to-be wants nothing to do with you…well, it doesn't do your ego any favors.

In spite of her bravado, she nibbled at her cuticles in her seat in coach, a habit my mother had never quite managed to drum out of her. As if hearing my mother's sharp reprimand, Katherine lowered her hand to double-check her seat belt was cinched tight.

Then she trained her attention out the window, though we were still on the ground and there was nothing to see yet.

That hair was her crowning glory. If she'd been playing it smart, she would've worn a hat, at the very least, but then, Katherine was a hothead, passionate to a fault and sometimes reckless.

Case in point: her decision to run away before our wedding.

In certain circles, I was considered quite a catch—rich, handsome, fit—but Katherine saw only the man who'd broken her heart when he'd been too stupid to realize that a woman like Katherine came along only once in a lifetime.

I had a week to prove that I'd changed. Starting now.

I peeled away from the attendants' area to make my way to my wayward fiancée.

"Leaving without me?" I tsked, startling her with the silky censure in my tone.

"Luca," she gasped in open dismay, her brow furrowing as her nose wrinkled, as if she'd just stepped in something putrid. "What are you doing here?"

"I could ask you the same thing, love."

"Don't call me that," she warned with a glower that could flash freeze meat. "God, you're like gum on my shoe. Go away."

Not a chance. "And why would I do that?"

"Because I don't want you here," she answered, cutting me a hard look.

I stared pointedly at her ringless finger, hating that she seemed to the world an available woman, when she belonged to me. "Where's my grandmother's ring?" I asked, moving slightly so other passengers could get past me, but I was already causing a logjam.

"It's too heavy and it's gaudy."

"It may be gaudy, but there's a lot of history in that ring," I said. "Once we're married, you'll only have to wear it on special occasions or when we dine with the family. Mother has particular expectations about gifted family heirlooms."

"I'm never wearing it," Katherine returned flatly, "because I'm not marrying you."

Her declaration hit me like a punch to the groin. She'd never outright stated she wanted to call off the wedding, but I should've seen it coming.

"That's a big decision to make. I hardly think making it when you're angry is a good idea," I warned, glancing at the people trying to push past me.

"Luca, you're blocking the way," Katherine said, embarrassed. "Just go home and I'll call you when I land."

"Sorry, that's not going to happen. Where you go, I go."

Before Katherine could hit me with a retort, the sharply dressed attendant made her way to us, her expression polite yet annoyed that I was standing in the aisle as she said, "I need you to take your seat, sir. Perhaps I can help?"

Katherine was really going to be pissed, but it couldn't be helped. "Yes, actually, my bride-to-be seems to have gotten the wrong seat assignment. I was just sharing with her that we've been upgraded. Can you help us out?"

Relieved to find the fix so simple, the attendant smiled and looked over my tickets, her expression breaking into a wider, more accommodating smile. "Of course, Mr. Donato." She gestured to Katherine. "I am so sorry for the mix-up. Your seats are in first class. We'll get that squared away right now."

"Excellent," I murmured, smiling apologetically at Katherine, knowing she wouldn't risk a scene.

"Upgraded?" Katherine's gaze flitted from the attendant to me, indecision marring her beautifully expressive face. Tiny freckles danced across the bridge of her nose and onto her cheekbones because she refused to wear enough sunscreen when she went out. She wanted to tell me to shove my ticket up my ass, but I knew she wouldn't, not with so many people watching.

"Miss, if you'll just come with me," the attendant prompted, gesturing again, and I knew Katherine wanted to murder me. I'd take the risk.

"Fine," Katherine finally relented with a sour look she didn't even try to disguise, but I didn't care. I needed more privacy—and legroom—than coach could provide for what I had to say to my runaway fiancée.

In a world filled with daisies, Katherine was a wild blood rose—willful and breathtaking yet dangerous with sharp thorns.

But even roses needed tending.

And Katherine had broken her contract by running. I could be a dick and just drag her off the plane, reminding her that our marriage was a business arrangement that neither of our fathers would allow to be dissolved, but that tactic would only make things worse between us.

"Sweetheart," I murmured, settling my hand on the small of Katherine's back as we fell in behind the attendant. I caught her subtle stiffening at my touch and I prepared myself for an uphill battle, dragging a wagon filled with cement—oh, and the wagon was probably on fire.

Katherine gave the attendant a tight smile and lowered into the luxury seat. "I can't believe you. How dare you chase me down like a fox after a rabbit. I'm not your fucking property," she said, crossing her arms and skewering me with the heat in her eyes. "How did you find me?"

I paused, accepting a champagne flute from the attendant, then answered, "Alana told me. She also said you quit your job at Franklin and Dodd." She'd been working there for over a year.

"Damn you, Alana," Katherine muttered, exhaling an irritated breath. "I knew I shouldn't have told her where I was going."

"True enough, but why did you quit your job?" I asked with a frown. "I thought you were doing well in their marketing department."

Katherine ignored my query and simply shook her head, disappointed in her friend's loose lips. I couldn't blame her, but she should've known better. I'd never understood their friendship to begin with. Alana was the stereotypical rich girl, raised with wealth and privilege. She was somewhat clueless and out of touch.

I thought Katherine kept Alana grounded, but I had no idea what benefit Alana provided Katherine.

Katherine rubbed her forehead, trying to ease the furrows in her brow. "Damn, damn, damn," she muttered before leaning back against the headrest, her jaw tense. "I should've just bailed and not told anyone."

"Probably."

She narrowed her gaze. "Thank you, peanut gallery. Nobody asked you."

"Does your father know?" I asked.

She cut me a short look. "Of course not. He wouldn't understand any more than you would."

I swallowed the insult of being lumped in with her blowhard of a father, but in truth, while Bernard Oliver had more in common with my own father, Giovanni, I was nothing like either man.

"Why California?" I asked, settling in for the long flight, trying to make conversation.

"Because it was on my bucket list. And it was far enough away from everything associated with my life in New York. And yes, that includes you."

I barked a short laugh even though I was starting to bristle at her constant jabs. "So you picked San Francisco in January? I hope you packed warm clothes, because you're going to freeze your pretty little ass off."

"I'm well aware of the weather. I'm not made of glass—I'm sure I'll survive. Besides, nothing could be worse than a New York winter."

"I wouldn't be so sure about that. The marine layer creates a thick fog that eats into your bones. I think I prefer snow."

"The point was to get *away* from you. Anyplace would've been preferable as long as you weren't there. Even a swamp. And before you start pointing out that I've never been to a swamp, so I can't make that assumption, just stop before you start. You've screwed up my entire travel plan, and I'm really not in the mood to hear your mansplaining bullshit."

I knew her well enough to recognize that she wasn't playing.

"You know, I would've thought two years was long enough to lose your quills, but if anything, you've only gotten worse," I said, reluctantly ditching any hope I might've had that we could pick up where we'd left off all those years ago—back when she *didn't* think I was the devil. "Jesus, Katherine, I thought I'd given you plenty of space to do your own thing so we could make this work when the time came to marry."

She stared me down, shaking her head as if I were an idiot. "That right there is why I could never marry you, Luca. You *gave me space*? We broke up because you were caught messing around, and to add insult to injury, your actions were plastered all over one of those stupid paparazzi rags. You broke my heart and humiliated me."

"I told you that was a misunderstanding."

"And I told you, you're full of shit. I won't be one of those women who simper at your feet and believe whatever nonsense you happen to be dishing out."

I bit my tongue. Arguing with her about the past wasn't going to solve anything, but I did point out, "I never asked you to be that woman," because it was true. A simple and vapid woman would bore me to tears. In all the years I'd known Katherine, *boring* was never a word I'd use to describe her.

That photo had been unfortunate, but I'd learned a valuable lesson. Don't let cute starlets sit on your lap when you've had too many whiskeys and not enough food. The paparazzi had snapped the pic because of the girl, not because of me, but it'd sold quite a few tabloids.

It was pretty condemning, considering she'd been kissing me…and she was topless.

My father had been outraged, my mother had been mortified and I'd lost the woman of my dreams.

In all, it'd been a shit day.

"Why'd you wait until now to call off the wedding?" I asked. "Seems if you were still pissed about that incident, you would've called it all off before this dramatic exit."

Katherine's blue eyes flashed with ire at being called dramatic. She couldn't help it—it was the red hair. The Scottish heritage was hard to tamp down. "Because you aren't the only one with obligations. I wanted to call it off then, but my father interceded."

By *interceded*, it was a fair guess he threatened to cut her off if she didn't go through with the wedding. Bernard believed in brute force to get what he wanted. When our households were joined together, the connections in the business world would grow exponentially. An arranged marriage today wasn't all that different from an arranged marriage back in medieval times.

It was all about the power exchange, the advancement of a family's reach and influence.

"I wasn't given much of a choice. I was a semester away from getting my degree, and I wasn't going to let everything I'd worked for go down the drain because *you* chose to be a jackass." She drew a breath and blew it out, adding with a shake of her head, "Honestly, I thought I could go through with it, have a marriage in name only, but these last six months… I realized I can't.

And I won't. I'm not going to live my life to someone else's standards. So…I'm out."

"It won't be that simple," I told her, distracted by a whiff of her hair as she purposefully turned away and a wash of memories hit me hard.

Hemlock trees and sage, the heat of summer, coconut-scented sunscreen mingling with her signature white-citrus-and-cucumber body spray and the feel of her beneath me as I took her virginity.

I could still feel her tight wetness clasped around me, the way she shuddered and gasped as I gently pushed myself deep inside, breaching her lithe body for the first time.

She'd been eighteen; I'd been twenty-two.

The way she'd cried out, her teeth worrying the full pink flesh of her bottom lip, seconds before she came on my cock, her sweet sex clenching around me, greedy for more.

In spite of the slight chill of first class, sweat dampened my forehead as I took a deep swallow of my champagne.

Jesus, now was not the time to think of that memory if I wanted to keep my head on my shoulders.

"I'm not looking for an easy way out. I just want out," she said.

Time to move the subject to safer ground. "If I were going to run away, I'd at least pick someplace warm with a secluded beach and a well-stocked bar," I shared, clearing my throat and my head of the pornographic things I wanted to do to my not-so-sweet bride-to-be. "I mean, San Francisco in winter…kinda crappy."

"Perhaps if things don't work out for you being CEO of the Donato empire, you can start a travel agency," she quipped with a dismissive glance before adding, "I picked San Francisco because I wanted to experience the cultural vibe of a liberal city. Not because I wanted to get a tan on some beach."

I smothered a grin. She'd always been curious and artsy—a big film buff, Coppola to be specific—so I could understand why the city appealed to her. "Well, that's good, because the San Francisco beaches smell like dead fish and they're barely nice to look at, much less lie around on the sand. The homeless are particularly fond of the beaches, as well."

"I know what you're doing," she said, bored. "Trying to scare me off with all your negative press, but I don't care. It's time for me to live life on my own terms, and I want to see the West Coast."

"You could've asked me. I would've made it happen."

"I don't want to ask you or anyone for anything." She turned to me. "Do you realize it was never my choice where to go to school or even what I would study in college? Your family made *all* my choices based on what would benefit the Donato name when we married." She huffed out a breath. "I am more than a doll you can dress up and prop in the corner, waving and smiling as the perfect, uselessly educated housewife. I never even wanted to go into marketing. I wanted to be a veterinarian, remember? But your father deemed my choice of profession *inappropriate* for a Donato. So the decision was made for me."

I remembered Katherine's desire to work with animals. I also remembered my father's disdain for such a career choice. I should've stuck up for her, but I'd remained silent. At the time, I'd had my hands full finishing up my own degree and learning the business at my father's side. I hadn't had the spare brain space to fight Katherine's battle, too.

But still, I regretted not saying something.

Everything she said was true, but it didn't mean I'd had any say, either. I couldn't give a shit what degree she had or what career she pursued. Maybe it was my misfortune to have fallen in love with my arranged bride, unlike others in similarly wealthy families that treated marriage alliances as business transactions.

"So, you quit Franklin and Dodd. What's your plan? Become a vet?"

"Maybe. I don't know, but when I decide, it'll be my choice."

God only knew it would've been so much easier if I'd felt nothing for the troublesome redhead. If I'd felt nothing but obligation to produce a kid, I would've written off Katherine a long time ago, selected any of the numerous women trying to get that gaudy ring on their finger, put a kid in her belly and moved on with my life.

But I loved her. That was the inescapable truth that made it impossible for me to walk away without one hell of a fight.

"So…did you pack appropriately?"

"Of course I did," Katherine said, adding sardonically, "Did you?"

"I didn't pack anything. Whatever I need, I'll buy new."

"Of course." Katherine's gaze returned to me, accusatory. "I preferred my original seat."

"No one prefers coach over first class."

"I do."

"Was this the entirety of your strategy?" I asked, drawing attention to how poorly she'd planned her getaway. "Liquefy your accounts and then melt into the bohemian life of a hipster on the West Coast?"

"Maybe. As long as whatever I planned was on my own terms, the details were irrelevant."

"I beg to differ. My family has a significant investment in your welfare. Did you think that if you breached the contract, it would go without some sort of compensation or penalty? My father isn't going to let this insult pass without consequence."

Katherine fell silent. I knew she'd given this possibility thought, but she was resolved to follow through. "I'll have to take the risk," she finally said.

"You really hate me that much?" I asked, all levity fading from my voice.

It was the minute hesitation that gave her away and filled me with hope—maybe misplaced and wildly irresponsible hope, but hope nonetheless.

Before Katherine could answer, the flight attendant returned with a refill of the champagne. I preferred scotch, but since I'd already started with champagne, I figured it was best not to mix. I needed my head on straight if I was going to find a way to get Katherine to love me again.

"I don't hate you, Luca," she said, glancing away. "I just don't love you any longer."

I didn't believe her. One thing I'd learned about human nature was that strong emotion betrayed vulnerabilities. In the last six months, she'd done everything in her power to avoid being alone with me. If there weren't residual feelings messing with her judgment, she wouldn't have needed to avoid me.

Maybe I was basing my opinion on my own wild hope, but I believed she still loved me. Somewhere deep down she loved me like I loved her, but she was afraid to trust me again.

I could sense her agitation with her sitting so close to me; her fidgeting fingers gave her away. Memories of growing up around each other, falling in love, having sex…they were all in there, rubbing against the memories that hurt. It was my guess that Katherine was running from *every* memory between us.

"I know you remember how good it was between us."

"I try not to live in the past."

Ouch. "It could be that way again," I told her. "If you'd just give us a chance."

She answered with heavy silence.

I tried again. "Katherine—"

"I want out of my contract," she blurted.

"Excuse me?"

"I didn't stutter and you have perfect hearing. Let me out of our marriage contract or I'll spend the rest of my life embarrassing your family, starting with an exposé on your family that begins with how I was essentially purchased to be your bride."

She'd thrown down a goddamn gauntlet.

"If you do that, you'd ruin your own family, as well,"

I pointed out, narrowing my gaze, trying to gauge if she was bluffing.

"I owe no allegiance to my father. He made this mess—he can deal with the fallout. I was never asked if I wanted to marry into the Donato family, but then, I was only a kid. Who cared what my feelings were, right?"

I knew Katherine had as strained a relationship with her father as I had with mine, but unlike me, Katherine seemed uninterested in gaining her father's approval.

Resolve shone in her eyes, and I understood the hard line she was willing to draw to be free of anything remotely connected to the Donato name.

Her demand was like a punch to the gut. I'd never expected her to go that far. I could give her the world on a silver platter if she'd only let me, but no, she wanted fucking out.

"You're willing to go that far to satisfy a bruised ego?"

She shook her head, obviously seeing things differently than me. "You'll never understand, Luca. That, above all else, is why I can't marry you. When people show their true colors, it's best to believe them. And I don't like your colors."

My mother would fall over in a perfumed faint if a scandal of this proportion reached her little social circle. My father would lose his temper and bring all the attorneys under our employ down on Katherine's head for breach of contract. He would ruin her. She had no idea the fire she was playing with.

I'd done this.

I'd turned a sweet, loving girl into a Donato-hating shrew who found me to be the devil.

I couldn't let Katherine's broken heart ruin our second chance before we even got started.

It would be ugly.

That blue-eyed gaze slivered, sending spikes through my heart as it raced. In business I was known as a boardroom shark. I could sense the tiniest drop of blood before my opponent even knew he was in trouble. Nothing scared me.

Except the thought of losing Katherine for good.

"Give me a week to change your mind," I proposed, my gaze pinning hers, willing her to agree to my deal. I needed this to work. "If by the end of the week, you still want to be free…I'll do what I need to release you from your obligations to the Donato family without penalty, as long as you promise to keep the details of our contract confidential."

Katherine stared with suspicion, clearly believing my offer was pure crap. "You're lying. I don't believe for a second that your family would walk away from an investment."

She was right, but I planned to win, so the consequence of failure was a nonissue. However, I couldn't exactly say that without sounding like an arrogant ass. Instead, I said, "This isn't about an investment—it's about me and you. Give me a chance to change your mind."

"I'm serious, Luca. I don't want to marry you."

"You've made yourself perfectly clear."

"Then let's skip the experiment and just call it done. You go your way, I'll go mine."

Never. "If you're so sure your feelings won't change, where's the harm in letting me spin my wheels?" While she considered my point, I pressed my agenda, saying, "Give me one week," because I wasn't going to stop until she agreed.

The fact was, I loved her. I didn't want anyone but Katherine.

Now it was up to me to remind her why, once upon a time, she'd loved me, too.

CHAPTER TWO

Katherine

WAS LUCA ACTUALLY offering me a way out of my contract? Was it that simple? Agree to spend a week with him and at the end he'd let me go?

Offering the deal went against Luca's nature—he was hardwired to go after the win, no matter the cost.

In business, he was ruthless and vicious. His reputation in certain circles was downright scary, and yet he was offering me an opportunity to walk, free and clear.

My belly trembled at the implication, even as there was the tiniest sliver of hesitation that perhaps I didn't want to be free.

Of course I wanted to be free. Why else would I have made such a bold move to get away from the Donato family?

Because maybe you wanted him to know heartbreak, too?

I shoved aside that annoying voice that seemed to whisper in my ear at the worst moments. I felt nothing for Luca but contempt. I wasn't going to hitch myself to someone I couldn't imagine looking at from across the dining table without wanting to throw the saltshaker at his head.

But even more so, I couldn't give my heart to someone I couldn't trust. Giovanni had taught his sons that fidelity was expected of their wives but was not necessary for men. The more I'd gotten to know Giovanni, the more I knew I wanted nothing to do with his family.

Especially after Luca had proved he was nothing more than a chip off Giovanni's block.

But I knew that if I didn't at least give Luca the appearance of having a shot at winning me back, he'd never give up, and I didn't look forward to the idea of Luca chasing me from state to state.

"What would this week together entail?" I asked warily. I knew without his admitting it that he, no doubt, thought if he could get me into bed, I'd melt like chocolate in his hands and stumble over my own feet just to walk down the aisle with him. *Not fucking likely.* The sex had been good—but had it been *freedom* good? Yes. I couldn't even begin to delude myself into thinking otherwise. Sex had been the one thing between us that had worked spectacularly. So the answer was obvious—avoid anything that put our naked bodies in close proximity. A slow smile followed as I tacked on slyly, "What if I said there would be no sex between us?"

He shocked me with an easy shrug, saying, "Then there's no sex."

Yeah, right. I barked a short laugh. "I don't believe you." Luca needed sex the way the human body needed air.

"You have trust issues, Katherine," he admonished,

as if I didn't already know he was a man slut who fucked anything that walked. "It's an unattractive trait in a woman."

"If I do, I do because of you."

He exhaled, the subtle twitch in his jaw the only indication of his irritation, but Luca did his best to seem reflective. "I've made mistakes. I was young."

"If that's your idea of an apology, you suck," I said.

Donatos didn't apologize. Every action was deliberate, good or bad. From Luca's viewpoint, he had nothing to apologize for. I could already hear his argument. Was it his fault that I'd given him my heart before he was ready? Was it his fault that I hadn't been able to go with him to that stupid yacht party? In Luca's mind, I'm sure the blame for *his* mistake landed squarely on my shoulders.

Since our breakup, I'd had time to figure out who I was and what I wanted in my life without Luca's blinding influence clouding my judgment.

"It's true, I probably do," Luca conceded with a modicum of humility that momentarily shocked me. "I can't say I've had a lot of practice, but believe me when I say I'm sorry for hurting you."

I didn't want a life with a man who couldn't take responsibility for his fuckups—and offering a blithe semiapology years later didn't count.

Where was his apology when it'd happened? When I was broken into pieces, sobbing my heart out, utterly betrayed? My lips pressed together to keep from venting all the frustration that he wouldn't listen to years ago from vomiting out. Why couldn't I let it go? Whatever had happened had happened years ago. *Live in the now, not the past,* as Alana liked to say airily, because she didn't give two shits about anything deeper than when the newest Prada bag was dropping.

But I wasn't that way. *Okay, sue me—I hold grudges.* Deep ones.

Especially when I was made to feel stupid and naive.

And that day, I'd felt dumber than a box of hair for believing that Luca Donato could ever be satisfied with only one woman.

I blinked back hot tears, instantly irritated that Luca still had the power to hurt me, if even in memory. I narrowed my gaze, letting him know that I didn't trust there was much weight behind his apology, saying, "We'll see," and left it at that, grateful the plane had begun to taxi. I needed the distraction.

The truth was, I didn't actually enjoy flying. Anxiety fluttered in my chest as the plane started to eat up the runway. I gripped the armrest tightly, closing my eyes as the plane lifted into the air, the power of the jet engines rumbling beneath our feet.

I focused on my yoga breathing—from the belly, in and out. Flying was safer than driving, so they said.

I had no idea who *they* were, but I had to assume *they* knew what they were talking about.

"Are you all right?" Luca asked, interrupting my belly breathing. "You look a little pale."

"I'm fine," I snapped, returning to my relaxation techniques, but now I was a little dizzy. "I just get a little anxious during takeoff."

"Here, take a sip. It'll help soften the edges," Luca

said, holding out his champagne flute with the remainder of his drink. I shook my head, refusing his offer. He gave me a look that said I was being childish, but I didn't care. I didn't need Luca tending to me, in any way. Not even if his suggestion would lessen the sudden tightening in my chest.

"I just need to breathe," I said, demonstrating my yoga technique. "See? In and out. I feel better already."

"Suit yourself." Luca finished his champagne and set his glass in the elegant cup holder until the attendant could retrieve it once we hit thirty thousand feet.

Thirty thousand feet.

Eek! If human beings were meant to fly, we would've been born with wings! Panic started to override my breathing, and instead of controlled inhales and exhales, I was suddenly panting and spots were beginning to dance before my eyes.

"You're so damn stubborn," Luca said.

I couldn't spare the oxygen to tell him to shove his opinion up his piehole, so I settled for sending him a dirty look. Damn it, I was going to have to take something to ease my anxiety, which I did not want to do with Luca sitting beside me, looking as handsome as he ever was, reminding me that I wasn't the only woman who had eyes in her head.

Jealousy, now? Luca made me feel out of control. I wanted to tell him "go fuck yourself" in one breath, yet when women inevitably gave him fuck-me eyes, I wanted to tattoo my name on his forehead just so they knew he was mine.

But he wasn't mine, because I didn't want him.

It didn't make sense in my own head, so I couldn't possibly explain my feelings to anyone else, which became readily apparent when I'd tried to talk to Alana about the situation.

"You do realize you're walking away from a gazillion-dollar family, right?"

"It's not about the money, Alana," I'd reminded her, flopping back against her plush luxury sofa the night after my last dinner engagement with Luca. "I just can't do this. All the rules, the obligations, the expectation that I simply nod, smile and look pretty... And his mother! I'm more than a walking uterus. I was made to do more than pump out Donato babies!"

"But your babies would be *so* cute," Alana had protested, picking up on the least important detail in my impassioned declaration. "I wonder if they'd have your red hair or his black? That Italian heritage is hard to override, but your red hair is something even Photoshop can't replicate. Oh! What if they had his black hair but your crazy curls? That would be fab."

I had snapped my fingers in front of Alana's dreamy gaze. "Focus, Alana. I'm not marrying him. I can't. Marrying Luca would be admitting that I'm good with sacrificing everything that I am, just for money. I'm not that person."

"You're so dramatic," Alana had said, rolling her eyes and reaching for her phone. "Have you seen Georgie's newest Insta post? She's such a bitch. I can't believe she had the balls to say that Carolina's party was a dud. It was way better than her lame masquerade debacle at Halloween."

"He broke my heart," I'd reminded Alana, dragging her back on point. "Remember?"

Alana had blinked, then seemed to remember. "Of course, darling. He's a dick. But aren't all men? Fidelity is a unicorn, sweetheart. A fun bit of fiction we cling to as little girls, but then we grow up and realize variety is far more fun, and even better than that is having the money to go and *do* whomever we choose. Okay, so you *think* he cheated on you, but honestly, it's actually a good thing because you guys broke the seal before getting married—now you don't have to cling to those silly, outdated and impossible standards. Besides, you were in college when it happened. Have fun, baby girl. And if you really feel the need to console yourself, do it with his money."

That was, *literally*, the worst advice I'd ever been given, but I didn't fault Alana. The truth was, as much as I loved Alana, her advice just cemented the belief that I would never fit into Luca's world—and I didn't want to.

When I chose a husband, I wanted someone who shared the same philosophies about love and marriage. Not someone who believed people were interchangeable and disposable.

"So what are we going to do in California?" Luca's voice dragged me back to the present, and I reluctantly popped an anxiety pill.

I closed my eyes, willing the medicine to work quickly before I freaked the fuck out and jumped from the emergency door to end up as Flat Katherine.

"I haven't agreed to your deal yet," I reminded him

with a weak frown, my heart still thundering in my chest. "I don't know if I can stomach spending a whole week with you."

He cast a derisive look my way to quip, "You really know how to punch a guy in the nuts."

I shrugged. Luca's feelings weren't my concern. "Just being honest."

I was grateful Luca didn't feel the need to offer a rebuttal, which gave the medicine a chance to calm my racing heart and settle my nerves. By the time Luca asked about the plans, I could actually think straight again.

"Did you have a plan when you ran away?" he asked. "A place to stay? Anything like that?"

I opened my eyes, feeling more confident and in control. "Yes, actually. I've found a cute hostel in Berkeley that's cheap."

Luca's distaste might've been comical if I hadn't been so irritated that he was tagging along. "A hostel?" he repeated, his lip curling. "Have you ever stayed in a hostel?"

"No, but it looked fine," I answered, enjoying his displeasure. "Not everyone needs the Ritz. I certainly don't."

"You know you have to share a bathroom with strangers, right?"

"Of course I know that," I said with fake sweetness. Okay, so I'd never done it before, but it wasn't a deal breaker. I was sure everyone was hygienic and polite. I'd been curious about backpacking since college. Hearing my friends regale me with tales of their summer travels made me yearn for an experience I'd always been denied. The daughter of Bernard Oliver didn't gallivant around the globe staying in hostels, especially not with students whose families didn't belong in our social circle. So, maybe this wasn't quite the same, but hosteling in San Francisco, testing out my new freedom, would be exciting nonetheless. "I'm actually looking forward to the adventure."

"Adventure. That's an apt word for it," Luca responded drily. "Unlike you, I actually stayed in hostels when I did a trip after high school with my friends. It was mostly a drunken crawl across Europe, which was fun but also disgusting. You've never stayed in a hotel with less than a five-star rating."

"Hence the adventure," I returned with a glare. "Don't poop on my plans. I'm going to have fun, and you can't stop me."

"May I make an alternative suggestion?"

I decided to humor him. "Such as?"

"Let me take you to Fiji. I can guarantee the allure of sharing a composting toilet with a bunch of hipsters will fade a lot more quickly than the experience of lying on a pristine white-sand beach with crystal clear waters lapping at your feet."

He knew I loved the beach and Fiji was one of those places we'd always talked about when we were younger. I hated that he'd remembered that small detail. I hated even more that a part of me wanted to say yes, but I wasn't changing my plans.

"I want to experience life like a *normal* person, and a normal person in their early twenties is usually *broke*.

A hostel is within my budget. But I can understand how that might not be your scene. Feel free to bow out. You're a little overdressed anyway," I said with a small smile as my gaze flicked to his suit.

"When in Rome, do as the Romans do," he said with a shrug. "Jeans and hoodies, it is."

"You're really going to stay in a hostel with me?"

"Why not? Sounds fun. Maybe I'll diversify my portfolio and buy one for a tax shelter."

My sound of disgust was followed by "Just like a Donato. Not everything is for sale."

"That hasn't been my experience."

"Life is about more than what can be bought."

He agreed, leaning over to whisper in my ear, "Life is about good sex."

I gasped, and he chuckled at catching me off guard. If he thought keeping me off balance would tip the scales in his favor, he was wrong. Even if his voice in my ear had just started percolating my blood with a heat I remembered all too well.

I swallowed, forcing a smile. "Yeah, well, we're not having sex, so…" *Keep telling yourself that and you might believe it.* It was absolutely essential that neither one of us was naked around the other—that was just asking for trouble.

"Let's make this week interesting," he proposed with a playful glint in his eye. "We will compromise—"

"Donatos don't compromise," I cut in flatly.

"There's a first time for everything," he countered with a small smile. "Are you interested in hearing my proposal?"

No. Yes. Well, maybe. "If only out of sheer curiosity," I answered, one brow climbing with skepticism. "What is this compromise?"

"If you agree to splitting our days between things I want to do, I will agree to do what you want to do without complaint. I get three days, you get three days, with the last day reserved for travel."

"Technically, someone is going to get shafted, because today is a travel day, too."

"Unfortunately, as you've already picked hostel living for our first day, you've used up one of your days," he explained, matter-of-fact. "Unless you'd like to change your mind about staying in a hipster hotel. I'd be happy to make arrangements at the Four Seasons."

I hesitated, weighing his offer. I could tell by the way his gaze intensified that he sensed victory, but he never made the rookie mistake of celebrating too early. He knew I was intrigued by his offer. I was even curious as to how he'd choose to spend his days when I'd taken sex off the table.

But I also knew giving a Donato room to wiggle was dangerous.

"Why do you care, Luca? Wouldn't it be so much easier to just walk away?" I asked, exasperated by the allure of the game beginning between us. It felt too familiar, too entertaining. I didn't want to feel anything remotely positive with Luca, because I didn't want to question or regret my decision.

Luca offered a brief smile before saying with a shrug, "You signed a contract. If being a part of this family has taught you anything, it is that you honor your commitments."

Not because he loved me, but because Donato men didn't walk away from an investment. I smothered my disappointment. "Very *Game of Thrones* of you, but I'm no Lannister—nor am I a Donato. You and I both know that contracts entered into with a *child* are illegal and, thus, nonbinding. Your family and my father conducted an illegal sale of a person. Even with all your money, that's still illegal—and despicable, I might add."

"Have you wanted for anything?" he returned, that tiny twitch returning to his jaw that gave away his temper. "Have you been mistreated in any way?"

"Not the point," I said stubbornly, shaking my head. "Still illegal."

"The finest schools, the best opportunities, every need provided for… Yes, I can see how you received the sharp end of this deal." He stopped me before I could jump in, adding, "And not to put too fine a *point* on your argument, but you were perfectly amenable to the arrangement until your ego was bruised. Suddenly, you were a victim and we were the devil. So, please, when you're forming your narrative in your head, be sure to paint yourself with the same colors as you've assigned everyone else."

No one liked to be called on their bullshit, and I was no exception. "Well, even the devil was an angel before he fell" was all I could offer by way of an excuse, because he was right. There was a time when I'd been blissfully happy, blessed even, not because of the money and the privilege, but because I'd been in love with a man I thought felt the same way about me.

"Better to reign in hell than serve in heaven," Luca said with a flippant shrug. "Let me know your decision before we land. Now, if you don't mind, I'm going to catch up on some sleep. Feel free to glower out the window, but do so silently."

"I don't glower," I muttered, but he'd already tuned me out and my anxiety medication was making me sleepy. There was no point in arguing an unfortunate fact. Yes, I'd been in love with Luca, and being his bride had been my favorite daydream.

But things changed. People woke up. And rose-colored glasses often broke under the pressure of reality.

I couldn't marry Luca—not if I wanted anything that was truly me to survive.

CHAPTER THREE

Katherine

IN SPITE OF the medication, I couldn't sleep, unlike Luca, who slept like a baby without a care in the world. While I tried to find a comfortable position, he snored lightly, deep in dreamland.

It was just like a Donato to manipulate a situation to their advantage in any way possible. I sneaked a glance at his profile. Dark hair, sharply barbered with perfect edges, his clean-shaven jaw without a single nick, as if even the blade was afraid of failing a Donato.

But I remembered a time when Luca wasn't so concerned with the appearance of perfection.

When he'd smiled with warmth, when his blue eyes had sparkled with mischief and fun.

I squeezed my eyes shut against the unwelcome memories that began to spill forward with the slightest encouragement. That was the thing about opening a door, right? Hard to slam shut once the wind started pushing against it.

"You're so beautiful…"

Luca's voice echoed, a distant remnant of a different time between two different people.

It'd been a humid day in the city, and my prep school graduation from Dalton loomed. Luca had spirited me away with a promise of a private celebration between the two of us.

I remembered everything about that day—the smell of the wind as it made my hair dance through the open convertible top of his Maserati—how I couldn't keep the hem of my sundress from rippling up my thighs and Luca couldn't keep his eyes on the road.

"We're going to crash." I'd laughed, gesturing at him to stay focused, but I was drunk on his affection, his seeming obsession with me. I teased him with flirty looks cast his way, knowing I was driving him nuts. "Where are we going?" I asked, grinning.

"You'll see."

I loved the way he took control. I always felt safe with Luca. He seemed so worldly, so accomplished.

Of course, he was the Donato heir—the expectations were high. Giovanni Donato had groomed him from the time he was a kid to take the reins when the time came for the mean-eyed bear to retire.

Giovanni scared me and always had. It amazed me that Luca sprang from Giovanni's DNA. Luca was nothing like his father. Luca was kind, sweet, caring and so romantic, whereas Giovanni was cold, manipulative and quite comfortable playing the bad guy if need be. To be honest, I avoided Giovanni whenever I could, which wasn't difficult, as Giovanni paid as little attention to me as he would the multitude of servants looking after his palatial mansion.

But who cared about Giovanni Donato, anyway? He wasn't around. It was just me and Luca, and I was his princess. The sleek car ate the road as we headed to our unknown destination. The joy in my heart was near to bursting. I was living the dream. How'd I get so lucky?

Just as I was about to scream from the building anticipation, Luca pulled into a dirt driveway lined with a white picket fence for as far as I could see. Rolling hills with gently swaying dried grass waved as we drove by, and cows dotted the pastureland.

"Where are we?" I asked, delighted as we parked in front of a huge farmhouse, chickens clucking and scratching around the front yard. It was like the living embodiment of "The Farmer in the Dell."

"I thought you might like this place," Luca said, opening my door with a wide smile. "It's a sanctuary for animals that have been rescued from abusive owners."

My eyes widened as I exclaimed, "Do they have goats? Oh, please, say they have goats!"

"They have goats."

I squealed and jumped into his arms, wrapping my legs around his strong torso. His hands cupped my behind as he laughed at my enthusiasm while I peppered his adorable face with kisses. "You're the best! This is amazing! I can't believe you brought me here."

Luca knew I'd always been obsessed with goats; they always made me laugh and I'd tried, unsuccessfully, to get approval from my dorm manager to have one as a pet.

I hopped down and slid my hand into his as we walked into the farmhouse, a permanent smile on my face. The old hardwood groaned in welcome beneath our feet, and the smell of beeswax and lemon was the most heavenly aroma I'd ever known.

"You must be Mr. and Mrs. Donato," a plump woman said, coming forward as she wiped her hands on the apron tied around her ample waist.

I blushed at her assumption, biting my lip at the wild thrill of being called Mrs. Donato, but Luca corrected her with a coy "She's not mine yet, but hopefully someday." I wanted to pinch him playfully. Of course, I would marry him at twenty-three, after I graduated college, but no one knew that.

"Young lovebirds." She sighed as if remembering her own youth. "Well, I'm Mrs. Ellering, but you can call me Iris. Welcome to Knucklebocker Sanctuary. We've prepared a special day for you and your sweetheart. Just follow me."

Oh, that sneaky devil had prepared everything in advance, and I loved it.

"I heard someone is an animal lover?" Iris prompted as she led us to the large redwood barn.

"That's me," I piped up, squeezing Luca's hand as I beamed. "I hope to work with animals someday. Maybe go to veterinary school."

"That's a noble profession," Iris said, pushing open the barn doors. The scents of barn wood, hay and horse poop immediately assaulted my nose, but I liked it. It was so earthy and unlike the city that I drank in the ambience. Plus, the fact that Luca had arranged every-thing made it extra special.

"Harvard," Iris called out, "we have guests."

A bald, wiry man in faded overalls and a full white beard appeared from a stall where a horse nickered. "You them fancy folk from the city that's bought us out for the day?" he asked.

I tried not to blush, but Luca answered for us both, saying good-naturedly, "What gave it away? My soft hands?"

"Oh, go on now, be nice." Iris waved at her husband with mock disapproval, but it was easy to see they were both playing around. My heart melted a little at how easily the older couple flowed together, an obvious by-product of a long, happy marriage. I tightened my grip on Luca with a wistful sigh. *That will be us, someday...*

I awoke with a start, realizing that I'd been dream-ing and we were landing. Luca was already awake, his attention focused on his phone.

What a difference from then to now. Gone were the smiles, the laughter...the sweet, good-natured Luca who went out of his way to make me happy with an over-the-top gesture, replaced by this manipulative carica-ture dressed in a ten-thousand-dollar suit.

I absently rubbed at the dismal chord that twanged in my chest. If I cared, I might've mourned the loss of the man I used to know, but I didn't care. Disdain had replaced any pain that lingered, and I was grateful. Just as Luca wasn't the man he used to be, I wasn't the girl he used to know, either.

If Luca thought he could persuade me to forget the

past with this phony seduction act, he didn't know how much I'd truly changed. Of course, Luca probably felt secure in the idea that he could win this little wager; otherwise he wouldn't have extended the offer.

Time to negotiate. "I want our deal in writing," I said.

"You don't trust me?" He tsked as if I were being unfair. When I didn't budge, he relented. "Fine. Anything else?"

"Yes, I will give you seven days, but at the end of those seven days, when I haven't changed my mind, you will not only agree to end my contract, but you will not seek any damages from the breach and you will leave me to live in peace. I never want to see you or another Donato again. Clear?"

"If I can't change your mind," he repeated, but there was something about his tone that sent a warning chill dancing along my skin. "But I will change your mind, Katherine. I have no doubt that by the end of the week, possibly sooner, I'll be between your legs and you'll be gasping my name."

I sucked in an embarrassed breath, glancing around quickly to see if anyone had caught what he'd said. "I said no sex," I said with a sharp hiss. "Absolutely no sex. No touching, no sucking, kissing or licking…nothing."

His knowing chuckle undid me, and I suffered an intense need to run far and fast. It was as if he could sense that my heart rate tripled when he was around, that my skin heated and my toes curled inside my shoes against my will.

My attraction to him was mortifying. My dignity cringed and wailed, *Remember how he destroyed you without skipping a beat? Do you want to be tied to him for the rest of your life? Afraid of when he'll, no doubt, do it again?*

God, no. Then suck it up, buttercup, and get ready to win at all costs. I swallowed the lump stuck in my throat but held my ground. "No sex," I growled.

"Fine." He sighed but then added with a silky whisper against the shell of my ear, "But I promise I won't think less of you in the morning if you change your mind."

A tremble rattled my knees. Was I afraid that he was right? That it wouldn't take much for me to crumple beneath his touch if I so much as gave him one single opportunity? That if I did let him in, I'd willingly bare my neck for the slaughter as I sank into the pleasure that I knew he could wring from my body? Okay, maybe that part was a *little* dramatic, but my life was on the line. And as much as I hated to admit it, sex with Luca had been pretty good. Okay, *spectacular.*

True story—after one particularly long and exquisite orgasm, I temporarily went deaf. Yeah, that had done wonders for Luca's already healthy ego when I'd shared that phenomenon with him.

But no one had been able to deliver that kind of pleasure since, so I knew Luca had some skill.

Immaterial, I reminded myself when I started to drift. I didn't want to live my life as a Donato Stepford wife. I knew that for certain, and no amount of stellar sex was going to change that fact.

I just had to keep my eye on the prize—my freedom—and everything would work out in my favor.

I could handle seven days.

Lifting my chin, I held Luca's stare, reiterating my terms. "In writing, please."

There went that damnable smile again as he said, "I'll have my lawyer draft something immediately."

And I wasn't sure if I'd just made a very big mistake.

CHAPTER FOUR

Luca

TRUE TO MY WORD, I had a draft contract, simple and concise, emailed to me within an hour of checking into the roach motel passing itself off as a hostel. As Katherine perused the wording with the diligence of a woman signing away her soul to the devil, I wondered how quickly she would notice that the single bed in the room was quite small.

If she thought I was going to sleep on the floor, she was nuts. I'd seen toilets in third-world countries cleaner than this dingy, faded linoleum, and I wasn't touching it with my bare feet, much less my backside.

"Everything in order?" I asked.

A subtle frown pulled on her forehead as she double-checked everything. Her frown deepened as she regarded me with irritation. "The bedroom clause? I told you no sex."

"Are you saying you can't sleep beside me without tearing off my clothes and having your wicked way with me?"

"Please—" she rolled her eyes "—you know *I* won't have a problem, but *you*, on the other hand… I don't believe you can keep your hands to yourself."

Oh, sweet Katherine, you're going to beg for my hands—and tongue—by the time I'm through with you.
"I guess we'll have to see," I said with a small shrug. "Anything else?"

The indecision as she vacillated between refusing to sign and going forward was intriguing. I think of the many things I enjoyed about Katherine, it was her stubborn refusal to simply do as she was told. Maybe I was tired of people always jumping when I barked. I wouldn't put it past Katherine to rip up the contract out of spite.

Finally, she signed her name with flourish, chewing her plump bottom lip as she finished. "There. Done. You get one week and then I'm gone."

"So the contract says," I agreed, causing her to cast a suspicious look my way. I smiled. "Now that the legalities are out of the way…shall we discuss the schedule?"

Katherine drew a deep breath and exhaled with a nod. "Might as well."

"We can do this one of two ways. You can take all your days consecutively or we can trade off. Which do you prefer?"

"I prefer not having you in my space at all," she answered with a perfunctory smile. "But seeing as I just agreed to this ridiculous game, we'll switch off."

"Excellent," I said, already ready to vacate this trash bin. I would have the penthouse suite booked at the most exclusive hotel in the city for tomorrow. At the very least, I'd get a decent shower, which I knew wasn't going to happen here. "On to the second order of business… as you can see, the bed is quite small."

"I wasn't counting on company," Katherine said, but she could already see where I was heading. "I guess you'll have to sleep on the floor."

"You and I both know that's not going to happen."

"The contract says one bedroom, not one bed," she pointed out. "So, technically, if we're still in the same room…it doesn't mean that we have to be in the same bed."

"You can take the floor if you like, but I'm taking the bed," I said, enjoying how her upper lip wrinkled in subtle distaste for the same reasons mine did. "But if you're amenable to sharing the bed, I'm not opposed to it."

"I don't mind sleeping on the floor," she bluffed.

"Excellent. Then it's settled. Maybe we can get an extra blanket for you. San Francisco is quite chilly at night."

Especially in January.

"You would make me sleep on the floor?" Katherine asked.

"Of course not. You're the one insisting on sleeping on the floor."

"I am not," she refuted, scowling a little. "*You* are by not being a gentleman."

At that I laughed. "Have I ever been accused of being a gentleman?"

Katherine opened her mouth but stopped short. I would give anything for a window into that overactive brain of hers. What memory had popped in before she ignored it? I would ask if I thought she might admit it, but I wasn't going to waste the energy. Not yet, anyway. "Fine," she agreed through gritted teeth. "But I swear to God, if you touch me…"

I waved away her threat. "Sweetheart, I promise I won't touch you…until you beg for it."

Katherine flushed red but managed a haughty "Like that's ever going to happen" before she left me alone in the room, supposedly to use the communal toilet. I cracked a grin at imagining how Katherine would shriek at the bathroom conditions. She talked a good game, but she was out of her element. As much as she wanted to play the hippie flower child, she was just as accustomed to wealth as me. I doubted the "charm" of her accommodations would last long.

Perusing the small room, I chuckled at the memories of Europe—young, dumb and full of come, as they say— me and my buddies traipsing through London, Athens, Paris in one long, endless summer of debauchery.

All those foreign, exotic women—I limited myself to nothing. Curvy, thin, short, tall, thick. And wild, shy and timid—I enjoyed the smorgasbord of female options and learned a few things, too.

We often joked it was a miracle we'd escaped alive with our cocks intact. Although Ryin had caught a particularly nasty infection that'd required a stringent round of antibiotics—but at least it'd been curable.

And speaking of debauchery…

I grabbed my cell and dialed my friend Dillon Buchanan.

He surprised me with a quick answer. "Fucking A, Luca Donato? What are you doing? Are you in town?"

"I am, and I'm looking for a little entertainment. You and your brothers still own that club?"

"We do—damn source of contention with the wives, but yeah. You interested in playing while in town? I could set you up with some playmates."

"Thanks, but I brought my own. My fiancée, actually. I want to treat her to the wonders of Malvagio before we head back at the end of the week."

Malvagio, originally owned by Dillon's twin brothers, Nolan and Vince, was an exclusive sex club, intensely private, invite only, and it took an act of God to gain an invitation from a sponsored member. The shit that happened between those walls was pure hedonism, catering to certain fetishes with a definite *Eyes Wide Shut* vibe to the entire operation.

The obscenely wealthy needed their diversions, and the Buchanan brothers had found a way to cash in on that need.

Not that they needed any money—the Buchanans were billionaires in their own right—but hey, nobody turned down more cash, right?

"Fiancée...holy shit. Never thought I'd see that happen. Is she mentally challenged?" Dillon joked.

"Ha-ha," I retorted. "Coming from the man who found a woman to marry him, in spite of being the biggest asshole in the city."

"I'm only an asshole to you. To my lady, I'm Don fucking Juan. What are your plans for tomorrow night? The auction is on the calendar. Interested?"

I grinned. Each year Malvagio opened its membership to women hoping to gain a sponsor into the club, but in order to do so, they went on the block and sponsors competed for the prize.

It was sexist as hell, but everyone seemed to enjoy the show, so no harm, no foul.

"Sounds fun," I answered, already picturing Katherine's expression of shock. "Put me on the list with a plus-one."

We exchanged a few good-natured insults and then said our goodbyes.

By the time Katherine returned, I was smiling like the Cheshire cat.

CHAPTER FIVE

Katherine

I DIDN'T TRUST that smile. Luca had something up his sleeve. I didn't expect him to cough up his master plan, though. All I could do was remain vigilant and deflect any attempts at seduction that he might try.

Oh, yes. I knew he was going to pull out all the stops. Probably try to woo me with fancy dinners and sickeningly trite flattery, because that was all he knew of me from our past, but I was long past that girl.

He'd broken me two years ago. And even before then, I could feel myself changing as my perspective of the world shifted. I guessed higher learning did that to you. He could waste his time plying me with useless trinkets and hollow conversation, but I was immune. I would endure this week and then finally walk away from the Donato family forever. Starting fresh was scary, but there was something exhilarating about the prospect, too. I couldn't wait.

A moment of disquiet intruded on my budding elation. I'd known the Donato boys as long as I could remember. Nico, Luca's youngest brother, and I were friends. I didn't care for Dante much—he was too much like Giovanni—but the point was, they'd always been part of my life. I didn't know what life would be like without their influence casting a shadow, both good and bad.

I guessed I would find out.

"I'm hungry," he announced, checking his watch. "Let's get some dinner."

Ah, here it comes. "Let me guess…a candlelit dinner for two atop the highest building in the city? A glorious view of the bay, stars twinkling, the mood just right… so cozy, so romantic," I mocked. *Like I'm going to fall for that.* I folded my arms across my chest, smug. "But it's my day to pick."

He frowned. "A simple 'no, thanks' would've been fine."

"Like you weren't angling for some romantic night out," I said, calling his bluff.

"Not unless you consider a burger down at the corner pub romantic," he said, his expression clearly saying, *Calm your tits, crazy lady,* but I wasn't buying it. He grabbed his coat. "You coming or not?"

"Not."

"Suit yourself."

My certainty faltered as Luca headed for the door. Was he actually going to leave me behind? My stomach growled in protest. "Are you really going for a burger?" I called after him, grabbing my coat to join him. He shook his head with open annoyance at my suspicion, then he kept walking. He exited the hostel and stepped onto the sidewalk, his stride so damn confident that even passersby took notice. I couldn't help staring just a little. Everywhere Luca went, he attracted attention. If it wasn't for his looks, it was his demeanor. He had a way of walking into a room and instantly taking control. It was as if the universe engineered every circumstance to his advantage, and that drove me nuts.

Even if it was a *little bit* sexy. Okay, maybe *a lot* sexy, but I wasn't going to feed his massive ego by admitting it. If anything, I would deny it until I died, just to prick a few holes in that giant head of his.

The pub wasn't far, true to his word, and I could smell the aroma of something delicious the minute we were within a few feet. My stomach clenched with hunger, reminding me that I hadn't eaten since that morning at Alana's, and I was privately glad I'd decided to tag along. I'd let Luca spend his money so I could keep what I had in reserve.

An Irish pub, the interior dark paneling punctuated by import-beer signs and raucous laughter, the place had a fun vibe that was hard to dislike. We slid into a cozy booth, and a terminally cute and bubbly waitress named Erin bounced over to our table.

"Welcome to Harrigans. What can I get you to start off with?"

"Murphy's Irish stout," Luca answered, earning a smile from Little Miss Easily Impressed.

Her gaze lingered for a second longer than necessary before she gestured to me. "And your lady?" she asked, clearly on a fishing expedition.

Might as well help the girl out. Do her a solid.

"I'm not his lady," I corrected her, shooting Luca a pointed look, daring him to say anything different, but the man simply sat there, waiting for me to give Erin my drink order, which only made me look like a bitchy shrew. "We are…uh…business associates," I clarified with a smile. "And I'll have a Guinness."

"*Oh*, my mistake. You two look so sweet together I just kinda assumed. I'm so sorry. Be right back." She beamed and bounced away like the human equivalent of a bunny rabbit with giant boobs.

"I think she likes you," I said, hoping to goad him into saying or doing something that would cement my disdain for him, but he didn't even nibble at the bait. I tried harder. "Supercute, too. Those boobs, right? Pretty big. If you like that sort of thing. I mean, of course you do. All guys lose their minds over big tits. I think it's etched in your DNA."

"You seem pretty obsessed with our waitress's breasts," he observed, amused.

Heat climbed my throat to heat my cheeks. "That's not what I meant… Oh, forget it. Never mind," I said, letting it go. He wasn't going to do something so overtly offensive as coming on to the waitress on the first day of our deal. *What an amateur move.* If I wanted to win, I had to stop thinking so small.

Erin returned with our drinks, and after we both ordered the house burgers, I fidgeted a little, unsure of what to do with my hands. Finally, I settled with my hands in my lap, but I was intensely aware of how an entirely too-small table was the only obstacle between us. Our knees were practically kissing beneath the table.

Was I supposed to make small talk? I had two settings around Luca—head over heels in love and despise with the force of an EMP blast—I didn't know how to be neutral.

And his seemingly relaxed, taking-in-the-ambience attitude wasn't helping things. Why wasn't he acting like he normally did—arrogant or patronizing—so I could find my bearings?

I didn't know how to reconcile that Luca with this chill *dude*.

"How'd you know about this place?" I asked, breaking the awkward silence. "Have you been here before?"

"Nope. Dinner locale courtesy of Google Maps. It was the closest to the hostel and had a good Yelp review. I figure we had nothing to lose, seeing as we were already taking our lives for granted by staying in the murder motel for the night, but, hey, life is for the living, right?" He lifted his bottle in salute and tipped it back. "Plus, it reminds me of a few pubs me and my buddies frequented in Scotland. Good times, except for the time I was persuaded to eat haggis on a drunken dare."

I dragged my gaze away from the spectacle of those sensual lips wrapping around the bottle top and focused on my own drink. I didn't care for Guinness, but it seemed sacrilegious to order anything less in an Irish pub. Besides, the beer helped loosen the tension cording my shoulders, so I continued to slug it down. "How'd that end?" I asked.

"With my head stuck in a dirty toilet and a bunch of locals laughing their asses off," he answered wryly. "Never touched haggis again."

I bit back a laugh, but I rather liked the image of a young Luca puking his guts out in a foreign country.

"You like that, huh?" His slow grin did terrible things to my stomach. "Then you'll love the story of how I woke up after a wild night in London to find my face a different color than when I passed out. The fuckers sprayed me with the darkest sunless tanner they could find. I went to bed white and woke up a mottled dark brown, and that shit did not scrub off easily. I spent the rest of the week looking like I'd caught a skin disease until it wore off."

At that I really did laugh. "Was this during your European pub crawl after high school?"

"The very same. How'd you know? You were pretty young then."

"I always knew what was going on. My circumstances weren't exactly normal."

He conceded my point with a silent nod, but before either of us could say much more, our food arrived and we both let it go, choosing dinner over uncomfortable topics.

And I was grateful. I didn't want to have a deep, soulful conversation with Luca about anything, much less my unorthodox childhood, thanks to his family, and he'd seemed on the verge of saying something distressingly nice or even apologetic.

I couldn't risk buying into anything he had to say, even if a part of me craved it more than I wanted to admit.

I'd long since stopped wondering how things might've been different if Luca had apologized in the slightest for breaking my heart… I wondered if I would've granted my forgiveness. I knew the answer— of course I would've. I'd been helplessly in love with the jackass. I was pretty sure stars had twinkled in my eyes like a cartoon character whenever he'd been around.

Hard to imagine being that way with anyone now— nor did I want to. I liked who I was, and I had no interest in returning to that caricature I'd been before.

Food was a great buffer, and by the time we were finished eating in silence, not needing to speak as we shoveled burgers into our mouths, I'd lost some of my prickles.

I felt more secure about making it through the week without succumbing to Luca's charm. I just needed to keep at the forefront of my mind the reasons not to marry him. Good sex did not a relationship make. I mean, it was important, don't get me wrong, but I didn't want to raise my kids the way the Donato boys were raised.

For one, Giovanni was an old-school misogynist, and even though Luca wasn't that way, his brother Dante certainly leaned that direction. I didn't want my kids around that kind of influence and keeping any Donato grandchildren away from the family would be near to impossible.

"Thank you for the dinner company," Luca said, patting his belly in the most comically unrefined way. "That burger hit the spot. Can I tell you a secret?"

My smile faded into quizzical curiosity. "I guess."

"I'm not into fancy food. Never have been. Most

times I'd rather just have a burger, fries and a milk shake, but it seems I'm in the minority."

"No, you're not. I hate fancy food," I admitted. "You remember that time your mom had the chef prepare duck in blood sauce? I thought Dante was going to throw up all over your mother's fine china."

"God, yes. Who knows what possessed Mother to have the cook serve that disgusting dish. Thankfully, she never did it again."

As much as I wanted to forget everything I'd experienced with the Donato family, there had been good times. My family was small, just me and my father after my mom died, and our home had always felt quiet. The Donato family home wasn't exactly cozy, but it felt fuller than mine. Nico and I had perpetrated some world-class pranks, but after getting caught one too many times, we'd realized we had to stop if we wanted to get into any worthwhile university. He was a good friend, but I was prepared to walk away from all of them.

The breath hitched in my chest when I realized the magnitude of what I was doing—walking away from everything I'd ever known—but I couldn't let myself travel too far down that road.

I had to do this.

But there was no sense in ruining a decent dinner, right?

We shared some light and totally safe memories, laughed a little, and by the time we walked back to the hostel, I was actually smiling.

Until we entered our room and my gaze fell unerringly on that tiny bed.

Could Luca actually lie beside me without making a move?

Would I be able to sleep with him smashed up against me?

I guessed there was only one way to find out.

CHAPTER SIX

Luca

KATHERINE PUT UP a good front, but the minute we crossed the threshold of our room, I could sense the tension in her shoulders. I wanted to knead the bunched muscles between my fingertips, hear her moan as I released the knots. But I knew if I touched her, all the progress I'd made at dinner would go down the toilet.

So I ignored her and went about my normal evening routine.

I settled on the bed with my phone to check emails, disregarding her completely. I pulled my shirt over my head and shucked my trousers. Katherine's sharp inhale made me turn in question.

"What are you doing?" she asked, gesturing to my near nakedness. "You can't sleep like that."

"No, I can't sleep fully clothed," I corrected her.

"I mean, you can't sleep with *me* like that," she said, her cheeks blaring with heat, even as her gaze kept dipping to the way my boxer briefs hugged my ass and cupped my cock.

"When did you turn into such a prude?" I asked. "I remember you being a lot less…particular."

"I'm not a prude," she protested. "I just don't want to feel your man parts bumping into me all night, that's all, but whatever. As long as you can keep your hands to yourself…I can handle it."

"No problem on my end," I lied, giving a convincingly real yawn even though I was wide-awake. Indeed, keeping my "man parts" from nudging her might be a challenge. My cock was already threatening to plump like a Ball Park hot dog on the grill at the thought of being next to Katherine all night. "I hope you don't snore."

"I don't snore."

"I'll let you know in the morning if that's true or not."

"The bed is smaller than I realized," she admitted, biting her lip. "You take up more than half of it."

"What can I say? I'm a big guy," I said without apology, sliding beneath the blankets. "Not much I can do about that."

"I know, I was just saying…it's a little small."

Yes, a California king would've been preferable, but I looked forward to a night with Katherine doing her best not to let our bodies touch. I suspect she would be so miserable by morning that she'd agree to leave this dump almost immediately, which worked for me.

"Close your eyes," she demanded as I plugged in my phone to charge for the night. Katherine stood, clutching her nightgown to her chest like a Victorian lady.

"Seriously?"

"As a heart attack."

I sighed and deliberately shut my eyes. She killed the light before changing. The mattress gave under the weight of Katherine's body as she slid into the bed, drawing the covers to her nose. "Is it safe now?" I asked in an amused drawl.

"Yes," she answered, her voice slightly muffled. "But don't you dare try anything tonight."

I grunted my acquiescence and rolled onto my side. I smothered a laugh at Katherine's rigid body next to mine. At this rate she'd wake up cranky and with a stiff neck. Hell, I would, too, if the springs piercing through this thin mattress were anything to go on.

But all in all, this was working out far better than I'd imagined.

Except for the raging boner now threatening to split my Jockeys in two.

I stifled a groan as I rolled away from her, my dick digging into the bed. If I could survive this night… everything would fall into place.

Hell, at this rate, I might not even need a whole week to have Katherine eating out of my hand—and sucking my cock.

CHAPTER SEVEN

Katherine

A SIGH ESCAPED me as the morning sun caressed my forehead. The comforting weight of a big body behind me, an arm wrapped around my waist drawing me close and a slow, even breath on the nape of my neck drugged me into a contented lethargy.

Something familiar yet foreign pressed against the cleft of my behind, and I instinctively wiggled, pushing against it.

A groan followed as the arm around me tightened. I wasn't awake yet, but I was slowly becoming aware. The tingle in my belly intensified as I arched against the sweet sensation of that rock-hard length pushing against me, insistent, eager. It'd been so long since I'd felt this wild need, this all-encompassing hunger to have him inside me.

It was too early to fight the need; my brain wasn't in control just yet. There'd always been something about Luca that had drawn me, even before I was old enough to realize how my future had been sold to the Donato family.

Before that awareness, Luca had simply been that enigmatic older boy with the devilish smile and the blue-eyed stare that made me want things I had no idea how to verbalize.

Don't wake up.

If I opened my eyes, I'd have to acknowledge how much I missed his touch, how easily I could roll to my back and open my legs for him. The feel of Luca filling me, stretching me like the first time—the memory taunted me. If Luca's fingers sought out my folds, he would find them damp and ready.

Pretending that none of this was real was better than admitting that I missed him, that a part of me still yearned for the taste of him on my tongue, still fantasized about all the things he used to do to me, how he'd introduced me to the tantalizing world of sexual pleasure.

No. Sex was sex. Orgasms were a dime a dozen if you knew what you were doing. Luca didn't have some special hold on me.

At least that was what I told myself every day, and I'd keep telling myself that until it became true, because I wasn't going to marry him.

My eyes snapped open and I tried to scoot away, but his arm remained locked around my waist.

"Luca," I said, trying to inch out of his sleepy grasp. "Luca…" But if anything, he seemed determined to keep me close. I gasped as he nuzzled the back of my neck, sending an army of dancing soldiers traipsing down my exposed skin. My nipples pearled to aching points, and I think my ovaries popped like a bottle of champagne. His tongue teased the smooth skin where my shoulder met my neck and I shivered, my eyes fluttering shut as my toes curled. His hand crept down my belly, seeking between my legs. Was he still asleep? It was possible. Luca was a deep sleeper. Or he could be wide-awake and playing that he was asleep so he didn't have to take responsibility for mauling me. *If only I wasn't dripping for more...* Suddenly, he moved, expertly rolling on top, his solid weight pressing me into the mattress. My legs automatically opened, leaving my core exposed and accessible.

Damn it.

"Good morning," he said, dipping to taste my lips before I could offer a word. His cock fit perfectly against me, the only protection between us the thin fabric of our underwear. He rubbed against me and swallowed my moan. The wanton, sex-starved lunatic hiding in my brain screamed, *Fuck me, Luca!* but I was doing my damnedest to shut that crazy bitch up.

Luca was the most masterful kisser I'd ever locked lips with, and that hadn't changed. If anything, he'd gotten better. He teased, nibbled, penetrated and commanded, leaving me breathless, all the while driving his cock against my sensitive mons, grinding until I was practically writhing beneath him, nearly ready to beg him to just stick it in already.

Where was my sense of control? No one touched me like Luca. Maybe I could delude myself into believing that the sex hadn't been as good as I remembered, but with his tongue in my mouth, my legs trembling with need, it was impossible to cling to that flat-out lie.

The thing was, I might not want to marry him, but maybe a romp for old times' sake wouldn't be a terrible idea.

I wanted him to bend me over the bed and sink into me, stretching my softness with the thick length of his cock. He could reduce me to a quivering ball of flesh with the talent of that tongue, and he knew it.

"I still remember the way you taste," he murmured against my lips, allowing only the slightest breath before plunging his tongue back into my mouth, evoking memories of how he'd done exactly that to my insides.

A groan escaped as he traveled to my neck, nibbling and kissing, sucking and licking, and I wanted to push his head between my thighs. I wanted to lose myself in the power of an orgasm only Luca could give.

Seriously, he was like a sex ninja, with skills that were damn near mythic.

For a brief moment, I was content to simply lose myself in the pleasure of being touched by Luca. My entire body yearned to feel his fingers and lips on my skin.

"Kiss me, Luca," I murmured, expecting him to slide down my belly to sink between my thighs, but instead he returned to my lips, plunging his tongue in, demanding and coaxing an equal response from me.

My nipples tightened to tiny, hard points of aching need as they rubbed against his chest, abraded by the thin fabric of my T-shirt.

His cock, rock solid and urgently pressed against my slit, teased me with the promise of pleasure. I wrapped my legs around him, desperately seeking that delicious friction against my clit. I was so aroused that I could've come from a single stroke of his tongue or even a few judicious flicks of his finger against the swollen nub nestled between my folds.

I couldn't take it anymore. I needed release or I would go insane.

But just as I was about to lose my dignity and beg, he rolled off and climbed from the bed to dress, leaving me panting, confused and disappointed.

"What are you doing?" I asked, struggling to catch my breath.

"Getting dressed," he answered, plainly obvious. "I thought we could check out this place called Mama's. Maybe get some banana pancakes if the wait isn't more than forty-five minutes. Supposed to be the best in the city."

"You want breakfast?"

"Yeah, I'm starved."

Two seconds ago his tongue had been buried in my mouth and now he was all about banana pancakes? What game was he playing? I should be grateful, not insulted, right? I'd told Luca I wasn't going to have sex with him. If I were an idiot, I'd assume he was being a gentleman by adhering to my wishes, but I knew Luca wasn't born with a chivalrous bone in his body.

So he was playing me. He wanted to pretend that he wasn't into me to prove a point.

Fine by me.

"Pancakes sound fab," I agreed, smiling with false brightness as I scooped up my clothes from last night.

I would change in the bathroom. "Give me a second and I'll be ready."

He nodded and pulled his trousers on. Luca wearing the same clothes from yesterday seemed like a sign of the coming apocalypse. He hadn't packed anything because he knew he could just toss down his credit card and buy whatever he needed, but still, seeing him so carefree was throwing me off-kilter.

I escaped the room, disappearing into the communal bathroom once it was free.

The smell of the previous occupant was enough to make me gag, but I was determined to put a good face on things. I couldn't give Luca the satisfaction of knowing that I kind of hated the hostel. It was definitely more appealing on a website or in a story than in reality. For one, my back was killing me from sharing that crappy mattress. I rolled my shoulders, trying to loosen up. I wanted a long, hot shower…in a private bathroom. One glance at the shower stall that had seen better days told me that'd have to wait.

God, I hadn't considered myself a snob until this moment—and the realization wasn't very flattering.

Still, there was no way I was admitting any of this to Luca. For all he knew, I was digging this lifestyle and I wanted to get dreads and a butterfly tattoo on my lower back.

And what the hell? Kissing and nibbling on me like that? That clearly violated our predetermined rules.

But seeing as we'd both been half-asleep, I guessed I could give him a pass—once.

I closed my eyes and swallowed the sigh that threatened to follow. The man had a magic touch.

Would I ever be able to forget how his fingertips felt grazing my skin? Not likely, if he kept doing it.

Just get through this week. After that, I can move on.

Dressed and ready, I met Luca outside, the bite in the air nippy enough to make me shiver. I probably couldn't have picked a more terrible time to visit San Francisco, but I hadn't been thinking—other than to get as far away from New York as possible. The dreary clouds hovering overhead were anything but cheery. Or warm. Right about now, Luca's offer of Fiji would be highly appealing—if not for my pride.

So, I'd just have to make the best of San Francisco.

"Mama's is only a few blocks. I thought we could walk," he suggested with a cheerful smile. He didn't wait for my approval, just set out with a healthy stride, leaving me behind. I hustled to catch up just as he started talking. "Man, it's been a while since I've visited the Bay Area for pleasure. In January it always reminds me of London with its damp and chilly weather. Just smell that bracing sea air!" He drew a lungful for emphasis. "Pretty refreshing. You're right, this was much better than some overrated pristine tropical beach."

I clenched my teeth to keep them from chattering. I'd always considered myself in decent shape, but my calves were burning along with my lungs, yet I was still freezing. "You can stop with the act, Luca," I gasped. "I'm onto you. This sucks and you know it."

But no, he was going to ride this out to the bitter end, I realized, when he insisted, "Not at all. This is one hundred percent me. I love the rain and the damp air. Makes me feel alive."

My gaze narrowed. I couldn't actually tell if he was lying. He seemed to genuinely enjoy our four-mile walk uphill. Who was this guy? He had me so turned around I didn't know which end was up right now.

Luca the uptight businessman had left the building, and in his place was…chill-dude Luca.

This had to be a game. Luca was trying to keep me tottering from one foot to the other. I hated to admit it was working. Not to mention, keeping up this pace was grueling. All I could do was huff and puff and chase after him. I had no more oxygen to argue.

We found Mama's, and the line to get in wrapped around the building and continued down the street. "Are you kidding me?" I complained, my stomach growling loudly. "I'm starving."

"Well, we came all this way. Might as well see what the fuss is about, right?"

I glared mutinously, blaming Luca for my burning calves, my pissy attitude and my grumbling belly. "These better be some utterly fantastic pancakes," I warned, folding my arms across my chest.

Luca chuckled, earning some appreciative glances from the closest women, and I wanted to bare my teeth at them like a wolverine defending its territory. *Knock it off. You don't want him, remember?* I drew a deep, calming breath and tried to find my center. "If you enjoy the Bay Area so much, why do you stay in New York?"

"New York is where my family is," he answered, adding with a shrug, "and New York is my home."

"Do you like New York?"

"I like some aspects of it, others not as much. But I can travel anywhere I want, so it doesn't really bother me to keep New York as my home base."

Yes, obscene wealth had its perks, I thought drily.

But there was something about his admission that gave me pause. Did Luca want more than what his family expected of him? I'd always assumed that Luca bought into the Donato empire without question.

Disquiet seamed my mouth shut. I didn't want to see Luca as *complicated*. I didn't want to look too closely at my own biases, because that opened a can of worms I wasn't ready to wrangle.

My stomach growled again, and I repeated, mostly to myself, "Those pancakes better be life changing," because it was far safer to focus on pancakes than anything else currently crowding my brain.

CHAPTER EIGHT

Luca

IF THERE WERE an award for ignoring a herculean boner, I would've won it.

I might've even suffered permanent damage from walking with giant wood trying to bust through my jeans.

But whatever the cost, it'd been worth watching Katherine struggle to make heads or tails of my unexpected behavior.

She expected me to try to get in her pants—and God knew I wanted to—but the stakes were much higher than satisfying a need to fuck.

I wanted Katherine to want me as much as I wanted her. I had no doubt I could get her in bed—that was an easy but ultimately hollow victory. Hell, I could've fucked her six ways from Sunday with her blessings this morning, but it wouldn't put my ring on her finger.

Overcoming her pride was the first hurdle to returning her to my bed for good.

I knew better than to try to sweet-talk Katherine

when she was hungry—the woman was ruled by her stomach, and right now she looked ready to start eating her way through the line of people—but forty-five minutes was a long time to simply stare at each other without conversation.

"Would you like to know our plans for today?" I asked solicitously.

"I would," she agreed with a wary expression, as if I were going to trick her into getting married at a courthouse. "Does it involve more walking? Because my feet are dead."

"No more walking," I promised her with a chuckle. "Since you've never been to San Francisco, I thought we'd do the tourist thing for the day. Alcatraz, the Presidio, etc."

Her expression brightened slowly with a smile. "That sounds fun," she said but added, "What's the catch?"

"No catch."

"I don't believe you."

"Katherine…you have to give me a chance to show you I'm not the man you think I am," I pointed out, mildly amused by her stubborn desire to paint me as the devil. I mean, I suppose in certain circles I was evil incarnate, but with her…I would be her white knight. "We could even check out the observatory, hit a museum or two…whatever you'd like."

"Really?" She still didn't trust my motives. *Smart woman.* "And then?"

"And then a little shopping," I suggested with a small smile, gesturing to my clothes. "Obviously I didn't come prepared to sightsee."

"And tonight?" Katherine pressed, watching me intently. "Where are we going tonight?"

"Well, first we are going to check out of that heap you call a hostel and into something less bohemian before dinner and a show. Sound good?"

"It sounds incredible," she agreed, but her gaze narrowed. "You're planning something."

"Even if I were…you're committed to doing whatever I choose, as it's my day and evening," I reminded her. I doubted I'd get much pushback on the hotel—she played a good game, but I could tell she hated the hostel, too—but if I told her about my true plans for us… she'd bolt. No, it was better to leave a little mystery. "But let's enjoy the day. I haven't been a tourist in a long time. This should be fun."

I brightened as I thought of something else to add, saying, "Let's check out the pier where the sea lions hang out. Those fat fuckers are pretty entertaining."

Katherine's gaze widened at my casual attitude. I guess it was my fault that I'd spent too much time in business mode, neglecting my future wife. I should've been wooing her way before now, but I'd taken for granted that she would be there when the time came.

Somewhere along the way, Katherine had changed from an adoring teen to an independent, way-too-fucking stubborn woman who didn't believe a word that came out of my mouth and was prepared to call me on my shit.

To be honest, the new Katherine was hot as fuck.

The challenge fired me up in ways I hadn't felt in a long time.

After an interminably long wait—I secretly agreed

with Katherine that the pancakes better be life changing—
we were seated in the cramped eatery/bakery.

San Francisco was a foodie town, and they were serious about their eats. I wasn't accustomed to waiting for
anything. As a Donato, I was seated at the best tables
and never asked to wait longer than it took to check my
coat at the most pretentious restaurants in New York,
and I'd forgotten how the other half lived.

But I enjoyed the wait with Katherine. The way the
morning sun kissed her crown, lighting up her face,
made up for the crease that seemed punched on her forehead. My bride-to-be was such a grump when hungry.

We ordered, and within a relatively short time, our
food arrived.

I was suitably impressed with the service, but before
I could sample the food, Katherine was already diving
in, stuffing her face with banana pancakes.

Syrup dripped from her lip as butter melted in a
gooey pool on top of the stack. Her tongue darted to
lick the syrup away and I nearly knocked the table over
from the instant erection that sprang from my pants.

She groaned with open delight, and I forgot about
my own quickly cooling breakfast.

"It's good," Katherine admitted, closing her eyes as
she chewed, savoring each bite. "God, it's good."

I swallowed and managed to drag my gaze away before she found me staring like a starving man who'd
just stumbled on a fresh deli sandwich. "Yeah?" I said,
clearing my throat and focusing on my plate. What the
hell did I order? Oh, right, eggs and bacon. Definitely
not as exciting as a carb-loading free-for-all. I shoveled

in a bite just to do something to short-circuit my intense need to lick the sweetness from her soft lips.

"You were right—worth the wait," she said with a giggle, the sound tickling my groin. "What do they put in these things? Crack? So good!" She paused midbite to ask, "Want to try?"

I looked up and saw her with a forkful in offering. How could I resist? I opened my mouth like a baby bird. Damn, she was right. "My money is on crack," I agreed. "That's unnaturally delicious."

"Right?" She laughed, returning to her plate. "Who knew the secret to happiness was to be found in a tiny, crowded bakery in San Francisco?"

I shared her laughter, returning to my food. "Maybe I could entice the chef into returning with us. I wouldn't mind this for breakfast every day."

I caught my mistake the minute the careless statement dropped from my mouth. I glanced up to find Katherine's smile fading. I wasn't surprised when she said, "*Us?* I'm not returning with you, Luca. I thought I was clear about that."

"I'm an eternal optimist."

"And I'm a realist. You get one week. No more. I want to be free of the Donato family, and that includes you."

"Thank you—you've made that very clear," I returned sharply, angry at myself for being so stupid as to lose my lead over something so trivial, but snapping at her wasn't going to gain me any points, either. I tried for levity, saying, "My mistake. Finish your crack pancakes before they get cold."

But the moment was gone.

I swore privately. I didn't have time to fuck around and play these games. One wrong move and I was screwed.

My cell buzzed with a text.

All set for tonight. Is your plus-one going on the block?

Any other time I might've laughed at the innocent question, but I was too irritated at myself for the stupid mistake to find the humor. I texted back, Not for sale. But we will be there to enjoy the show.

I could practically see Dillon's smirk as he sent back, Password: Bacchanal.

Katherine hadn't looked up from her plate as she finished quietly. All that progress...down the drain.

Back to the starting point. I tried for something out of my wheelhouse. "I'm sorry. I didn't mean to sound presumptuous."

Katherine inhaled a short breath, taken aback by my apology. I'd offered precious little of those in my lifetime, and she knew it. For the time being, the ball was in her court.

"I know you think I'm going to change my mind, but I won't," she told me quietly. "You have no idea how it feels to have your future decided by someone else—or worse, by committee, which is how it feels knowing our fathers pushed this on us. It wasn't my choice to be part of your family. Our fathers orchestrated this entire thing for professional gain, and I was too young at the time to understand the gravity of what it meant. I was sixteen when I signed that contract, for God's sake!" she hissed, running a hand through her hair. "But I'm not a kid anymore. What your family and my father did to my life…it wasn't right."

Discomfort mixed with annoyance flashed through me. I hated talking about the contract. I'd had nothing to do with it, and I hadn't been given a choice, either. The Donatos and the Olivers had been allies in business for years, and our fathers wanted to ground that in something solid and binding—the marriage of their children. I was the Donato company heir, but Katherine's father felt he didn't have one, especially after his wife died. Bernard could've offered Katherine a chance to take over the business. Instead, he'd archaically— with my family's help—groomed her to be a rich man's wife. And ensured it with the contract. Oh, she'd have a career, but she wasn't meant to be a CEO. Any children of ours—any sons, our fathers would insist—would inherit both companies and keep them running aligned for years to come. The situation wasn't pretty, but it was the situation we were in, and while I sympathized with Katherine, I couldn't lose her.

"Look, you've already conceded you haven't been mistreated. And you act as if arranged marriages aren't common in certain circles," I said, shaking my head. "Or as if you weren't perfectly amenable to it at one time."

"Yeah, well, I was naive," she shot back, her voice dropping to a harsh whisper, her gaze darting to see if anyone was listening. "Since having time to think about our situation, I came to realize that no one has the right to barter someone else's future. Wouldn't you rather choose your own wife instead of having your father dictate to you who you'll marry?"

The words burned on my tongue to admit that it didn't matter that my father had orchestrated the contract between us—I would've married her without a contract—but I doubted she'd believe me. She would probably think I'd say anything to get what I wanted, which under any other circumstance might be accurate, but I wouldn't lie to Katherine.

"The world we live in isn't like that of normal people, no matter how much you wish it was. This is our life, Katherine," I replied, unable to stop the chill from frosting my tone. I didn't enjoy being schooled, not by her, not by anyone. "And we are not free from our obligations."

"You're hopeless," Katherine said, giving up. "I don't know why I thought you might be different from the rest of your family. Thanks for reminding me that you're cut from the same cloth."

I might have caught the sheen of tears in her eyes or it might've been my imagination, but it didn't matter. Katherine didn't stick around long enough for me to solve the mystery.

CHAPTER NINE

Katherine

IT'S A BLESSING, I told myself, each angry step more force-ful than the next as I left the eatery. Better to know now that Luca still viewed this as an obligation that couldn't be questioned. He was incapable of seeing my perspec-tive, both in terms of the contract and when it came to a lifestyle other than the one we were raised in.

Yes, I went to an exclusive school. Yes, I was blessed with an incredible education, but I'd used that to get a taste of what life was like outside the Donato circles. All through college, I'd kept myself on a reasonable bud-get, not dipping into my trust fund when I went over it. Even when I was desperate for decent food, I told myself other students didn't have that luxury. I wanted to see if I could live more modestly. And it turned out I could.

I wanted to do something worthwhile with my life, not spend it lunching and one-upping each other with mate-rial goods. I wanted to work with animals, find a small, cozy apartment and enjoy love without the expectations and petty judgment of those typical of wealthy circles. I wanted something genuine—not the facade.

At one time, I'd thought Luca was different, too. Before he'd started working for Giovanni. The more time Luca had spent climbing the corporate ladder (granted, he was the heir to the empire, so the climb probably wasn't arduous), the less I recognized him.

He became closed off. He'd put in long days with Giovanni and be too distracted or too worn-out to talk after. The cunning business sense his father bragged about seemed at odds with Luca's compassionate nature. Unlike Giovanni, Luca had a kind heart. Giovanni never would've orchestrated something as touching as Luca's trip to the animal sanctuary because he didn't place any value on sentiment. But not Luca. Luca had always been Giovanni's opposite. Even so, self-doubt weighed on me while I worked through a degree my heart wasn't in. I needed him and he wasn't there.

The incident at the yacht party with that starlet was just the final straw. And when he didn't apologize, it proved his true colors.

I wanted Luca to be different. Maybe that was why it hurt so much that he wasn't.

I wanted Luca to be the man I'd foolishly believed he was when I was younger. Kind, generous, funny… compassionate…

It was foolish to wish he was someone else, but sometimes I thought I caught glimpses—especially when he was out of his usual element—like today, wearing yesterday's trousers, looking wrinkled and adorably disheveled from sleeping in the world's worst bed. And yet somehow still managing to find the most amazing place to eat on such short notice.

Yeah, he was charming when he wanted to be.

But it was all an act. That was the lesson I'd learned years ago, and I didn't really see the need for a refresher course. If I was still that love-struck girl, I'd pin my hopes on the flimsy possibility that Luca had real feelings for me—but I wasn't that girl.

I knew Luca was trying to live up to his father's expectations. Giovanni and my father—not necessarily Luca—wanted this union. That point had been hammered home with painful precision.

It didn't take long for Luca to catch up to me outside the restaurant.

"Caught your second wind?" he joked, his long stride matching my short, angry one. "Are we training for a five-K?"

"Stop, Luca," I demanded, skidding to a halt. "I don't feel like playing this game. We are not friends. We are not lovers. We are *nothing*. Got it?"

"Wrong." He surprised me with a twist of his lips that was both sexy and dangerous at the same time. He closed the distance between us, and I didn't have the good sense to back away. "You are my fiancée until the end of this week. When my time is up, we'll see where the chips fall. Until then, you're my bride-to-be."

I opened my mouth to shoot him down, but he grabbed me by the waist and jerked me to him, stealing a kiss as brazenly as a thief in broad daylight. My knees threatened to buckle. I instinctively clutched his shoulders, my mouth opening under the onslaught of his lips.

Luca's tongue darted, going straight for mine—taking, not asking. The shivers started immediately, mocking my weak protests until they were a memory. This was what I feared most—losing myself to the pleasure that only Luca could give, forgetting why it was crucial that I free myself from the Donato golden cage.

Luca was the jailer, even if he presented me with diamond-crusted handcuffs.

Even knowing all that, I was helpless to stop him, because a part of me desperately yearned for the bliss I found in his arms.

Luca nipped my bottom lip as he slowly pulled away, his grip still holding me tight. "One week, my love," he murmured, my foolish heart skipping a beat at the endearment. "You owe me one week…and the terms are nonnegotiable."

I wanted to blurt, *Screw the deal!* but I didn't. There was something in his eyes that invited no argument. Luca had never been a bully, but neither was he a push-over. Tension pulsed around us, weaving a sultry web, tightening until I could barely breathe. He knuckled my chin, forcing my stare. "Are we clear?"

I swallowed but managed a short nod. "One week."

A slow smile spread across his lips before he dipped to taste me again.

When he released me, we were both breathing hard. It didn't matter that we were standing on a busy city sidewalk, parting people like Moses and the Red Sea as they went around us. For a brief, heart-stopping moment, it was only him and me.

I wiped at my mouth as reality returned. Luca would

use every second of the week to try to convince me to marry him. Perhaps in addition to his need to please his father, it was a game and his pride was on the line. It couldn't possibly be because he truly did love me.

I wouldn't entertain something so foolish.

But I could do this kicking and screaming, fighting the entire way, or I could concede for the sake of a smoother ride to the end. Could I beat Luca at his own game? Could I shut off my heart and play the part of his fiancée, knowing full well I intended to walk away when it was all done?

Honest answer? I wasn't sure. I wanted to be strong enough to follow through with my plan, but there was a part of me that still yearned for what I'd thought I was getting when I was sixteen.

God, I'd loved him so hard.

They always said first love was the most powerful. Win or lose, the experience left a mark. I would bear Luca's mark on my soul until I died.

Dramatic? Perhaps, but there was no other way to explain the hold he had on me.

Time to forget all that. Time to play to win.

"Okay, Luca," I finally said, my tongue darting to taste where his lips had been. "I will stop fighting you on this and play the part of your fiancée until our deal is up. Where to next, *honey*?"

He slipped his hand into mine, answering, "On to Alcatraz, then shopping. I have a few places in mind, and I think you're going to love them."

I forced a smile and allowed him to pull me along, keeping step with his stride.

From the outside looking in, we might've looked like lovebirds out on the town, but I knew the truth.

At least... *I think I do.*

CHAPTER TEN

Luca

I DIDN'T TRUST Katherine to accept our deal without argument for the rest of the week. My fiancée wasn't malleable or meek, and knowing she would tell me to shove it was invigorating.

I know—stupid—but she captivated me in a way I couldn't explain, not to my father, not to myself. All I knew was I would do anything to keep her.

If that meant lying, deceiving, strong-arming… I was beneath nothing, but if she wanted to play games with the master, I'd certainly indulge her. She thought that by playing the part of the sweet fiancée, she'd play me, then walk.

I would never let her walk.

But if she expected me to play fair, she was naive.

My cock hardened at the thought of tonight.

The moment Katherine walked over the threshold of Malvagio, the sensory overload would start.

Sights, smells, sounds—the club was a smorgasbord of consensual debauchery.

Katherine was a powder keg of repressed need. All it would take was a spark and she'd ignite. And I fully planned to be the one holding the match.

Maybe it was playing dirty to push all her buttons at once, but I didn't have the luxury of slowly wooing her. Seduction was my best chance.

Once on the ferry to Alcatraz Island, the wind whipping her hair across her face, I pulled her into my arms to shield her from the bracing cold. She shivered and settled against me, choosing warmth over pride. Her scent teased my senses; her soft behind pressed against my groin. I sprang an erection nearly immediately, and I didn't try to hide it. If anything, I pulled her closer so that she knew exactly how she affected me.

Her sharp inhale told me she knew.

I leaned down to whisper against the shell of her ear, "You have the best ass. The memory of bending you over the bathroom counter…sliding my hard cock into you…it still turns me on to this day."

Katherine swallowed but recovered enough to quip, "Hold on to that… No repeats are scheduled on this trip."

I laughed, knowing she was struggling. Her shallow breath and the restless wiggle of her backside against my cock was evidence enough that she was lying through her teeth, but I enjoyed the chase.

Pressing, I said, "That's a shame. You have the sweetest O face. The way your toes curl and your mouth goes slack, your eyes squeeze shut as your breath is held captive in your lungs…it's the hottest thing I've ever seen. When I jerk off…it's your face I picture."

"Do you kiss your mother with that mouth?" she shot back, her tone breathless.

"I haven't kissed my mother since I was ten," I told her, allowing my mouth to drift down the column of her neck. "But I remember the way you taste. The sweet tang of your pussy haunts my dreams. The way your belly trembles and your thighs quake when you reach your climax…the way you gush, flooding my mouth when you come…your taste is an addiction I can't quite quit."

"Stop," she demanded, but the word was weak at best. "No sex."

"Who's having sex?" I questioned with false inno-cence. "We're just talking."

"But you're talking about sex."

"*Ah*, well, you never said we couldn't talk about sex," I reminded her, neatly snaring my little spitfire with her own words. "Now, where was I? Ah, yes, the scent of you on my cock…teasing me throughout the day, re-minding me of how perfectly I fit inside you…the way you moan, clutching the bedsheets as you come hard… yeah, definitely my favorite memory."

"Luca…"

I ignored her plea. The ferry was moderately full, the nasty weather having put off many of the tourists hoping to see the infamous prison island, but there were enough people to make touching impossible and I wanted to slip my hands down the front of her pants to see if her core was as wet as I believed it would be.

The inability to do as I pleased only heightened the

anticipation for tonight. I savored my own frustration as I continued to stoke hers.

"Do you think of me when you touch yourself?"

Her quick no was telling.

I sighed, tightening my hold around her waist, my thumb lightly stroking her belly over her sweater. "Want to know what I think? I think when you close your eyes at night, your hand drifting down to your dripping pussy, you finger yourself with me in mind. I think you come with my name on your lips."

"You have quite the imagination," she said, glancing around the ferry to see if anyone was listening. "I don't think of you at all."

"No?"

"Nope." She added with a sniff, "I have slept with other men, you know."

I stiffened. "Careful." Unlike my family, I hadn't expected Katherine to remain celibate until I married her, but I didn't want her past lovers rubbed in my face.

But I realized my mistake too late.

"Oh, yes, when I really want to get off, I think of—"

I turned her roughly to face me. "You like to live dangerously," I said, my tone low, daring her to continue. The more I thought of someone else with Katherine, the more I wanted to break something. "Don't let your mouth overload your pretty ass."

Her angelic smile was anything but. "Jealous?"

"Territorial."

"Is there a difference?"

"Jealousy is an emotion reserved for those who want but can't have. Territorial is the need to protect what is already yours." Katherine held my stare, her chin lifting in a subtle motion. Defiance flitted through that expressive face, but she remained silent. "Make no mistake, Katherine, you are mine," I murmured, brushing my lips across hers. "Always."

The tiny shiver in her frame was the only confirmation I needed. She talked a big game, but Katherine was a quivering ball of need, her body reacting to mine with delicious readiness, no matter how vehemently she protested.

"Alcatraz Island," the ferry operator called out, and Katherine wasted no time in scuttling down the ramp, putting distance between us.

But it was the quick glance backward that did her in.

Her cheeks flushed, her beautiful eyes wide, her sensual mouth plump from my kiss…she wasn't running from me. She was running from the desperate hunger she couldn't deny.

A slow answering smile curved my mouth.

Victory was a dish best savored slowly, so as to fully appreciate its subtle nuances.

Tonight couldn't come fast enough.

CHAPTER ELEVEN

Katherine

I DIDN'T KNOW what scared me more—Luca's steadfast assurance that he would win or my fear that I might want him to.

I was grateful for the distraction of the Alcatraz tour so I could get my bearings again. Being pressed against Luca was hazardous to my resolve. The memory of each sculpted hill and valley of his physique was imprinted on my brain. My knees seemed to be made of jelly when he touched me.

But as we walked the tour, our attention drawn to the historical facts of the most infamous prison of its time, the tension coiled in my gut slowly lessened.

"To be locked up in this place…it must've been awful," I murmured, peering into the cell on display, the metal cot with its thin, worn mattress, the saddest thing I'd ever seen. Some of the most dangerous criminals in the United States had been housed here at one time. Luca was similarly engaged with the self-guided tour, his brow furrowed with interest as we listened through our headphones, and I took a private moment to regard him without his knowledge. Why was the man so beautiful? His skin glowed with his Italian heritage; his nose, strong and firm as his jaw, spoke of authority and inborn confidence.

Luca was hard to forget—even harder to push away when he wanted to stay.

But I had to steel myself against the onslaught of feelings that came into play whenever Luca was involved. The fact that he was playing to win only pinched harder. Why hadn't he cared this much when he'd broken my heart?

He hadn't tried very hard at all back then. If anything, he'd seemed irritated by my refusal to believe his thinly patched-together excuse. His clichéd "It isn't what it looks like" had been an insult to my intelligence.

Tears stung my eyes. I wiped them away quickly. Why did I care? I might have wanted Luca's love at one point, but I didn't anymore. Now he was just a threat to my freedom.

I thanked the part of me that was still looking out for my best interests, instead of the part that just wanted to open my legs and feel him inside me again.

The self-guided tour ended, and we found ourselves back at the gift shop. I was prepared to walk back out, choosing not to purchase anything to commemorate this trip, but Luca was on a buying spree.

He grabbed two sweatshirts, a ball cap, several key chains, two coffee mugs and a handful of Alcatraz-themed T-shirts. When I gaped, he just grinned and donned the ball cap with a charming grin, saying,

"This is how places like this survive. Gotta keep history alive." After paying for his purchases, he handed a wad of cash to the astonished docent, tipping the ball cap with a charming "Keep up the good work. The tour was great" before exiting the gift shop.

"Th-thank you," the guide stammered with a delighted smile. "What a generous donation! Alcatraz thanks you!"

I flashed a quick smile and followed him out. "That was unexpected of you," I said, standing beside him on the bluff overlooking the cold Pacific. "How much did you just give as a donation?"

He shrugged. "Just whatever I had in my billfold. Probably five hundred. I think when I get home I'll make a bigger donation. Places like this need support in order to make it."

The crust around my heart cracked a little bit, but I just nodded and left it at that. I suppose it didn't matter if his donation was all part of his scheme to seduce me, because historically relevant places *did* need donations to survive, so I let it be.

The ferry came to return us to the city, and Luca had a sleek town car waiting at the pier.

I was secretly relieved to have a nice place to relax, as the walk around Alcatraz hadn't been a leisurely stroll. Much like everywhere else in San Francisco, it seemed, there were steep hills and the misty air had nearly frozen my lungs.

We returned to the hostel, collected our things and checked out, then we checked into a different hotel, one of Luca's choosing.

The Loews Regency Bridge to Bridge suite was more in keeping with Donato expectations. The view from the private terrace was stunning with the Bay and Golden Gate Bridges both visible on good days. I tried not to sigh with relief at the sumptuous king-size bed dominating the room, but my bones were eager to sleep in all that luxury after suffering through a night in the hostel bed.

I'd almost forgotten how nice Luca could be. Whereas some people with obscene wealth were wretched to servers, Luca was different. Although firm, he always treated them, from the housekeepers to the valet, with respect, and he believed in rewarding those who performed well.

I had to admit, it was a tiny notch in his favor. I abhorred assholes who treated other people as beneath them.

After tipping the bellhop, he closed the door and immediately started making calls, all the while instructing me to enjoy a bath while he handled some business before our dinner tonight.

"I thought we were going shopping," I said.

He paused in his call to say, "Clothes will be delivered within the hour. By the time you're finished, you'll have clothes to wear to dinner."

Of course. I bit back a sigh. I could only imagine what would be awaiting me when I finished my bath. I didn't like the feeling of being dressed up like a doll, but he was already in business mode and anything I said would be a waste of energy.

Besides, it was only for a short time. No matter what

he had in store for me tonight, nothing would change my mind.

The fact was, even if I was in love with Luca—which I wasn't—I would never stay.

The fear that I couldn't go through with the wedding had started six months ago. I couldn't shake the horrible feeling that I'd be walking down the aisle toward someone I didn't trust.

I wasn't hardwired for a business-type marriage. I wanted the real deal, the love and butterflies, the romance.

If we chose to have children, I wanted those children conceived in love, not obligation.

Luca's mother had already started talking about the appropriate timeline for her first grandchild, which had really put me off.

Maybe I didn't want to get pregnant on her social schedule. Maybe I didn't want to have kids at all—I didn't know—but I did know that someone else wasn't going to be in charge of my fallopian tubes.

Luca was expected to take over the family business once Giovanni retired, but seeing as the old grump seemed to sip on the spring water of eternal life, I suspected he'd outlive us all, which meant we'd never escape his influence.

Much like the Donato boys, I'd been raised by a nanny, but from the time I was thirteen, I was invited to the Donato mansion for their social events, which were frequent, so sometimes I felt I knew the Donato home better than my own. Once I turned sixteen, I was invited to private dinners so I could get to know my future husband under the watchful eyes of our parents.

It's amazing what kids can adjust to.

I'm not sure if it was a tragedy or a blessing that I'd fallen in love with Luca on my own.

I sank into the bath, blissing out in the luxury of the massive sunken tub as the jets pulsated beneath my sore muscles.

Walking anywhere in San Francisco was like training for a triathlon, and I was sorely out of shape, if my screaming thigh muscles were any indication of my fitness level.

A short knock at the door interrupted my contented sigh. "Yes?" I asked, wondering what Luca could need.

"May I come in?"

It was stupid, but I was charmed by his courtesy. Luca made no secret that he wanted me, but thus far, we'd avoided having sex. "Y-yes," I answered, my voice catching. I cleared my throat and tried again with a clear yes.

Luca came in, shirtless, I might add, and handed me a flute of champagne—my favorite drink—along with a small tray of chocolate-dipped strawberries.

I grinned, not bothering to hide my excitement at the welcome snack. We hadn't eaten since brunch. He placed the tray next to me and went to the sink to rinse the sweat of the day from his face. My belly tingled as I toyed with an outrageous offer, knowing it was a bad idea, but the allure of danger had always been my downfall.

"If you want to join me, you can," I offered politely. I mean, he had brought me delicious goodies, and it seemed only fair to share the tub before dinner so he could use the jets on his muscles, too. Between last night's awful sleep and then walking around all day, he must be suffering as much as I was.

"You sure?" Luca asked with an uncertain smile that was both endearing and sexy at the same time—*yep, dangerous*. "Aren't you afraid I'll catch an illicit eyeful of titty or I might offend you with my naked body?"

"Your body was never the problem" dropped from my mouth before I could stop it. *Damn champagne, loosening the gears on my jaw, apparently.* "Look, we can be adults. We've already seen each other naked plenty of times, but the bubbles provide a modicum of privacy and you look like you could use the jets, too."

"All right," Luca said with a nod, popping the button on his jeans with a deliberate motion that made all the nerve endings in my body wake up and take notice. I pretended to be unaffected by his seemingly unintentional strip tease and looked away just as he dropped his boxer briefs.

Luca slid into the tub, giving me the all clear with a "Your virgin eyes are safe," the laughter in his voice coaxing a smile from my lips.

His deep sigh as he sank lower into the water did terrible things to my determination, but I'd put myself in this situation, perhaps as a test. I was in a giant bubbly tub with Luca, undoubtedly the sexiest man I'd ever known.

And we were both naked.

Because we were in the tub.

Together.

If I could get through this without succumbing to

my baser desires, I was golden. I could get through the week, no problem.

Oh, Mother Mary. My fingers itched to curl around his cock. If he wasn't hard already, I knew it wouldn't take long. I sank lower into the bubbles so he didn't see my nipples pearling, ready.

I might have overestimated my own strength. My own hubris might've just screwed me harder than Luca ever could.

"Admit it…you hated the hostel," Luca challenged with a teasing grin. I laughed, relieved to draw my focus away from the pornographic thoughts populating my brain. "C'mon, just admit it. I know you well enough to know that, for you, sharing a bathroom with strangers was the worst thing ever."

"I didn't love it… Sort of like dorm life, " I hedged, not quite willing to concede that my booking had been a terrible idea, insisting that the run-down roach motel had a "certain charm." But I couldn't sell the outright lie with any conviction and we both knew it. I relented with a resigned bite into another strawberry. "Okay, yes, I hated the hostel. It was awful, but to be fair, the pictures on the website were far more quaint and boho chic."

"You thought it was going to be like 'glamping,'" he correctly assumed with amusement, and I both hated and enjoyed that he knew me so well.

"Nico told me about that time you and your brothers got the bright idea to try camping behind your house. None of you had ever pitched a tent before, but you refused to ask for help. Nico said you nearly suffocated when the whole thing collapsed in the middle of the night."

"That was Dante's fault. He was in charge of the poles, but he took shortcuts and I was practically brained when the top pole came down on my face. I had a black eye for a week."

"What'd you say you got the black eye from?"

"Sailboat accident," he answered with a grin. "Sounded much better than how it actually happened. Did Nico also happen to share that he was the first to run back to the house like a giant baby, leaving us in the dust? He'd thought a bear attacked the tent."

"He did not share that part," I admitted, laughing. I could believe Nico booking it back to the house, shrieking. "To be fair, he's the youngest. He was probably pretty freaked out."

"We all were," Luca said, sharing my laughter. "You try being woken out of a sound sleep by the sound of tearing nylon and poles clattering all around you. I think Dante pissed his pants."

I giggled at the vision of Dante, the smug prick, wetting himself. "I might enjoy that vision a little too much."

"You and Dante were never close," Luca said, shaking his head.

"He was always so mean."

"Probably had a crush on you. Lord knows, half the guys in your class did—Nico told me. Can't say I blame them... I felt the same way."

Luca's quiet compliment caused a strawberry to lodge in my throat for a brief second. I swallowed, meeting his gaze, shocked, not so much by his admission but because it was the first time Luca had ever shared something so private and real with me.

Luca broke the spell, saying with a crooked grin, "Not a bad first day in San Francisco. Bet your feet are killing you, though."

I jerked a short nod, tangled momentarily in the complicated threads that wound around us.

Luca surprised me by finding my foot beneath the water and gently rubbing the insole. I groaned without thought.

He shifted, murmuring, "Keep making sounds like that and I'll start rubbing more than your feet."

I bit my lip before challenging him to go for it. I was playing with fire, but I'd forgotten how addictive the heat between Luca and me had always been.

When we'd been together, the sexual tension had been off the charts. It was no different now, except everything *was* different.

We weren't young lovers anymore. There were only expectations and family drama between us now. Something Luca had mentioned earlier rose up in my memory, and it occurred to me that I'd never considered how the pressure to live up to Giovanni's expectations might weigh on Luca.

Neither of us had been given a choice in the way we were raised and how we were expected to fulfill our obligations.

"Do you love your father?" I asked.

My question took him aback. "That's an odd question," he said slowly, trying to figure out where my head was. "Do you love your father?"

"No." My answer was simple. "How can I? He's a stranger. My mother died when I was two. Instead of raising me with love within a real father-daughter relationship, he tossed me into the arms of a nanny. I was expected to be polished and pretty so that I reflected well on his image, but I was nothing but a bartering chip to him. When he and your father arranged this marriage, I'd served my only purpose. Why would I love a man like that?"

Luca nodded, a hint of shame coloring his cheeks. Did it embarrass him how I'd come into his life? I knew Luca didn't approve of his father's actions, but he'd been young, too—what choice had he had?

Both of us had been powerless to affect the situation we were put into.

But I wanted to know, did he love his father?

"Pretty deep question for a soak that's meant to be relaxing," he finally answered, his brow lifting in question. When I didn't let him off the hook, he sighed, saying, "I don't know. My relationship with my father is…what you'd call strained. But I suppose somewhere, deep down, I love him. He is my father, after all. He afforded me many opportunities, and he's taught me how to succeed in a cutthroat world. I owe him my respect, if nothing else."

"That sounds like something you'd say about an asshole mentor, not your father."

"He's a difficult man."

I suppose that was a fair answer to an unfair question.

"Let me wash your back," he suggested, changing the subject. I hesitated, but we were already in the bathtub naked together, and it'd been my idea—not sure how I could possibly try to maintain some sort of distance now. I turned around and scooted toward Luca, sliding between his legs.

The soft washcloth on my back felt good. I closed my eyes and enjoyed the simple pleasure.

Then I felt Luca's lips brush against the top of my shoulder and I shuddered with a tiny sharp inhale, the only sound between us.

"Every inch of you is perfection," he murmured, pressing another kiss to the column of my neck. I arched slightly, giving him better access, which he took without reservation. "Your taste, your smell, the way you cry out when you come. You're all I ever think about."

His hands reached around to cup my breasts possessively. There was such hunger in his touch I practically vibrated with the need to feel him inside me. There was something so arousing about the way he held me tight, his palms filled with my tits, the hardened nipples poking out between splayed fingers. He knew how responsive my nipples were. All it would take for me to lose all sense of reason would be for him to latch onto my breasts with that greedy mouth.

"We should get ready," he said against my skin, pressing one last kiss against my bare shoulder as he released me.

I fought to control the rush of disappointment. "Good idea," I agreed with false calm as I scooted away so he could climb out of the tub. This time I didn't avert my eyes. A smile curved my lips as his cock sprang out, hard and ready, from the nest of dark hair.

At least I wasn't the only one suffering.

But this was good, I told myself. Sex would only complicate an already messed-up situation, and it might contaminate my judgment. I didn't want anything to veer me off course.

Eventually, I'd forget how good we were together between the sheets.

Eventually.

CHAPTER TWELVE

Luca

DRESSED IN A sharp black suit, my shoes gleaming in the soft light, I'd just finished straightening my cuff links when the door opened and Katherine emerged. I'd been waiting for her to finish her hair and makeup, which had given me time to assemble her wardrobe choices for the night.

Fluffy white towel wrapped around her, Katherine stared, her mouth dropping at the glittering diamond accessories that accompanied each outfit choice. I wanted to ensure she had the pick of whatever style she wanted, so I'd had my assistant send samples from every designer in the city and had those matched with appropriately decadent jewelry choices.

Diamonds, rubies, emeralds, pearls, sapphires…it was an assortment of breathtaking jewels fit for a queen. The Donato name carried enough clout that I was able to get the gems on loan for the evening, likely because the jeweler hoped I would purchase at least one of the offered beauties by morning.

Katherine stood at the edge of the bed, staring down at the selections. "Are you insane? Where are we going to dinner, the Taj Mahal?"

"You'd be surprised how difficult it is to get reservations," I quipped with a small smile. She glanced up in question, her brow furrowed. "I wanted to ensure that wherever we went, you were the brightest diamond in the room."

She flushed and bit her lip, reluctantly flattered. "But, Luca... I...I don't know what to say except I can't wear any of this..." she said, even as her eyes were drawn to the brilliant sapphire drop pendant that was my personal favorite. She would look stunning in the blue dress with that pendant around her neck.

"Why not?" I asked.

"This is all too much."

"They're loaners for now, and I promise you don't have to accept any gifts you don't want. You like the sapphire?"

Her gaze returned to the gem, blinking as she swallowed. "Yes, but..."

"Then you shall wear it," I said, moving to clasp the pendant for her. It hung like a blue teardrop just above her cleavage, a promise of pleasure to come. I hardened instantly at the thought of Katherine wearing the sapphire and nothing else. My fingers itched to relieve her of the towel, but I refrained. Instead, I said, "And the dress? What do you think?"

She dragged her gaze away from the pendant, looking toward the dress. All she could do was nod, finally admitting, "It's gorgeous, too."

"Excellent." I felt the tension lift from my shoulders. "Do you need help slipping it on?" *Please say yes*, I practically begged with my eyes, but she carefully scooped up the dress and disappeared into the bathroom, closing the door behind her. I chuckled and rubbed the sudden damp from my forehead. If she liked the blue dress, wait until she saw what I had planned for dessert...

When Katherine emerged from the bathroom moments later, the deep blue of the dress clinging to her curves like a second skin, the sapphire pendant winking from her throat, I nearly buckled in an embarrassing display of total weakness.

I'd never met another woman who made me feel the way Katherine did. I was old enough to realize I never would.

With her hair swept up into a messy bun and a little makeup on, she was perfect. Katherine had a natural beauty that most women would kill for.

Frankly, I thought she was gorgeous from the moment she opened her eyes in the morning, bedhead and all, but now was not the time to share that sentiment. She was too skittish yet to hear anything so raw. When she'd been ready to hear it, I hadn't been ready to share, and now we were playing on opposite sides of the field. I suppose I was to blame, but a Donato didn't look backward. *Push forward to victory.*

Unsticking my tongue from the roof of my mouth, I offered a sincere compliment, saying, "Stunning. I'm glad you chose the blue."

She blushed, and her fingers found the pendant. "As

long as I don't get robbed at gunpoint later," she joked. "It's like wearing a giant target on my chest."

"You'll be perfectly safe," I assured her, crooking my arm for her to slip her hand into. We left the room and got into the elevator. In truth, I would tear apart with my bare hands anyone who dared to hurt Katherine. Did that threat extend to my own family? My father was a stubborn bully, but would he actually go through with ruining Katherine if I intervened? I couldn't let him do that. Defying my father wasn't high on my list of desirables, so I'd just have to make sure I didn't lose.

"Are you okay?" Katherine asked, noting the sudden tension in my body. "You have a pensive expression."

"I'm fine," I lied with an engaging smile. "Just wondering how I'm going to keep my hands to myself during dinner when I want to do unspeakably dirty things to you in that gorgeous dress."

She gasped and blushed, but this time she didn't hit me with a disapproving glare. Could it be Katherine was softening? I wasn't about to look a gift horse in the mouth, but I wasn't going to celebrate prematurely, either. We got off at the ground floor and exited the hotel.

"So where are we going for dinner?" she asked as I helped her into the waiting town car. "Although I think I'm too nervous to eat. What if I spill on this incredible dress? I'm such a klutz. What if I end up with a buttered roll between my boobs?"

"Then I would be a gentleman and fish it out." *With my mouth.* At her shy smile, I added, "You're the only woman I know who can find some way to wear her food at some point during the meal." When she started to frown, I hurried to add, "And I find it one of your more endearing qualities, believe it or not."

"I don't believe it," Katherine responded, smoothing the lines from her dress as she settled in her seat. "But you always were a smooth talker. I won't hold it against you."

"That's a plus," I said with a rueful chuckle, returning to the subject of dinner. "Tonight, we have dinner reservations in the private section at Cafe Zoetrope. I think you'll love the ambience."

At the mention of filmmaker Francis Ford Coppola's San Francisco restaurant, Katherine stilled the anxious fidgeting of her fingers on her matching clutch. I pretended not to notice how her breath had become shallow and her eyes had widened. "The actual Cafe Zoetrope?" she asked breathily.

I pretended ignorance. "You've heard of it?"

"I think I read something about it online," Katherine hedged, not willing to divulge her true pleasure at my choice. This woman would concede no easy victories. Under normal circumstances, I would enjoy the challenge, but I needed a win.

"Thank you for tonight," she said, her gaze dipping with a bashfulness that I found incredibly alluring. "You didn't have to do all this, but I appreciate the thoughtfulness."

My pride swelled. Being able to coax a smile from Katherine's supple lips was the best feeling in the world, but it made me greedy for more. I wanted to throw diamonds and whatever else she might want at her feet if it meant earning genuine happiness from her. "It suits you. The blue compliments your skin tone perfectly. You should trust me to always know what will make you shine."

The budding warmth fled from her eyes as she looked away. "I like to figure out for myself what works and what doesn't."

Damn it. My damn arrogance would be my downfall when it came to Katherine. Swallowing my pride, I said, "Of course. I'm humbled that you agreed with my choice."

She shot me a quick, rueful glance as if to say, *You? Humble?* And I wanted to admit, *Yeah, hard pill to swallow, but I'm truly trying.* However, I said nothing. I didn't trust my mouth not to fuck it up.

We arrived at Zoetrope, entering through a private door reserved for VIPs and members of the Coppola family, and were seated at a cozy table surrounded by memorabilia from Coppola's films throughout the years.

In spite of my gaffe only moments prior, Katherine was entranced with my restaurant choice.

"This is incredible," she breathed, her eyes sparkling with wonder. "I love his films and his spirit. This is a man who never gave up on his dreams and goals, no matter that to others he seemed to fail several times. I'm in awe of that kind of grit and talent. And entrepreneurship! I mean restaurant, winery, filmmaker, father…the man is an inspiration."

And I'm in awe of you.

She caught me watching her, her smile faltering before she asked, "How'd you know I would love a place like this? I've never told you about my fascination with Francis Ford Coppola."

"I pay attention to the things that matter to you," I answered. "You own every one of his movies on DVD, and you once mentioned that you wanted to take a trip to California to see his winery." Not to mention, I knew she'd recently sent her résumé to the winery's marketing department.

Her cheeks flushed a becoming shade of pink. "You remember that?"

"Of course."

It'd been a casual comment, but when she'd talked about Coppola, my jealousy had flared. I'd wanted to be the sole reason her face lit up like a Christmas tree. I'd been too young to appreciate that learning what made my woman tick was a gift, but then, I'd fully taken for granted that Katherine was mine and always would be, so I hadn't spent much effort in ensuring she was happy.

The waitstaff, impeccably trained, took our orders and left us to ourselves. The wine helped ease the tension, but I was suddenly agitated. Too many thoughts racing through my head. Too many pitfalls to stumble onto and break my neck.

Confidence had always been my strength, my armor. My fear that none of my usual tricks would work left me flailing with a flimsy strategy, and with the stakes as high as they were, I couldn't afford to make stupid mistakes.

I needed Katherine in my bed, but it had to be timed perfectly. Each time I pushed and pulled away, I drove her frustration higher so that when I finally got between her legs, she'd remember why we were so good together.

Bone-melting orgasms were going to be my secret weapon to cracking open that locked heart.

"When did your fascination with Coppola begin?" I asked, seeking safe ground.

"I don't know when it happened, exactly, but it might've started with the first time I saw *The Outsiders*."

"The movie with Matt Dillon?"

She bobbed her head. "Yep. Here's the thing, it was on late-night television, I was up studying for exams, and I put it on for background noise. But slowly I started to catch snippets of the movie, and before I knew it, I was totally engrossed and bawling my head off by the end. Something about that movie just touched my soul." She risked a short laugh. "I know that sounds corny, but the movie is pure genius, and that, of course, sparked an interest in who directed the film, and I found Coppola. The rest just seemed to flow into a genuine obsession that I can't explain, but it's my guilty pleasure."

It was the first real bit of personal information Katherine had willingly shared all week, and I was eager for more, even if I wanted to be the one who created that megawatt smile instead of an old filmmaker she'd never met.

Our food arrived—*linguine alla vongole* for me and *bumbola ai broccoli e salsiccia* for Katherine—and we enjoyed the culinary perfection of old-world Italian cooking.

"Reminds me of my great-grandmother's linguine,"

I said with a bit of nostalgia. "Nonna was a feisty thing, but, damn, she could whip up a mean table."

"That's the one who lived in Italy, right?"

I nodded. "My father's grandmother Francesca Donato. She died when I was ten, but she made sure to teach her daughters how to make fresh pasta the Italian way."

"Your nonna would've loved Greta," Katherine quipped with a knowing grin.

Our cook, Greta, ruled the Donato kitchens with an iron fist. She was the female version of my father. She believed in old-school traditions and would skin alive anyone who dared to take shortcuts when it came to what landed on the Donato table.

"That she would," I agreed. The stout Italian woman had starch flowing through her veins, but she could make your mouth orgasm with her culinary skills. If Dante kept eating Greta's pasta the way he did, he'd end up fat as a summer tick. Actually, I'd like to see that—the asshole could use something to take him down a peg. I rubbed my belly, suffering my own indulgence. Time to walk off some of this dinner, but first, "Dessert?" I asked.

"God, no." She shook her head and groaned. "I can't fit anything else in my stomach."

"Me, either." I signaled for the check, paid, and we made our way into the brisk night air. Fog had begun to settle. The pale, misty blanket cloaked the city streets with an eerie elegance, but it chilled to the bone quickly. We managed a few blocks before we hurried back to the awaiting town car, our noses tingling with the cold.

"What now?" she asked, curious as she rubbed her hands together to warm them. "We could see a movie... We could probably even find a theater showing Coppola films."

I laughed at her not-so-subtle hint. "As much as I would love sitting in a darkened theater with you, I have different plans."

"Oh? Do tell."

"It's a surprise. I recall that you used to enjoy surprises."

"I was younger then," she reminded me, her expression wary.

"True. I guess you'll just have to trust me."

My next move was a gamble. It could blow up in my face or put her in my bed. What I was about to expose Katherine to was above and beyond anything she could possibly imagine.

I didn't have the option of taking the safe route. It was go big or go home.

We returned to our hotel, and as directed, a new selection of outfits awaited Katherine.

Only this time instead of jeweled necklaces for accessories, there were ornate masquerade-style masks.

"What the hell... Where are we going?" Katherine asked, her gaze roaming the beautiful masks and their accompanying corsets of black, red and purple lace before turning to me for answers, balking openly. "I'm not wearing any of those anywhere in public."

I closed the distance between us with strong, purposeful steps until I was close enough to draw her to me. She melted in my arms even as her gaze remained cautious. I brushed my lips across hers as I murmured, "I can promise you...where we are going is very, *very* private." I released her reluctantly, her lips still dewy from my kiss. "Time to get dressed. We don't want to be late."

CHAPTER THIRTEEN

Katherine

MY HEART HAMMERED in my chest. The lingerie on the bed beckoned with wicked fingers, promising a night that would live in my dreams forever—but was I willing to allow such a memory to exist?

"No sex?" I repeated the question, my throat suddenly dry. "If I wear this...will you still stick to our agreement?"

"Darling, I've been good so far," he reminded me, and I blushed. *Yes, I am the one who's having trouble remembering our deal.* In hindsight, I should've forbidden all kissing when we struck our deal. Too late now.

"I will not fuck you until you beg for it," he returned, but his blue eyes glittered with a secret that I didn't trust and desperately needed to know. Still, I hesitated, afraid that he was going to find a way to put me on my back, in spite of our deal. Mostly afraid because I wanted him to. The tension coiling in my body was enough to crush a Smart car. I craved his touch, craved the feeling of him inside me, pushing me toward that brink of disaster, but I was trying to remain strong. As long as he kept his promise…I could get through this.

"I don't beg," I answered, my fingers trailing across the lacy texture of the black corset, the long garter straps dangling in wait. The accompanying mask was a thing of art. I perused the selections, each more beautiful than the last, but my eye was drawn to the black. I wanted to slip it over my face, to lose myself in the illusion of being someone else, if only for the night. I caught the voracious look in Luca's eyes as I teased my fingers across the fabric of my favorite corset. If anyone would beg, it would be Luca. "And what are you wearing if I'm to wear this ridiculous getup?"

"Nothing quite as beautiful."

The smart part of my brain warned that I should refuse, that wherever Luca planned to take me was a bad idea, but the other part of my brain couldn't quite resist the temptation of finding out.

Curiosity would ruin me; mystery was my Pied Piper.

"Which one should I wear?" I asked coyly, enjoying the subtle bobbing of his Adam's apple. "Do you have a preference?"

"The black," he answered, his voice rough. "The same one that you can't keep your hands from."

"You always did have excellent taste," I murmured, slowly plucking the lingerie from the bed and clutching it to my chest as I headed to the bathroom. "I guess you'd better get changed, then," I said before closing the door behind me.

Was I doing this? Even though I knew it was a bad idea? That I would likely end up with Luca's cock inside

me? I shivered, trying not to buckle at the sheer pleasure of that thought. How could I miss him so much and
yet hate him, too?

You don't hate Luca, a voice whispered. *You're still
in love with him.*

Stunned, I rejected the silver-tongued devil in my
head and carefully removed the exquisite designer dress
to change into the equally gorgeous lingerie. The steel-
boned corset accentuated my waist, flaring my hips,
pushing my breasts up like an offering, my nipples
barely covered. In fact, the dusky rose of my areolae
flirted with the edge of the lace trim purposefully. One
slip and my nipples would pop free, hard and pearled
for Luca's hungry mouth. I caught my breath, my fingers shaking as I snapped the sheer garters into place.
I pulled out the pins holding my hair in place. Waves
tumbled to my shoulders, and I fitted the mask to my
face. My lips, red as sin, pouted and promised ruin. This
was insane. I was in dangerous territory, but the secret
thrill at my image in the mirror was far more powerful
than any voice of reason.

Drawing a deep breath, I opened the door and found
Luca waiting. He'd changed into sleek, soft leather pants
that on anyone else would've looked corny and trying
too hard, but on Luca they looked absolutely sinful.

His shirt, casually sexy, was slightly open, hinting at
the hard, muscled chest hiding beneath. My own breath
hitched in my chest as warmth flooded my pelvis. If he
slipped a finger inside me, he'd find me wet and ready.

"You're fucking gorgeous," Luca muttered, almost as
if he were angry, but I knew it was simply raw, primal

lust that roughened his tone. I knew without needing to touch that he was rock hard. I could practically feel the sexual pulse between us like a desperate heartbeat. His searing gaze left scorch marks on my soul. "Shall we?"

He produced a long, elegant trench coat for me, slipping it over my shoulders before clasping my hand in his and leading me from the room to the car.

My gaze kept drifting to Luca in question. The mystery of our destination was more than I could stand, but I savored the torture.

We pulled into a dark alley and exited the car. I remained close to Luca, the area looking sketchy as hell. He knocked on a door that I hadn't even realized was there, and a small panel opened as two eyes peered out. "Password" was all the voice said.

"Bacchanal," Luca answered calmly, and the peephole shut with a rusty click as the door opened, revealing a hulking man with a bulbous nose and a mean-eyed squint, but he stepped aside so we could pass.

We traveled a long hallway until we turned a corner, revealing the most incredible view I'd ever seen—a private world of tits and ass, throbbing music and open sexual acts happening in full view of anyone who cared to watch.

"What is this place?" I asked in shock, my gaze riveted to this buffet of sensuality.

"Welcome to Malvagio, my love," he answered with a broad grin. "Where anything goes as long as it's consensual."

"This is a...sex club?" I managed, still staring, my gaze snagging on a woman on her knees sucking a man's cock as if her life depended on the come jetting down her throat. She was naked, aside from the tiny pasties attached to her nipples and the thong that barely covered her pussy. I should've been horrified. Disgusted, even.

But I wasn't.

There was something intoxicatingly exciting about the taboo place. Everywhere I looked there was something illicit and forbidden happening right before my eyes.

After spending my life under the shadow of who I was supposed to become...the idea of being whoever I wanted within these walls had my heart hammering with instant arousal.

Damn Luca for knowing my secret perverted heart.

Luca graced me with an inquiring look as if to ask, *Shall we stay?* and I gave him a small nod and tremulous smile in answer.

The sensual energy in the club twisted a knot around my senses as we wound our way through the crowded dance floor to a raised section where a table awaited us. Luca seemed comfortable, familiar even, with the place, and I immediately had questions I shouldn't ask.

The puffed burgundy leather booth was grotesquely ornate, ostentatious and borderline in poor taste, but that was what made it perfect for the surroundings. Everything bore a decadent yet used quality that spoke of the hedonism found in this place. I couldn't stop staring, my breath suspiciously shallow, as I was bombarded with sights and sounds that were usually reserved for private moments.

A tall, broad-shouldered, dark-haired man with a curvy woman on his arm approached with a knowing grin. "Fucking Luca Donato, you son of a bitch, you came after all." He clasped Luca's hand and pumped it vigorously before they embraced in a man hug.

"Dillon Buchanan," Luca returned with an equal smirk before turning to the curvaceous woman with a respectful bow. "And you must be the woman who made an honest man out of this asshole."

Dillon beamed, making introductions. "My beautiful wife and business partner, Penny. Penny, this is Luca Donato. We used to run together back in the day."

"I won't hold that against you," Penny promised with a sweet smile before turning to me. "And you are...?"

Luca answered before I could. "My fiancée, Katherine," he said.

I quickly followed with "Pleasure to meet you," before shooting Luca an uncertain look. It was obvious Luca and Dillon knew each other from connections I had no access to. I had so many questions, but now was not the time to ask, and besides, they seemed very nice, in spite of the surroundings and the fact that I could almost see the woman's nipples overflowing from her tight bustier. I shifted a little, knowing my nipples were similarly in the danger zone of popping out.

Well, when in Rome, I guess.

"Pleased to meet you," Penny said, looping her arm around her husband. "Are you here for the auction?"

"The auction?" I repeated, confused. "What is that?"

"Darling, don't ruin the surprise," Dillon admonished when he realized I was clueless. To Luca he said,

"I'll have some champagne sent over. If you need anything, don't hesitate to drop my name."

The Buchanan couple left us, and I immediately turned to Luca. "What the hell is the auction? You're crazy if you think you're selling me to the highest bidder in this place."

He laughed as if my fear was absurd. "You should know by now I don't share."

I relaxed a little. "So, what is it, then?"

"Malvagio is very exclusive, very difficult to get into. Prospective members must earn a sponsor. Tonight, the hopefuls will step on the stage in the attempt to snag someone's interest. It's quite entertaining. I didn't know the auction was tonight when I called Dillon, but I think you'll find it worth a watch."

An auction where people hoped to be bought. What a foreign concept. I'd been bartered in a business transaction before I'd understood the meaning of the word, and yet the people here *wanted* to be bought.

Luca sensed my disquiet and leaned over to whisper in my ear, "Darling, it's all a game. A consensual game where the ultrarich get to pretend and forget their obligations for a night. No one is truly bought and sold." I relaxed until he amended his statement, saying, "Actually, that's not entirely true. Once a sponsor makes a purchase, that person is obligated to please their sponsor in any way they choose for a year. It's all in good fun, though. No one is asked to do anything against their will or comfort level."

It all sounded reasonable, except I imagined that their comfort level and mine were vastly different.

"Have you ever…sponsored someone?" I asked, though I didn't know why it mattered.

"No." I couldn't hide the whoosh of air released from my lungs, and he laughed. "Aw, if I didn't know better, I'd say my woman is a bit jealous."

"Don't flatter yourself," I replied, but the burn in my chest at the idea of Luca pleasuring anyone aside from me was telling. It also ignited a memory I'd rather forget. I settled against the plush cushions. "So, what now?"

"Now we wait for the show to begin." The champagne arrived, and he handed me a glass. "How about a toast?"

I raised my glass. "What shall we toast?"

"New beginnings?" he suggested with a cheeky grin, which I immediately countered with a brief smile.

"Closure."

The glitter in his eyes told me he wasn't pleased, but I didn't care.

I would prove to Luca that it would take more than our sexual chemistry to make me forget why I needed out of my contract.

But as I sipped my champagne, the bubbles tickling my nose, my masked gaze watching the people on the floor writhe and move to the music, a strange exhilaration loosened my inhibitions.

Tonight, hiding behind my mask, I was free to do as I pleased.

Perhaps that even meant allowing myself to have sex with Luca, one last time.

Maybe.

CHAPTER FOURTEEN

Luca

THE LIGHTS DIMMED and the crowd roared as a voice over the loudspeaker announced the beginning of the auction. All eyes went to the stage as the thick velvet curtains rose, and one after the other, the hopefuls walked the stage, the announcer listing their attributes.

"Carli is a sweet girl from a good, upstanding family in Rhode Island, but when she's not volunteering to help orphaned animals, she's taking it up the ass! That's right, Carli loves a fat cock up her ass. Who would like to plug this lovely beauty tonight? The bidding starts at ten thousand!"

Katherine giggled and clapped her hand over her mouth in delighted shock. "I can't believe this is happening. Do they write their own stuff or is this just made up?"

I shrugged. "Who knows? All I know is that just as her real name isn't Carli, I doubt any of these people do any volunteer work. Malvagio is all about satisfying the most jaded of appetites, if you know what I mean."

Katherine nodded and her eyes sparkled as she watched the carnal show. One after the other, women, all impeccably groomed and fanatically physically perfect, walked the catwalk, their talents shared with the potential sponsors.

Once the sponsor made the purchase, a golden collar was clasped around their necks, then they were led off the stage by a thin gold chain to do whatever they were asked to do.

By the end, our bottle of champagne was gone and Katherine was itching to dance.

I laughed as she grabbed my hand and dragged me to the dance floor.

Closing her eyes, she lost herself to the beat of the music, her hips swaying and grinding, a visual that nearly had me busting a nut right there on the floor.

God, she was hot.

Appreciative, and some downright hungry, glances were thrown Katherine's way, but she was oblivious, which worked in my favor, because that meant she also didn't catch the *back the fuck off* vibe I was sending to the wolves in the den.

Katherine looped her arms around me, each part of her body a perfect fit with mine, and I knew she felt the erection in my pants, but she simply laughed—the sound like gasoline on my raging libido. "Is that a banana in your pocket or are you just happy to see me?"

My strained chuckle was my only answer as I ground against her. I wanted to bury myself inside that sweet pussy—that wet haven I wanted all to myself. The restraint it took not to drag her to a darkened corner was almost more than I could bear.

But when she reached down to cup my shaft through the leather, my knees threatened to collapse. "What are you doing?" I asked, hardening even more, if that was even possible. I feared my skin would split in two at this rate.

"Probably what I shouldn't." She lifted on her tiptoes to kiss me, her tongue darting against my lips, teasing. "But then, you know that."

I whirled her around so that her ass was against my cock, holding her in place by a firm hand on her belly. Against the column of her exposed neck, I murmured, "Careful, baby girl. You're playing with fire."

"I know you want to fuck me," she dared, pushing my buttons. "And I know you think you're going to seduce me into leaving with you at the end of the week."

"And if I did?"

"Then you'd be wrong," she said, but when I surged against her, she gasped. Still, she managed with a certain "Even if I slept with you against my better judgment, breaking my own rules…it wouldn't matter. I'm not going home with you."

I growled, tightening my grip on her. "Then why tease me like this?"

"Because I miss the feel of you inside me," she admitted breathlessly, and that was all I needed. She thought it would be so easy to fuck me and walk away? She'd obviously forgotten how electric our chemistry was. *Well, guess it's time to remind her.*

Her hand in mine, I pulled her away from the dance

floor, up the stairs and down the hall to the private rooms. The doors were coded, and I knew the Buchanan men had a private room that only they were allowed to access.

I also knew their code.

Bypassing the dungeons designed for those who enjoyed BDSM, I went straight to the Buchanan suite and punched in the code, knowing ahead of time that the suite would be empty and available.

We were seconds across the threshold with the door locked behind us when I hoisted her into my arms and her legs wound around my waist as if they belonged there.

Feverish to taste and touch, we were both out of control. The burgundy walls, black decor and giant bed in the center of the room were a blur as we stumbled out of our clothes. Her soft skin, etched by the boning of the corset, trembled beneath my fingertips as I laid her on the black satin bedding.

Her hair fanned out, long, wild tendrils that begged to wrap around my hand. I reached for her mask, but she stopped me. "Leave it," she said, and I nodded. I would eagerly agree to anything she wanted tonight. I was so desperate to taste her again, to feel her close around my cock, to hear her moan my name as she came.

I slid the thong from her thighs and tossed it away. Her sweet pussy, tantalizingly bare, beckoned with a dewed slit. I licked my bottom lip, nearly insane with need. My heart almost stopped when she slowly opened her legs for me, inviting me in, spreading herself like an offering.

It was like a fevered fantasy materializing before my eyes. I knew her body so well, from the location of each mole or freckle to the delicate folds that hid her bashful clit.

"Jesus," I breathed, taking a moment to simply stare at the woman who'd become everything to me. Fuck everything else in life. I trembled with the urgency to taste her, to know her again. I wanted to sear the unique flavor of her into my brain so that all I had to do was close my eyes and be right back in this moment, my face between her thighs.

A moan escaped my lips as I nibbled that sweet, swollen nub. Tiny pulses beneath my tongue danced in time with her gasps, drawn breaths and keening cries.

"Luca!" she groaned as my tongue played and teased, my fingers sliding into her honeyed pussy as she dripped with need. I lapped at her sweetness, the musky feminine scent driving me into a raw, primal state where only one thing mattered—Katherine.

I wanted to taste every inch of her. I wanted to know how she'd changed, how she'd remained the same.

I'd introduced her to pleasure, but years had passed since that time in our lives. I was eager to show her the difference between a foolish young man and a man who'd learned the importance of patience and timing.

I wanted her to moan my name until the ringing echo of the pleasure I could give her obliterated the memory of anyone else.

Maybe I didn't have the right to believe she would always be mine—that I'd taken something so precious for granted—but when it came to Katherine, I wasn't interested in playing fair or following society's rules.

Pushing her to the edge of climax, just when I knew she was about to come, I slowed my attention and her tiny groans of desperation made me smile against her damp flesh. "So greedy," I murmured, relishing the way her body spasmed and her legs quivered. As soon as she caught her breath, I started again, slipping a finger deep inside, strumming her G-spot.

"*Oh*, God," she gasped, arching, her fingers digging into the bedding. "I can't… I can't handle it…" she pleaded, sucking air, her beautiful breasts heaving, nipples tightening. "Luca!" And then she gushed in my mouth, shattering completely.

I lapped at her, in carnal heaven. I could have buried my face between her folds and died a happy man, but I was greedy for so much more.

I climbed her body, pausing to suck a taut nipple before moving to her mouth. I wanted her to taste herself on my tongue, the unique flavor that drove me insane with need and want.

She groaned, clutching at me as I plunged my tongue into her mouth. "You taste that, baby?" I grinned against her mouth as she gasped. "That's all you, and it's hot as fuck. I love the way you taste, woman."

I swallowed the small whimpers coming from her open mouth as she recovered, her thighs splayed open as I maneuvered myself to her opening. I delved into the small bowl of complimentary condoms, sending foil packets bouncing to the floor as I fished for one. I sheathed myself with shaking fingers and then slowly fed my shaft into her slick opening.

She clasped around me like an oiled glove. My eyes rolled back as a groan escaped my slack mouth. Raw heat enveloped my cock, searing my nerve endings with intense pleasure.

Katherine clutched at me, her legs locking around my waist, driving me deeper.

"I'll never get enough of you, Katherine," I said, my voice strained as I railed her without control. She drove me insane. The suave lover had left the building and in his place was a rutting beast, but Katherine took each thrust with wild abandon, crying out, urging me on.

"Yes, Luca!" she moaned, arching against me, squeezing me from the inside, milking my cock for every drop I could possibly give her.

I couldn't hold back any longer. I wanted to last, I wanted to wow her with my sexual prowess, but I was simply out of my head with the need to reclaim what had once been mine.

I came with a shout, my hips thrusting on autopilot as I emptied myself, jet after jet. If only that fucking thin piece of latex weren't between us. I wanted her dripping with my come. I wanted to watch as it slid from her core and dribbled down her legs, so I could slip my fingers inside her, knowing I'd filled her completely.

Primal, territorial pride suffused my chest as I continued to thrust against her even as I was beginning to soften. Her tiny whimpers were like embers landing on tinder, igniting fresh sparks.

I could spend my life buried inside her, fucking her

until we were old and gray and prone to breaking a hip if we fucked too hard.

"Luca." She breathed my name, soft and fluttery as butterfly wings. My breathing harsh, I held her tight, afraid to let go. Being inside her again, feeling her clench around me—I knew if I couldn't make this work between us, I'd never feel this way again.

There was no one but Katherine for me. I wanted to tell her—to bare my soul in a way I'd never tried—but the words were stuck in my throat.

Maybe if I told her what a jackass I'd been to dick around the one person who'd known me best, the one person who'd loved me unconditionally, she might see fit to forgive me. No more manipulations or carefully thought-out seductions for the sake of winning. Just me and her, naked, rediscovering one another as lovers should.

Just do it. Open your mouth and say the words she needs to hear.

But I couldn't. I was pussing out.

Ah, hell. Katherine needed to learn to move on from the past, right? I would give her the world if she'd let me…but I couldn't fucking apologize for something that had never actually happened.

Yeah, the thing was, I'd never cheated on her, but I was guilty of something else.

When that pictured had blown everything up—I'd been relieved.

We were too young, and everything was happening too fast.

I knew Katherine had fallen hard for me, and I was

getting there, too. But Katherine still had college to get through, and I never wanted her to regret marrying me too young.

So I'd been fucking relieved when I'd inadvertently blown everything to shit with one stupid decision.

I thought with time we'd laugh about it, maybe even joke on our wedding night about how young and stupid we'd been.

I never expected our breakup to be the catalyst that propelled Katherine right into the decision that she was through with everything associated with our lives before that moment.

Including our engagement.

CHAPTER FIFTEEN

Katherine

TINY PULSES ECHOED in my body, every nerve ending alive. The satin beneath my skin, the scent of our lovemaking—everything seemed more intense, more vibrant.

How could I ever hope to be free of Luca when I knew I would forever be addicted to this feeling? Luca was in my soul, marked from the moment I gave myself to him at eighteen.

Malvagio was the epitome of sin and ruin wrapped elegantly in luxury, drugging me with its promise of secrets and anonymity. Nobody would know what we'd done here, on this bed, except me and him.

The freedom to breathe for the first time in months overrode the faint voice of reason, telling me to stop whatever was happening between us before it became a runaway train.

I pulled off my mask, my heart still fluttering like a butterfly on meth. When I finally could talk without sounding Marilyn Monroe breathless, I asked with a curious yet sated smile, "Why did you bring me here?"

I didn't regret what'd happened, even though I'd sworn on a thousand Bibles it wouldn't. A part of me had desperately wanted to be in Luca's arms. No matter what it would cost me. Therein was the crux of the issue. What I was trying to escape wasn't so much Luca, but myself. How could I respect myself if I sacrificed my will and dignity just because I couldn't end this ridiculous obsession with Luca Donato? The answer was simple—I couldn't. "Seems a lot of effort to go to just to have sex."

"Sex with you is never too much effort."

I shivered at the sensual caress of his answer.

"What if I told you that I wanted you to experience something dangerous yet safe, something that you would never forget no matter where life took you from this moment? I wanted you to be free to experience something unique, something only I could provide for you."

My breath caught as I searched his gaze. As if I could ever forget.

Who was I kidding? The writing had been on the wall from the moment I agreed to his deal. Maybe a part of me had always known, as well. "You always knew you would get me into bed. Your confidence never wavered. Why does it matter to you so much?"

"Because you're mine and you always will be."

I think the words came out of his mouth before he realized they were coming. Maybe it was on his mind and he'd just lost the ability to hold them back, but the effect was a punch to the face for both of us.

"I don't belong to anyone, least of all you." I started

to leave the bed, but he grabbed my arm and pulled me back, unwilling to let me leave without saying his piece.

"That's not what I meant. If you want me to say that I'm unhappy you were chosen as my future wife, I would be lying. You have always and will forever be the one that I want."

My breath hitched in my chest as an unwelcome emotion crowded my reason. "Why?" I asked, even though I didn't want to hear his reasons for fear of falling all over again for the man I needed to run from.

"Why does there have to be a reason? Why does there have to be a logical explanation? You, of all people, should understand that sometimes emotion and feeling do not correspond with logic and reason. It's true I could have my pick of any woman in society—there are plenty of well-heeled women who would not only throw their daughters at me but also pin their hopes on landing a Donato in some fashion—but I'm not interested in them."

How many times had I hoped and wished to hear those very words from Luca when I was hopelessly in love with him? When I'd been that starry-eyed girl believing everything that came out of his mouth. But he'd shown me that words were easy, actions were hard.

"Luca, you have always been very eloquent with your words. Doesn't mean I believe them. Not anymore. Have you forgotten? I know you better than anyone."

He surprised me with a firm shake of his head. "No, you *knew* me. The person you remember was a foolish boy who didn't understand the value of things or people. I'm not that person anymore, but you're determined to keep stuffing me into that tiny box for *your* comfort level. If you gave me the chance, I could show you that I've changed."

I regarded him intently—questions racing—while digesting his statement. Was I being foolish and narrow-minded by refusing to let Luca in a second time? The stakes were so much higher now. I wasn't just risking a broken heart; I was risking my future. Once I took those vows, I would never be able to walk away from the Donato family. *Ever.* They didn't believe in divorce. It was death do us part.

"I want to marry you, Katherine," he said, breaking into my thoughts. "I want to pledge my life to you and give you everything you deserve. All you want to do is run without even giving me a chance."

"I did give you a chance—you ruined it."

Luca's grunt of frustration grated on my nerves. I wasn't the one being difficult.

"Stop living in the fucking past. I told you, I was a kid. I wasn't ready to settle down and I hurt you. All I can say is I'm sorry."

"So you're saying now you're ready to be a faithful partner?" I didn't buy it. He could talk all he wanted and fill my head with pretty lies, but it wouldn't change the truth. Donatos followed their own code of conduct, and it was biased toward the family. They did not bend to the will of another person, and they did not take other people's feelings into consideration. "Luca, there's a reason the Donato family has managed to carve a permanent place in the top echelon of society. I'm not stupid, and I'm not blind. I know the Donato family is feared *and* respected. I also know that I don't want to be part of that anymore."

Luca looked as if he wanted to shake my head from my shoulders. I could understand his frustration, as he wasn't used to being denied, but I would never be the wife he wanted.

"Jesus, Katherine," he muttered, shoving his hand through his hair. "Why is it always the same damn argument?"

"Because you never listen to me," I returned, folding my arms. "Trust me, I'm doing you a favor."

"How so?" he asked, as if humoring me.

I tried not to bare my teeth at his condescension. "I will never be the subservient, doting wife who walks two steps behind you and defers to your judgment in any and all things like some modern-day geisha."

"I never said I wanted that!"

I startled at his sudden shout.

His nostrils flared as he cast me a dark look, but I wasn't backing down.

"That's how your entire family works," I said. "You've been raised to take over the Donato family empire. How can I know for sure you'll be any different? There's an expectation, and I have no interest in fulfilling the role of your wife under those conditions."

"And what if I said screw the traditions? I just want you. I want you in whatever way that you would be willing to have me."

My mouth opened in surprise. Was that a hint of desperation in his voice? Couldn't be. Luca was always in control, always pulling the strings behind the scenes.

Luca took my silence as an opportunity to jump in. "Let me show you the man I can be. Let me show you how it can be between us. All I want is you by my side, and if that means bucking tradition and forging a new way for the Donato family, I am willing to do that. But you have to be willing to give me a chance."

Everything he said was true. I was afraid of giving him the chance to prove me wrong. If I admitted that he had changed and that there was a possibility that he and I could actually ride off into the sunset, happy, just like I'd always hoped and dreamed, it would mean taking a chance on an unknown future where anything could happen—both good and bad. Luca had the power to destroy me completely. I was afraid of taking a chance, of giving him the keys to my happiness.

But a part of me desperately wanted to run straight to his arms, close my eyes and allow everything that Luca was envelop me. I knew it was a contradiction, but when I was with Luca, I felt safe. In those moments, I knew that Luca would never let anything happen to me, that he would destroy anyone or anything who threatened me. The irony was that he was the one who had hurt me in the first place.

I should have stuck to my guns and just kept him at a distance. Sex clouded judgment. My body still echoed with his touch—I could smell him on my skin.

"Luca, if I were to give you the opportunity to show me how different you are, what would we do?" I asked, unsure. I was walking on an iced lake, each step a gamble, but a part of me wanted to believe in the fairy tale, if only for tonight.

"Anything you want," he answered without a hint of artifice or manipulation.

Fear and uncertainty fought a battle with hope and longing. Was I willing to see Luca differently? Was I willing to put my heart on the line for a second time when the stakes were so fucking high?

"Say yes," he urged, my entire future riding on one seemingly small choice. "Say yes, Katherine. *Please.*"

"I'm afraid," I whispered. "What if you hurt me again?"

"I won't."

"You don't know that."

"Let me show you."

Luca held my gaze as we both held our breath. The energy in the room swirled with possibility. I swallowed. My brain knew the right way to respond, but my lips were moving before conscious thought could stop them.

"Okay, Luca…"

And it was done.

Brain, zero. Heart, one.

CHAPTER SIXTEEN

Luca

I IGNORED THE pinch of guilt as I gathered Katherine into my arms, squeezing tight. I had broken through the first barrier. Someday she would realize that this had been the right choice.

"Thank you," I murmured against the crown of her head, inhaling the citrus scent of her hair. "I will show you that I'm a different man."

That part wasn't a lie. I wasn't the same kid who had carelessly broken her heart without realizing the depth of his consequences.

Of course, in some ways that was a good thing and in some ways it wasn't. I knew the value of having solid people in your corner, but I also knew that you couldn't always afford honesty.

But for now, we were cocooned in Malvagio's nest of iniquity, safe from prying eyes and free to be whomever we chose.

And in this moment, I chose to be her willing everything.

I rose and poured cold artisan water into frosted glasses for us both. She accepted the water and finished it with greedy gulps and a satisfied sigh. "Perfect," she murmured with a smile as I agreed.

Once finished, I climbed back into the bed and pulled her close. I would worship her body many times tonight, but for now I was content to just hold her.

Her arms closed around me as her head nestled on my chest.

"Tell me about this place," she said with a small giggle. "I mean, a sex club operating right under the nose of the snootiest people in society? I would kill to see the looks on some of those snobby matrons if they found out who exactly was a member."

I tapped her nose playfully. "That's the point—they never will. Malvagio's member list is a closely guarded secret. That's why it's so difficult to get a sponsor and even more so to become a member."

"So what's the point? All this cloak-and-dagger, secret passwords, anonymity…it's kinda silly, don't you think?"

"Of course it is, but as you know, the wealthy bore easily. Malvagio plays to their twisted sense of privilege, and the Buchanans were brilliant enough to take advantage."

"How do you know the Buchanans?"

"Dillon and I met in grad school. Jesus, he was crazy. I never saw a man treat his body the way he did and not die as a consequence. But he dropped out of grad school before getting his degree—something about his old man cutting him off. We lost touch until a few years later, when I saw him by chance in a bar, still abusing his liver with impunity, but he'd changed from a reckless asshole to a ruthless prick who'd amassed quite a fortune on his own, without his daddy's money. I was fucking impressed."

"That is impressive," Katherine agreed.

"I was happy for him. His dad…what a piece of work. You think my father is an overbearing dick? Dillon's father made my father look like Santa Claus."

Katherine looked up at me. "Seriously? That's pretty bad."

"Yeah, the Buchanans got all messed up. Honestly, I don't even know how Dillon managed to find a woman like Penny to straighten him out. All the Buchanan boys have changed for the better, but damn, I never would've thought it could happen."

Katherine cast a dubious glance my way, saying, "Well, they do own a clandestine sex club—they can't be all that lily-white and reformed."

I laughed. "True enough. I guess they were lucky enough to find accommodating women."

"I guess so."

She traced a small circle around my nipple, causing it to perk immediately. I sucked in a tight breath. "Careful, or you're going to get fucked again."

"I'm not complaining," she answered coyly. "If there's one thing you do well, it's what you do in bed."

"Perhaps I should put it on my résumé."

"Perhaps."

I resisted the urge to push at my growing erection. Any touch would only make things worse. I tried to focus. Clearing my throat, I said, "The club was actually started by Nolan and Vince, Dillon's twin brothers. Dillon only just recently acquired the club when Nolan decided he no longer wanted to be in the sex club business. Actually, it was his wife that suggested he find someone else to run the club, and he was eager to make her happy."

"You mean his wife didn't like her husband running a sex club? Go figure," she said, chuckling.

"The Buchanan boys are the most wild, lecherous, fun-loving perverts I've ever known in my life. But once they got married, they became downright respectable. A little boring, if you ask me."

"So you think marriage makes men boring?"

I answered her no doubt calculated question carefully.

"No, I think *they* got boring. I think that if you and I were married, there wouldn't be a boring day for the rest of our lives."

That part was true. I didn't doubt that there would always be sparks and fireworks between Katherine and me. Our chemistry couldn't be faked. There were some people in your life who interconnected with your soul in a way that was rare and precious. I wasn't saying that the Buchanan men hadn't found that—hell, maybe they had—all I knew was that I saw no reason to give up a harmless hobby just because another person said so.

"How long have you been coming to Malvagio?" she asked.

"Over the years, a handful of times. It isn't one of those places where you want to spend too much of your time. It's like eating a finely crafted dessert—too much of it is just too much."

"Have you ever bought someone at the auction?"

"No."

"Why not?"

I chuckled. "Because as much as I enjoy Malvagio, I'm not interested in sponsoring someone into the club. It takes too much time and effort. You have to understand most of the people who frequent this place are trust-fund babies who wouldn't understand the concept of working for a living. I don't have that problem. Boredom has never been my issue. I'm running the Donato empire, so free time isn't something I have too much of."

I enjoyed my captive audience. For the first time in years, Katherine was actually listening.

"And, to be honest," I added with a shrug, "it's fun and games when you're drunk and everyone's naked and fucking, but by the light of day, it's like the mornings at a strip club—sad, run-down and smelling of stale beer and bad decisions."

"This is the nicest strip club I've ever seen," she joked. "But I get what you're saying. It is a little on the sleazy side, but in an intoxicating way. As in, you know it's bad, but you want it anyway."

I laughed. "Dillon will be happy to hear his branding is hitting the mark. That's exactly how it's supposed to be. He doesn't want people trying to live here. It's a place where people can indulge their fantasies, have fun in a safe environment and leave in the morning with a secret. That's pretty much it. And because they don't need the income, the money that the club makes actu-ally goes to help fund a women's shelter."

Katherine lifted her head to peer at me with ques-tions. "What do you mean?"

It wasn't common knowledge, as the Buchanans liked to keep their business private, but sharing this information with Katherine would go a long way toward showing her that I wanted to be different.

"A handful of years ago, someone gained access to one of the Malvagio dungeons and nearly killed a woman named Lana Winters. Lana's sister, Emma, came to Malvagio with the intent of exposing the club but ended up a victim of the same person who'd as-saulted her sister. Vince tried to save the club by help-ing Emma, and they ended up falling in love."

"That's some love story," Katherine said wryly. "And by help...you mean..."

"Oh, Vince totally kidnapped her to keep her from going to the police, but he made sure she had the best care while she recovered."

"He *kidnapped* her?"

The story was not your typical meet-cute, but noth-ing the Buchanans did was ever by the book. I'd learned to just go with it. "But they fell in love eventually," I reminded Katherine, adding when she gasped in femi-nine outrage, "And the incident left an impact on the Buchanan brothers. So they wanted to make sure that even though Malvagio might look like Sodom and Go-morrah at its finest, at the end of the day all proceeds go to help various nonprofit organizations, which are routed through the Buchanan trust, so as not to embarrass anyone."

Katherine lost some of her ire. "I guess that's admirable. What kind of donations are we talking about?"

I laughed. "Let's just say it's more than enough to keep the nonprofits comfortable and doing their good work."

"I guess that's one way to keep the balance," she supposed, pausing to straddle me. Katherine regarded me with an arched brow, her hair tumbling around her shoulders. "And how many women have you fucked in this place, Luca?"

It was a loaded question. "You know there's a law about self-incrimination," I teased, reaching up to tweak her rose-hued nipple. "Surely you aren't asking me to divulge information that might make me look like an asshole when things were going so nicely between us."

"Withholding information doesn't make the truth any less of what it is," she said.

I anchored my hands at her waist, loving the feel of her hips beneath my fingertips. "Are you sure you want me to answer?"

"I wouldn't have asked if I didn't want to know. I have no illusions that you've been celibate all these years, Luca. For that matter, I haven't been, either."

My fingers tightened. Her smile told me she knew exactly what she was doing.

I surged against her, impatient to claim her again, no matter how many men she'd been with. "You really want to know?"

"I do."

"I don't know the number. I never kept track. But I will tell you this," I said, rolling her to her back, rising above her. "You're the only one that matters."

Sealing my mouth to hers, I silenced any further questions about past lovers. I didn't want to know about hers, and I certainly didn't want to share about mine.

I'd been with scores of women across the globe, from wild to mild, but I'd never found a woman who ignited everything inside me the way Katherine did.

In some ways Dante was right—my brother had always maintained that Katherine was not a good fit as my wife. She would never be malleable or dutiful, content to be arm candy, happy to serve my every need. *Thank God.*

I wanted exactly what Katherine was—the exact opposite of whomever Dante and my father thought I should marry.

I kissed her hard and deep, the thoughts in my head crowding the lust in my heart. I didn't want to think about strategy, even though I should.

In truth, if I had never hurt her, she wouldn't have grown.

I know, I was a bastard for saying it, but it was no less true.

If I'd never broken her heart, she wouldn't have been forced to be the woman she was now, the woman capable of standing beside me. The one who would fight with and fight for me—but I couldn't say this to her without sounding like the arrogant ass she already believed I was.

Private epiphanies were best felt by the heart, not forced down your throat.

"You're so damn beautiful," I whispered, my lips blazing a trail down her silky skin, returning to her soft mouth. I drank in her breath as she groaned, our bodies pressed against each other.

"Luca," she moaned as I dragged my mouth down to her molten core. I could taste her over and over and still delight in the discovery of her flavor on my tongue. She sucked in a tight breath as I suckled that tiny, swollen pleasure nub, loving how her hands twisted and pulled at the bedding, her thighs shaking and trembling as I pushed her harder toward her climax.

I lost myself in her shuddering cries, drinking in her pleasure as she shattered beneath my tongue. Before she could recover, I flipped her onto her belly, taking a brief moment to admire the perfection of her ass, then went to reach for a condom, but before my fingers reached the bowl, I hesitated.

It was wrong, but a part of me knew that if I got Katherine pregnant, I'd never lose her. A baby might be the only foolproof way to get her to marry me.

But even as the ruthless Donato creed—Win at All Costs—urged me to simply drive myself unprotected into her womb, I couldn't do it.

Doing so would betray her trust in the worst way, and we'd never recover. If I was going to win her heart, I had to show her that I would never sacrifice her wants and needs for my own.

Not even if it meant losing so *she* could win.

I grabbed a condom and slid it over my erect cock

before feeding my shaft to her hot, wet southern mouth. Her folds swallowed my cock, and I lost myself in the exquisite torture of being inside the woman who was my entire world.

If I were lucky, someday Katherine would give me fine sons, strong, smart and capable. She would grace me with incredible daughters who would keep me on my toes and make me wish for the opportunity to be the man that my little girls would believe I was.

I would not be like my father. I would be kind and loving and adoring to my children.

But that wasn't tonight.

Her hot sheath closed around my cock, a tight, wondrous fit. We were made for each other. I lost myself in the pleasure of knowing that she, in this moment, was completely mine. In this bubble of sheer perfection, hiding within Malvagio's walls, I lost myself in everything that was incredible about this woman. The smell of her musk on the air was sweeter than French vanilla.

I would fuck her raw and give her such incredible bone-melting pleasure that all she could think of was when she would get her next fix. By the end of this week, I would have her so cock-drunk that she would not know where I stopped and she began.

I came quickly with violent spasms, spending completely inside her. Relief that I hadn't made a terrible choice in a weak moment made me cling to her all the more. I'd come so close to fucking everything up before I'd had a chance to show her that I was worthy of being her husband.

Thank you, God, for knocking some sense into me, I thought with a grateful heart.

But I wouldn't lie—the thought of Katherine carrying my child was the most incredibly mind-blowing concept. How ironic that I'd spent my adult sexual history doing everything that I could to prevent an accidental pregnancy, but now I wanted nothing more than Katherine swelling with my child.

I was jumping the gun. I hadn't won her heart yet. I couldn't start registering in the baby department at Neiman Marcus.

At our core we were still animals. Turned on by scent, aroused by the visual cues of a soft pussy and beautiful tits. Katherine was physically perfect in every way. And I didn't mean that in some generic, plastic Barbie sort of way.

I loved that her hips had grown faster than her body could handle. Those tiny silvery lines that she deemed imperfections were absolutely beautiful to me.

And when she swelled with my child, I would lovingly bathe her with any oil or cream or anything she desired just so I could worship her body.

Instead of going through the motions of my mother's silly courtship rituals, I should've been doing exactly what I was doing right now. Loving the shit out of her. Fucking her so hard and so often that all she could think of was me.

Instead, because of my arrogance, I'd half-heartedly followed a stupid plan set up by my parents with the belief that Katherine would come around eventually.

I'd known this woman nearly her entire life, but

maybe I'd never truly known her at all. If anyone was having an epiphany, it was me. I was thunderstruck. And all of this happened in the flash of a blinding orgasm, when everything came together in a giant cataclysm of emotion, physical response and striking clarity.

I couldn't even gasp her name, but I was screaming it in my head. Never in my life had I lost myself like this. It was scary and heady at the same time, but there was something so visceral about the way we came together.

Katherine would have to come to grips with the fact that I would chase her to the ends of the earth and take every opportunity to seduce her into loving me again if need be.

Katherine was hardwired for me, even if she didn't know it yet.

I collapsed and rolled to my back, gasping hard. Neither of us spoke. The faint sound of music from the upper floor was the only sound. The air was dense with the energy we had created together. I knew she could feel it, too. I slowly turned to regard her, waiting.

Something had changed between us. Something deep.

Did she feel it, too? Of course she did. Was that fear I saw in her eyes? No. It was something else, maybe something she wasn't ready to put a name to or define. I caressed her jaw in silent understanding. There was so much I wanted to say, so much I wanted her to know. But it was too soon. Too soon for her to recognize that she and I were meant to be together. And so I simply waited.

When she said to me in a small voice tinged with

happy exhaustion, "I'm starving," all I could do was hold her in my arms with a grateful chuckle, feeling as if I'd just been given the secret to eternal happiness— a redhead with a voracious appetite.

My woman wanted food. Damn straight that was what she was going to get.

CHAPTER SEVENTEEN

Katherine

I WAS FALLING AGAIN. Maybe I'd overestimated the depth of my disdain for anything associated with the Donato family. My own arrogance had led my heart to betray me.

I'd been so adamant that I would never be that stupid girl who begged and scraped for Luca's affection when he grew tired of me. I wasn't so naive as to believe that his interest would never wane.

Rich men were accustomed to having whatever they wanted at the snap of a finger, so when someone didn't fall at their feet, it was the challenge of the chase that interested them, not the actual person.

I'd seen it a million times. The chase was fun, the catch boring.

But Luca's game face was pretty convincing. Even if the small voice in my head kept whispering that it was all a lie, my body insisted what was happening was real.

That shattered part of myself was finally coming back together, puzzle pieces sliding together as if drawn by magnets. I would never forget how this moment felt—no matter if I died an old woman surrounded by cats or if a crosstown bus mowed me down tomorrow.

This was classic addiction behavior, and Luca was either the drug or the dealer—maybe both.

I was better than this. Stronger.

Maybe if I kept telling myself that, I would believe it.

I was losing my mind.

"What if I said I never want to leave this room?" I murmured, no longer in control of what flew from my mouth. I glanced at him quickly to gauge his reaction. I wasn't disappointed.

"I would say that I felt the same way."

The intense truth in his blue-eyed gaze struck me to the core, and I melted fresh.

Damn the Donato charm—it was their gift when they chose to use it. Dangerous if you didn't arm yourself against it.

Even sweet Nico, one of my oldest friends, had broken so many hearts it should be a crime.

But safe in this bubble with Luca, I could savor this moment for the simple pleasure that it was.

I could just wrap my legs around him and be in this moment and nowhere else.

"A quiet woman is a thinking woman," Luca said, regarding me with a subtle smile. "Should I be worried?"

I chuckled, but he was right. My thoughts were racing. I closed my arms around him, snuggling close. I was still going to walk away, but I wanted to savor the way it felt when he touched me, the way my skin ignited, the way my nerve endings came alive—the way my heart stopped in exquisite agony.

We fit together so perfectly, so poetically. I wanted to find someone else who touched me the way Luca did, but I knew I wouldn't.

My previous relationships had all lacked substance and I'd been eager and ready to let them go when the time came, because Luca had always managed to occupy space in my heart, no matter how many times I'd tried to oust him.

"Has the world landed on your shoulders?" Luca asked as he rose to grab a handful of green grapes from a decorative bowl on the marble-topped entry table. He popped a grape into his mouth, offering me one. I chewed slowly, holding his gaze.

Luca knew me so well—my subtle nuances, the things that I wanted to hide.

"I know enough to admit that what we have isn't normal, that our situation was never normal and never would be. What if what I want is something more mundane than what you could give me?"

"Clarify."

Was I ready to jump into the deep end of the pool? I supposed I owed Luca some sort of explanation, some kind of closure. I drew a deep breath and let it out slowly, gaining strength before beginning. "Luca, I don't see myself raising my kids in an environment where extreme wealth is the norm. I want my kids to have a normal life, the life I wasn't given. Now, before you get all pissy because you think I'm judging you for something you couldn't control, just listen to me. I want a normal life for my children, and I don't think you'd recognize normal if it had a sticker on its forehead."

"I'd say normal is subjective," he countered, his gaze narrowing just enough to give away his irritation.

"Did you know that I put myself on a reasonable budget when I was in college? Even though I had access to a trust fund and I could've lived large just like everyone else in our fucked-up little circles, I didn't want to. I wanted to live like a normal student. I learned a lot about life that I was oblivious to before that decision. I had the opportunity to meet people who struggled and yet still managed to make a difference in other people's lives. It made me realize that some challenges were a blessing, and I know you will never understand that concept."

"Good grief, Katherine, don't try to sell a romanticized version of strife to me. Everyone has obstacles, no matter the size of their pocketbook. Your point is both shallow and naive."

I blinked back the sudden hot tears that threatened. Why did his opinion still have the power to cut me off at the knees? Lifting my chin, I continued, undeterred, "Your elitist attitude only proves my point further. Struggle has never been part of your vocabulary, and I'm not saying it's your fault. I'm just saying that I don't want to raise my kids in that environment. And let's be real, Luca, there's no way that you would be willing to live in a modest home instead of a palatial compound that displays your wealth to the entire world just so that your children could live in a way that is relatable to ninety-nine percent of the world."

A wry, almost patronizing smirk toyed with the corners of his mouth as he reminded me, "I backpacked across Europe with nothing more than what I could carry. I've seen plenty of struggle, and I also know there's little to romanticize about it."

"At any given moment, you could've had money wired to you," I refuted, shaking my head. "Not the same. That was just more Donato playtime. You always knew that you could pick up the phone and have a private jet drop out of the sky to pick you up and change whatever situation was happening at the moment. There was no danger, no threat to your well-being. You will never know what it means to have to reach down inside you and pull out grit and raw determination to survive."

"Neither do you."

I stared, momentarily quiet before conceding his point. "Perhaps you're right. I walked away from wealth, but I knew it was always available. I knew that I could access a bank account and get what I needed. I chose not to touch the trust so I could learn how to stick to a budget, and there were times I had nothing but ramen noodles to eat for days because they were the cheapest food I could find and still pay my rent. That's what I'm talking about."

I seemed to have hit a nerve.

"Katherine," he said, his clipped tone accentuating each consonant, "I am trying to drag a company that is mired in the past into the twenty-first century so we can evolve. I'm fighting my own father to let loose of the reins so I can make things happen, but the *son of a bitch* is tenacious as fuck. I don't want my kids used as bartering chips like you and I were. For fuck's sake, I want my kids to know what it's like to simply fall in love with whomever they choose, but I can't do that. Not until I have some control—which my father refuses to relinquish—and the freedom to refashion our business into something we can all be proud of. Dante is breathing down my neck, and my father gets some sick pleasure from threatening to make Dante his heir. So I have to bide my time walking the line between forward progress and whatever my father wants, and chasing after you hasn't helped matters. So, yeah, I know *struggle*, even if I've never had to pick between eating a meal and paying rent."

His impassioned response was more than I'd expected. He so rarely talked about his stresses, I guess I'd convinced myself he didn't have any. I couldn't wrap my head around the possibility that Luca felt the same way as I did—that he wanted something more for his kids.

God, at one point I'd dreamed of our babies. I'd dreamed of what it would be like to look into the eyes of my child and see Luca staring back at me. I held back the tears that threatened to betray the depth of my yearning.

"Luca, I *hate* all of the circles you run with. Most of those people are assholes and entitled bitches. I can't deal with that lifestyle. I want a small house that I can clean myself. I want to do laundry and make dinner. I want to have a career and take care of my own children. When I go on vacation with my family, I want to pile into a minivan and go on a road trip, not some crazy ostentatious private island bullshit. My kids will not attend private school, and they will understand that whatever they want in life they have to work for. Does that sound anything like something you could provide?"

Luca blew out a heavy breath with a defeated shake of his head. "Katherine, what do you want me to say? We were born into wealthy, well-connected families, and nothing can change that. I want to give my kids the best I can provide them with. I don't want them to want for anything. Fine, we'll buy a fucking house in the ghetto someplace so we can raise our kids next to drug dealers and prostitutes."

"That's the point. I don't want them to have everything given to them. Struggle isn't always bad."

Luca shook his head. "I don't see how struggling is good for anyone, least of all kids."

This was going nowhere. "Forget it, Luca. You and I are just too different…and we want different things."

I wanted to get dressed and leave, but Luca wasn't finished.

"Hold up," he said firmly when I moved to shimmy into my panties. "You're not going to withdraw because you're afraid of taking a chance on seeing something different that goes against what you *think* you know. You have to give people a chance in order to determine whether or not they're capable of reaching your expectations."

I ignored his pointed look and grabbed the discarded bustier, crumpled on the floor. "Life lessons aren't exactly in your wheelhouse, Luca. You should stick to what you know. Go acquire some failing corporation and tear it to pieces for scrap. Leave the heavy lifting to those who are qualified."

My barb glanced off without the desired effect. Luca's lip curled with disappointment. "I never realized how cowardly you truly are until this moment."

"Excuse me?"

"You are more willing to run from the possibility of happiness because it challenges some twisted belief you've got locked in your head than take a chance and face the unknown. That's chickenshit."

"Don't tell me what I am," I fired back. "You don't have that right. *You* broke my heart. You are the one who ruined everything. Don't sit there and condescend to me that I'm not the one willing to give people chances, because that's not true. I gave you everything that was mine to give and I loved you, Luca, and you cheated on me!"

Crap! I bounded away from him, jerking on the ridiculous lingerie I'd worn into Malvagio. I felt more vulnerable and exposed than being completely nude. I didn't want Luca knowing that my feelings for him went deeper than I was willing to admit.

"I want to go home," I said, tears crowding my eyes. A mental breakdown felt imminent, or at the very least an ugly sobfest. Emotions, both good and bad, crashed into me like snowballs from every direction. "Luca, now!"

At the near-hysterical note in my voice, Luca sprang from the bed and pulled me into his arms. I wanted to push him away, but my arms had no strength. All I could do was allow him to fold me into his embrace and hold me so tight that all the broken pieces inside me had to knit back together, even as I struggled to keep them apart.

No, I wasn't ready to love him again. I wasn't ready to give him exactly what he wanted. He could not win!

Finding my strength, I pushed against him. "Stop. I want to go home."

Luca let me go. "Home? And where is home? You have no home here in California. You left without any solid plans. You're so goddamn hotheaded you didn't think this through."

Luca stalked away from me, striding naked to the bathroom. The slamming door echoed behind him. Alone in the room, I let the tears fall. He was right.

I was scared. I was hotheaded. I was reactionary.

And in that moment I felt like I'd gotten everything wrong—which I hated even more.

How could he possibly turn the argument around so that I was the one who felt terrible? As if I'd based my opinions on fake news and gossip.

There was nothing fake about the ache in my heart. The memory of seeing that woman perched on my boyfriend's lap, immortalized in print for everyone to gawk at, was still very clear in my mind.

I could almost look back and say, *You know what, we were both young and stupid.* But that did nothing to ease the pain and the suffering I went through after he broke me!

I was damaged because of him, and it was hard for me to wrap my brain around the fact that the person who had damaged me the most was the one I still wanted.

Luca reappeared, a specimen of male perfection even as every muscle was rigid and taut with anger. No matter what, he still had the power to take my breath away. I supposed I could add that to the stack of crosses I had to bear when it came to Luca.

Seemed fitting, because the truth was pretty brutal.

No matter how far I ran, I would never escape the fact that Luca would always be in my heart.

CHAPTER EIGHTEEN

Luca

THE RETURN RIDE to the hotel was silent. I'd lost all the ground I'd gained, and I was kicking myself for playing my hand too soon.

I could practically feel Katherine vibrating with anger and hurt, too many memories from the past standing between us.

If I tried to explain, it would come off as justifications, and that was the last thing she wanted to hear right now.

I wasn't going to grovel over an incident that was so fucking stupid it was practically a nonissue. I hadn't cheated on Katherine—I'd never even kissed that woman—but appearances were everything, and she'd been on my lap, topless.

What Katherine didn't know was that immediately after the paparazzi took the picture, I removed the drunken starlet from my lap and went to unload the tequila I'd downed as I'd puked my guts out.

I'd tried to tell Katherine, but when she hadn't believed me, I hadn't tried very hard to fix the misunderstanding. Like I said, I'd been shamefully relieved.

Maybe I'd wanted to be free for a time before getting married.

Maybe subconsciously I'd wanted Katherine to experience more of life before tying herself to me for the rest of her life.

Hell, I could spend hours coming up with a dozen different scenarios that might justify why I hadn't just tried a little bit harder to clear the air and heal the hurt.

But at the end of the day, my silence had been the loudest.

I half expected her to take a stand and demand that I take the pullout sofa in the living room of the suite rather than the sumptuous luxury king, but she didn't, even if her glance did flick to the sofa before she trudged to the bedroom.

I supposed that was a good sign, right? *Better not count your blessings just yet.*

"Are we going to talk about this?" I ventured, removing my shirt and tossing it, peeling myself from the leather pants with equal disregard for where they ended up.

"Nope," she answered, disappearing behind the bathroom door with her nightclothes. I much preferred her naked, but the chances of that happening were slim to none.

I sighed and removed my watch, setting it on the nightstand, and climbed into the bed. Katherine reappeared a few moments later, her face scrubbed, her hair tied up in a bun. If she thought she was going to deter me by going with the schoolmarm look, she was sadly mistaken.

What my future bride didn't realize was that she could be wearing a paper sack and I'd still find her the sexiest creature alive. Even if she wasn't the friendliest at the moment.

"Kath—"

"I'm tired."

I shut my mouth. Nothing was going to happen tonight. Tomorrow would be about damage control.

I had a plan. All I had to do was follow through and see it done. My eyes drifted shut, and I found sleep relatively quickly.

So quickly, in fact, that morning came within a blink.

I awoke to an empty bed, alarm chasing the sleep from my brain. Bounding from the bed, I called out for Katherine, only to find her at the table, sipping her tea and reading the delivered newspaper, fully dressed as if she'd risen hours before me.

The little vixen hadn't wanted to leave anything to chance. She'd known if given a shot I would find a way to make love to her again, and this was her way of thwarting me.

Well, I wasn't so easily deterred. "I never took you for an early bird. What happened to the girl who said she was a night owl?"

"She grew up."

A short and sweet answer delivered with a perfunctory and bland smile.

"Good," I said, surprising her when I didn't engage as she'd hoped. "I have big plans for today."

"As do I, seeing as it's my turn to pick our activities," she said with another smile, only this time there was an edge to the corners. "Today, we are going to volunteer at a local soup kitchen."

No, today we were going to Sonoma County. "Yes, technically, it is your day," I conceded, rubbing my chin at the dilemma. "I guess I overestimated how much you would enjoy spending the day at Coppola's winery... We had so much fun last night at Cafe Zoetrope that I got ahead of myself and booked a private tour. But I can cancel. Volunteering at a soup kitchen sounds equally fun."

I knew her weaknesses.

"It's impossible to get a private tour on such short notice," she said, calling my bluff.

"For a Donato, nothing is impossible," I reminded her with a shrug. "Our tour is scheduled for this afternoon, which means we need to get moving if we want to make it to Geyersville on time."

"I know what you're doing," she said, narrowing her eyes. "And it's not going to work."

I was a bastard and probably going to hell, but it would be worth it. I tried to make the decision easier for her. "How about a compromise?"

"What do you mean?"

"Helping others is the main goal when you volunteer, but there are other ways to help... Would it ease your conscience if I wrote a fat check to the shelter of your choice so that we could go enjoy our day without the guilt?"

"You can't just toss out money everywhere you go

to solve your problems," she said with a scowl, my plan backfiring. "Coppola will just have to wait. We are going to the soup kitchen."

The firm set of her jaw told me she would rather cut off her nose to spite her face than admit she'd much rather spend the day in Geyersville. I silently swore at her damn stubborn nature, but a deal was a deal.

I sighed. "I'll make some calls. Coppola will be disappointed. There aren't many filmmakers who are willing to personally give the tour, but I'm sure he'll understand."

Katherine's jaw dropped a little, but she didn't take it back, even though it was killing her. "Francis Ford Coppola was going to give the tour?" she asked, wincing. "Are you kidding me?"

"No, but it was a onetime deal. He's a busy guy, as you can imagine. Anyway, I'm going to shower and then we can be off."

I smothered the chuckle bubbling to the surface and left her to think about what she'd just sacrificed for her stubborn pride.

Soup kitchen, here we come.

CHAPTER NINETEEN

Katherine

WITHOUT REALIZING IT, Luca had made my point. He was much more willing to throw money at something than experience it himself if the situation didn't align with his personal comfort. There was no growth or learning curve in cheating the experience like that. I didn't want my children to learn that lesson, either.

But to be honest, I'd thrown out the soup kitchen idea believing that Luca would refuse. Charity I was familiar with—I'd been to more charity balls and benefits than I could count. Giving time had always seemed more genuine to me than giving money, but I'd never actually done it before. Why? I'd never been in a homeless shelter, just as I'd never actually slept in a hostel before the other night, either.

And so far I was not all that enthused with what I'd discovered, which only made me feel like a spoiled diva—the one thing I was trying my damnedest not to be.

When Luca reappeared, dressed and ready to roll, I

averted my gaze when I felt the urge to stare with long-ing. The man could make anything look like the height of fashion, even jeans and a soft gray henley.

My mouth dried as memories of that hot body jabbed at me. How could I be so addicted to his touch, even after all these years? It was as if no one had ever existed until Luca touched me. Total bullshit. Especially after last night had gone down in flames. I was above that moony girl stuff, and I would prove it by completely squashing those irritating tingles dancing in the pit of my stomach.

"You ready?" I asked, grabbing my purse.

"As ready as I'll ever be," he answered with a grin that melted me just a little.

Grateful that Luca didn't feel compelled to talk about last night, I spun on my heel before he could start. "Let's hit the road, then. Our ride is waiting." It seemed highly inappropriate to arrive at a homeless shelter in a town car, so I'd ordered an Uber. Secretly, I was hoping that Luca was appalled, but he wasn't. The damn man climbed into the modest sedan without blinking an eye. "You can still change your mind," I told him. "It won't hurt my feelings at all."

"I'm looking forward to experiencing an adven-ture with you," he replied, and I nearly swallowed my tongue.

"It will probably smell," I said, trying to paint a pic-ture that wouldn't appeal to him. "And the people will probably smell, too."

"Probably."

"And that doesn't bother you?"

He shrugged. "Human beings without access to showers and basic hygiene products generally smell. I'd smell just as bad, if not worse, if I couldn't shower and brush my teeth." He cast a smile my way, adding, "Even you would stink. Humans are dirty creatures."

Who was this guy? I nodded but didn't trust my voice, grateful when I didn't have to find something to fill the silence, because we'd arrived.

The building, covered in graffiti, was nothing to look at from the outside, but I'd read that this particular shelter was known for accepting anyone, even drug addicts and criminals, if they were in need and there was a bed available.

Run by the sisters of the Immaculate Conception Nunnery, the shelter was bustling by the time we walked in. I'd already set up the volunteer hours with Sister Mary over the phone, so after being directed to her office, we found ourselves seated opposite a stout older woman with a rather stern countenance.

I could totally imagine Sister Mary wielding a ruler to slap the knuckles of unruly children.

"Welcome to our humble shelter," Sister Mary said, her round face breaking into a brief smile. "We appreciate new volunteers."

"Happy to help," I murmured, shooting a glance at Luca. Was he going to throw his checkbook at her, or would he go through with volunteering? I held my breath, waiting.

"My fiancée is so kindhearted she insisted we spend some of our vacation helping those less fortunate," Luca said. "I'll admit it wasn't my first choice, but now that

I'm here, I'm looking forward to getting my hands dirty."

Sister Mary smiled with approval. "That's a good man," she said for my benefit, and I wanted to roll my eyes but didn't. She produced some paperwork and slid it over to us. "I just need you to sign a few forms, acknowledging that you are choosing to volunteer and that you will not hold the Immaculate Conception Nunnery responsible for any injuries you may sustain while in service."

"Injuries?" I repeated with a confused frown. "What do you mean?"

Sister Mary folded her hands and answered, "My dear, sometimes our guests are unstable. They can't help themselves—they are unwell. We do our best to keep our volunteers safe, but sometimes a guest will become unruly and scuffles happen. But not to worry, we have security for those events and rarely does anything truly harmful occur. However—" she tapped the documents "—we all have to take precautions so we can continue our good work."

I nodded and signed my name, but maybe I'd bitten off more than I could chew. I looked to Luca, but he didn't seem deterred in the least. In fact, he looked ready to get started. His strong, solid signature sealed the deal for the both of us, and I realized this was happening.

I wrestled with the cowardly urge to back out. Nothing was working as I'd planned. Luca wasn't playing his part as expected. Each time I thought I had him pegged, he spun around and did something completely out of character, challenging what I thought I knew, and that was beyond dangerous.

I was already teetering on the edge of the cliff—a part of me had never stopped loving Luca—but I didn't want to be roped into the Donato family lifestyle and obligations. I shuddered, hating the thought of Luca becoming anything like his father. If it weren't for those undeniably strong Donato genes, I'd question whether or not Giovanni's blood ran through Luca's veins.

Wouldn't that be a kick in the pants for the old man if it turned out Luca was someone else's kid? I smothered an inappropriate giggle. My nerves were jangled enough to show through the mask I was hiding behind, and Luca could see I was struggling, plain as day.

I didn't know which was worse, realizing that I wasn't as bohemian as I tried to be or that Luca could see right through me.

I guess it didn't matter. I was going to see this through, simply because I refused to let Luca have the last laugh.

Accepting gloves and an apron with forced cheer, I followed Sister Mary into the dining hall, where the rest of the volunteers were already serving breakfast.

But when I expected the nun to put us together, she sent Luca in one direction and me in another.

I chewed my lip, watching as Luca went off with a smiling volunteer with big, bouncy red hair and even bouncier boobs, and I was delivered to a not-so-smiley nun with a pinched mouth and hard eyes.

Within a heartbeat, I'd been sized up and found wanting, but another set of hands was still useful.

"This is Sister Bernice," Sister Mary said in quick introduction. "She'll be your supervisor today. Sister Bernice, this is Katherine. Have a blessed day and thank you for your contribution."

And then Sister Mary left me with the battle-ax.

"We're kitchen detail," Sister Bernice said flatly, turning and expecting me to follow, which I reluctantly did. We rounded the corner and entered a huge working kitchen, bustling with activity. Everywhere I looked, people were passing to and fro, hands filled with giant bowls of food, heading for the serving hall. I figured I was going to be cooking or chopping, something food related, but when Sister Bernice pointed to the stack of dishes crowding the oversize sink, I felt like Cinderella staring at an impossible workload, except I didn't have any mice or birds to help me with the job.

"I'm pretty good with cutting and chopping," I offered helpfully. "I can chop with the best of them."

"We have all the choppers we need," Bernice stated with a brief lift of her lips that might have passed for a smile in a different life. "We need someone to wash dishes."

"Of course. No problem." I offered a wan smile and went to the monster sink and the mile-high dishes crusted with food. I slipped the rubber gloves on and grabbed the industrial-size nozzle to start rinsing.

Each time I cleared a spot, another cartful of dishes appeared, until I couldn't pretend to smile anymore, but I didn't quit. Quitting would only prove that I was exactly the type of person I didn't want to be. Maybe all this time I'd been playing the part of an independent woman, knowing full well that I could access my trust at any time. Just like Luca had accused.

I used my forearm to wipe the sweat from my forehead before it dripped into my eye. It was cold as a witch's tit outside, but in this kitchen, it was roasting.

"You look thirsty," a voice said. I turned and saw a young man offering a bottled water, which I gratefully accepted. "How'd you end up on dish duty? You give Sister Bernice attitude or something?"

I chuckled, shaking my head. "I didn't say two words to her before she sized me up and stuck me here." I guzzled the water, out of breath by the last swallow. "Thanks," I said, smiling. "My name's Katherine. What's yours?"

"Bart," he answered, extending his hand in welcome. "Let me guess…community service for…a drunken sorority prank?"

I laughed. "No, I came because I thought it would—" *make my fiancé run back to New York* "—be fun."

"Are you having fun?" he asked, his brow rising. "Because you look miserable."

I started to protest, but I didn't have the energy to lie. "I'm…totally miserable," I admitted. "So why are you here?"

"Community service. Drunken frat prank," he answered with a wink. "Anyway, the sisters are always good for signing off on community service, so they have a pretty steady stream of volunteers to put to work."

"Spoken by a repeat offender?"

Bart shrugged without commitment, but the impish grin said it all. "So, you're not from here... Let me guess... East Coast? Maybe New York?"

"Does my accent give me away?"

"A little." He made a pinching gesture with his fingers. "But it's cute. I love girls with accents."

I laughed, shaking my head. Bart was definitely flirting, but when I realized that my first thought was I wished Luca could see a cute guy flirting with me, I knew I was officially a terrible person. "I'm here with my fiancé," I said, letting Bart down gently. "He got lucky. Sister Mary sent him to the serving hall."

"Fiancé?" He groaned, covering his heart as if shot. "Just my luck. All right, whoever he is, he's one lucky bastard."

Divulging the odd truth of my relationship with Luca would only serve to create more questions I couldn't answer, so I just smiled and nodded in thanks.

"Let me see your hands," Bart said. When I simply stared quizzically, he laughed and repeated his request, adding, "I promise it's nothing weird." More curious than anything else, I removed my rubber gloves. Bart grasped my hands and turned them this way and that, finally revealing his reason. "Sister Bernice always puts the people with the softest hands in the kitchen, and the ones she thinks need the most humbling, she puts on dishes."

My mouth gaped. "Me? Why would *I* need humbling? It was my idea to volunteer."

"Let me tell you, Sister Bernice has the eyes of a hawk. She can see what others can't."

The heat crept into my cheeks. I'd been judged?

How was it possible that *I'd* failed the test while Luca had passed with flying colors? I rolled my shoulders to release the gathering tension. "Well, I can guarantee Luca's hands are softer than mine," I groused, but I knew that probably wasn't true. Luca loved being active, and he wasn't afraid to get his hands dirty.

"New college grad?" Bart surmised with a knowing grin. Not as new as he thought, but a close guess. "You have that highly educated but ultimately useless look about you." My pride pinched, I scowled in response, but Bart just laughed. "Hey, not judging, cutie, just making an observation. My older brother has that same look, and I have no doubt as soon as I graduate in the spring I'll have that look, too. I think it comes with the degree. After this last shenanigan, my dad put his foot down, saying, *It's time to get serious, son*," he said, in a mockingly parental tone. "But, I don't know, nothing really grabs me."

"Actually, I had a job with a high-powered marketing firm, Franklin and Dodd, but I quit to come to California. I'm thinking of a career change."

"Brave," Bart said. "Your fiancé cool with that?"

"It's not his decision, it's mine, but…yeah, I think he's okay with it." Luca didn't care where I worked. He just wanted me to marry him. The quiet truth hit me hard. This trip hadn't exactly turned out as I'd expected. It was a sobering thing to realize that the soapbox you were perched on was quickly breaking down. I'd spent a long time believing that I was unequivocally right about certain things, but Luca had me questioning what I thought I knew.

Bart and I were fairly close in age, but unlike him, I didn't suffer from a lack of ambition or drive. If anything, I had more than I could possibly put to good use, which was why the thought of becoming a society matron scraped at my last nerve. I didn't want to be a useless piece of arm candy.

"That your man coming toward us with a look like he wants to beat me with my own arm?" Bart asked with fake fright. "Jesus, he's tall."

I hid the smile that immediately bloomed. Yes, Luca was delightfully tall and broad shouldered. And he did, indeed, look as if he might want to thrash Bart for flirting with me. A warm tickle danced in my belly. There was something undeniably sexy about the way Luca looked at me. Sometimes when his blue eyes fixed on mine, I felt as if he could see straight to my soul.

I smothered the wistful sigh that threatened.

None of that.

"I came to ask if you'd like to sign on for another four-hour shift or if you'd like to go," Luca said, shooting a cool look Bart's way.

Bart thrust his hand toward Luca. "Bart's the name, and you, big guy, are one lucky son of a bitch for locking down this hottie."

My cheeks heated, but I laughed. To my surprise, Luca's tension released and he accepted the hand offered. "Pleasure, Bart. And yes—" his gaze flitted to me with warmth "—I'm a lucky man."

Bart grinned and said, "Well, I've still got another four hours on my tab, so I'd better find Sister Mean Eyes and get my assignment. I'd say you two did your good deed for the day—go find something more interesting to do. I know what I'd be doing if she was my girl..." He sauntered off with a wink.

My amused smile caused Luca to pull me into his arms, circling my waist possessively before I could stop him. "I can't leave you alone for a second," he murmured with a low growl, sending shivers down my back. His lips nibbled at the soft skin of my neck, and my knees threatened to buckle. "Stay or go?" he asked.

"Go," I answered breathlessly.

Luca pulled away, his lips twitching with knowing, but I didn't care. I didn't want to wash dishes anymore, and at the moment I didn't care to examine my reasoning with a magnifying glass.

"Good." Luca grabbed my hand and led me from the hot, stifling kitchen to sign us out with Sister Mary. "You do good work here," he told the nun as he handed her a business card. "Call my office on Monday for a proper donation."

"Bless you, Mr. Donato," Sister Mary said. "Thank you for your service and donation."

Luca dipped his head in acknowledgment and we left the shelter, only this time Luca had called for the town car.

As I settled into the plush back seat, a question nagged at me.

Was I fighting out of spite, or was this a battle truly worth fighting?

At this point...I didn't know anymore.

CHAPTER TWENTY

Luca

I'D ONLY EVER been territorial with one woman, and that was Katherine. I knew there was nothing to the harmless flirting between Katherine and the smiley-eyed little bastard, but that didn't stop my teeth from baring. It wasn't that she was talking to another man…it was the fact that a stranger could so easily make her smile and laugh when all I could do was make her suspicious of my motives.

Spare me the lecture. Yeah, I knew this was a problem of my own making, but that didn't make it any less difficult to deal with, and right now, all I wanted was to feel Katherine beneath me.

I drew her to me, my hand cupping the back of her neck, and sealed my mouth to hers, letting my hunger override any hint of cunning or strategy. My tongue sought hers, tangling and twisting with an urgency that she could feel in my touch. When she responded in kind, my cock hardened to stone, violently ready to pin her to the motherfucking black leather.

"L-Luca," she breathed against my mouth, pushing against my chest with furtive glances at the driver, who was doing his best to keep his eyes on the road. "What are you doing?"

"Isn't it obvious?" I asked, toying with the buttons on her jeans.

She gasped. "But the driver," she whispered, covering my hands with hers.

"The driver is paid to mind his own fucking business," I growled, dipping forward to kiss the base of her throat. Leaning back to catch her eye, I asked, "May I?"

She gave a furtive glance to the front seat before turning to me again. "Yes. God, yes," she said, scrambling to unbutton her jeans.

I reached for her jeans and panties, swiftly tugging them down and off completely, responding to the way her body quickened to my touch. I could smell her arousal, that sweet, musky feminine grace that only Katherine possessed. I grabbed her legs and pulled her to her back, one leg splayed over the seat, the other anchored over my shoulder as I nibbled my way to her tight pussy.

"Oh, God," Katherine moaned, clapping her hand over her eyes as her teeth worried her bottom lip. I dipped a finger inside her, withdrew and licked her essence clean, groaning with pleasure. Katherine was sweetness personified. I couldn't wait any longer. My hunger wouldn't wait. I needed to feel her shatter so I could drown in her release. I went straight for the tiny, swollen piece of her that throbbed beneath my tongue, sucking and teasing until her entire body was shaking and twitching with each stroke. Her skin dampened as her breath became stilted, muscles tensing. I wanted to draw it out, tease her until she was mindless, but I couldn't help myself. I was delirious with the taste and sound of her and I couldn't stop.

Come for me, baby.

As if hearing my silent demand, Katherine stiffened and cried out as she hit her climax, gripping the seat cushion for dear life as her entire body spasmed. She gasped, her mouth falling open as her chest rose and fell like a boat on a turbulent sea, but I wasn't satisfied. I needed to be inside her, to take her as only I could. No one touched her like I did, and I knew that for a fact.

I moved away from her so I could release my cock, popping the buttons on my jeans with shaking fingers. No sooner had I sprung free and sheathed myself with a condom than Katherine climbed on top, knees straddling me so I could slide in.

Her honeyed pussy sucked me into her body, and I groaned as intense pleasure gripped my cock. I clutched her hips as she moved, rubbing herself against my shaft, her cheeks flushed and her hair wild. The air in the car became stuffy, but the driver knew well enough to keep his fingers away from that window divider switch that maintained the barrier between us. I wanted to taste, smell and immerse myself in everything that was Katherine.

I wanted to lick the sweat from her body, swallow the cries from her mouth. She rocked against me, finding her own pleasure even as I rocketed toward mine. I was inside her—heaven—just me and her. This was how we connected and how we'd always connect. Our bodies knew the truth even if neither of us was willing to commit to the words.

Katherine braced herself on the ceiling as I anchored her hips; her thrusts became erratic and I surged inside her. The liquid heat between us pooled and sizzled until I couldn't hold back any longer. I jetted hard, straining with the effort it took to keep from breaking the windows. Dimly, I heard Katherine follow with a feminine cry, slumping against me, her head lolling on my shoulder as her walls pulsed around me, milking every drop from my balls.

My arms closed around her, my cock still buried deep. I could sleep for days just like this.

Primal emotion flooded me. I would fuck her raw if given the chance, not only because fucking her felt right, but because I simply couldn't get enough.

"Air, please," I said, my voice raw, and the driver discreetly levered the window to allow some fresh air to circulate. It was then Katherine came to her senses and met my gaze, her embarrassment evident, but I simply kissed her again, saying, "Wealth has its privileges."

That, she couldn't deny, and she didn't try.

Nodding, she slowly climbed from my lap.

As we adjusted our clothing, Katherine said, "You're making mincemeat out of my declaration that I wouldn't have sex with you."

We broke into shared laughter as I said, "I never take my eye off the prize." I buttoned the final button on my jeans, saying, "And if you really want to know, I'll admit that I plan to fuck you at any opportunity given me." Color flushed her cheeks prettily. I took a chance and added, "But tell me if I'm wrong… I don't think you mind."

"I don't," she admitted with an unhappy sigh, tucking her feet up under her. "That's the thing, Luca…sexual chemistry was never our problem. Our problems were much bigger and went way deeper."

"You said *deeper*," I teased, cracking a reluctant smile from her lips.

"I'm being serious."

I exhaled. "Yeah, well, most couples do have problems. We're not immune."

"We're not a couple, Luca."

I met her gaze. "What do you want, Katherine? An apology? Do you want to hear that I would change things if I could? That I would take back hurting you? Yeah, I would do anything to take back what happened on that damn yacht, but I'll never apologize for wanting to marry you. I want you, Katherine. It's always been you. I don't really give a shit how it came about… maybe we were always destined to find each other and this was just the particular way things shook out for us, but I don't care. I love you."

The words tumbled from my mouth without forethought. I confess, I'd thrown around the *L* word before, but there'd been nothing behind it. Only when I thought of Katherine did the word take on a different meaning, hold a significant weight.

And I'd never said those words to *her*. Not even when we were younger. I'd always said things like "There's no one like you" or "You're my number one girl," which

Katherine had been fine with, because she'd known that we were going to marry.

She'd said the words to me plenty of times—and I'd squirmed each time.

Not because I hadn't felt things…but because I'd felt things I wasn't ready to deal with.

I'd been a kid. Barely out of college. She'd been a teenager. Each time she'd looked at me with those stars in her eyes, I'd cringed. I hadn't been ready to jump feetfirst into what I knew was in store for the both of us. I'd told myself hurting her had been a fucked-up blessing, but in all honesty, I'd been a damn coward.

But the words were out there now, sitting between us like a fat cat that'd eaten too much cream and wasn't going anywhere.

"You shouldn't use words you don't understand," Katherine warned in a cold tone, but the bright sheen in her eyes gave her away.

Maybe it was time to actually come clean and admit what I'd always known but had been too afraid to show. It was probably lousy timing, but time wasn't something I had in surplus. I still had to deal with my father when all this was said and done. I drew a deep breath and reached for her hand. She looked at me sharply but didn't pull away, which gave me hope. "I've always loved you, Katherine. I just wasn't ready."

"What?"

"I've always loved you."

"You don't cheat on the people you love."

"I agree. I didn't cheat on you."

She looked at me sharply before pulling away, putting distance between us. "Come again?"

"I told you then, I'm telling you now… I didn't cheat on you. I was drunk. The woman sat on my lap and kissed me, but I didn't kiss her back. Right after, I removed her from my lap and promptly threw up."

"You're expecting me to believe that you had a topless Chrissy McMichael on your lap and it was totally innocent?"

"Oh, hell no, I didn't say it was innocent. I shouldn't have let her sit on my lap. It was an error in judgment, but then, I was also fucking drunk off my ass. But I didn't mean for you to be hurt."

"Convenient. Too bad you weren't willing to own up to anything back then."

"I tried telling you what really happened. You weren't interested in listening. Not that I blamed you. I'll be the first to admit it looked bad."

She didn't respond, just continued to gaze at me with reproach.

"It's the truth," I told her, laying all my cards on the table. "But I fucked up that day by not admitting what I really needed to say."

"Which was?"

"I thought it was better if we took a break. I didn't have the balls to admit that I was relieved that you broke it off."

Her eyes widened with incredulity, and she shook her head as if she couldn't quite wrap her head around my admission. "You wanted to break up?"

"Yes and no. But mostly yes. Not for the reasons you might think, though."

"Oh, I've got to hear this," Katherine mocked, fresh anger leaking into her tone. "This ought to be amazing."

"I needed you to experience life. Hell, *I* needed to experience more before I settled down so that when we did actually tie the knot, I would be ready. I wanted that for you, too."

"That's some backward-ass logic." She rubbed at her nose with a sharp, agitated motion. "I mean, Jesus, Luca, you didn't need to break my fucking heart just to get some space."

"I was stupid" was all I could say in my own defense. "I know that now, but I can't take it back. All I can do is learn from it and move forward. But be honest with yourself for a second…would you have understood if I'd said, 'Hey, babe, let's take a small break so we can both do some wild and crazy shit without each other'?"

She didn't bother lying. "No."

"See?"

"I don't even know what to think about this, Luca. How am I supposed to react to this information? Just laugh it off and say, 'Oh, all is forgiven!' because you've decided to come clean about your true reasons for hurting me?"

"I'm trying to be honest with you. If we're to have any shot together, I want to start with a clean slate," I answered quietly, because it was the truth. "I don't want to keep anything from you ever again. A pretty lie is what started all this. I should've just knuckled down and given you the ugly truth and let the chips fall where they may. I think we would've been able to get through that far easier than what we're doing now."

"Maybe." A beat passed between us. "But that's not what happened, is it? So we have to deal with the reality of our situation."

"And the reality is?"

"I can't marry you."

I rejected her declaration, heart and soul. "You're mine and you always will be. I will chase you to the ends of the earth until you realize we were meant for one another."

Katherine threw her hands up in an exasperated motion to wipe at the tears that had begun to track down her cheeks. "This is so classic Luca. Pulling out the big guns for the win, because winning is everything. But I'm not a prize to be won. I'm a human, flesh and blood, and you broke my heart. I don't care that you weren't ready for what you were feeling. It still sliced me to ribbons, and now it feels even worse somehow, knowing that you actually hadn't cheated on me but you didn't try to convince me otherwise. You let me think that I wasn't enough for you. I don't think I can forgive you for that."

"I could say I'm sorry a million different ways, but it wouldn't change how I handled myself. All I can say is…I am so sorry for hurting you."

"Wouldn't it just be easier to let me go?" she asked in a plaintive cry that tore at my heart. "I mean, love isn't supposed to be this hard."

"Bullshit. Love is love. Whether it's hard or easy depends on how we handle what comes our way. I love you, Katherine Cerinda Oliver. I've never wanted anyone more than I want you. I'm ready to be the man you need me to be. Just give me a damn chance to show you."

"How do I know you're not just playing me to get what you want?"

"I don't chase after what I have no interest in catching. Woman, I'd chase you until we were both in wheelchairs. A lifetime doesn't seem nearly long enough for all the things I want to experience with you. Does that sound like someone who's just playing?"

"Crap," she muttered as fresh tears dribbled down her cheeks. "Now look what you've done. I'm a giant crybaby mess."

"I think you're beautiful," I said, proving it by kissing her tearstained lips. Salty and sweet, that was my Katherine. I kissed her softly, brushing my lips across hers with a tender touch. I wanted everything with her, even if it meant weathering the ups and downs of a volatile relationship. I was in, 100 percent.

I sensed the crack in her armor as she sagged against me, opening her mouth so my tongue could slide inside. Her breasts begged for my touch, and I was happy to oblige as my hand crept beneath her sweater to caress a pert, pouty breast. I wanted her nipple in my mouth, but I could wait.

Nibbling the column of her neck, I inhaled the sweetness of her skin, losing myself to the intoxicating pleasure that was solely Katherine.

"Luca," she moaned, the sound of her anguish going straight to my heart. I slowed to a stop, even though I wanted to devour her a second time. She peered at me through wet lashes. "I just can't. I'm sorry."

"Why not?" I pressed, needing to find that stubborn bone of contention stuck in her mind. "Tell me. I'll listen."

Katherine paused, gauging my response, as if testing whether or not she could trust me. The moment felt heavy—everything was riding on which path we took. Would she trust me enough to share her true fears? Or would she withdraw and push me away again?

God, Katherine, please let me in.

CHAPTER TWENTY-ONE

Katherine

HE'D SAID THE WORDS—*I'm sorry*—I'd wanted to hear for so long yet had given up hope I ever would. Donatos didn't apologize. They were stubborn and stoic, marching to the beat of their own drum. Even if I was stunned by the apology, I had to recognize the ugly truth—my problems weren't so easily solved. An apology was simply words uttered to create an effect. Luca would say and do anything to get what he wanted, that much I knew.

"How can I trust you're not saying what you think I need to hear?"

"Trust is a leap of faith. You have to let go of whatever you're holding on to in order to make that jump."

I skewed my gaze at him. "Since when did you become such a philosopher?"

"When my fiancée kept doing everything in her power to push me away."

"Why do you keep calling me your fiancée when I've

told you repeatedly that I'm not going to marry you?" I asked, exasperated.

He chuckled. "Because I'm an optimist."

I looked away, refusing to let his charm get to me. There was something stubbornly romantic about the way he refused to take no for an answer. "You're impossible," I said, shaking my head. "What am I going to do with you?"

"Marry me."

His simple answer took my breath away, and tears started fresh.

Luca slipped his hand into mine. His gentle touch was tender, speaking of genuine concern, but I questioned if any of it was real. Nothing felt right in my head right now. When I'd bailed on New York, I'd known in my heart I was making the right decision. Now? I was turned around and upside down, and it was all because Luca wasn't performing to the script.

It was as if we'd just stepped into a time warp and he was once again the Luca I'd fallen in love with—kind, funny, considerate, *sexy*...well, *that* part had never changed—and I was falling all over again, faster than I could stop myself.

Instead of confidence, fear was my traveling companion. Fear of myself, of what I'd been denying since Luca had broken my heart, of losing myself in the Donato vortex, fear of being exactly the kind of person I'd been disdaining since I'd discovered that ugly mag with my boyfriend's picture on the cover with that sloppy-drunk starlet.

To be honest, the whole situation at the shelter had

thrown me for a loop. The person I thought I was might not be real at all. Sister Bernice had summed me up in a glance simply by looking at my hands. It pinched to be judged so quickly, but there was a level of truth to her conclusion, and that killed me inside.

"I don't like your father, and your mother is iffy," I said abruptly, readying myself for a fight, but Luca just nodded. My sails deflated.

"Sometimes my family is hard to like," he said with a shrug.

Couldn't argue with that.

"Your father scares me."

"I will never allow anyone to hurt you," Luca promised.

"What if you can't prevent it?"

His low growl surprised me. "I will break anyone who tries."

There was something real and deeply rooted behind his gaze, something I'd never seen before. Was it possible Luca truly loved me? My heart skipped a beat at the thought. I desperately wanted Luca to love me, *really* love me, not because I was his arranged bride, but because he'd chosen me above all else.

"How can you know that what you feel is genuine, that it won't fade?" I asked.

"You're the only one questioning their feelings. I've always known how I felt about you. I always knew you were the only one for me. I just had to be ready to go all in."

My eyes burned with unshed tears as my heart ached with the need to hear exactly that, but my brain was determined to question everything that came out of his mouth and I was breaking from the strain. "I can't think anymore," I cried, losing it. "I just can't. Luca, I—"

"Shh," he crooned, drawing me into his arms. "Then don't think. Just let me do the thinking for now. We're on our way to wine country, where we are going to enjoy being tourists, okay? I want you to think of nothing more than which wine you want to sample next. No more picking at problems bigger than whatever the moment can provide."

It sounded so tempting—turn off the brain and just enjoy the day with the man I was impossibly crazy about—but could I actually do it? God, I wanted to enjoy this day with Luca. I wanted to hold his hand and walk through the vineyards, eat good food and laugh at silly jokes.

So do it.

The voice I'd been trying to ignore was louder than my fears this time.

I wiped at my tears, nodding slowly. "Okay," I said, swallowing the lump in my throat. "I can do that. I think."

Luca smiled and kissed me again.

Everything felt right when his lips were on mine. Was it possible to say *screw the world* and just chase my happiness?

Could I convince Luca that a life with me was better than a life slaved to his family? Was I really going to ask Luca to choose between me and the Donato empire?

Two seconds into my attempt to stop thinking, I was already breaking the rules. I exhaled a long breath and drew a halting one. "I'm ready to be a tourist," I told Luca, earning a grin from his sexy lips. "And just be with you."

"Good," he murmured, sealing his lips to mine.

Yes, today…I was Luca's.

Tomorrow? I wasn't going to think about that.

CHAPTER TWENTY-TWO

Luca

NESTLED AGAINST ME, Katherine drowsed in the hotel bed after a long day at the Coppola vineyard. She had been delighted to learn everything about the wine-making process on the private tour, even though the filmmaker hadn't been our tour guide.

Watching her eyes light up had been worth every inconvenience the trip had caused to my work schedule. I hadn't planned to spend so much time wooing Katherine, but I couldn't deny that I'd enjoyed every minute. I should've been doing this months ago.

Maybe I'd been scared to get too close. Maybe I'd been caught up in my own arrogance—the Donato way striking again.

Either way, I was man enough to admit I'd gone about it all wrong and now I was faced with damage control. I wanted to wake up with Katherine by my side every morning. I wanted to taste her kiss and swallow her cries for the rest of our lives. Falling in love with your arranged wife… I guess it wasn't the usual thing, but I didn't care. I loved Katherine and I had to find a way to convince her that I was being genuine.

Today had been a good start.

Katherine sighed in her sleep, her hand curled under her chin.

As if sensing I was having a good moment, my father called.

I hesitated, tempted to send him to voice mail, but I eased myself away from Katherine and out of the bedroom to take the call.

"What's the status?" Giovanni asked gruffly. No hello, no *how are you*, just plain business. I'd long since stopped hoping my father would find his humanity in old age, but I knew Dante still hungered for that fatherly affection and that was a constant irritant between us. I'd settle for respect. I wanted to grab Dante and say, *Open your eyes, you idiot*, but Dante was as stubborn as a Donato could be, so I didn't waste the energy.

"I'm making progress."

"What does that mean?" Giovanni asked, irritated. "Are you bringing her home or not?"

"She's not a piece of luggage," I said, matching my father's clipped tone. "Don't worry about my fiancée. I have everything under control."

"I'm going to call her father, have him bring her to heel. I need you here, not chasing after some silly twit."

"Watch your mouth, old man."

"Have you forgotten who you're speaking to?" Giovanni shot back in warning, but I didn't care. I was tired of my father bullying everyone around him. Times were changing, yet Giovanni was anchoring the family to an antiquated and frowned-upon tradition. I mean, Jesus, we weren't in feudal Italy any longer. "Mind your own business. I have things handled."

"I want details."

"Details? What the hell does that mean?"

"How do you have things *handled*?" Giovanni replied, his disbelief evident.

My father was the last person I would accept relationship advice from. He and my mother were strangers to each other, and it seemed they preferred it that way. My mother was content to doodle around, lunching and gossiping with her matron hens, and my father was off trying to remain in the power seat when he should've retired years ago. I was sick of his bullshit.

"Just back off," I told him, ready to get off the phone.

"You forget your place," Giovanni said, unimpressed with my stance. "I want you on the next flight home."

"I'm not leaving without Katherine. I'll be home when we come together."

"Don't be stupid. I should've found you a different girl, a better one, two years ago. One girl is not worth this much trouble."

This one was. "Don't talk about things you know nothing about. Just keep your nose out of my business and we'll be fine. Cross that line…and you're no longer my father."

The silence on the other line was deafening. Would Giovanni get the message that I wasn't playing around? I wouldn't let anything come between Katherine and me. Never again. "You might have introduced her into my life, but she was meant to be mine, so back off and leave me to my business."

"You love her?" he asked, shocking me with the bald question.

"Isn't it obvious?" I answered.

He exhaled in irritation, but he didn't question me further. I hadn't made a conscious choice to defy my father, but the time had come. My father was the kind of man who would push for as long as someone allowed him. That time was done.

"So when are you coming home?" Giovanni asked by way of concession.

"In a few days. I'll be at the office on Monday."

"I suppose that'll do."

"It's the only offer on the table."

There was a long pause, and then my father said, with uncharacteristic paternal concern, "I just want what's best for the family."

"Then trust that I will do what needs to be done to protect the Donato name, but you have nothing to fear from Katherine. She's going to make a fine Donato."

Giovanni harrumphed as if to say, *That remains to be seen*, and then said, "I'll see you Monday."

The line went dead and I clicked off.

A sound caused me to turn. Katherine leaned against the doorjamb, dressed in a T-shirt and nothing else—just the way I preferred her, actually, but her expression was questioning. It didn't take much brainpower to realize she'd heard at least part of the conversation.

"Who was that?" she asked.

"My father."

"What's going on?"

I could level with her—take the chance that she could handle the ugly truth—or I could lie.

The urge to smooth things over with a lie was strong, but I knew if I was going to make a fresh start with Katherine, I had to start with complete honesty.

"My father wanted me to come home. I told him I wasn't ready."

"Does he need you back at the office?" she asked with a confused frown. "I didn't think Giovanni needed anyone, the way he seems to be in control of everything."

"He likes to think he's in control," I corrected her with a small smile. "But he's not in control of this time between us right now. I'm dying to know what you have in store for us today."

Since I'd taken over half of her day yesterday, it was her turn to plan the activities. Somehow I doubted we were heading to another soup kitchen, but as long as I was with her, I'd board a ship to the moon if that was where she wanted to go.

If she was charmed by my answer, she didn't let on. I knew she wanted more details about my conversation with my father, but I wasn't going to let anything ruin our day.

"So what's it going to be?" I asked.

Realizing the subject was finished on my end, Katherine pursed her lips, disappointed, but took my cue. "Today we are cleaning kennels," she answered, watching for my reaction.

"Kennels...for dogs?"

"Yes. There's a rescue group for sled dogs, and they always need volunteers to help brush the dogs, feed and walk them, as well as just socialize with them."

"So, we're going to play with dogs today?" I clarified, just making sure I had the way of things. At her nod, I said, "All right, then, jeans, tennis shoes and a hoodie."

Maybe she expected pushback, because I'd never been all that into dogs, but it wasn't going to happen. Besides, how hard could it be to play around with a few of them?

"I'm ready when you are," I said, taking the opportunity to steal a quick kiss. She gasped and tried not to smile, but her futile attempt at seeming stern was laughable...and cute. I released her so she could get dressed, and she scuttled back to the bedroom, closing the door behind her.

As if that would stop me from totally undressing her in my mind every second of every day.

For the rest of our lives.

CHAPTER TWENTY-THREE

Katherine

LUCA HAD STOOD up to his father—that much I'd gathered—but there was something else…something that'd caused Luca to growl at his father like a wolf, and that was a side of Luca I'd never seen.

I bit my lip as I leaned against the closed door, processing what I'd heard and what Luca had shared.

Luca had always done his best to be the dutiful son. He bore the weight of his family's expectations without complaint, but something his father had said had made Luca openly bristle.

Had Luca been defending me?

I frowned in thought. What could Giovanni have said to make Luca react like that? I guess it didn't matter, but Luca's reaction created a chain reaction in my thoughts that felt suspiciously like pride.

Luca was more than capable of handling himself in the business world; he didn't need Giovanni shadowing his every move any longer, yet he tolerated his father's influence.

Except today.

Today, he'd stood up to Giovanni and basically told the old curmudgeon to back off.

For me.

A warm, cozy, tingly feeling crept from my belly to my heart.

And now we were going to Nor-Cal Rescue to play with fluffy dogs. I couldn't imagine a better start to the day.

I dressed quickly, and by the time I exited the bedroom, ready, Luca had already ordered an Uber to pick us up. Before we left the room, he teased, "Should I prepare for another hostel experience, or shall we be staying here for the duration of our trip?"

"Kiss my butt, you know the answer to that," I said, shaking my head with a small laugh. "I don't want to stay in another hostel, thank you very much. And screw you for making me realize that I'm not cut out to be a boho hipster. You dashed my dreams, Luca."

His eyes lit up at my teasing. Our playful banter was something I'd sorely missed, even if I was loath to admit it.

When he slipped his hand into mine, I didn't pull away.

We arrived at Nor-Cal Rescue, a small shelter run by volunteers and kept afloat by donations, and were greeted by the coordinator, Emmett George, an affable man with twinkly eyes and a bushy beard.

I shared a look with Luca, knowing we were thinking the same thing—Emmett was the people version of a husky.

I liked him immediately.

"The lady here says you two are from New York...
Business or pleasure?" he asked, looking from me to
Luca with an engaging smile. "Either way, it's right
decent of you to volunteer some of your time with our
pups."

Yips and yelps echoed in the background, and I
smiled, eager to get started. I'd always wanted a husky,
but my father hadn't been interested, so I never got the
chance.

When I discovered there was a rescue group in San
Francisco, I knew there was no way I was leaving without cuddling with some big fluffy dogs.

Luca, far less animal crazy than me, looked just as
excited as I was to help out, and that only intensified
the confusion in my heart.

There were no easy answers between us—I should
probably stop looking—but in the meantime, I was
going to give myself permission to simply enjoy the day.

Emmett brought us into the compound, a clean but
small space where every kennel was occupied by some
type of northern breed, from Siberian husky to malamute.

And they were all freaking gorgeous.

"How could anyone abandon a dog like this?" I asked
as Emmett leashed a beautiful red husky with eyes as
blue as Luca's. "She's amazing."

"She's a runner," Emmett explained with a sigh as he
hooked up a fluffy malamute for Luca. "This purebred
lady is an escape artist. Apparently, her previous owners couldn't keep her occupied and she got bored. And

when huskies get bored, they find mischief. In Cora's case, the owners gave up and surrendered."

I made a sad face. "That's awful."

"Well, some people see a husky or northern-type breed and all they think is 'Wow, pretty dog,' with no thought as to how the breed must be cared for. The overwhelming crime for each of these dogs is that their previous owners simply didn't know what they were getting into when they purchased from the breeder."

Animals were my weakness. I wanted to throw gobs of money at the shelter to ensure that the pups remained safe and cared for. As if keying in on my desperate desire, Luca said, "I'd love to make a donation, if I could."

"We never turn down cash," Emmett said, smiling. "Feeding these hungry beasts doesn't come cheap. We feed the pups a grain-free diet, as most get skin allergies from that crap that most people feed their dogs. Not here, though. Nothing but the best. Hell, sometimes I even go without just so these beautiful rascals get a good meal."

"It's official, I love you," I said to Emmett, casting a glance at Luca, who was chuckling. "You are an incredible human being to give so freely of your time and resources. Yes, please, let us leave you with a donation. It's the least we can do."

"Sounds like a plan to me. Why don't you take Cora and Togo for a walk, and when you come back, I'll have the paperwork drawn up for your donation. It's tax deductible, you know." He fake whispered to me, "I always try to tack that on so that people feel free to be generous."

I laughed, knowing that Luca would probably be ridiculously generous, and I was grateful for his willingness to reach into his pocketbook, even if it was only to score points with me.

We set out with a brisk pace, which helped mitigate the bite in the foggy air. The city was certainly not sunny today, not that the dogs minded one bit. For the pups, this was perfect weather.

Togo, the malamute, was leading pretty hard, but I was impressed with how Luca handled the big dog. My dog, Cora, was more playful than anything else, wanting to sniff and investigate everything, turning to look at me every now and again with a doggie smile.

"They are pretty cute," Luca admitted as our dogs kept pace with each other. "Let me guess, you want one."

"And if I did?"

"Then we'd leave with a dog, I suppose."

Luca made everything sound so simple.

Want a dog? *Get one.*

Don't like your career? *Get a new one.*

Love me? *Get married.*

I withheld my response. I was utterly confused about where to go from here, but if I decided to back out of the contract and stay in California, I had no doubt that my father would cut me off, leaving me penniless.

Knowing that, I really shouldn't bring a dog into my life, but there was something about Cora that I couldn't quite shake.

But there was also something very appealing about how easily Luca took to the pups.

"Did you ever have a dog?" I asked.

He laughed. "No. Mother wouldn't hear of it. The thought of an animal loose in her home? She'd rather die. But I never felt the need to have a dog, either. I guess I'm ambivalent about animals."

"My dad wouldn't let me have a dog, either. But unlike you, I always wanted one. Dogs are amazing. They never judge you, and they're always happy to see you. How can you not love that?"

He shrugged. "Guess I never gave it much thought."

"So, even though you aren't really into dogs, you were willing to do this with me today?"

"Katherine, I would do anything you asked. Spending time with you is all that matters, whether it's in a private sex club or a soup kitchen filled with homeless people. You are the only factor that matters in the scenario."

Tiny flutters tickled my heart. Togo whined and immediately found a spot to poop. I burst out laughing at Luca's chagrined expression. I fished out a plastic poo bag from my pocket and handed it to him.

Togo, finished, glanced up at Luca, very proud of himself.

"I feel ya, buddy. That's how I feel after a good poop, too," he said, causing me to laugh harder. Luca flashed me a quick grin before scooping up the pile and throwing the bag in the nearest trash can. "That might be why I never felt the need to get a dog," he admitted as I wiped my eyes, still giggling.

I looked to Cora, wondering if she was going to

follow suit, but she seemed ready to resume our walk without relieving herself.

We walked a few more blocks, admiring the architecture, sharing likes and dislikes, until we returned to the shelter, where Emmett had a few new jobs for us.

"Oh, goody, more poop," Luca remarked wryly as we started cleaning out kennels while Emmett took the rest of the dogs to the small yard to stretch their legs a bit. Luca paused to rest on his shovel. "If I did have a dog, I would feel zero guilt hiring someone to handle the dirty work."

"I would be okay with that," I admitted, wrinkling my nose at the odors in the room. "This is a little more than I bargained for."

"Big dogs, big poops."

I laughed again. "Yes, that seems to make sense."

We finished up in the kennels, and Emmett funneled the dogs back into their cages. It broke my heart to see such beautiful dogs stuck in cramped little cells. "It's like prison for dogs," I said with a sad face.

"That's exactly how I see it, too," Emmett agreed, but there wasn't much he could do to change the situation. He was doing the best that he could with what he had. "But our goal here is to find forever homes for these pups, so this is a temporary pit stop to wherever they're going to end up. We never put a dog down, but we are limited in our space, so we can only take the dogs that are easy enough to rehome."

"Careful, Emmett, you'll have my softhearted fiancée offering to build you a new structure to house all the poor, abandoned and neglected dogs in San Francisco."

Emmett laughed, seemingly oblivious to the fact that he was standing next to one of the wealthiest men in the world. What good was all that wealth if you couldn't put it to good use? "If you were to build a new compound, where would you build it?" I asked, curious.

Luca just shook his head, knowing the direction my thoughts were traveling.

"Ah, hell, I don't know. Hard to say with real estate prices the way they are here in the city. I haven't even looked. Don't want to put my energy toward something that will never happen. But before I start sounding like a downer, we do all right here. We have some pretty generous donors that keep Nor-Cal Rescue alive, so I'm not complaining."

I seriously loved this man. So kindhearted and humbled by every blessing. I looked to Luca, practically begging him with my eyes to make this man's dream come true.

"Can I get a business card?" Luca asked with a small sigh, and my smile widened.

Emmett fished around in a pocket and found the saddest, most crumpled-up excuse for a card and handed it to Luca with a chagrined expression. "No one ever asks for business cards. I just keep that one in my pocket so I don't forget our 501(c)3 identification. Sometimes our donors want that info right away."

Luca hesitated. "If you need to hold on to it…"

"No, you keep it. I needed to get a fresh one out of my office at some point anyway. Besides, in light of that sweet donation and your time, I think I can let loose of one card."

I shared a secret smile with Luca as he pocketed the card and looked to me. "Are you ready to go, sweetheart?"

I took one last lingering look at Cora and Togo, hoping with all my heart they found loving homes soon, and nodded. I didn't even mind Luca using the endearment; my heart was filled with sap and goo.

We walked to the awaiting Uber and climbed in.

Sweaty, smelly and starving—but I couldn't imagine a better day.

Maybe I'd been wrong to assume things about Luca.

He'd spent this entire time with me, without complaint, just to show me that he was different.

That I was worth the trouble he was willing to face by refusing to leave me behind.

A suspicious tingling tickled my nose. Luca misinterpreted my emotion as sadness for the dogs, pulling me close to say, "Don't worry, those dogs will find excellent homes. I'll see to it, I promise."

I barked a watery chuckle and buried my face against his chest. I wished concern for the dogs was the reason for my sudden urge to bawl. *Stop being so damn amazing*, I wanted to shout, but I didn't. Instead, I just let him believe that was the reason and simply nodded.

"Thanks for being so generous with your donation," I said, finding my voice again.

I heard Luca's smile as he said, "What can I say? I'm a sucker for a pretty redhead with a soft heart."

I laughed and rested my head against his shoulder.

Yeah, and I was a sucker for the sexy Italian who'd stolen my heart when was I just seventeen.

But I wasn't going to admit it...at least not yet.

CHAPTER TWENTY-FOUR

Luca

WE RETURNED TO the hotel, showered and ordered room service.

I was surprised Katherine hadn't dragged us to some farm-to-table restaurant where we had to slaughter our own chicken or something, but she seemed content to ease up on her attempts at pushing me away.

I wasn't going to look a gift horse in the mouth, but I could fairly feel the weight of her thoughts.

I tilted her chin to brush a soft kiss across her lips.

She gazed up at me, a wealth of unsaid words shining in her eyes. How could I get her to see that I wanted nothing more than to make a life with her?

"What did your dad say to upset you?" she asked.

I knew she'd heard more than she let on. I didn't really want to have this conversation, but I supposed there was no point in running from it if I wanted to start fresh with Katherine.

"He was going to call your father to pressure you into marrying me."

"That wouldn't have worked," she said, scooting up to face me, a stormy frown marring her expression. "I'm not afraid of my father. When I left, I'd already factored in the reality that he would cut me off. As long as I was free from living under anyone's thumb, I was willing to take the risk."

"I don't care if it would've worked or not—I don't want you to marry me like that. When you say *I do*, I want you to say it because you want to."

Katherine softened a little, almost against her better judgment. She was fighting a battle within herself, but I had no idea if I would end up on the victor's side.

"I meant what I said," I told her in earnest. "All that matters is you and me. I would do anything to make you happy."

"Even if it meant walking away from your family?" Katherine challenged, watching me closely. "C'mon, Luca, you know that's not even possible. You're the heir to the Donato empire. Your father would never let you walk, not for any reason."

If she were asking for the moon, I'd find a way to give it to her.

"You mean more to me than anything money can buy. If that means I step down as my father's heir and walk away from everything I've ever known to live in squalor, as long as I have you…I'll have everything I'll ever need."

Katherine blinked suddenly as a dam broke. She said with a watery chuckle, "You living in squalor? I can't even picture that. For that matter, how would *I* fare living that way when I could barely stomach the hostel?"

"I have my doubts," I agreed, wiping away her tears gently, "but I'd follow wherever you go."

"I'm so confused," she said, shaking her head. "Everything in me says this will never work, but I have to admit…this week with you has challenged everything I thought I knew about who you are."

"Do you love me?" I asked with blunt seriousness. "Do you? It's very simple."

"It's anything but simple," she disagreed with a scowl. "Nothing about *us* is simple."

"It is to me."

"How is it that you can see so clearly when I feel as if I'm peering through mud?"

"Because I know what matters."

"What about your family?" she asked, unsure, but there was something about her faltering tone that gave me hope.

"Fuck them."

She sucked in a surprised breath. "What about your father?"

"He's an old man. It's time for him to retire and butt the fuck out of my business," I growled.

Stunned, Katherine stared. "Really?" she asked, her voice barely above a whisper. "You would do that?"

"Losing you would be the end of me. What do I need with all that material stuff if I'm broken inside? You are my heart."

Suddenly, the mud Katherine had bemoaned cleared, and I knew something had shifted for her. She could finally hear me. I dared to hope. I grasped her hands and kissed both softly. "Marry me…Katherine."

I held my breath, knowing this was the moment that would make or break everything. I'd never questioned her love for me. Even though she tried, I'd always known her heart was with me. I'd just needed her to realize it, too.

Was it finally happening? Was I stupid to hope?

Just as the moment stretched painfully long and sweat began to dampen my forehead, a tremulous smile formed around the words as she answered with a happy shake of her head. "Y-yes, Luca. Yes, I will marry you."

Thank God. "You've just made me the happiest man on the planet," I said without exaggeration before sealing my mouth to hers. As our tongues twined and danced, I drank in the future with her by my side. I would always support her dreams and goals. If she wanted to go back to school to be a veterinarian, I would be her biggest champion. Whatever she wanted, I would make happen.

A weight of epic proportion fell from my shoulders as she flung her arms around me, hugging me tightly. I could melt into her, losing myself in the sweetness of what I'd cherish for the rest of our lives.

"Luca," she gasped, closing her eyes as I pulled her panties free to sink between her thighs, ready to seal our union with my tongue and breath, but she stopped me, her hand gripping my hair, her expression serious. "Don't ever make me regret this decision," she warned, and I knew exactly what she was saying.

"The next starlet who wants to sit on my lap can sit on the floor," I promised with a crooked grin, and she released my hair.

"Good boy," she said, gesturing with a wide smile. "Continue with what you were about to do."

I laughed and then set about turning her inside out in ways only I could. Until the day I died, the sound of her gasping in pleasure would forever be the greatest gift she could ever give me.

I was the luckiest man alive to have Katherine Oliver by my side.

And I would never forget it.

EPILOGUE

"You sure you're ready to do this?" Nico asked, adjusting my tie, looking to me for confirmation that I wasn't going to ditch my bride and run on cold feet from the Gothic Catholic church. The bells rang out through the city, announcing a Donato was tying the knot.

I smiled at my little brother without a hint of jitters or nerves. For the first time ever, I felt 100 percent sure that what was happening was right.

"Nic, she's everything I ever wanted before I knew what I wanted."

Nico grinned ruefully, saying with a lifted brow, "I have no idea what that means, but if that dopey smile on your face is any indication that you're ready…I guess you are. You look drunk, by the way—and by God, if you say *drunk on love*, I'll fucking vomit."

"I hope you get to experience what I'm feeling right now someday."

"No, thanks," Nico said with good humor. "I'm not the marrying kind. No offense to your girl, but I need more variety than one woman for the rest of my life."

"When you find the right woman, a lifetime spent with her will never be enough."

"I'll take your word for it."

Dante appeared, his hard expression barely softening as he said, "It's time." I'd hoped that Dante would loosen up after our father retired, but if anything he was more wound up than ever, and we'd gone head-to-head more than once at the office.

But today was about my bride, and Dante, at the very least, respected that boundary, even if he looked like he'd sucked a lemon before donning his tuxedo.

I laughed and clapped Nico on the shoulder. "Let's go make an honest man out of me."

"That would take an act of God, and I really don't think anyone checked that off on the gift registry. But, hey, we can at least manage hitching you to one fine woman. How's that?"

"Sounds good to me." I tugged at my jacket sleeves, ensuring everything was perfect, and exhaled slowly. "Let's do this."

I walked with my brothers, ready to marry the woman of my dreams, and I was struck by an incredible sense of gratitude. I could've lost her. Someone must've been on my side, because there was a moment when the scales could've tipped the other way. I shuddered to think of how things could've gone wrong.

Everything had worked out—that was all that mattered.

We took our places at the front of the church, Father Gabriel smiling. Familiar faces stared back at me, some smiling, some not. A Donato wedding was a spectacle for East Coast society. Everyone sitting in a pew was among a select few, and some wore their smug satisfaction as surely as their girdles holding every bit of flesh in their designer clothes.

The popular bridal song "Canon in D" by Pachelbel began and everyone turned as Katherine, my incredible lady, appeared, a vision in cloud white, a gown fit for a queen.

The crowd murmured at her beauty, stunned by the upswept red hair, blazing tendrils caressing her porcelain face, a dainty tiara perched on top.

My heart swelled with so much love, tears sprang to my eyes.

But fuck it, I didn't care who saw me cry.

My eyes were locked on her.

Life was too good to be true.

My father had retired, and with him went his old-school ways. I was in the process of rooting out the lingering aftertaste of his archaic policies, and I'd burned any evidence of my soon-to-be-wife's contract.

Katherine was my equal—my partner—she chose me as much as I chose her.

And she was pregnant.

We weren't telling anyone just yet. The baby was our little secret.

She fucking glowed.

I couldn't wait to carry her over the threshold of our new place—a modest house we'd picked out together—that was a far enough drive from the Donato estate to create a buffer, but not so far that my mother would squawk about not being able to see her new grandchild.

A tiny shiver skipped down my back, and Nico caught the subtle movement. "You okay?" he murmured, shooting me a worried look. "You got this?"

I responded with a slow, sure smile. Oh, yes, I had this—and I was never letting go.

* * * * *

LET'S TALK
Romance

For exclusive extracts, competitions
and special offers, find us online:

 facebook.com/millsandboon

 @millsandboonuk

 @millsandboon

Or get in touch on 0844 844 1351*

For all the latest titles coming soon, visit
millsandboon.co.uk/nextmonth